Advance praise for DOUBLE CROSS

"*Double Cross* sucked me in from the start and I couldn't put it down until the last page. I want the next one—*now*."

—SHILOH WALKER,
nationally bestselling author of *Veil of Shadows*

Praise for MIND GAMES

"*Mind Games* is a violent U-turn in a fresh direction, signaling the dynamic and welcome arrival of both Carolyn Crane and the most unique urban fantasy heroine I've seen on the page in a long while, Justine Jones. And like Justine, Midcity is brightly imagined, beautifully dangerous, and perfectly flawed. Flashy and stylish, this is urban fantasy's new shot in the arm."

—VICKI PETTERSSON, *New York Times*
bestselling author of *Cheat the Grave*

"Carolyn Crane writes with deft and evocative flair, creating a fantasy-noir world touched with comic book cool. With a twisty plot, a unique heroine, memorable supporting characters, and an amazingly fresh premise, debut novel *Mind Games* is a delicious, unforgettable delight. I can´t wait for the next book!"
—ANN AGUIRRE,
national bestselling author of *Blue Diablo*

"With a twisty, edgy storyline, a unique premise, and a fascinating heroine, *Mind Games* jump-starts a smart and original urban fantasy trilogy. A fabulous debut!"
—MELJEAN BROOK,
author of The Guardians series

"Masterful worldbuilding, sly humor, and fantastically quirky characters. I can't say enough good things about this book. I loved, loved, loved it. A+"
—JILL SORENSON,
author of *Set the Dark on Fire*

"A wonderful start to a new series."
—EllzReadz

"Wow! Crane's writing style brings to mind old-school noir, with the compelling attitude of superheroes from a graphic novel. A masterful blend of dark and light, good and bad, and all the grays in between, it will draw readers thoroughly into her tale, as they root for the good guys—while trying to figure out just who the good guys are. The ending promises more adventures, and that is a very good thing."
— *Romantic Times* (four stars)

"Carolyn Crane's debut novel is a brilliant original in every way. Just when I think that urban fantasy heroines are becoming too clichéd and predictable, *Mind Games* blows me out of the water with its unique premise. Justine does not wield a katana, or ride a Harley, or kick like a ninja. Instead she fights with her mind, and speaking as a nerd myself, I find that concept oh so sexy."
— dirtysexybooks.com

"*Mind Games* is a fast-paced book from start to finish, you never know what's going to happen next! It is completely different from any other urban fantasy."
— Wicked Little Pixie

By Carolyn Crane

Double Cross
Mind Games

DOUBLE CROSS

CAROLYN CRANE

SPECTRA
25 YEARS

BALLANTINE BOOKS • NEW YORK

A Spectra Mass Market Original

Copyright © 2010 by Carolyn Crooke

Published in the United States by Spectra, an imprint of The Random House Publishing Group, a division of Random House, Inc., New York.

SPECTRA and the portrayal of a boxed "s" are trademarks of Random House, Inc.

ISBN 978-0-553-59262-7
eBook ISBN 978-0-345-52272-6

Printed in the United States of America

www.ballantinebooks.com

9 8 7 6 5 4 3 2 1

Acknowledgments

There are so many people I want to thank for *Double Cross*!

First of all, I am endlessly, lavishly grateful to my critique partner, Joanna Chambers (a.k.a. Tumperkin), who has been such a brilliant and important co-creator of this book. I feel so lucky we took a chance on each other! And also my husband, Mark, the most amazing brainstormer, draft reader, and sentence-punch-up guy ever, and an extraordinary writer in his own right. I'm grateful also to early readers Elizabeth Jarrett Andrew, Marcia Peck, and Teresa Whitman, who brought insight to the beginning. And to Jessica Miller, who came through with a late-draft read and some key thinking that greatly improved things.

Warmest thanks to Cameron McClure—you continue to be a treasured ally, giving me hard, smart, creative input on my work, and being a great agent in every other way. And I'm hugely grateful to my wonderful editor, Anne Groell, as well as David Pomerico and all the other hard-working people at Spectra.

Also, I owe a tremendous debt to so many book bloggers—your support of the series, your friendship, and all of our creative interaction has meant so much to me. And I should specifically thank Sarah (Sharrow) and Rachael Dimond, who both gave me specific earworm song ideas in a contest ages ago—songs I ended up using on these pages.

Finally, so many authors have reached out to me in so many ways: Ann Aguirre, Meljean Brook, LB Gregg, Vicki Pettersson, Jill Sorenson, Shiloh Walker, Penny Watson, and others. Thank you! And I especially want to thank the talented, generous authors in the League of Reluctant Adults—I feel so lucky and happy to have the benefit of your kindness and insight, and to be in on your mayhem.

Chapter One

EZ THE COAT CHECK GIRL, a.k.a. the Stationmaster, draws her face right up close to the glass window of her little booth and fixes me with a piercing gaze. Her fine features and short blonde hair lend her a certain elfin beauty; it's hard to believe she's a mass murderer. Honestly, how does a dream invader even kill people? People have bad dreams all the time. They're just dreams. I should have asked when Packard assigned me her case.

"Do you get a lot of patients coming to your clinic with, you know, Morgan-Brooksteens parasites colonizing their organs?" she asks.

"Oh, yes." I run my finger along the semicircular hole at the bottom of the window. The coat check booth is situated along a kind of balcony overlooking the glamorous piano bar below. They call this place the Sapphire Sunset. Soft music and voices rise up through the air, punctuated by occasional hoots of laughter.

"What happens to them?"

"Well, once a person's organs are colonized . . ." I shake my head.

"But I thought there were promising new medications on the horizon!"

" 'Promising' may be overstating it. Just between us, we don't want people scared if they have symptoms."

Ez stiffens. "People should be scared if they have symptoms?"

"No, I said we don't *want* them to be scared."

"Which implies they should be scared!" The conversation winds on like this for a while. It's easy to frighten a hypochondriac once you understand that it's just an adult version of monsters in the closet.

I study the booth as she describes her symptoms. Stationmaster Ez is separated from the world by two panes of glass; tokens are passed back and forth along a metal gully under the semicircular holes. To the left is a coat carousel, like a revolving door for coats. Patrons hang them on hooks and Ez spins the coats to her side. She slides a token across the gully for each coat, and then she hangs it up and rollers off lint. You'd never know it's been her prison for three years. The curtain behind her probably hides where she sleeps and bathes.

Cut off even from touch! Otto only reserves this level of security for his most dangerous offenders; usually when he makes a force-field prison, non-prisoners can pass in and out. That's how it was when he had Packard imprisoned in the Mongolian Delites restaurant.

A new tune noodles up from below. "Muskrat Love."

Ez lowers her voice. "Whenever he plays that, I want to shove an ice pick in my ear."

"I bet." I'd like nothing better than to discuss the insanity of that song, but I can't let her get off subject. "Look, I could take your pulse and examine your skin tonus," I say. "That would provide certain indicators."

She points to the window. "Antiburglar force field."

I nod. So that's how she explains it. Probably only the owner knows she lives here. Her eyes grow huge as I pass my hand through. I have to be touching a target to zing her.

"How'd you do that?"

I'm ready with my story: as a nurse, I have a descrambler that unknits fields just enough for me to pass through.

"I never heard of that!"

"What if you were having a heart attack? How would I treat you?" I don't tell her the device is the chain bracelet I'm wearing; she might try to rip it right off. "Come on, let's see."

Cautiously she places her hand in mine and I pull it toward me, back across the gully, and pretend to inspect her skin as I stoke up the fear I'm going to zing her with. The abnormally large amount of fear I'm able to generate is the reason Packard drafted me into his psychological hit squad, and the reason he could teach me to dump it into other people just by touching them. Later, others from my squad will do the same thing to her, with different emotions. We're like a demolition team of neurotics.

I focus on one of my triggers: the plastic hospital tray where you put your jewelry before an operation. I feel the panic thicken my throat, speed my pulse. The room goes bright.

I hate this job more every day.

"Can I get one of those? A descrambler?"

"Medical professionals only. Let's see the other one."

She extends her other hand toward mine. It occurs to me that this is probably the first time somebody has touched her in years. I feel like such a fiend.

"Can I just *see* the descrambler?" she asks. "I'd really like to just see it."

"Sorry, I'm not supposed to show it around." I concentrate on ripping the hole between our energy dimensions in the area beyond my fingers. The hole acts as a kind of siphon tube, allowing my dark, roiling emotions to rush out of me and into her. Out they flow, faster and faster. I try to maintain my composure, standing there inspecting her hand, but I feel this incredible levity as the heavy fear leaves my body, my mind, my entire being.

When it's all gone, there's only the sensation of wind

inside my fingers, and exquisite calm. My shoulders drop. Everything's new.

Ez's face has gone ashen. "You see something! I know it. Shit!"

They never suspect my touch; they always think the fear is from the conversations. Which is exactly why we have the conversations.

"I have it, don't I? The parasites are in me! They've colonized my body!"

Before I can answer, fingers dig into my shoulders and I'm jerked backward. My hand separates from hers, which is forced back inside the field.

I spin around. "Packard!"

He grabs my elbow and pulls me across the catwalk and down the wide, carpeted stairs, down into the sea of people.

"What are you doing?" I ask, nearly tripping down the last few steps.

He drags me into a corner below the coat check catwalk, where Ez can't see us. This sort of rough treatment would make me a lot angrier if I hadn't just zinged out all my negative emotions. All the same, I shake him off, and I do my best to fix him with a good glare. "Don't ever do that again," I say.

His green eyes burn into mine. "Or what?"

I have nothing to say to that, unfortunately.

"You zinged her!" he says. "I told you to wait for me."

"You were an hour late," I say.

"What have you done?" Packard's handsomeness doesn't come from being pretty and finely sculpted; he has a more brutal handsomeness, with big rough-hewn features that look as if they were carved with caveman tools. Tonight, his shortish cinnamon curls are a bit wilder than usual. He glares at his hands, then at me.

I should probably be more concerned at this point, but after you zing out all your fear and darkness, life seems pretty great. Glory hour, we call it. Most people think happiness is about gaining something, but it's not. It's all about getting rid of the darkness you accumulate.

It's here I notice spots of blood on his white shirtfront and cuffs. His fine black jacket is darker in spots, too. "Oh my God, what happened, Packard? Are you okay?"

"How long did you touch her?"

"Just enough to zing her."

"How did you get through?"

"Otto made me a descrambler." I hold up my arm with the bracelet. "What's going on?"

"I'm the one to hand out the descramblers if and when people need them."

"Well, Otto gave me one."

"She's a dream invader."

"I know," I say.

Packard frowns. His roguish allure appealed to me at one time, but that was before I realized he'd tricked me into being his minion for life.

I cross my arms and look away, struggling to maintain my usual grudge against him. Everything and everyone is way too enchanting during glory hour. And if a person was alluring to you before glory hour, their allure increases a millionfold. Hell, even breathing is a wonderful, sensual experience during glory hour.

He says, "Once she touches you, she has you."

"How was I supposed to zing her without touching her?"

Packard pulls a pair of long silver gloves from his pocket.

I take them. No wonder he wanted me to wear my silver dress. "They're lovely." I run a palm along the smooth cool silk. Everything is so wonderful during glory hour!

I look up to find him staring at me strangely. Packard is the most intense person I know. Even when he's just stirring his coffee or adding up columns of numbers, he has this intensity to him. Like white-hot lava churns inside him, 24/7.

"Let me put this in a way that even your glorying mind can understand. I touched you while you were touching an extremely dangerous dream invader. She's probably linked to us both now."

"Packard, why do you have blood on you?"

He stares at my shiny shoes. I grab his sleeve. "Packard. The blood. What *happened*?"

Silence. Then, in a whisper: "Rickie and Francis were shot."

"No! Are they . . ."

"They're both alive. Rickie needs a lot of surgery. Francis was just hit in the shoulder."

"Shit!" Now I'm focused. Rickie's a telekinetic Packard took under his wing; Francis is a regular human and Packard's right-hand man.

"Three figures. Hooded gray sweatshirts," he adds.

"The Dorks."

He nods gravely. The trio of serial killers known as the Dorks has been terrorizing Midcity for two weeks. Five shootings and eight dead. Regular people think it's random. It's not.

Packard gives me the details of Rickie's condition. It's bad.

"So they shot Francis? They're going after us humans, too?" Up until now, the Dorks have only targeted those with highcap powers.

"No. They were specifically targeting Rickie," Packard explains. "It was only when Francis shot back that he became a target."

"It doesn't make sense," I say. "Even DNA testing can't identify you guys."

"Somehow the Dorks can tell," Packard says grimly. "They *see* us. I don't know how, but there's no other explanation. Eight dead. Six injured. All highcaps except Francis."

"Maybe it's a coincidence," I say.

"A highcap is a one-in-a-thousand mutation. You don't get coincidences like that."

"Could the Dorks have a list of you guys?"

"A few of the dead were so secretive, even the highcap community didn't know they were highcap until after." He bites his lip. "They can tell."

It means they can tell Packard's a highcap. And Otto, too. Otto would never have been elected mayor if people knew he was a highcap.

Midcity's mainstream media rarely cover the local highcap phenomenon unless they're making it into a Bigfoot or UFO type of infotainment feature. Nevertheless, a growing number of Midcitians suspect that highcaps are real, or at least they suspect it enough to fear and loathe them.

Packard pulls me closer to the wall as a squadron of fancy revelers squeezes past. "It gets worse. Before Rickie was shot a second time, she tried to send loose rocks and gravel at them, but as soon as her projectiles neared them, they dropped out of the air. As if the Dorks are shielded somehow, or possess a kind of counterpower. A personal dampening field . . ."

Across the room, the piano player starts up a rendition of "The Look of Love" and gathered people start singing along.

"Remember the precog who was killed last week?" Packard says. I'd thought that was strange, because if there's anything a precog will pick up, it's killers coming after him. Can the Dorks shield themselves even from a precog? Maybe operate in a slice of future a precog can't pick up? And, obviously, the telepath they shot last week didn't hear their thoughts. Everybody said they took her

by surprise. You don't take a telepath by surprise with
something like that, I don't care how much you're
skunking your thoughts. How do they see us, and make
it so we can't see or affect them?"

I suck in a breath. "Any leads?"

He shakes his head.

The killers are called the Dorks because one of Otto's
decrees, in the week he took office as mayor, was that the
city papers can't give serial killers cool names anymore.
The names are prechosen, like hurricane names, and kept
in a vault to be selected randomly. Privately, Otto told me
other D names include Doofus, Dolt, and Dickweed.

"You won't need those gloves for Ez anymore. The
damage is done. She's in, and there's no getting her out
until she wants out."

"I'm sorry I didn't wait for you."

Slowly Packard turns to me. "It'll almost be worth it,
just to see the look on Otto's face when he finds out. You
and me, conferenced into each other in dreams."

"Why should Otto care? So she screws around in our
dreams."

"Dreams that she creates from our memories. She uses
memories as her raw material."

"So what?"

"Do you have any memories that you'd prefer not to
revisit—with Ez and me along for the ride, experiencing
everything from your point of view? Think of the experiences you'd most prefer to keep private. Those are the
ones she'll grab. Ez is like a collage artist, and the easiest
memories for her to use are the ones with the highest
emotional charge. The ones you work hardest to suppress.
The ones you avoid, yet return to over and over. It's
those we'll relive together. Along with what you felt and
thought."

It's here I get nervous.

He looks into my eyes. "That is the one silver lining in all this. I'm thinking of certain moments at Mongolian Delites." He places a finger on my throat, trails it down my chest. "The way you felt with me. The way anything was possible."

I grab his finger. "Don't." He hasn't touched me like that since last summer. The way I'm bending his finger has to hurt, but he doesn't show it. Naturally.

I say, "How do you know it won't be the playback of *your* most secret memories?"

"Because," he says, "it won't." His hesitation tells me he's not so sure. That he's maybe even worried.

I let go. "As if it would even be that memory. A couple of stupid kisses."

"That's what you call it?" Packard laughs. "No, no, Otto's not going to like this one bit, when he hears."

"Can we get to the part where she's actually a threat in some way?"

"With every dream, she increases her hold on you," Packard says. "She gets deeper into your mental content and gains power, then starts you sleepwalking. Eventually she gets you committing crimes in your sleep. By the time Otto sealed her up, Ez had gangs of sleepwalkers rampaging on her behalf. Remember the Krini Militia three years back?"

"The cannibals? The ones who'd . . ."

"Break their victims' arms and legs? Then tear into their stomachs with their teeth and eat them? Yes. Those."

"I thought that was a Satanic cult."

"That was the official explanation. Unofficially? They were sleepwalkers under the control of Stationmaster Ez up there. As her hold deepened, she'd merely plant suggestions during the day that she'd activate at night. She'd make them file their teeth to get them sharp, then go out and kill."

"Shit." I touch my tongue to my teeth.

"Poor devils would wake up in the morning with bloody faces, and think they were having nightmares, along with a tooth-grinding problem that involved bleeding gums. They had no idea they were roaming and cannibalizing as they slept."

The pianist starts up a rendition of the Everly Brothers' "Dream." I can see from a quirk of Packard's lips that he caught it. He gives me a look; he sees that I caught it, too. No discussion necessary. It's amazing how unhealthily well we've gotten to read each other in the past year.

"Dentists helped Otto's men break the case," he adds.

"And now she'll enter our heads through our dreams and command *us*?"

Packard tilts his head in the way he does that means yes.

"As we sleep?"

"With some influence while we're awake, but not much," he says.

"What are we going to do?" I'm coming out of glory hour hard.

"Disillusion her. Fast." He heads over to the bar and I follow. He orders a bottle of ginger ale and hands it to me.

"Thanks." I sip. It's like cool velvet fire on my tongue.

"We have a while until she gains that level of control," he tells me. "At first she'll just construct dreams out of our charged memories." He straightens. "The Stationmaster is officially fast-tracked. After you get her fully obsessed with her mortality, Vesuvius will destroy her considerable pride in her accomplishments. Then Carter will crank up her rage and self-loathing." He looks up at Ez; from where we stand, you can see her head and torso framed by the window. "The Stationmaster lives in a vicarious state, which makes her psyche fragile."

He's reading her psychology; I can tell by the trancelike tone of his voice. He can't see thoughts, but with the power to read psychology, he sees what's behind thought.

"She's likely had few meaningful experiences of her own," he continues. "She'll feel as though she's never really lived—especially now that she's trapped in there. Highly intelligent, hates authority, easily annoyed by stupidity. Odd. The cannibal bit seems extreme for her psychological structure . . ." He trails off.

"What does that mean?" I ask.

He squints, still in his reading trance. "Hmm. When I read her the other day, her structure didn't strike me as being aberrant. At the time, I thought it was the gestalt of the moment, but here it is again. Somebody who committed that level of crime usually looks more askew. I'm rarely wrong on reread . . ."

"Maybe she's a sociopath."

Packard shakes his head. "Sociopaths are full of gaps. Swiss cheese." He pauses. "She never did confess. . . ."

"She didn't? Wait, are you saying she could be innocent?"

Packard turns to me, startled out of his zone. He regrets what he just revealed; I can see it all over his face. "No. I'm not saying that at all."

"I think you are. Shit! If she's innocent, that changes everything."

He clutches my shoulders. "In very little time, she'll have total control over our sleeping minds and bodies. Is that really acceptable to you?"

"But what if—"

"Stop. I see patterns and weaknesses, not a person's past. There can be numerous explanations for her seeming balance."

"Go and read her some more."

"No. Disillusionment is the only way besides death to force her to break the link. We have to put ourselves first."

"Even if she's not planning on doing anything awful?"

"That's right." He takes the half-finished bottle from me and drinks it down. Then he wipes his wet rosy lips with the back of his hand.

I cross my arms. "Here's *my* plan. I'm going to get back up there and finish for today, but then I'm going to do some research and make sure she's guilty. And if she's innocent, I'm going to tell Otto to let her go."

"You're willing to lose even more autonomy?"

"I won't wreck somebody's life just to save my own ass."

"I think you will," Packard says. "You're saving your own ass each and every time you zing somebody. Because you don't want to be a Jarvis."

I picture catatonic Jarvis in his La-Z-Boy, staring vacantly at the TV, a glistening line of drool descending from his bottom lip. Jarvis is like the disillusionist bogeyman for what happens when you break away from Packard and stop zinging—one of those things I wish I'd known up front.

"Finish her," he growls.

"We'll see."

He scowls, then turns and walks off, long and lean and loose, leaving a wake of fascinated onlookers.

It's not his looks, or his outfit, or the blood on his shirt—which isn't so obvious, really—that makes people stare. It's his presence. People notice him. They feel him. They watch him, even from across the room.

I wander out into the crowd as he climbs the stairs. At the top, he turns and strolls, cool and lanky, down the catwalk, and past the coat check window. The exit sign at the far corner makes his cinnamon curls glow fire-engine red in the instant before he pulls open the door and disappears into the darkness.

I head for the stairs and climb slowly, hoping to hell that Ez really is guilty of the cannibal thing.

She has to be guilty. Otto would never imprison an innocent person; his standards of right and wrong are far too high, and mentally maintaining these force fields costs him too much.

Ez sits behind her window, staring at her hands, stricken by my terror. Packard used to say I have so much terror, he couldn't believe I wasn't in a straitjacket. That was one of the things that enchanted me last summer—that he alone admired how screwed up I was.

"Hey," I say.

She looks up. "How could you leave me hanging? You saw something, I could tell. You saw indications with my skin tonus!"

I go through more concerned-nurse charades. We have another scary disease conversation.

Ironically, there's a photo of Otto Sanchez on the wall behind her. It shows Otto standing tall and proud at his mayoral inauguration, his medals and finery gleaming, dusky curls falling carelessly around his big brown eyes. The inauguration photo was taken from a lowish angle, making Otto—already a strong, tall bull of a man—seem even more imposing. The whole city is crazy about Mayor Otto Sanchez, including me. But I'm the only one lucky enough to have a date with him tonight. Our fourth date since our hiatus for the election. Our "do-over," we call it. I'll ask him about Ez. Surely Otto can give me some sort of reassurance about her guilt. But what if he can't?

Much as I hate to admit it, Packard's right: I don't want her to be able to control me in my sleep, even if it's just to send me to the 7-Eleven at two a.m. for a carton of milk.

"Don't you think it would be good if I had a force-field descrambler?" she asks. "What if I suddenly need medical attention while I'm here at work, and the force field malfunctions or something and nobody can get in . . ."

"I can't give it to you."

"What does it look like?" she asks. "Do you keep it in your pocket?"

"I can't reveal details about it."

"I'm picturing you giving the descrambler to me. You walk up, carrying it in your hand with that same silver nail polish you have on now—which, by the way, is quite hot—and you slide it through to me. I'm picturing you standing right in front of this window and you so want me to have it, and pass it through . . . I can picture it so vividly . . ." She narrates the scenario in weirdly extreme detail.

Stifling a gasp, I pull my hand away. She's planting the idea so she can work with it later. She's attacking me psychologically—just what *I* do to people! I cross my arms. "I'm more concerned about your immediate problems," I say. "Namely, Morgan-Brooksteens parasites."

We go back and forth and somehow wind up on the topic of ingestion. She mentions the fact that eating crushed-up diamonds rips up your intestines, like it's something everybody knows.

I find this shocking. "I've never encountered a case of that directly," I say, hoping she'll explain further. As the nurse, it would be weird to quiz her too much about it.

But the moment is lost when an elderly couple approaches. I move to the side. The man places the token in the metal tray. Ez uses a stick shaped like an L to pull it through.

I can't wait to tell Otto. He'll find this diamonds tidbit as fascinating as I do, even though digestion isn't our specific obsession. Otto and I are more concerned about vein star syndrome. We bonded over it exuberantly when

we first met. God, we bonded over so many things. It tore
me apart, because Packard had me convinced Otto was
this cunning crime boss I had to psychologically attack.

I zinged Otto while we were having sex the first
time—a despicable praying mantis moment I regret intensely.

"Diamonds," she says once the couple is gone. "Not a
hungry girl's best friend."

I chuckle. She really is funny, but then it occurs to me
that her obsession with harmful substances in the belly
connects to what she made her sleepwalkers do.

"Nurse Jones!"

I know who it is before I turn, but of course I turn.
And of course it's Simon, sauntering down the walkway.
Simon, my fellow disillusionist.

He slides up between me and the railing, dark blue eyes
shining against his pale skin and jet-black hair. Simon always reminds me of one of those translucent deepwater
fishes, and the crazy outfits he sometimes wears do not
diminish this otherworldly effect. Today he's donned a
long, ratty, white fake fur coat and white vinyl pants,
with no shirt—all the better to see the many dragon tat-
toos on his chest. He looks like a space-age pimp. Simon
and I used to argue about which of us was more screwed
up. Why did I ever think it was me?

I make a face, meaning Nurse Jones is at work. He
flicks his black hair out of his eyes. "I have news. Catch
up with me." ASAP, he means. He heads off.

I turn back to Ez, but she's staring at Simon, cheek
pressed to the glass to keep him in view as he leaves.

"He called you Nurse Jones," Ez says. "Did he used to
be a patient or something?"

"That's confidential."

"I love his outfit. I would love to shake his hand for
wearing that outfit."

"Sorry."

"What? You can make your descrambler work for other people, can't you?"

I don't answer.

"What's wrong with wanting to shake a person's hand? And I'd like to check his coat, if you know what I mean."

A coat check joke. "You don't want to check *his* coat, believe me." Leaning on the counter, I describe the appearance of a Morgan-Brooksteens parasite-riddled spleen in gory detail.

You always want to close with a disturbing image.

Chapter
Two

IT'S JUST AFTER SIX when I step out of the piano bar into an evening alive with the sound of police sirens and the chop-chop of helicopters. Searchlights illuminate the dusky sky down toward the lakefront. Did they corner the Dorks? I pull my heavy black coat tight around me against the January chill, wishing I had big winter boots instead of heels.

A helicopter's searchlight sweeps my way, flashing on a row of leafless trees. I pull out my phone and call Simon, who directs me to a bar across the way. We click off without niceties.

The bar is dim and long, and it smells like stale beer. A line of people hunches on stools in front of a presiding bartender. I spot Simon's ratty white coat in a dark corner. He's leaning on the jukebox, staring at nothing, looking every inch the unhealthy, unwholesome person he is. Packard loves to claim he saved all our lives, but with Simon it might actually be true.

As I draw nearer, I notice Helmut sitting next to him. Helmut is a large, elegant disillusionist with a clipped little beard and a vicious talent for infusing people with despair about current events. That's his disillusionist specialty. Simon's, of course, is gambling and recklessness.

Simon hands me an ouzo. "Your coat check girl, she's

really . . ." He gets this faraway look, like a connoisseur searching for the perfect description.

"She's Ezmerelda, the dream invader," I say. "Thanks for distracting her."

Helmut stands. "*The* dream invader? The Krini Militia?"

"Yes."

"She's hot," Simon says.

Helmut rolls his eyes.

Simon swirls the ice in his drink. "I want to meet her. You have to introduce us."

"She's dangerous," Helmut says.

Simon turns to him. "And your point would be . . ."

Helmut grunts disgustedly. I sip my ouzo and close my eyes, enjoying the licoricy warmth in the back of my throat.

"You're glorying," Helmut observes.

"On the end of it. And I don't have much time."

"None of us do," Helmut says darkly. "Especially now. That's what we're here about. We need to do something about Packard."

"In what way?" I ask.

Helmut frowns. "Did you not hear about the Dorks going after Rickie?"

Simon says, "Don't mind Helmut. He's overreacting."

Helmut turns to him angrily. "It's not overreaction; it's self-preservation."

"What are you guys talking about?"

"The Dorks," Simon says. "Now that they have the mutant radar—"

"*Highcap* radar," Helmut corrects. "You know Packard was almost a shooting victim, too?"

I jerk to attention. "What? I thought he arrived after."

"Moments after," Helmut says. "He was on his way to meet with them—barely a block away, as I understand it. If he'd left seconds earlier, he could've been the one shot."

I feel hollow, shaky. "Oh my God."

"Not even a block away," Helmut says. "And he won't wear a vest, you know. I bought one for him, but will he wear it? It's probably still in the package."

I picture Packard, splayed and bloody on the pavement, green eyes devoid of their bright challenge. I fumble for a chair and sit. "He should wear a vest at the very least."

Simon smirks. "Vests are for pussies."

Helmut says, "When he gambles with his life, he gambles with all our lives. Of course I count him as a friend, and yes, the man saved me. But a man can't develop a symbiotic relationship with a group of people and then go out risking his life. I don't have to remind you what happens to us if we lose Packard."

For the second time in an hour, I picture the drooling, catatonic Jarvis.

Simon raises a finger. "I'll put a bullet in my head first."

"So will I," I say.

Simon turns to me. "Maybe we can do a bullet-in-the-head exchange. I wonder if there's a way to work it into a game of Russian roulette."

I smile. Simon's as devious as he is messed up. I don't always like him, but I've come to see him as a kind of ally.

"It won't come to that if we protect Packard," Helmut says. "Now, I'm proposing that we hire human security professionals to shadow and secretly protect him. I'm taking a disillusionist poll, and if the majority is for it, we're going to do it, and support the team and help make their jobs easy. And we will *all* participate."

"You're overreacting," Simon says again. "If Packard

wants to take chances, that's his business. You're into freedom, Justine. Shouldn't a man be free to gamble with his life?"

Helmut's dark eyes flash. "His own, fine. But not ours."

"Oh, we'd figure something out," Simon says. "Maybe he's made contingencies."

"I'm not betting my life on it," Helmut says.

"How boring of you." Simon crosses his lanky legs.

Helmut's black beard catches the light as he turns to Simon. "Our gambler prefers to gamble. Now *that's* boring."

"Excuse me if I see the upside," Simon says. "For one, with Packard out of the picture, his deal with Otto would be off and we wouldn't have to go around rebooting all these prisoners."

"Nobody's stopping you from walking away," Helmut says.

"I'll walk when it suits me," Simon says.

Helmut snorts.

"You don't like rebooting the prisoners?" I ask Simon.

"Too much like shooting fish in a barrel."

Helmut crosses his arms over his big belly. "We're forcing killers to turn over a new leaf."

"I liked it better when we were vigilantes." Simon wraps his shaggy coat around his chest and raises a hand, preacher-like. "Reverse emotional vampires, doomed to roam Midcity, on the hunt, shooting our crazy, fucked-up darkness into our victims."

"Stop it, Simon." I hate when he calls us reverse emotional vampires. "We're human beings."

"And they're killers," Helmut says. "Those are killers he's got sealed up."

"I have one who might not be," I say. "When Packard looked at Ez, he was like: *That's funny, she doesn't look like somebody who'd be a crazed murderer.* He was reading her structure when he said that. And I was like:

Well, shit! What if she's innocent? He wants me to disillusion her anyway."

Simon sniggers. "Packard would disillusion Mary Poppins if it kept him out of that restaurant." He turns to plunk a few quarters into the jukebox.

"Well, I'm going to talk to Otto," I say. "I need to know for sure." An old Hank Williams tune comes on. "What if it's a mistake? And he's got her cut off from touch. I need a descrambler just to touch her."

Simon looks intrigued. "The highest security."

Helmut looks disgusted.

"I have one of those coming up," Simon says. "Belmont Butcher. Chop-'em-up telepath. Otto has him in a butcher shop."

This surprises me. "Otto sealed the Belmont Butcher in a butcher shop?"

Simon shrugs. "Keeps him a productive member of society. He gave me a descrambler to get around the counter."

Helmut turns to me. "You know you're not going to get much assurance about Ez's guilt. Weren't you following that whole story online back then?"

"I'm not the news junkie here," I say.

"Ezmerelda was in hiding for weeks," Helmut says. "Extensive manhunt. Supposedly she was the lead Satanist." He makes air quotes for *lead Satanist.* "She gave all these online interviews to the highcap watcher sites and *Midcity Buzz,* places like that, where she revealed her status as a dream invader, but claimed her innocence on the Krini Militia. She said it was her boyfriend, this guy Stuart Dailey, and that she couldn't free those people from the dream link because it wasn't hers to break. She offered to talk to telepaths, but naturally a girl like that knows how to skunk her thoughts." He pulls his swizzle stick from his drink and regards it with a thoughtful air. "The authorities had a great deal of physical evidence, but it linked her *home* to the victims, not her. And this Stuart Dailey claimed never to have met her, and they couldn't find anybody who ever saw them together or would corroborate the relationship."

"Right," Simon says, turning a chair backward to take a seat across the table. "But who would rat on a guy who might make sleepwalking cannibals eat them alive?"

"You," I say.

Simon grins.

"Soon after that, she disappeared," Helmut says. "Sophia, Otto's assistant, likely revised the memories of friends and family to make it seamless, so who knows what they think? Meanwhile, Ez is stashed in an obscure bar. But here's the thing. As soon as they sealed her up, the fifteen remaining sleepwalkers all climbed to the top of the tangle and threw themselves off."

"The tangle?" The tangle is the dilapidated, complicated, and dangerously curly system of highway entrances and exits that has long been the symbol of Midcity's decrepitude. It's maybe twenty stories high. "How did I not hear about that?"

Helmut says, "Think of the PR nightmare. Crumbling rustbelt city, and then mass suicides."

"Definitely didn't make it into the *Midcity Eagle*," Simon says. "The big jump, they called it on the blogs. Some of those sleepwalkers were tying themselves to their beds toward the end, right? So they couldn't move without waking up. But other sleepwalkers came and untied them, and then they all threw themselves off. Like lemmings. Fifteen of them. It was the clincher on Ez's guilt, because it looked retaliatory."

Helmut says, "They say some of the bodies are still down there in the tanglelands."

"Wait," I say. "If I was imprisoned and had command over a group of people, the last thing I'd do is make them kill themselves. I mean, at the very least, they could bring me stuff."

"Piping-hot pizza pies," Simon says.

"What if it *was* her boyfriend?" I ask.

Helmut raises his swizzle stick. "Then why did the killings stop when she got sealed up?"

Simon shrugs. "Smart boyfriend?"

"One never really knows for sure on cases like these," Helmut says. "Most juries would've convicted on less than that, though. All those people dead—"

"Maybe the acquaintances would talk now," Simon says, "especially to somebody who's not the cops. I'll have a look into it. If there was a boyfriend threatening them, that might be over now."

"You would look into it for me?" I ask. Simon is an excellent investigator.

Helmut eyes Simon. "Aren't you the humanitarian."

Simon shrugs. "I didn't know she was so hot."

"I don't know what I'll do if she's innocent," I say.

"You would make Otto free her," Simon says.

I nod. "Of course." I don't tell them about the complication that she'll have nightly control over Packard and me.

Helmut raises his swizzle stick again. "Justine, I need you on board with this bodyguard plan. You have the most contact with Packard."

"No, I don't."

"Yes, you do," they say in unison.

"You just saw him," Helmut says.

"He had to deliver some gloves to me," I explain.

Helmut raises an eyebrow. "And he couldn't have sent them with one of his people?"

I don't answer. I'm thinking about those pretty gloves, clearly chosen to match that specific dress of mine. So thoughtful. Did he pick them out himself?

Helmut snorts. "And what was he wearing?"

"A dinner jacket," I say, "but just to blend in with the crowd."

"And did you share any food or beverage—"

"It wasn't a date."

Simon tips his glass into his mouth and chews ice loudly.

"It wasn't a date. And yes, Helmut, I'm on board with your plan."

Chapter
Three

THE EL BURRO MEXICAN RESTAURANT occupies the ground floor of a brick building that's squeezed between a little grocery and a pawnshop on the southwestern edge of town.

I pull the door open and step inside the spicy warmth. Blocky wooden furniture and stained glass windows of sylvan forest scenes say *German restaurant*, but colorful tapestries and sombreros say *not anymore*. Otto and I have dined here every Monday for four weeks now; it's our special secret rendezvous spot for our do-over. Not only is the food great, but the place is full of hidden nooks and cubbies. We like to be incognito when we go out. It's as much for me as it is for him.

I spot Otto way back, nose in a book. He's partly obscured by a riot of plants, as well as being in disguise, which means he's taken off his beret and put on blue-tinted wire-rimmed aviator glasses. Technically, it's not much of a change, but it's all he needs. His beret is so much his trademark that people don't recognize him without it.

Sometimes he jokes that if he took off his beret and walked around the eighth floor of the government building, his own staffers would throw him out. Most people think he wears the beret as a fashion statement, or to cover a bald head. The truth is that he wears it to protect his head from bumps that might precipitate a vein star episode. In rare cases, a sharp bump on the head can aggravate the condition, or even cause a vein to rupture if it's already bulging. Though I share his paranoia, hats were never a permutation I had. It's a bit extreme, no doubt, but I'm hardly in a position to judge. It's a great compliment that he's willing to remove it to facilitate our secret dates, because I know how he hates to go without some head protection. Probably he still sleeps with it on, or at least he did last summer. We haven't slept together, in any sense of the word, since then. Our do-over isn't up to that point yet.

He looks up, as though he feels me coming, and smiles. I smile back, and walk a little faster. He could wear the most ridiculous glasses in the world and they wouldn't detract from the dark elegance of his features, the kissable arc of his curved nose, the dark wavy hair that brushes his shoulders, or his nobility and goodness. He's the only real hero I've ever known.

Soon I'm in his arms, laughing, locked in a kiss. For a second I forget we're still not on solid ground yet.

He draws back. "Hello."

"Hi," I whisper.

He presses his lips to my forehead, seeming a bit somber suddenly. He's heard about Rickie. I sigh, breathing in the scent of his neck.

He snakes his hands under my coat, pushes it back off my bare shoulders. "Oh," he says.

I still have my pretty silver cocktail dress on. Overdressed. His bodyguard, Covian, won't approve. Covian doesn't like us to be noticeable when we're sneaking around.

Otto kisses my cheek. "My lady in silver."

I smile, enjoying his whiskery goodness on my cheek. Back when my hair was dyed blonde, I would've never worn silver. But it works for a brunette. My real hair color.

"Ah. It would seem that Covian wants us to sit."

"I don't even see him," I say as we settle in. Same side.

"Three tables over," Otto says without looking.

I glance casually through the fern fronds and spot Covian, Otto's bodyguard, staring sternly, juice in hand. He's one of the few black men in here. His angular cheekbones are set so high, they seem to squish his eyes upward, and his short hair clings to his head in small, defined curls that look almost carved. He wears a beige khaki shirt. Beige is his favorite color, he told me once. I tease him about it whenever I can. I mean, beige?

Covian's a highcap, of course. A precog, which means he can sense things before they happen, *like ocean waves from the future,* he says. He lets his perception flood out all around him.

"So you heard," I say.

Otto nods gravely. "They say Rickie will be okay, but . . ."

"You'll figure it out. You'll catch them."

A crease forms between Otto's heavy brows. His long silence tells me he's not so sure he'll catch them. He says, "People are staying in. It's happening all over again."

"Not like before."

"Just wait. Snipers have a way of emptying streets." He sighs heavily. "If the citizens knew it was only us highcaps being targeted, they wouldn't be so fearful. I wish I could tell them, *People, don't hide. If you aren't a highcap, you have nothing to fear.*"

I tuck a stray lock of hair behind his ear. "All you'd do is destroy your credibility. It would be like announcing that only Martians are being targeted."

"A lot more people accept our existence now. I've heard as high as forty-five percent."

"If you go out there and start talking about highcaps, you'll just give the citizenry a new fear. *Guess what, Midcitians—the good news is, the Dorks aren't targeting you. The bad news is, all those rumors about highcaps in your midst having freaky powers? They're true.*"

"Sometimes I wonder if it would change things if I stepped forward and announced that I myself am a highcap. Would it help citizens to see that we aren't to be feared?"

"No way. How many times have you said the citizens aren't ready for highcaps to be officially acknowledged?"

"Will they ever be ready?" Otto says. "And this ignorance of highcaps prevents the police from investigating the Dorks properly."

"Packard has people on it."

"Packard has *highcaps* on it—the very people who can't touch the Dorks. Did you hear about that part?"

"Yeah," I say, rubbing a circle on his back.

"They're shielding themselves somehow." Weariness has robbed his voice of its usual richness. Here he is, a new mayor, and his beloved city is being terrorized, his secret identity threatened, and all the while he's mentally maintaining countless prison force fields. He's seemed gloomier lately, too, but who can blame him?

I say, "I'm sure he's got nonhighcap thieves and thugs all over the case, too." Packard commanded Midcity's underworld before Otto sealed him up eight years ago. "Send a thug to catch a thug," I add, trying for levity.

Otto stares sullenly toward the front window.

"It's okay," I whisper, continuing the steady circles, palm warming. "I wish I could do something more to help."

"You are helping," he says. "Right here, right now. You have no idea."

I decide it's a bad time to question him on Ez's innocence, and it's definitely the wrong time to tell him about

Packard and me conferenced together in dreams. Otto can't take much more.

The waitress makes it back to take our order. Otto has some questions about the new tamales.

Will Ez really try to go into our minds tonight? And what if she does stir up memories about my time with Packard at Mongolian Delites? I don't want Packard to have access to my side of that memory. I barely want it myself. God, am I charging it up even now?

Otto opens his napkin. "Who are you working on this week?"

"Ezmerelda. Dream invader."

"Very dangerous."

"We'll handle her," I say, and with that I allow another opportunity to tell him about my screwup to slip away. Am I a coward? *Yes,* I think bitterly.

But from Otto's point of view there's nobody worse I could be connected to than Packard. Something horrible happened between them, something that made them hate each other. All I know is that it stretches back two decades, back to when Packard and Otto were boys, living with a gang of kids down by the river in an abandoned school, discarded for being devil-children like so many highcap kids are. Otto was known as Henji back then, but he hates it when the name is uttered. According to rumors, there was an epic battle between them. The school was reduced to rubble. Packard and Otto clearly have a pact of secrecy about it.

I've come to hate the secret. I feel like it's huge and formative, and my ignorance of it prevents me from truly knowing Otto—or Packard, for that matter.

"I saw Simon and Helmut today," I offer. "Helmut wants to put bodyguards on Packard."

"I bet he does," Otto says. "That's a good idea."

"And Simon said disillusioning your prisoners is like shooting fish in a barrel."

Otto harrumphs. "Yes, it would be exactly like that if we were killing the people, but we're not. We're doing them a favor. We're inducing them to turn over a new leaf and setting them free."

"What if they don't *want* to turn over a new leaf?"

The corners of Otto's generous lips turn up. "Oh, Justine."

"Seriously. What if a target would prefer to stay the way she is, and stay imprisoned for life, instead of being law-abiding and free?"

Otto gives me a thoughtful look. "I think most targets *would* choose to stay what they are, but it doesn't matter what they want. When you take people's lives and terrify the citizenry, you give up certain rights. We've got to look at this from the point of view of what's best for Midcity, not what's best for the criminal. But yes, they probably don't want to change. People rarely want to."

"Then do we really have a right to change them? Isn't it a human right to be who you've become?"

"It's not as if you're brainwashing these people. You're rebooting them."

"Still—" I pause as the waitress delivers our sodas and chips and salsa.

He touches my cheek. "Evil is an aberration of nature. You're rebooting them, restoring them. Righting them. You think a prison is somehow more humane, or moral, where the aberrations only get worse?"

I take the wrapper off my straw and stick it into my soda.

"If you went to them after they turned positive and asked which they'd prefer, they'd be grateful for your turning them. The work we're doing together is helping me keep the streets safe, so children can play in parks, and people can live free, and businesses can feel confident about locating here. Besides, I believe that, deep down, everybody yearns to be good." He unwraps his straw. "At

any rate, I certainly can't keep them all imprisoned with
my mind, they can't go to human prisons, and they can't
be freed the way they are. So even if what you're doing is
wrong, which it *isn't*, sometimes you have to choose."

I examine a tortilla chip, considering this.

"You're overthinking it," he adds.

"And they're all for sure guilty?"

He furrows his brow. "Of course."

I dip my chip into the salsa.

"I spoke with the lead Dorks investigator earlier," he
says. "Their latest theory is that all the victims were wearing something blue."

"Like the Dorks hate the color blue? That's why they're
killing people?"

"Something like that."

I crunch my chip disdainfully.

"What else are the detectives to think?" Otto says
"They don't know what connects the victims. If somebody trustworthy informed them that the victims are all
highcaps—"

"But somebody trustworthy *can't*."

An hour or so later we step outside into the chilly darkness. Otto's town car waits at the curb. After the last time
we ate here, we walked a few blocks to the West Side
Bakery for dessert. This is a perfect moonlit night for a
walk, not so cold, though you can still see your breath.
But there are the Dorks to think about.

Otto mentions the idea of a walk to Covian, who peers
up and down the sidewalk. Across the street, the mirror
windows of a mod 1960s gas company building reflect
the moonlight.

I wait, thinking about something Otto once said, about
how disturbing it is to highcaps to have their power
thwarted. I could especially see it upsetting Covian. He
takes his bodyguard work so seriously.

"I leave it up to you, old friend," Otto says. "You're the guard."

Covian stares at the sky for a while. Then he says, "Their pattern's been every three days, and always nearer the lake." He looks at Otto. "And they hit once today. It's not common for serial killers to change patterns."

Otto nods.

"But then, this is a gang of three, which adds unpredictability," Covian reasons. "Then again, twice in a day? And out here?"

Otto waits. Otto believes in people. Sometimes when he looks at you, his trust and faith feel like a warm breeze inside. I always think that's part of why he was elected—people like it when other people believe in them. I know I do.

"They struck once today," Covian says. "We're fine." Covian goes to the curb to send the car ahead.

Otto turns to me, brushing a stray hair off my cheek. "A short after-dinner stroll, a cookie, and then home . . ." The way he says that, my heart drops through my chest. *And then home . . .*

"Sounds wonderful," I say.

"I needed time," he says, "but I'm back." He means with me.

I want to say a million different effusive things, but before I can embarrass myself, he takes my hand and we set off down the block.

Covian catches up with us; then he drops behind, into shadows, then comes back near. That's how he guards, walking loose, open to waves from the future.

We'll have sex tonight; I can feel it. Does it mean Otto's over my attack on him? Of course it does. I squeeze his hand. Everything about this night has turned magical, and this dark, quiet neighborhood is suddenly the center of the universe.

We round a corner and stroll past shuttered storefronts. Across the way, a glass office tower is held up by giant concrete pillars; it looks like it's on stilts. During the day, cars park under there.

That's where the three loud booms come from. Boom-boom-boom.

Glass shatters. Car alarms wail. I freeze, bewildered.

Suddenly two louder booms sound like cannons in my ear. It's Otto, gun out, shooting at the pillars.

I didn't even realize we'd let go of each other's hands, but there he is, running in the other direction, returning fire. *And drawing theirs.*

He yells, "Get him behind that car!"

I see Covian on the ground, clutching his thigh. "Covian!"

More gunfire. More windows break around us. Alarms are going crazy.

"Go!" Otto says.

"Shit!" I help Covian to safety behind a car a couple yards down. Otto continues to shoot.

"Get down, boss," Covian yells, face a tight mask of pain. He unfolds onto his back on the cold sidewalk. "Don't let him—"

"Shhh," I say.

Otto's positioned himself behind a lone car at the other end of the block. The long stretch of sidewalk between us sparkles with broken glass.

"How is he?" Otto calls over the cacophony of alarms.

"I think he's hit in the thigh," I call back. There's a major artery in the thigh I'm worried about, and I press the heel of my palm where I think it is. Covian breathes heavily.

"Team on the way," Otto calls. "You need my help?"

"God, no!" Covian yells.

"We're fine!" I add. We're not, but neither of us wants Otto crossing the open space. Covian clutches his thigh; then he lets go, like he can't decide what to do. I can't tell if he's trying to help stanch the blood or lessen the pain. Sometimes he touches the side of his stomach. Blood's on his pants, his hands, my hands. It's getting cold. My fingers are numb.

"I'm okay," Covian says.

The bloodstain creeps wider on his pants leg. I feel so helpless.

"I'm pushing on where the artery is," I explain to Covian. "Applying pressure. Okay?"

Covian grunts his assent, then there's more gunfire. "No!" Covian yells.

I look over and gasp. Otto's sprinting across the empty sidewalk. More gunfire. He slides in like a ballplayer.

"Damn it!" I say.

"Covian." He crawls over and touches Covian's forehead, then he takes his hand.

Covian watches Otto's face, like he's finding strength there. The car alarms wail on.

"You're okay," I say. "I'm just keeping up pressure."

"Don't worry, Covian," Otto adds. "Between the two of us, we have a great deal of vascular knowledge. You're in excellent hands."

"With you two?" Covian barks out a laugh. It seems to cost him.

Otto smiles, but his eyes stay dark with worry. Sirens scream in the distance.

Covian whispers, "I couldn't feel them coming!"

"Of course not," Otto says. "It's the Dorks. It's not your fault." He pulls off his coat and settles it over Covian.

I gape at the red bloom of blood on Otto's shirtsleeve. "Your shoulder!"

"Flesh wound," he says.

"Well, God," I say.

With a burst of energy that surprises me, Covian reaches up, grabs Otto's collar, and pulls him down, almost like he aims to kiss him. "Don't go out again until they're caught! Promise me you won't take any more chances! Promise you'll stay inside!"

"I can't make that promise," Otto says.

The sirens are closer. "Promise me!"

"I've canceled my speeches," Otto says. "All public events."

"You have to promise to stay inside!" Covian is really freaked out. They have a bond, those two. They came up together on the force, highcaps in hiding.

Red flashes on dark walls. Gently Otto removes Covian's hands from his collar. "You need to trust that I'll be all right." He whips off his glasses and hands them to me, then he pulls his beret from the pocket of the jacket he'd draped over Covian and puts it on his head, transforming back to flamboyant Mayor Otto Sanchez.

The EMTs arrive and we give them room to work on Covian. Otto tells a pair of detectives what he saw. Officers are placing tabs next to bullet holes, examining the alley across the street. Only now do I think about the fact that Otto was carrying his gun. Dorks precaution?

Otto introduces me to the detectives Wang and Mulligan as his consultant, our usual ruse. The publicity of being a celebrity mayor's girlfriend would destroy my ability to work as a disillusionist. It would also connect Otto to the world of the highcaps and to Packard, a known crime boss. In short, it would connect Otto to all the secret operations of his own administration.

Detective Wang and his partner ask me questions about what I saw. Nothing, I tell them. They don't interview us hard, being that Otto was once a superstar detective and their boss. They're interested in the fact that neither of us is wearing blue, though, and also that Otto noticed that one of the Dorks had eyeglasses. Squarish, brown, possibly tortoiseshell rims.

They're putting Covian in an ambulance. His vitals

look good; that's all they'll say. Otto and I head down
the block where Jimmy the chauffeur is waiting, leaning
against the car. He opens the back door and Otto and I
climb in.

"Midway General, please," Otto says.

Jimmy nods. Maybe he already knew that. Like Covian, Jimmy's a short-term precog—certainly a good thing
for a driver to be. He puts up the partition window.

Otto rests his head back against the seat as we zoom
away. "He gets shot in my service, and all he can think
is that he let me down."

"He's going to be okay."

Otto stares out the window. The hum of our tires
mixes with the roar of a nearby motorcycle. After a long
silence, he turns to me. "I won't have us victimized like
this, Justine. I won't." There's an edge to his voice that
I've never heard before.

I put my hand on his arm. "We'll stop them," I say.

Otto gives me a weary gaze. "I'm so glad you're here.
You help me," he says. "So much."

I smile. It's not the most romantic thing a man might
say, but it means a lot to me.

He shifts and arranges himself to fit perfectly next to
me, chin on my head, like we're two puzzle pieces. We've
always fit well together; that's one of the big things about
us. Even last fall, in the chaos after I confessed that I'd
been sent to disillusion him, we'd attended a charity ball
together. We managed to have a nice time of it, in spite of
it all.

But soon after, he told me he needed to step back—*to
repair*, he'd said. And there was the election to think
about. He'd decided to run, and needed to focus on that
for a bit. And we disillusionists regrouped and began disillusioning the prisoners Otto's holding with his mind.
That was the deal: Packard's freedom in exchange for us

disillusioning Otto's prisoners. Every one we turn loose reduces the dangerous strain on Otto's brain.

Otto runs his thumb back and forth along the silky lining of my coat in a motion that seems almost self-soothing. Otto doesn't trust hospitals any more than I do; we're both acutely aware that more people die in hospitals than anywhere else.

"I couldn't make that promise to Covian," he says suddenly. "I won't let fear make me hide. But I'll tell you this—I won't use highcap bodyguards anymore. Even Jimmy." He gestures toward the front. "I won't put the highcaps who work for me in danger just because I won't hide. Human bodyguards and human drivers *only* until this is over."

"You should wear a vest, too."

"I do," he says.

"Good." I nestle my head on his shoulder, glad I didn't bother him with our Ez problem. All of these imprisoned highcaps are twisted and dangerous, but we disillusion them and it's over. The Ez situation is so minor when you compare it to what happened to Covian.

Jimmy's voice comes through the intercom. "Side entrance or ER?"

"The ER door," Otto says.

We arrive at the ER entrance. It's understood that I can't go in, with all the press that will be there. Otto kisses me, warm and light.

"Call me," I say as he gets out. "Call me when you know."

I watch Otto disappear through the double door.

Jimmy lowers the panel between us. "Home?"

"Yes, please."

Chapter Four

JIMMY STOPS THE TOWN CAR on my modest, well-lit block of cheerful storefronts and eateries tucked below brick apartments. We say good night and I get out in front of Mr. K.'s jewelry shop window, with its row of empty, black velvet necks. I pull open the door on the far side of Mr. K.'s and enter the tiny tiled entrance area.

Three flights of stairs later, I'm at my door. Even as I unlock it, I sense him. Sure enough he's in there, waiting on my couch like a bad guy in a B movie.

"You are so pathetic," I say.

He puts aside his newspaper and crosses his legs. He's wearing beat-up jeans I know well, particularly a rip in the thigh. I used to fantasize about sliding my hand in there.

"How's Covian?" Packard asks. "I got the report."

"Vitals looked strong. Otto's there now." I kick off my shoes, switching them for my fuzzy slippers from the closet. When I look up, his eyes are twinkling. "What?"

"Your slippers."

I look down at my beloved bunny slippers, only one ear between the two of them. "What about them?" I ask, defensive. I never go around in front of people with my bunny slippers. Even Otto has never seen my bunny slippers.

"I like them," he says.

I roll my eyes, but actually it makes me feel good. "Anything else?"

"That's what I want to know. All I got was the official report. Can you tell me anything they kept out of it?"

"Otto thought one of them wore eyeglasses. Sort of squarish brown frames."

"Eyeglasses," Packard says. "Another victim thought that."

"Same old thing otherwise—three guys in hoodies. They went for Covian first. And Otto's shoulder was grazed—he's fine, in case you're wondering." I walk around my little counter to get a glass of orange juice.

"He's not fine. The Dorks know he's a highcap now."

"No way. There's no way they recognized him." I come around with a glass for Packard. "Here, even though you don't deserve it for breaking in." As he reaches out for it I catch the glint of his blue metal chain bracelet—his friend Diesel's bracelet, actually. Diesel died in one of Otto's makeshift prisons. When Packard put on Diesel's bracelet last summer, he said he wouldn't take it off until he strangled his nemesis with his bare hands. That's never sat right with me. Packard's a highly imaginative criminal, but he's no killer.

"Why wouldn't they have recognized Otto?" he asks.

"Because he was wearing sunglasses and no hat when they came at us. It's weird—even just when he takes off his beret, nobody thinks it's him. It's this disguise we use. People never see through it."

Packard grunts.

I sit across from him, steadfastly not looking at the torn area of his jeans. It's strange to have him there, legs crossed, arm slung over the couch back—not so much sitting in it as completing it, as if the couch has been waiting for him.

"He's upset about Covian," I say. "He feels responsible. He's thinking about letting people know highcaps are the targets, not humans, and maybe even coming out as a highcap himself—"

Packard cuts me off. "He won't do that."

"He sounded like he might. He's pretty upset."

"He won't come out."

"Well, you weren't there."

"I don't need to have been there, Justine, to tell you what Otto will and won't do."

"You can't predict everything about a person from seeing their psychology."

"Yes. I can. It's simple pattern recognition. Otto will do what he needs to do to stay in control."

"You don't know that."

Packard smirks.

"Unfortunately, Packard, pretending you're a psychic won't make you a psychic."

"Seeing psychology is better than being a psychic," he says.

"Are we done?"

"You, for instance." He sits back. "One of the things about you is your tendency to insulate people from the reality of who you are. You hide the hard things. The things you think people won't like."

"I am so tired of your pop psychology insights. Maybe it works on the thugs and thieves you live off of—"

Packard turns his gaze on me. It's not that he wasn't looking at me before, of course, but it's different suddenly—like his gaze is burning a laser dot into my forehead. "Remember how you hid all those truths of your life from Cubby? Not just being a disillusionist, but all kinds of things."

It's here that I get a very bad feeling.

"You have the same sort of relationship with Otto. Which is why, even though this bit about the dream invader conferencing our sleeping minds together is something Otto would desperately want to know, you couldn't bring yourself to tell him."

A guess, but of course he's right. I feel the heat rush to my face.

"Fear. Guilt. It's inevitable with you," he continues. "You feel responsible for her compromising us in the first place, and you feel guilty about the feelings you still have for me—feelings that might be reinvigorated in the dream memories—and you think he can't handle that."

"His friend was just shot, for Chrissake."

"Waiting for the right time, are you? Or maybe you're just hoping the problem goes away so you'll never have to tell him, because you need to be perfect for him. Because you're worried that the real you will disappoint him."

This is like a shot to my gut, but I gaze at the ceiling as I sip my juice, pretending boredom.

"You'd be right, of course. Reality always disappoints Otto," Packard continues.

"Yeah, it does disappoint him, because he has a vision for something better, and he's working tirelessly to make it come true."

Packard smirks. "With the help of me doing his dirty work. And by extension, you and everyone else. It's our darkness that makes Otto's brightness possible."

"Why am I even talking to you? I didn't invite you here."

"The information about the glasses is good. That'll help."

"Tons of people wear glasses like that."

"I've got psychics moving through the city looking for anybody whose thoughts they can't read. Glasses helps narrow it down." He rests his arm along the back of the couch. "He's going to want to know. About our little secret."

"You better not tell him. It's for me to tell him." I'm thinking of Otto's hatred of being kept in the dark. I should tell him.

He smiles. "Fine."

I squint suspiciously. "Or maybe you *want* me to tell Otto about the dream invasion thing. Maybe that's what this is all about."

He raises his eyebrows. "The plot thickens."

"Screw you."

His eyes sparkle. "In your dreams. Sort of. We didn't quite get to that, as I recall."

"Not even in the same ballpark."

"Not that same ballpark at all," he says. "A kiss with the right person simply can't be compared to the drudgery of sleeping with the wrong one over and over."

I don't correct his assumption that Otto and I are sleeping together.

"Not the same," he says. "Not at all."

I put down my OJ and stand. "You think you're charging up that memory? Is that what you think? You are going to be so sorry when I dream about my experience of eating chocolate chip cookie dough ice cream yesterday. Now *that* was exciting. It's time for you to leave." I go and hold the door open for him.

"I'm sure I'll enjoy having that ice cream with you." This in a tone like it'll be really fun, in a dirty way.

I feel my face heat up. I hate it. I feel like I'm betraying Otto.

He comes nearer, his smile mischievous. "I can't wait to be inside you for it. I think it will be delicious."

Just like that, I lift my hand and I slap him. The high, loud sound startles me. His eyes widen.

The insides of my fingers sting, and my heart beats like crazy. I've never slapped anybody. I didn't know I had it in me.

"I'm with Otto," I say. "I'm committed to him."

Packard's right cheek is slightly pink, I notice with some surprise. "Do you have no sense of decency?"

He pauses, seems to think about this, then turns and walks out the door.

I slam it behind him.

Chapter Five

A DIM, ENCLOSED STAIRWELL—wide, with a metal banister up the center, and graffiti all over the cement block walls. *What is this place? Why is it familiar?* My heart pounds out of my chest as I breathe in mold and pigeon dung. Down below is the silent opening. It used to be a row of doors. One still hangs crookedly by a hinge, more decoration than door, with smashed chicken-wire glass still in it. Beyond, tall grasses sway in the moon-light.

With my bare foot I feel for the first crater in the cold stone steps. It's like walking on badly damaged teeth, but I know the good places to step, and I move down easily to crouch near the broken doors.

I'm on hyperalert, and I don't know why. It's as though I'm trapped inside a fierce river current of unfamiliar thoughts and feelings, and they're all about protecting this place.

A sound. I freeze. A crack—somebody or something stepped on a branch. I stay quiet as a ghost. Treetops rustle. Night birds call and whir. Another branch crack, and the rustle of wings.

A coon.

I breathe. Relief. *Nobody's coming.* I turn to go back up the steps. Back upstairs where it's warm. I picture shoes around a small fire. Food in cans.

Halfway back up the steps, something in the wall catches my eye—a new crack, jutting down like dark lightning through bright graffiti.

Alarm. Guilt. Heart pounding out of my chest. *No, not there.*

I scrabble across; sharp pain in my heel. Glass. I'll get it out later. I have to see.

The next thing I see is a hand—my hand, but not my hand—holding a lighter up to the crack, though it's more like a crevice; you could shove an apple in there. Breath, coming too fast. Closer now. I press an eye to the gap, thumb working the lighter's rough metal circle until a flame brings heat to my cheek, my eye, and light to the inside.

Bile rises into my throat when I see the ends of three dead, leathery fingers sticking right out of the broken wall into the gap, that seems a mile wide now. One has a creepy curved nail. Another has its fingernail hanging by a hair. The last is exposed to the knuckle, with no fingernail. No—the fingernail is embedded in the other side of the crack. I can't breathe. My throat won't work at all. I've dropped the lighter and I'm stuffing dead leaves and gravel in there. Anything to block it up.

I wake up gasping, coughing, neck thick with panic, eyes watering.

I put my hand over my chest, hoping to calm my heart, which is thumping dangerously hard.

Just a dream.

The red numbers of my clock come into view: 3:34 a.m. I tell myself that I'm not there—I'm here.

Here.

I breathe deep, nightshirt clinging cold to my spine, trying to shake the horrible image out of my mind. Fingers. I don't want to go back. There's a body in there.

I rub my face. I've never had a nightmare like that—so strange, yet horrifyingly real and familiar. It was so clear, and it moved almost in real time, not dreamtime. I picture the hand holding the lighter. Its knuckled shape reminds me of Packard's hand, except this hand was smoother and smaller.

And then it hits me: it *was* Packard's hand—young Packard's hand. And the dream was Packard's memory. It had to be! But who were those bodies? There were more—I knew that somehow. Or he did.

I think about the old abandoned school where he and Otto lived with other cast-off kids. I feel sure that's what that place was; it had the feel of grade-school architecture. The chicken-wire glass, that was the safety glass schools used to use.

I feel cold. How did bodies get into the walls? It's like a horror movie.

I get up and pad out to the kitchen in my clammy T-shirt, switching on every lamp I pass. At the sink I gulp down a glass of water, staring out the window at the market across the street, long green awning hiding its dark interior from my third-floor view, shuttered shops on either side. The dream lives in me still, its tendrils of dread reaching through to my nerves.

All that wariness and alarm. Bodies entombed in the walls, like secrets. Young Packard stuffing leaves and stones in to hide them. Something bad happens when they come out—and they do eventually come out. I knew that, too, when I was inside the dream.

A paranoid impulse makes me flip off the nearby lamp, feeling far too visible from the street. God, I'm still half trapped in the feeling of that dream. A creak from the direction of my bedroom—I freeze. No, it's nothing. Dreams can't come alive.

It's *nothing*!

But telling myself this doesn't help, and there is no way I'm going back into the bedroom now. Instead, I creep around to the sitting area on the other side of the kitchen, flop down on the couch, grab my phone, and call Shelby.

In addition to being my best friend, Shelby is also a disillusionist; her darkly enchanting despair about the pointlessness of life and the impossibility of happiness pulls targets into severe downward spirals. She's also fun to have drinks with.

Voice mail. *Damn.* I leave a message for her to call me and then I click off. She'd come over in a second if she knew I needed her. I throw the phone onto the cushion beside me. I could go over there except I'm feeling way too paranoid to venture outside.

I contemplate calling Otto, but our relationship is still too new and fragile for a middle-of-the-night call. Anyway, what would I say? That I had a nightmare? How pathetic would that sound?

It's been a while since I've sat awake in the middle of the night, weighing my need to call a man against my desire not to seem pathetic. Only it was always a hypochondria attack in the past. Everything else is the same: a man I *almost* have. A semisolid relationship that's not quite strong enough to withstand a freak-out.

But this is different. Because Otto is the perfect melding of every man I've always wanted, and he wants to be with me. In fact, I think I went after all those other men because I was intuitively searching for Otto, and none of those other relationships worked because Otto was the one I was destined to be with. Still, I can't quite bring myself to call him.

If I called Packard, he'd be here in a snap, but I won't be doing that, even though there's something comforting in knowing he would've had the same dream. And he'd let me zing my fear into him, too, and that would make me feel a whole lot better. Packard's the only one who can handle a zing. I don't know if that's because he's the inventor of the whole insane technique, or if it has to do with his highcap power. It doesn't matter; I won't be calling him. Packard is a Faustian bargain.

I read a sexy mystery book there on the couch for a while—a trick from when I'd be up in the middle of the night with a hypochondria freak-out, fighting with myself to not go online to look up symptoms.

An hour later, my mind feels separated enough from the awful imagery of the dream that I turn out the light next to the couch to sleep—fitfully—like some part of me is terrified to let go.

I officially rise at seven, exhausted and shaky. It's a fear hangover, which is where your source of fear is gone, but the fear was so strong that the chemicals and adrenaline are still in you, surging around. I'd get them off hypochondria all the time.

I measure coffee into my coffeemaker and pour in the water. Then I turn on the power and I just stand there watching the drips merge into a film that covers the bottom of the glass carafe.

Until my cell phone rings, startling me out of my stupor.

Otto. I hate talking to Otto before I've had my coffee. But what if he needs me? What if there's news about Covian?

I answer on the last ring. "Hey!" I say.

"Hey," he says, his warm, confident *Hey*. "I didn't wake you up, did I?"

"No," I say. "It's fine."

"You sound a bit—"

"I didn't sleep so well is all. Who cares. How's Covian?"

Otto updates me on Covian's condition. Apparently the bullet chipped his thighbone. There's some microsurgery technique they have to perform, and he'll be in a brace for a while, but he'll likely be able to jump back onto his soccer team by the end of summer.

"Ooh, I bet he's happy about that." *Drip drip.* "I'm so glad."

"I wish I could've stayed with you," Otto says. "I know that's why you didn't sleep well."

"It's not really why."

"Justine. You were involved in a shooting."

"I wasn't hurt or even the target." To push us off the subject, I report to him that watched coffee does not make itself fast, then we discuss our day. I tell him I'm going to work on Ez later on. I'm thinking maybe I ought to tell him about the dream invasion problem, but then I decide it can't be over the phone—it has to be in person.

"You know, Ez did give me a very interesting piece of information." I say this in my "something-scrumptious" voice, knowing he'll be intrigued.

"Oh?"

I'd been planning on saving this tidbit for a perfect moment that never came last night, so I spill it now. "She told me that ingesting crushed diamonds can rip up your intestines."

"What?"

"It kills you."

Silence. Then he whispers, "Could that be true?"

"She has a thing about internal organs." Which means she'd be the one to know. Hypochondriacs tend to be maniacally well informed on the subjects of their obsessions.

"My God! I've heard of people swallowing metal. But diamonds?"

"Remember that guy in the news who swallowed a whole car bit by bit?"

"Right. The VW," he says. "Could it be true? A man can swallow an entire car, but not tiny diamonds?" I knew he'd react this way; this is the sort of thing we can discuss for hours.

"Maybe you should ask at the hospital today when you visit Covian."

Otto laughs his warm, wonderful laugh. "What would it look like if the mayor began quizzing the medical staff on death by diamonds?"

"It would look like you're interested in a wide range of things."

"Justine. The mayor needs to maintain a certain amount of decorum with the citizens."

I smile. "I hope not with all citizens."

"Oh, no, I assure you . . ." Here Otto lowers his voice. "The mayor entertains distinctly unmayoral thoughts regarding a specific citizen."

My pulse races.

"The other citizens," he says, "would be scandalized."

"Well!" I say. I can't think of a clever comeback. Sometimes I'm like that with him.

"Be careful with Ez. She's dastardly."

"Dastardly?"

"I never thought I'd use that word about a woman, oddly."

I can hear the smile in his voice as he says this, and it makes me smile. And then I jump at the loud buzz of my doorbell.

"Is that your door?" Otto asks.

"Damn!"

"What is it?"

"Ally. Our rollerblading date—I totally forgot. We're doing the whole circuit."

"Good Lord, I hope you didn't drink too much of that coffee yet," he says.

"No, thank goodness." We both worry about an elevated heart rate while exercising. I may zing out my fear, but I certainly don't zing out my common sense. Or the knowledge that I'll always be in danger of vein star, and that I very well could have it.

I buzz Ally in as I get off the phone. She comes up and waits while I get on my sports togs, catching me up on the amusing little stories from Le Toile, the dress shop I used to manage and where she still works. The little stories make me feel connected to my old life, even though there are new girls who star in the stories. Ally also gives me a heads-up on a shipment of dresses from my favorite Italian line. They're insanely expensive—nothing I could've afforded back when I ran the place. But now I have a lucrative job in the security industry—at least, that's what they all think. I only pretend to be a nurse to targets.

"Actually, I may just put one aside for you," she says. "It's exactly your thing." She describes it in detail.

"I am so there." I'll go check out the dress and meet the new girls, so that the stories mean more.

I put on my hat and gloves, and I grab my face scarf. It's a loose weave, so you can wrap it around your face like a mummy and still see.

Ally smiles. "The security industry has been good to you, dude."

I swing my ice-traction-modified rollerblades over my shoulder and grab my key. "Everything has its trade-offs," I say.

I'm aware, as we head out into the bright, wintry morning, that she doesn't fully believe me when I say that. I used to not believe it when people said that sort of thing, either.

Chapter
Six

LATER THAT MORNING, I get in my car and start over to Mongolian Delites to say hi to the gang and grab a pastry before I see Ez. At a stoplight, I reposition the arms on the bendable Gumby doll I glued to my dashboard. I make it so that his hands are on his hips. Worried Gumby. I like to change Gumby to reflect my mood. I can't get the image of those fingers out of my head.

The outfit I've chosen for this day is one of my favorites—a soft gray cashmere sweater, soft jeans, a nice long corduroy jacket, and a bright hat that Shelby knit out of about nine clashing colors of yarn. I used to think it was part of her Eastern European fashion sense that drew her to colors that clash, but now I see it as a uniquely Shelby thing. A grim, hopeless girl swathed in colors at war.

I pull open the heavy double doors that once bore Otto's seal and enter the dim, candlelit dining room of tables and Persian rugs and tourist trinkets gleaming darkly on the walls. The place is just starting to fill with the early lunch crowd.

Delites is no longer Packard's prison—he'd never willingly set foot in here again—but the place still serves as a kind of clubhouse for us disillusionists. I make my way around the perimeter of the main dining area to the back booth area, hoping the whole gang is there. They've become family to me, and after that dream last night, I just want to be with them.

I smile when I spot Helmut and Enrique, our ennui guy, in the far booth. Enrique looks bored as usual, dark and suave, with a baby-smooth face and glinting diamond earring. Across the table is Carter, our anger guy, whose ash-blond hair is so pale it's almost metallic. Carter's complaining about the lack of snow with jerky arm movements, wide freckled face tight with anger. Good ol' Carter. I want to hug him. Instead, I order a bagel and coffee from a passing waitperson and settle in next to him.

Eventually, Carter runs out of ways to articulate the outrageousness of Midcity weather, and Helmut launches into a thing about his current target, the Brick Slinger—the telekinetic highcap who terrorized the city last summer, killing random people with flying bricks.

Now the Brick Slinger is a prisoner in a tollbooth on Highway 83. And he eats stinky food that annoys Helmut.

Helmut goes on to describe the conspiracy theories he and the Slinger have been discussing. The main one involves the FDA, the Trilateral Commission, and remakes of Disney cartoons.

The Brick Slinger's suicide—he smashed in his own head after Otto caught him—was described in gory detail by the reporter on the scene, but it actually never happened. Otto's revisionist assistant, Sophia, erased the reporter's memory and inserted a new experience of her own imagining. That's her creepy power.

"His political obsessions got so bad, the Slinger actually cut himself off from the news two years ago. I'm catching him up," Helmut reports. And his way of catching him up will be highly disturbing. You don't want to discuss geopolitics with Helmut any more than you want to discuss future hopes and dreams with Shelby.

Enrique snickers and twists his diamond earring. Helmut tells us he'll hand the Brick Slinger over to Vesuvius next for a crash in self-esteem; then Shelby will destroy his sense of hope.

Suddenly Helmut's waving, and a burly bald man with a gray mustache comes over. Helmut introduces him as Parsons, the head of Packard's secret bodyguard team. Parsons seems very in-charge and confident. Good.

Outside on the walk, I bump into Simon in his big crazy coat and ask him if he's got anything.

Simon shakes his head. "I spoke with three people, one a longtime coworker." He shoves his hands into his pockets. "They all think she made up the relationship."

"So the whole my-boyfriend-did-it story was a lie after all."

Simon screws up his lips, inspecting my face for a while. "You seem relieved."

"I want to get at the truth."

"We're not there yet. I have two more people to speak with."

"Three wasn't enough?" I ask.

"There was a sameness in their wording. . . . I have a gut feeling."

I smile. "Sure it's your gut?"

"I spend my time with liars and bluffers, Justine. I'm not done." He heads off.

I leave my car at Mongolian Delites and walk the seven blocks to the Sapphire Sunset piano bar. The air chills my lungs when I breathe deep, freshening me to my toes. My fatigue begins lifting.

Simon's right about my being relieved that Ez is looking guilty. Maybe it's wrong to be glad for that, but it simplifies things. I don't want to disillusion an innocent person, but I sure don't want to be a minion in my sleep. It's bad enough that I'm one when I'm awake.

Oddly, as I near the bar, my eagerness to see Ez builds.

Sapphire Sunset comes into view on the next block. It's a squat rectangle of blue stucco with black trim and shutters, and it sits right in the middle of a motley row of restaurants and antiques stores. Behind it is a hill that leads steeply down to the blocks along the lakefront. As I step up my pace, I spot a familiar blue car parked along the curb, with a familiar figure leaning against it, face turned to the winter sun. Packard.

I get a pang as I think of him so young and scared. And those corpse fingers in the walls! Him trying to cover them, block them.

Packard has a cardboard tray with two coffees and a bakery bag with an *M* logo. Maria's corner deli—the place where I'd get coffees for Packard when he was trapped. He points to one. "Cow brown."

Cow brown. His description for how I take my coffee—just a splash of cream. "Thanks."

"And the other's for you to bring to her." He hands me the stuff. "She'll respond emotionally to offerings like this."

"Okay, Packard. Thanks."

His eyes are light green in the sunshine, shot through with tiny bright lines. "What?"

"Nothing."

He tilts his head, whiskers a sparkle of sand below his cheekbones. "You dreamed something."

"Now I tell you my dreams?" I set the coffees on the hood and open the bag. The fragrant steam of banana nut muffins caresses my nose. My favorite kind.

"Let's have it. We need to know how she's working us."

"You had it too, didn't you?"

He waits.

"Fine. It was you. In that place. Bodies. It was horrible, Packard." I look at him sadly. "You were just a kid."

"Don't."

"I can't empathize?"

"No. You can tell me the facts."

"Fine," I say. "You were in a ruined stairwell upset about a hand embedded in a wall. Like a body was entombed in there."

Packard looks pale. "What did you make of the dream?"

"Why don't you tell me what I should make of it? Was that the abandoned school? What were those bodies?"

"Did you have consciousness during it? Thoughts?"

"I don't get to ask any questions?"

"This is important," he says. "I'm trying to determine how deeply she's linking."

I sigh. "I wouldn't say I had thoughts exactly. I knew vague things, like more than one body was entombed in there. I felt dread. Vigilance. And like I had this mission to protect the place, cover the bodies, not let them emerge."

A tanker truck pulls into the gas station over on the corner. Two men jump out, open a manhole on the ground, and pull out tubes, connecting things in a frantic fashion.

"That's it?" Packard asks.

"The dread was so intense—this sense that, what if the crack widened, and people saw what was in there? And there was also this sense of being under attack, like there were people outside in the night that might try to get in, and I had all this responsibility to handle it . . . or you did. A sense of guilt. And those bodies in there . . ." I turn to Packard. "What was going on?"

He presses his big, rough lips together—proud, exhausted, and clearly distressed.

"What happened in that place?"

He frowns. "Thanks to you, a deadly dream invader is parting the folds of our linked minds. Why don't you concentrate on getting us out of this mess instead of interrogating me?"

I flush with shame. "I'm working on it." A couple of people head into the bar. "Packard, what if we sleep in shifts? So we're never asleep at the same time?"

"The dream link is extratemporal. It doesn't matter when we sleep, only *that* we sleep."

"Should we *stop sleeping* maybe?" Curious as I am, I don't want to go back there.

"Have you ever stayed awake for more than a day or two?"

"No."

"You don't want to," he says simply. "You just need to go at her hard. And don't let on that you know. She's going fast, linking our dreams like this."

I nod.

"I've got Vesuvius giving her top priority once you're done. You need to zing the hell out of her. We have to make her release us."

I watch the gas station guys wind up the big hoses.

"You're not still having problems with that, are you?"

"As long as she's not innocent," I say.

"Did you enjoy having your consciousness invaded last night? She'll only go deeper."

"Don't worry—it's not looking like she's innocent anyhow."

"What do you mean not *looking*?"

"Simon's reinterviewing some people, but the stories are holding."

"Justine, we don't have time for this!"

"Look, I don't want her in my head, okay? But if she's innocent of murder . . ." I hold up a hand. "She's probably not, but I need to know for sure. It's bad enough that we're forcing these people to crash and transform and, you know . . . if the target's innocent . . ."

"Losing your taste for Otto's utopia?"

"Don't make it into something. I'm talking to you straight here. About disillusionment."

He looks at me strangely. "You no longer think it's right to disillusion criminals?"

"Do you?" I ask.

Packard draws his finger over the top of the side mirror. Says nothing.

"Come on, Packard. If things were different . . ."

He eyes me coolly. Something's there, I can tell.

"Can't you level with me about anything?"

He crosses his arms. "You're asking *me* about right and wrong? The man who runs thugs and thieves and whose word means nothing, as you so love to say? The man who stole your freedom in order to get out of that infernal restaurant? Now you're asking me how I feel about turning a few criminals around so I can stay free?"

"I guess."

"How the hell do you think I feel about it? I didn't see the sun for eight years."

"Right. *Of course.* I guess for a crazy moment there I forgot—"

"Well, don't. I never said I was a good person, did I?"

The ache in his words stops me from replying.

"And I'd do anything to keep from being trapped in that restaurant again. And you'd do anything to stay sane and alive, so don't pretend it's not true. And neither of us wants to hand over the keys to Ez to let her make us do Lord knows what in our sleep."

My heart pounds from his intensity, and I have the crazy idea that his pounding heart is making mine pound. I look away, feeling so sad, wanting to undo the conversation.

The breeze shifts and the gas fumes hit us. The gas station truck guys are hurrying to pack up. "They're acting like an Indy Five Hundred pit crew," I observe.

"Can you imagine if the Dorks shot that truck?"

"Oh, right."

More silence.

I ask if there are any leads, and I'm surprised when he tells me he has a suspect. His telepaths already nabbed a guy. I'm grateful for this spot of good news.

"We've got him at HQ," he says. "This suspect is immune to highcap powers and he wears glasses—that's why we picked him up. The guy doesn't feel like a killer, though I can't tell without seeing his structure. Telepaths can't read him. We're questioning him the old-fashioned way."

"I hope not too old-fashioned."

His expression is unreadable. "A little faith, Justine."

"What if this guy's innocent? That's all I'm saying."

He puts on his sunglasses. Mirrored glasses, and I get a pair of distorted Justine images—two long pale faces, long dark hair, dark eyes. I hate my reflection unless I'm steeled for it. It's the kind of thing Packard would know. *Screw you*, I think.

He turns and walks off.

Fine. I'm eager to get in there and see Ez anyway.

Wait—why should I be so eager to see her? I stop at the doorway, suddenly uneasy: my eagerness to see her feels like a leftover tidbit from a dream. Did she do something in my head as I slept? The idea of it creeps me out. I pull open the door. She has to be crashed.

"Nurse Justine! What a nice surprise!"

"Well, hey, Ez." I set my purse on the ledge in front of her window, eyeing a couple gazing over the balcony rail, wishing they'd leave. "How are you?"

"How am I? Aside from parasites probably colonizing my liver?"

She's fishing for me to say they're not colonizing her liver. I paste on a forced-looking smile and hold up the bag and coffee cup. "Look what I brought you." The coffee cup just fits through the window hole on my side if you pour some out and tip it a little. I set it in the gully between us. "And I wasn't sure how you take it so there's cream and sugars. . . ." I pull them out of the bag and plop them down on the metal tray next to the coffee.

She stares without touching the stuff. "You think I have them, don't you?"

"Did I say I thought that?"

"In so many words." She clutches her stomach. "Oh, my God. I have a deadly case of parasites." She looks up. "I sent off for Klosamine today. The topical and the pill. They're overnighting it."

"If it's an offshore pharmacy, you can't trust those, you know."

"I don't have much to lose, do I?"

"I don't know about that."

Her fine little features sharpen with fear. "That was a nonanswer!"

"No, it was a statement. I don't know about what you have to lose. Obviously, I just met you."

"Yet you don't deny it's a possibility that I may lose something."

I push the coffee nearer. "Don't let it get cold."

"Obviously I shouldn't have caffeine. Some nurse you are." She pushes the coffee back toward me. "God, I have to get out of here. I'm wasting my life away in this stupid job, and for what? For Morgan-Brooksteens parasites to set up an all-you-can-eat buffet in my liver? Fuck that."

The man nearby looks over. I'm sure our conversation sounds bizarre.

"You don't know for sure," I say.

"Another nonanswer! You think I'm dying! No, don't answer. Because I am going to get out of here, and I am going to set the goddamn world on fire. I am going to set every little corner of the world on fire, and the parasites won't beat me."

I take the coffee back, wondering how exactly I'm supposed to take this fire bit. I lift the bag. "Muffin?"

She eyes it.

"Banana nut."

She reaches out her hand and I push it through.

"So, you're thinking of switching careers?"

She pulls back the paper muffin wrapper. "Huh?"

"Getting out of here and setting the world on fire?"

A silence. "Yeah."

"To what? What career?"

"I've got a few possibilities."

"What's your favorite possibility?"

"Not this, that's what. I sure never planned on being this."

I nod. "I know the feeling."

"How can you say that? You're a nurse. You help people. You didn't want to end up being a nurse?"

"No, I always wanted to be a nurse." I pick a nut off the top of my muffin, feeling shitty. "Come on. What do you most want? If there was some perfect Ez life, your ideal situation, what would it be?"

She concentrates on her muffin.

I feel like kicking myself. What the hell do I hope to hear? That she dreams of turning over a new leaf to be a law-abiding person? Or that she plans to make more people into sleepwalking cannibals? So I can feel justified in zinging her?

She glares at me. "Like, be an actress in the Midcity Rep and marry some guy? And have kids and a Jack Russell terrier, and a lakefront condo, and we all play on the beach and have cookouts? Like that?" She breaks her muffin in half. "Right."

The speed with which she produces this portrait of a possible life suggests that maybe that *is* her ideal situation.

I could actually see her as an actress—she enunciates her words so carefully, and moves gracefully, as though she's conscious of her body in space. "Do you mean you don't want that, or you can't have it?"

"Don't act like you know me."

"I'm trying to know you."

She gasps. "You're trying to get me to not think of parasites!"

I'm about to protest, but then I think, *This is where I want her.*

"You think I have MBP. You're just trying to improve my last days!" She shoves the muffin away. "Oh my God!"

I go on to halfheartedly dissuade her, feeling guiltier than ever. Ten minutes in, we've worked up to me taking her hand to reexamine her skin and zing her, but a man comes up and practically knocks me out of the way.

"Hiya, Harry," she says.

I move aside. *Great.*

"Afternoon, Ez." He puts his coat in the carousel and she spins it to her side. He says something about the Midcity Maven's game last night and they have a jokey exchange.

I wait, not wanting to cramp her style or her tip proceeds. I'd hoped to finish and get the hell out, but now we almost have to start over. Zinging really is a bit like sex. You would never just release your dark emotions into somebody out of the blue; instead you talk with them, get them into the mood.

"That guy that was here the other day and yanked you away—was he your boss?"

"Pretty much," I say.

"A doc?"

"Kind of," I say. "But where were we? Because there was something important I was going to tell you."

"How long have you known him?"

"Not even a year. But Ez, on this liver thing—"

"Was he ever on a battlefield of any kind?" she asks.

"A battlefield?"

"Exposed to, like, atrocities?"

I stare at her. Is that what she made of the dream memory? Could she have picked up extra information?

"He spent time as a child somewhere under attack."

"Really," I say, waiting for her to go on.

She stuffs more muffin into her mouth.

He *did* feel like he was under attack in that decrepit, graffiti-covered stairwell. What the hell happened there? I know there was that battle between Packard and Henji, and Henji, at age eleven, left as a stowaway on a freighter out of Port Midcity, never to be seen again. Or at least that's what people think. The truth is that he returned a decade and a half later, a grown man with a new name— Otto—and joined the police. Rose to police chief, then to mayor. Most of the people who could connect Otto with Henji are dead.

Ez munches the rest of the muffin. Taking her time.

"What kind of attack?"

Ez gives me a sly look. "Show me the descrambler and I'll be happy to tell you all that I intuit."

"I can't do that."

"Is it in your pocket? Your purse? What harm can it do to show it?"

"It's the rules." My descrambler chain bracelet rests heavily on my wrist. I have this urge to show it.

"Nobody will know."

"Sorry."

Her beseeching look seems to tug at me, and I have this crazy sense that it will be a great relief to do as she says. She already has a kind of hold on me, I realize. Because I really, really want to show her the bracelet!

I take a deep breath. "You sidetracked me before I could tell you my thing—"

"Does he carry a field descrambler like you do?" she asks. "He's a doc. If you do, he should. Right?"

She wants a descrambler so she can get out. First order of business.

"Hey! Pay attention. Should he carry one?"

"Why? Are you worried about the parasites? Because I actually had some interesting news about all that."

She straightens to attention. "What kind of news, exactly?"

I narrow my eyes. "Not news. I mean, not news for the public."

She flings up a hand. "Don't tell me!"

"Okay."

"Wait, what kind of news?"

"It has to do with mutation."

"Shit! No, we were talking about the descramblers. You're giving me a descrambler, remember?" She goes on, but with less heart. It's the old hypochondriac Catch-22—you crave new information because you think it will calm your fears, but it usually does the opposite.

Soon enough I'm giving her the horrifying details of a deadly new viral mutation. It's just the sort of news that would've upset my dad—he was fixated on pandemics. He still keeps a level-four biohazard suit and top-grade respirator for me out at his place in the woods. *Always hazard gear for you here*, he says.

I sometimes dream of introducing him to Otto, but Pop never comes into the city. Too many germs. I drive the hour out there now and then and spend evenings eating frozen entrees and playing chess. Pop's impressed with my seeming sanity. He wouldn't be if he knew what it cost me.

Our conversation winds on, the two of us on either side of a coat check booth window, psychologically attacking each other. But in the end, I win, because I stoke up a whole lot of terror, take her hand, and zing

her. I strive to keep my expression impassive as my fear
whooshes into her. Slowly, the peace fills my head and my
heart, like cool, calming water.

She takes a shuddery breath.

I let go. Yes, I zing for public safety, to save Otto's
head, to save myself. But it feels great, and I love it. That's
the horrible truth.

Reverse emotional vampires. Maybe Simon's right.

She looks into my eyes, but it's that sort of gaze where
the person really isn't looking at you. At the end, after the
last of us is done with her, she'll be completely lost in that
inward attention. "You have to hurry back," she exhorts.

"I will."

Chapter Seven

THE DAY IS GORGEOUS—it has to be nearly forty degrees. I may be a reverse emotional vampire, but the sun is warm on my face and the sky is bright blue. I set back out toward Mongolian Delites to get my car, taking my sweet time. Halfway back, I treat my glorying self to a candy bar; I eat it on a bus stop bench while I watch pigeons tear at some garbage. Most enjoyable.

Glory hour is mostly over by the time I near Mongolian Delites. I can tell mainly because the reverse emotional vampire thing doesn't seem quite so amusing anymore. It seems horrible.

I recognize Carter's hair, like gleaming metal hay, from a block and a half away. He's leaning on the brick wall outside the restaurant building, talking to somebody. As I draw closer, I see that it's Daryl. They've positioned themselves in one of the few spots where the sun isn't blocked by buildings.

Daryl is one of Packard's thugs—a telepath and a jerk, which is an extremely unpleasant combination.

As I approach, I make a point of lodging the song "Wake Me Up Before You Go-Go," firmly into my head as a way of masking my thoughts from Daryl. Skunking your thoughts, it's called. Telepaths hate when you do that. They can still get in, but it's a whole lot murkier.

Carter's expression is calm. He's zinged a target recently. It's always a relief when Carter's had a zing.

"What's up?" I ask.

"Dorks got another one," Carter says. "Trio. Hoodies. Gunned a woman down about an hour ago."

"Is she—"

"Dead," Daryl says. Daryl wears a beret over his longish blond hair—the Otto look, which tons of men are sporting these days. If he feels vulnerable as a highcap standing out on the street, he doesn't show it. With so many highcaps in hiding now, the ones who do venture out are extravulnerable.

"Woman named Fern," Carter adds. "Telepath over in the university corridor."

"Packard said they got a suspect this morning," I say. "But if there was a shooting an hour ago with three Dorks present, it means the suspect is the wrong guy."

"Not necessarily," Daryl says. "There could be more than three Dorks and they switch off."

"That seems a stretch," I say.

"Daryl was just there," Carter says. "At HQ."

"That's right," Daryl says. "And the guy can't be read, just like the Dorks. And he recognizes us, too. He won't say how. Hell of a coincidence."

"Another guy with the powers of the Dorks, huh." I lean on a parking meter and twirl my car keys around my finger, making a bright silver blur, keeping the song going. "Huh."

Carter says, "Not good."

Daryl eyes a couple clipping up the sidewalk across the street. The couple eyes us back, maybe thinking we're the Dorks. We're three people, though we don't have the hoodies. "Won't say how he has the powers, but we'll get it out of him," Daryl continues. "We'll make him sorry he withheld."

I grasp my keys, stopping their bright orbit. "What do you mean, *make him sorry?*"

"He's gotta be one of the Dorks," Daryl says.

"He wasn't even at the last attack, but you want to make him sorry? This suspect gonna need a nurse?"

Daryl gives me the fish-eye.

Carter says, "Packard won't let a guy get really roughed up." Carter, of course, is Packard's number one fan.

"As opposed to partially roughed up?" I say. "I'm going over there."

"You're not a nurse," Carter says.

"But I'm *like* a nurse."

Carter gives me a pitying look.

"Sometimes," I add, turning back to my car.

I drive through the former industrial heart of Midcity. Years ago this was a bustling, prosperous area, but over the past decade it's become a ghost town.

I position Gumby so that his arms are crossed. Annoyed Gumby. "I *am* like a nurse sometimes," I say to him.

Gumby communes with me in his silent, silly way.

"Make a guy sorry?" I say. "When he wasn't even at the last Dorks attack? Screw that!" I drive deeper north, past long, low buildings crouching behind empty loading docks, and faceless factories full of machinery carcasses. Life in this neighborhood is centered around the corner bars and pockets of run-down houses these days, all hemmed in by weedy sidewalks.

I turn before I hit the tracks, heading up alongside the wasteland of rusted-out freighter cars under a web of high-voltage wires. I park behind the old depot—a small, historic brick building with a boarded-up front.

This is what we disillusionists semijokingly call HQ. It's the secret center of activity for our operations as well as those of the highcaps who support and assist the police—

without the police knowing, of course. And Lord knows
what else.

I go around back and ring the bell. One of Packard's
guys lets me in.

With its gleaming marble floors and fluted woodwork, the interior hearkens back to the time when
Midcity was a thriving center of everything; you can almost imagine old-time families waiting here for their
trains.

I settle onto a couch and nestle my first-aid kit onto
my lap while the man gets Packard from the back, where
the suspect is presumably being held.

After a few minutes Packard strolls out in coveralls
and rubber gloves. "Everything okay?"

I stare, horrified, at the rubber gloves. Why is he wearing rubber gloves? And coveralls?

"Ez came off okay and all that." His smile fades when
he spots my first-aid kit. It's my nice one—shiny silver,
with a red embossed cross on it. A gift from Shelby.

"I ran into Daryl," I say.

"And?"

"I know you all get a little upset when you're unable
to use your powers on somebody . . ."

A pause. "Just what do you imagine is happening here?"

"Why are you wearing rubber gloves?"

Packard raises his latex-covered hands between us.
"Few props make a suspect more nervous, or make a
person's imagination run more wild, than rubber gloves.
Greg found the coveralls in a closet. We thought they
were a nice touch."

"They're props?"

"Of course. I'm just wearing them to question him."

"Cripes, Packard. You're scaring him to death?"

"I'm not above scaring a man who knows something.
Somebody's got to do the dirty work." Packard pulls off

a glove, then meets my gaze with a defiant light. "Who better than me, right?"

I just stare at him with this weird ache.

"Stop that," he says. "What do you want?"

"I'm here to see about this poor guy."

"This *poor guy*?" He snaps off his other glove, eyes on me, like he's looking through me. Shit, he's reading me. "You're using this poor guy. Riding in with your first-aid kit to make sure he's okay. You're uncomfortable with yourself for what you're doing as a disillusionist, and you hope coming here will relieve some guilt, and restore your self-image as a good girl."

"I can't believe you're throwing that back in my face!"

"Want me to go in there and hit him so you can bandage his face?"

"Screw you."

"And if you can insult me while you're at it, that's all the better, since you blame me for all the ills of your life."

"You got that right."

"At the same time, you're desperate to be with me, to know what that would be like. But since I'm so morally degraded, you settle for these angry encounters."

I smile through the burn in my face. "And there we have it, ladies and gentlemen, proof that Packard is not an empath or telepath after all."

"Denying it won't make it any less true." He lays the gloves gently on the top of the couch back and whispers, "It'll just make it more powerful." Even the gloves seem oddly suggestive now. I'm conscious of my mouth watering, like I haven't swallowed in way too long. He sits on the couch arm. "And then there are those far-too-short moments at Delites."

"You're trying to charge up that memory again!"

"As if I need to."

"That experience will never be as salacious and suppressed as your and Otto's big secret."

Packard smiles and crosses his long legs. "So how does the ol' ball and chain feel about our new connection? Did you tell him yet?"

"I haven't even seen him since yesterday."

"Ah."

"What do you mean, *Ah?*"

He smiles.

"Stop it. Quit trying to manipulate me."

"I can't say *Ah* now?"

"No," I say sternly.

"Even if it's purely innocent? A genuine *Ah?* Not even that?" He makes a pleading face. It looks silly on him; he's never been the pleading type. He bats his cinnamon lashes once. "Not even . . ."

I try not to laugh.

He keeps the face going and finally I smack him on the arm. "Stop!"

He laughs and I laugh. It's like old times. But then it all falls away and I catch this flash of sadness in his eyes. Casually he turns from me as if to check the clock, and when he looks back, I get his usual hard look: domineering, out-for-himself Packard. But that fleeting break made me feel sad for him, and suddenly I think of the Dorks out there. What if Packard had been shot? The image of him shot and bleeding on the pavement makes me feel sick.

"You really think this guy knows something that can stop the Dorks?" I ask.

"He's able to recognize us like the Dorks can. And he's immune. He won't talk about how he got this way. *Yet.*"

"Has Francis tried to get him to talk?"

"Francis is still recovering."

"So it's only highcaps questioning this guy?"

"You have a point?" Packard asks.

"Let me talk to him."

"Now you want to help?"

"I think you need my help." I cross my arms. "You know what happens when you give a kid a calculator instead of teaching him math?"

He tilts his head, his eyes fetchingly bright.

"Sure he can do math that way," I continue, "but then if you take the calculator from him, suddenly he can't do any math at all, because he's learned to rely on the calculator. Your power lets you look at people and see exactly what it takes to make them tick. Or crumble. But without your power, you don't get people."

"No, I have a challenge for once. It's refreshing."

"I bet, when your power is gone, I'm the superior psychologist. Because I'm used to reading people the hard way."

"You really want to get in there and see him?"

"If he hates and fears highcaps, and there are only highcaps questioning him, how is that effective? I'm sure your just *being* a highcap antagonizes him."

"So *you* should talk to him?"

"Yeah."

"How do you know he wouldn't hate you more than he hates us? You'd be the conventional human who went over to the dark side."

"Let me go in there and see him."

"Are you interested in saving us, or saving him?"

This stops me. Packard waits, running his hand heavily along the back of the couch, palm along the nubby fabric. The motion makes a low whispery sound.

"Both, I guess," I say. "Why can't it be both?"

He studies my eyes for a bit, then levers himself up off the couch arm and walks slowly to the door, lithe and lanky, and slaps the metal panel next to it. A buzz. He pulls it open and disappears.

Is he mad? Is this his answer, then? End of conversation? I stand there stupidly, unsure what to make of the sudden sense of loss I get from Packard walking off and ending the conversation. It's like I've been pushing and pushing and pushing on something, and now it's gone. So that's *it*? I *was* sort of a bitch to him, but who wouldn't be in my place?

Just as I'm picking up my coat and kit, the door opens and Greg, another thug telepath—a short, pale man with a buzz cut he's kept since his mercenary days—storms out. I quickly skunk my thoughts with "Wake Me Up Before You Go-Go" as he passes. He heads for the exit.

Then Packard comes through the door. "Your turn."

"What?"

"With the suspect."

"Me?"

"You made a good case." Packard takes my first-aid kit from my hands. He opens it, pulls out my scissors and tweezers, and tosses them onto the couch. "No weapons." He snaps the lid shut. "Ready?"

"Just like that?"

"Apparently I'm not above much of anything." He turns before I can reply. I follow him through the security door and down the depot hall. He stops at the very end, before a door with no window, still holding my kit. "Even though it's possible he's working with the Dorks, I don't feel that he's dangerous—far more bark than bite. He's hungry, and mentally exhausted. He's almost there, but he just won't budge. Maybe he'll respond to the good-cop treatment. Or just a human face."

I think about what Simon said. That we're barely human.

"You're on your own in there. Keep in mind that it's soundproofed. I'll stay out here, but I can't listen. If you need me, you'll have to shout. I'll be right out here."

"What? No cameras or recorders or two-way glass?"

"What would highcaps need that for?"

"Right. Why spy when you can see right into people?"

"You want to do this thing or gripe?"

"What's his name?"

"Marty." He gives me my kit.

"Sending me in to be on my own with a suspect," I say. "Should I be flattered or worried?"

"Get us some answers and you can be whatever you want." He unlocks the door and I go in.

The room is plain white and bright, and a thickset fellow sits at a table in the center of it. He's in his late thirties with a shaved head, chubby cheeks and squarish tortoiseshell glasses, which give him an owlish look. There's an angry splotch on his jaw that will be a bruise tomorrow, and his lip is bloody.

I close the door with my foot. "Hi, Marty."

Marty frowns.

I set down my kit. "Can I take a look at that lip?"

"What are *you* doing here?"

"I'm here as a nurse."

"That's not an answer. You know these people are highcaps, right? And I'm being held illegally? I'm going to guess you know that." He wears a roomy tan canvas jacket over a red T-shirt and denim jeans—dark, like they just came off the store shelf.

"I think you should consider me an uninvolved party, here on your behalf. Like the Red Cross."

"If you were here on my behalf, you'd call the cops. Or at least bring me a sandwich."

I open my kit. For all my big talk to Packard, I don't have any idea how to deal with him. What can I possibly learn from a man this angry? I unpeel my cold pack and jerk the sides to activate it. "Hold this to your jaw. It'll cut down on the swelling."

"Oh, sorry, you mean hold it with my fucked-up hand?"

I gasp when he shows me his left hand, which features a fat, purple, crazily bent pinky. "Oh my God!"

"Wow, your bedside manner is impeccable. You think you can do something about it? Aren't you supposed to jerk it back into place or something so it doesn't heal crooked?"

I nod. He's probably seen that in movies. So have I.

I walk around to his side of the table and take his hand in mine, thinking about the anatomy book Otto and I sometimes study. "The fifth metacarpal digit."

He snorts. "You want a prize for that?"

"Can you move it?" I ask, cradling it, careful to not touch the pinky area.

He shifts it minutely, winces. "Ow." He looks up. "What do you think?"

"I'm not sure yet."

His owlish features darken. "This is what your friends did to me."

Carefully I turn his hand to look at it from a new view. The pinky points sideways, like somebody tried to twist it off, and it stuck in its twisted position. "Which one?" I ask. "That military-looking fellow who just left?" Greg, I'm thinking. Hoping.

"No, the other guy."

"Blond with a beret?" Daryl. Maybe it was Daryl.

"What does it matter to you?"

"It just does."

He glares at me. "They're all highcap."

It must've been Daryl. Probably why he's not here anymore. I release Marty's hand.

"You going to treat me?"

"I'm thinking." The movies where people pull parts of bodies straight are usually Wild West movies, but it seems like movies set in modern times show it too. The pinky definitely needs straightening. It seems like a matter of logic. "It *is* important to do this sort of thing earlier rather than later," I say. "You don't want it healing wrong. Or to lose the finger."

"Could you just get it over with?"

"I'm willing to try to set it, but here's the thing. While I have a certain kind of medical experience, I'm not really a nurse per se."

"Are you in nursing school?"

"No."

"What sort of experience? Have you set bones or dealt with things like this?"

"Not specifically."

He stares at me incredulously; the light overhead glints off his glasses and makes his bald head shiny. "You have no nursing experience at all?"

"Not really."

"Why in the hell would you say you were a nurse?"

"I'm here *as a nurse*. To act in the capacity of a nurse for you."

"Act in the capacity of a nurse? Christ, what is this?" He kicks the table.

I jump.

"Ow," he says, cradling his hand. "Fuck. This is fucking great." He grabs the cold pack with his right hand and holds it to his damaged pinky. Winces. He's a man at the end of his rope.

"Well, clearly you need some medical attention if you're going to save that finger."

"Fuck off."

I unwrap an antibacterial pad. "I'm going to clean your lip."

"No, you're going to fuck off."

I put the pad on its wrapper on the table. "I'll leave it in case you change your mind."

"How long exactly do you guys plan on keeping me here?"

"That's undetermined."

"So basically you're useless."

"I came to see that you're all right."

He leans forward and glares at me. Being in this room with this man feels like being confined with an angry wasp who might decide to sting me. Packard says he's not dangerous. Is he sure? Suddenly I wish he could listen in. Though if he was listening, he would've stopped things the minute Marty kicked the table.

I walk back around to my side and try to think what to do. Questioning a guy is weird. It's not like a normal conversation, even a normal fight. You're supposed to sort of be the boss. I'm not the boss type, or the predator type.

"So you think this is okay?" he suddenly asks. "All this? It's okay for highcaps to go around raping people's private thoughts? And then, when a guy like me does something to protect himself, they kidnap and assault me? That's all good with you?"

"You did something to protect yourself?"

"Listen, I don't have jack to do with the Dorks, as I've told them over and over. Don't you get it? The highcaps don't like that I can see them, that's all. And they don't like that they can't fuck with me. That's why I'm here."

"You're here because somebody's killing them, and those people have the same kind of immunity that you do."

"And as I've already told your friends, I don't know *anything* aside from the news. I didn't know it was highcaps getting it until, oh, about six harrowing hours ago." He blinks at his hand. "You don't think I'd actually lose my finger, do you? You weren't just saying that. . . ."

"If it's not getting blood you'll lose it, I know that much. You need medical attention."

"Maybe you should see that I get some."

"How could you tell I wasn't a highcap? How are you immune?"

"Don't you dare question me!" This, like I'm so beneath him.

"Did you always have these abilities?"

He clamps his mouth shut in the shape of a big frown.

"If you're innocent, why won't you say?"

"Because I shouldn't have to."

"You should if you know something that could prevent a crime."

"Then arrest me, huh?" He stands and shoves the table. "Why don't you turn me in to the cops?"

My pulse surges. I'm not good at this.

He breathes hard, nostrils going. Aerating.

"I'm trying to help."

"Well, you're not." He flops back in his chair, tan jacket hanging open. You can read his whole T-shirt now. Midcity University Beagles.

I pack up my first-aid kit, click the lid shut, and snap the latch.

He sits up, as if alarmed by my leaving. "I'm sorry," he says. "It's been a harrowing day, you know?"

I nod.

"I was heading to my son's ball game. My parents were going to meet me there."

I recognize this as *Captive 101*—you remind people that you have a family so they empathize with you. It makes me feel very weird.

"And I don't see why it's a crime. Having this, you know, capability."

"What's it like? The capability?"

"To recognize them? And they can't fuck with me? It's great, that's what it's like."

"Right." It's true that once you know about highcaps, it *is* disconcerting, to know they could do so many things to you and you're helpless, often ignorant about it. "So, like, if you were at a baseball game, you could just look around and instantly tell who the highcaps are?"

"That's right."

"And they can't do their thing to you?"

"Nope."

"Hmm." I trace the red embossed cross on the lid. "Sometimes when I know a guy's a telepath, I think of an awful song. Sometimes I do that Wham! song, "Wake Me Up Before You Go-Go." Or else, you know, "Who Let the Dogs Out?" . . . Woof. Woof woof . . ."

He says nothing.

I smile. "They hate it when you do that."

"You have to protect yourself," he says. "That's smart of you."

I study his face. "So your thoughts are secret and private. You're your own person."

"They have a hold on you, don't they?"

This stops me.

"Don't look so baffled," he says. "You're uneasy about their power, yet here you are. And why else would you say *you're your own person*? It doesn't make sense to the conversation. But it shows what's important to you."

"Important, huh?"

"That's right. I'm in sales. I'm always looking for people's priorities."

I give him the vague, knowing smile Packard sometimes gives me when he wants me off balance.

"You don't have to worry what you say in here," Marty says. "They can't hear. Did you know that? They don't have this room miked."

"What makes you think that?"

"I've been in this hellhole all day. Figured a few things out." Marty nods. "And it's clear you're not your own person, and that you would love to be."

He has no idea how *not* my own person I am, I think wistfully. How badly I'd like to be free. Even as a prisoner, Marty's freer than me. He's not a slave to zinging.

"Wouldn't you love that?"

"This isn't about me."

"Don't worry, I'm not one of them. You want to keep something to yourself? That's your right. We're on the same side, you and me." He crosses his legs. "Imagine if there was a way you could keep them from ever seeing into you, or using their powers on you. And you could tell who they are just by looking. Would that interest you?"

I narrow my eyes. He's talking like he can give me the power.

"You don't have to say it. I know you want it. And you deserve to have it. How is it right that some people should walk around with power over other people? Some guys can see your thoughts, but you can't see theirs? Some guys have the power to fuck with you and fuck with your stuff in totally outrageous ways, but you just have to sit there and take it?"

"It's not wrong to have different powers. If we met out on the street, you could probably beat me up if you wanted. Is that wrong?"

"Questions are good. It shows you're serious about this. And my point is, you should have the right to level the playing field, wouldn't you agree? And you can do that," he says.

He has no idea how wrong he is. It's way too late for me to level the playing field.

He sits up straight, adjusts his jacket. "What's your name?"

"Justine."

"Justine, I know not all highcaps are bad, but some of them are. Think how it was before Mayor Otto brought the hammer down for law and order. But Mayor Otto isn't standing on every street corner, is he? What's wrong with recognizing highcaps for yourself and guarding against them? It just levels things out." He claps his hand to his chest. "But they're holding me here because they don't want us humans to have that."

"It's not a crime to be like you are," I say, "but it's not a crime to be a highcap, either." This is all starting to get confusing. There are too many angles that seem right. "Look, my one and only function here is medical, and I feel strongly that you need medical attention."

He gets this wily look. "Will you help me"—he does quote fingers here—"*get medical attention* if I show you how to be like me?"

This is interesting. I want him to say more, but he's waiting. I look up at the cracked white ceiling, bare except for a decrepit light fixture in the middle with three lightbulbs. If this was a normal place a glass cover would be over them, making the bulbs less harsh. "I don't have a lot of pull around here."

"With what pull you have? Surely you could find a way to see that I get out of this."

"I really don't think I could, unless the case was solved."

"Maybe I'd show you out of the goodness of my heart. We're both trapped, and it makes us natural allies. Maybe I want to do that for you."

"I don't understand. You could *show* me how to be like you?"

"In a manner of speaking."

I consider this. Immunity to highcaps wouldn't be a bad power to have. It wouldn't get me out of being a minion, and it's too late for it to work against Ez; the damage is done, she's made the dream link. Still, it could be handy going forward.

But then I start wondering. *Why* is he offering to show me? What's in it for him? I narrow my eyes. "What's involved in this showing?"

"It's nothing weird or complicated." He runs his hand over his smooth head. "Just a little . . . sort of . . . something."

Everything in me goes on red alert. I've heard this sort

of talk before—it's how Packard tricked me into min-ionhood: he knew a technique I could use to get out of hypochondria attacks. He would just show me, that's all. Never mind that it would enslave me for life. I shake my head. "No. Forget it."

Marty pulls back in confusion. "Forget it?"

"Yeah," I say. "Forget it."

"You don't want the power?"

"No, I don't want it."

A vertical furrow appears on his forehead. "It's nothing to be scared of."

"If it sounds too good to be true it probably *is* something to be scared of," I say, wishing I'd thought of this when Packard offered me his cure.

"It's a simple little thing."

I fold my arms. "No way."

"This is silly. I want you to have the power. I mean, I'm not giving you the . . . thing. You'd have to get your own. But you can see how they work."

Thing? They? "No, I don't like it."

The furrow deepens. "I'm doing you a favor!"

He wants this way too much—suspiciously so. "I'm not interested," I say. "At all."

"This is a way to *help* yourself. You won't even help yourself? I'm your ally here. We're allies!"

"How do I know it's not a trap? Maybe I end up somehow beholden to you."

"You are the most paranoid person I've ever met! What's wrong? You don't want to be immune to high-caps? You don't want to be able to recognize them?"

"No," I say.

"For Chrissake!" He removes his eyeglasses and slides them across the table to me. "Just put them on."

"The glasses?"

"Go ahead, put them on."

"No."

"Don't be an idiot. I'm trying to help you! You can take them off if you don't like them."

I stare at them. "What do they do?"

"They give you personal immunity to highcap powers. And let you see them."

I touch the rim.

He says, "If I was a highcap, you'd see the blur around my head. Sort of like, you know on a hot day and you look at the sidewalk and see this blur above it? That's how highcaps look when you wear the glasses. Slight blur around their heads—it's the energy that their freak brains give off. At the same time, there's a chip implanted in the frame, right here, that disrupts the waves or something." He points to the area between the lenses, the part that rests above the nose.

"Do you make these?"

"No, they came from the Internet."

"You can get these on the Internet?"

"Twenty-nine ninety-nine, baby. Paradigm Factory dot com."

I sit up straight. Should I believe him?

"My brother buys all their conspiracy shit—lead-lined hats to guard against space rays, insoles for radiation from tectonic plates, you know." He lowers his voice. "He bought me this pair. Just for the hell of it, I tried them out on this guy at my chess club who I've always suspected of being a highcap cheater. Sure enough, the blur's coming off his head and suddenly he can't beat me."

"You're sure nothing will happen?"

"Only that you'll have the power."

"I mean, will they alter my brain chemistry or anything?"

"Your brain chemistry?" He squints like I'm talking crazy. "No. Just try them."

Now I'm totally suspicious, because I feel like he's

pressuring me. "Forget it, I'm not touching them. I don't want anything to do with these glasses."

"What is wrong with you? Christ!" He bangs the table—really hard this time. "I'm trying to help you!"

Another bang behind me—the door. I spin around. Packard is staring beyond me. I turn just in time to see Marty shambling the glasses back on, but it's too late.

"The glasses," Packard says. "It's the glasses."

Marty holds them fast on his face as Packard closes the distance between them and looms tall over him, his hard, angular frame in soft plaid—browns and burnt reds that match his shaggy curls.

"Take them off or I'll rip them off of you."

"Fuck you."

I back away from the table. I don't need to see Packard's expression to know it's intense.

"Fine! Okay." Marty pulls them off and places them in Packard's palm.

Packard jerks his arm. "Ah!" The glasses clatter onto the floor. "What the hell?"

My heart jumps. "Are you okay?"

Packard's inspecting his hand. "Yeah . . . just a kind of a bite. It's okay. I'm okay."

I glare at Marty, outraged.

"They wouldn't have done anything to you," Marty says, as though I've accused him of something. "They're antihighcap glasses, and you're not a highcap."

"Well, they did something to *him*, didn't they?" I snap. "They hurt his hand."

"He's a highcap!"

Packard stares at the glasses where they landed on the floor. Curiosity has made his features softer, more boyish. "Where'd they come from?"

Marty turns to me. "Don't tell him. Don't be a collaborator."

"Of course I'm telling him," I say.

Marty's eyes go dark; there's a rumbling in his throat, and then he spits—a longish goober that flies through the air, seemingly in slow motion, and lands in the center of my sweater, a shiny blob on gray cashmere, just above my belly button. I stare, dumbfounded. I've never had a person's spit on my clothes.

Out the corner of my eye I see Packard fly at Marty, pin him against the wall. "You do not do that! You do not!" He jerks Marty with every *not*. "You do *not* disrespect that woman, you understand me?" Packard speaks through his teeth, as if to bite back his fury. "It was your goddamn *lucky* day she decided to come in here. And you would spit at her? You were *privileged* she came in here!"

"It's okay," I say, unable to take my eyes off the glistening wad. I'm vaguely aware of buzz-cut Greg entering the room.

"What's up?" Greg asks.

I don't know how to answer. Packard jerks Marty again. "You have proven that you don't deserve her kindness, but she'll give it anyway, and you know why? Because she has a nobility of spirit."

I look up and see them struggling strangely; Packard's wrestling Marty's canvas jacket off, I realize. Greg goes over to help him. The next thing I know, Greg's holding Marty and Packard's coming to me with the jacket.

"So sorry, Justine." He kneels in front of me. "You mind?"

I shake my head.

Packard pulls my sweater gently away from my stomach and scrubs from the inside and outside at the same time, with the interior quilting of Marty's jacket. "You know, they say spitting is a legal form of assault, and there's a reason." He scrubs harder, getting every bit of moisture out, knuckles lightly brushing my bare tummy. "Here we go," he says.

"Thanks," I whisper, wanting badly to touch his hair, at the very least.

"You did such a great job." He looks up, gaze soft. "We would never have thought of the glasses."

Our eyes lock. The feel of his hand is still alive on my stomach.

"It was luck and blundering—"

"Don't discount it." He stands. "This is information that will save lives."

Behind me another of Packard's guys has edged in the door.

Greg nods at the glasses with a distant look in his eyes. "You can touch them, Justine. They won't hurt you. He wasn't lying."

I'm surprised Greg would know this until I realize he's taking dictation from Marty's mind.

I go pick up the glasses. All quite normal: plastic brownish rims, smooth, cool glass lenses.

Packard throws Marty's jacket back at him.

"Girl's paranoid of everything," Marty says. "Doesn't say much for whatever goes on around here." He shakes it out. "Can I go now?"

"Where'd they come from?" Packard asks me.

"Off the Internet," I say, meeting Marty's gaze straight on. "Paradigm Factory dot com."

Greg lets out a hiss. "How long have they been on the market?" he asks Marty.

Marty purses his lips.

Greg's listening to Marty's mind. "He got them around Halloween. First he heard." Then, "Damn it!" He turns to me. "You told him the song trick?"

"Sorry."

"Halloween," Packard says. "That's over two months they've been on the market at least."

"The place makes conspiracy products," I say. "Marty thought it was a joke until he tried these. Maybe they're not so widespread."

"Can I go?" Marty asks.

"No," Packard says.

"You have your information," Marty says. "You have your lead. You gonna kidnap everyone that has these glasses?"

"He does need medical attention for his finger," I say.

"Come here." Packard says. "But leave the glasses."

I sort of want to keep them, but it's not the time or place for that battle, so I set them on the table and grab my kit instead.

The door shuts behind us.

Some way down the hall, I stop and turn to him. "You're not really going to keep him, are you?"

"Just for now." Packard strides away.

I follow. "Why?"

We enter the little office at the end of the hall. I'm acutely aware that we're alone now. He walks around to the other side of the chunky wooden desk and grabs his phone.

"The man did just help us," I say. "The Dorks are Paradigm Factory customers. That's huge."

"I know," Packard says. "And the minute we release him, he's going to warn the people there that we're coming for their customer database."

"But it could take hours, even days to get that information. We keep him all that time?"

"No."

"Well, what?"

He gives me a look. "Sophia."

"No."

"We can't let Marty walk around knowing what he knows. Our faces. You. We have to use her."

I sink into the chair on the other side of his desk.

Telekinetics may rob people, other highcaps may read people, Ez may make you do things in your sleep, but Sophia steals memory. She takes a little part of who you are. She'll probably take the whole day from Marty. That's as much as she can do: one waking day.

"And afterward he gets to go home," he adds, then looks away. "Soph," he says. "Whatcha doing?"

Helmut told me that when a highcap is a small child, the highcap mutation is blank possibility; like a stem cell, it can evolve into almost anything. At some point, a highcap child's nature and personality determine what his or her highcap power will be. The child who wants things from outside his crib becomes a telekinetic. The child who yearns to know what others are thinking becomes a telepath—and telekinesis and telepathy are by far the most common powers. Then there are several oddball powers. As children, dream invaders wanted to interact with sleeping people. Helmut has speculated that Sophia had the impulse to hide the truth. Otto wanted to interact with buildings. And apparently Packard wanted to understand.

Leave it to Packard to turn understanding into a dangerous power.

Chapter
Eight

GETTING THE ADDRESS, phone number, or even a non-fake name associated with the Paradigm Factory is about as easy as finding the lost Lindbergh baby. All the website has is information on how to order, and a Yahoo email address. Even the ISP turns out to have false information on the firm. We end up having to get Otto on the phone, and Otto gives the job to the tech crimes unit of the police force.

We're counting on the outfit being local, since Midcity is the only city with a significant highcap population. Highcaps hardly ever move away; when they do, they're back within a year or two. Nobody knows why. I've heard people theorize that highcaps stay because they're connected to the Midcity River, because the mineralogical deposits under the city give them energy, and even that they long to be near the tangle.

I'm in the front room texting Shelby when Sophia arrives. The revisionist wears her red hair in a stiff, old-fashioned Mary Tyler Moore do—Shelby and I have decided it involves extensive hair curler usage—and her eyebrows are the most sharply groomed I've ever seen, just this side of evil. She wears a beige pantsuit—a hot, tight safari number—and tooled blond boots. The boots, I think grudgingly, are really wonderful.

"Hey, Sophia," I say. "Packard says to go right in."

She breezes past me without a word. Acting like I'm beneath notice is part of her campaign to suggest my unfitness as a partner for Otto. She slaps the entry panel. The door doesn't open. She slaps it again.

I smile. "If you ignore me and nobody's there to see it, are you really ignoring me?" I ask.

But just then, Packard comes through.

She kisses him on the cheek. "We ready?"

"Wait. We're bringing him out."

"Am I taking the whole day?"

"Most of it. We picked him up outside a coffee shop. So if you can take from the coffee shop on—"

"But after he drank coffee?"

"Yes."

"Good," she says. "Coffee's the ideal separation point. Got someone ready to hold him?"

Packard nods and fills her in on the details of Marty's abduction.

I've never seen Sophia do a memory revision, but I'm told she looks deeply into people's eyes, more or less hypnotizing them. Then she burrows into their short-term memory, finds a specific scenario, and erases back to it. Some people get creeped out by her staring into their eyes, and they need to be held. Sometimes their eyes have to be held open. Myself, I make it a point never to meet her gaze.

After the erasure, she plants fake memories. Packard told me she imagines whole scenarios and burns them over the portions she's erased. *Like planting movies in there,* he'd said. The images she plants "magnetize" the victims' memories, causing them to fill things in. *Utterly seamless, always convincing*—that's what he'd said. *Nobody ever comes back from a revise.*

I'd scoffed. It seems like a person would know.

No, he'd said. *The one who'd know they were revised*

is the one who was revised. The one who'd know is gone.

I sometimes wonder if there are vascular implications. Surely it can't be healthy, on a purely physical level.

Sophia and Packard are discussing whether she should plant a mugging. Packard thinks it would explain the lost time.

"A mugging's easy," she says. "Violence, confusion." Her lipsticky smile makes me queasy.

Greg comes out with Marty in handcuffs. Marty glares angrily at me as he's escorted toward the main door. "I was trying to help you," he growls.

"Sorry," I say, "but at least you're going home. And to get medical attention."

Greg opens the door and ushers him out.

Sophia smirks at me and whispers, "Is it really an apology if he's not going to remember it?" Then she swings out after them. She'll erase him in the van before they get to the coffee shop. She'll take the hours he spent here, and with those hours, she'll take the man he's become since morning.

I give Packard a disgusted look. "I'm going to take off, too."

"Once we get that address we might need a regular human," he says.

"Can't we just give this lead to the cops?"

"No, we can't. For about ten separate reasons."

"Is one of them that you don't want the cops to have the glasses?"

He looks at me straight. "You want me to get a different human?"

I realize that I don't. For about ten separate reasons.

Sophia and Greg are back an hour later, just about the time we get the intelligence on the location. The tech guys tracked it down through the credit card side.

Even though its real name is the Paradigm Factory, we've started calling it the Paranoia Factory. The name has a double edge—the place feeds on paranoia, but it's also causing paranoia, especially among the highcaps. When I went back to get my nurse kit from the room Marty was in, I found the door locked, with the glasses probably still in there. Like they wanted the glasses in confinement.

We gather around the office table. Packard punches up an address on his laptop. It turns out that the operation is located in a low-rent strip mall in Midhaven, a suburb fifteen miles southwest of Midcity.

When Packard does the satellite zoom-in we can see the shops. On the end there is a wallpaper outlet, and then there's a vacuum cleaner sales and repair shop. Next there's a place that manufactures custom cubicles, a uniform supply outlet, a Chinese take-out place, and a dollar store on the very end.

Packard gets a mischievous look. "I bet I know which one hides the Paranoia Factory. I don't even have to look at the addresses."

Sophia puts her hands on her hips. "How do *you* know?"

It hits me and I laugh. "I know, too."

Packard meets my gaze. "Sense of humor, these guys."

I raise an eyebrow.

"What?" Sophia demands.

"The vacuum cleaner store," I say.

Packard doesn't take his eyes off me. "Because who the hell goes into a vacuum store?" he says.

"Nobody, that's who." I turn to Sophia. "Have you ever heard of anybody buying a vacuum at a vacuum cleaner store?"

"One of the unsolved mysteries of the universe," Packard adds.

She frowns. "That doesn't make sense."

"Have you ever looked in the window of one?" I say. "The vacuums in them are always ancient, for one thing."

Packard says, "Nobody knows how they stay in business."

"We know how this one does," I say.

"Whatever," Sophia says.

I look over at Packard, who's studying the image. I'd never thought anyone but me wondered about the vacuum cleaner store thing.

Sure enough, when we zoom in on the addresses, it's the vacuum cleaner store. Greg wants to get some of the guys together to storm the place from the back.

"Greg," Packard says. "These people make products that protect against things like sunspots and highcap attacks. Can you imagine how much security they'd have? Booby traps. Panic buttons. Auto-destructs. And do you think every person there isn't wearing those goddamn glasses?"

Greg shrugs.

"We learn about them first," Packard says. "We have to do this right."

"And then we put them out of business," Sophia adds.

An hour later I'm driving Greg's white van through Midhaven. I'm wearing a curly blonde wig, bright red lipstick, and white tennis shoes. I have a bag of pretzels on my lap and a new appreciation for the power of bright white tennis shoes to fully destroy an outfit.

I turn into the strip mall parking lot.

Greg's van is windowless in back except for one shaded circle, like a kidnapper's van, and Sophia, Packard, Greg, and Rondo—a security surveillance expert and a telepath like Greg—are sitting back there.

I park several shops down from the supposed vacuum cleaner store, sort of in front of the dollar store, like that's where I'm going. I shove another handful of salty little toothpick pretzels into my mouth; I haven't eaten since breakfast, and now it's well past lunch.

We go over the plan. I'm supposed to waste time in the dollar store while Rondo examines the area around the vacuum cleaner showroom through binoculars and figures out where the cameras are. Then I'll walk over and buy a vacuum and ask somebody to carry it out for me. They'll grab the person and do a *read 'n' revise*. Packard's term.

I turn in my seat. "You actually have a term for it?"

"That's right," Packard says.

"That's disturbing."

Packard says, "You love to remind me that I'm a villain, Justine, but when I do something the least bit villainous, you act outraged."

Sophia snickers and I give her a withering look.

It hurts that he would say that. And it hurts that Sophia snickered.

I sit back like I'm annoyed, reminding myself that I'm here to stop highcaps from dying. If Francis was out of the hospital, he'd be the human who buys the vacuum cleaner, but he's not here; I am. And I'm good at this sort of thing.

I get out and button up my coat. The air is crisp and sharp, the winter sky a dazzling blue.

In the dollar store I find a plastic pen that has a floating smiley face inside it—a gift for Shelby. She'll hate it. She'll enjoy hating it. This cheers me up. I also find a troll doll key chain for myself. I deliberate over getting a Rubik's Cube for my dad, to replace one that my brother broke back when we were kids. Dad used to love solving and unsolving it, but that was right before my mom died, and the fun stopped. Will it remind him too strongly of the past? I decide to go for it anyway.

Packard's waiting in the van's passenger seat, eating my pretzels, when I climb back in. I show him the Rubik's

Cube. "For my pop," I say, twisting it. "He used to have one. You know, *before*." I'm still angry at Packard for being so cavalier with me, but I keep on, because I need his opinion. "I hope it doesn't make him sad, though."

I twist on, not looking at him.

"I'd think, after all this time, the pain would be less," Packard says. "It might feel nice to remember." He pauses, then says, "I've never read him, but that's how it goes with the distant past. At least for me. Remembering makes me happy, sometimes. Whereas it wouldn't have previously."

My ears perk up. Is he talking about his boyhood? About remembering when he still had a home and a bed? Or the time in the abandoned school before he and Otto fought?

"And you can soak it in disinfectant, too," Packard adds. "Really strong. So it smells."

"Pop would appreciate that." I'm touched at his thoughtful suggestion. He's never met my pop, but he's seen photos and heard me talk. I may have my mom's vein star paranoia, Packard said once, but I got my father's brown hair and eyes. *Faraway eyes,* he called them. Like the Stones song.

"Have you been back since Christmas?" Packard asks.

"No." I gaze out the window. "I know." It's just two weeks, but Pop's all alone. There's this silence where Packard doesn't comment further; I'm thankful for that. We all do what we have to do. If there's one person who appreciates that, it's Packard.

"Come take a look, Justine," Rondo calls from the back.

I clamber over the hump between the front seats. Rondo's sitting by the circular window. The binoculars look tiny in his big, muscle-bound hands. As he shows me how to adjust the focus, I notice he has the number 29 tattooed on the side of his neck. Black ink on brown skin; you almost can't see it. I take the binoculars and peer through; everything looks super close-up. Rondo points out the cameras perched on either side of the Paranoia Factory door, and the one farther out on a light pole. I move my view to the dirty display window, where three old-fashioned vacuums perch on podiums that seem to be covered with ratty-looking carpeting. "Somebody needs to vacuum the vacuum cleaner display," I say. "Who in their right mind would be enticed to buy a vacuum from that?"

"You," Sophia says.

The small showroom is lit by buzzing fluorescent lights. A series of podiums displays vacuum cleaners; each has a sign bearing the model name in 1970s-style lettering. Other vacuum cleaners hang from brackets along the cheap paneling that covers the walls.

A woman with short black hair and brown tortoise-shell glasses, just like Marty's, makes her way over from a little desk in the far corner. "Can I help you?"

I point to a heavy-looking machine on the far podium. "How's that one?"

"Good," she says. "Depending on your needs."

"I just need it for my employer," I say. "I think something heavy duty is best."

"Mmm," she says.

I wander over and pretend to inspect its chrome features. I'm thinking it'll be more convincing that I need carryout help if I buy a heavy one.

She sidles up. "This one's good." She crosses her arms and waits.

I walk around it. "Can I try it?"

Without a word, she yanks it down, unwinds the cord, and plugs it into the wall. Packard warned me not to act too interested in the place, so I don't look around, and I make a special point not to look at anything that appears to be a camera, or at the door in the center of the back wall, which clearly leads to the real operation.

I test that model, then two others, just to be convincing. In the end, I choose the first, and pay with the cash Packard gave me. The first was the heaviest one, but I'm still embarrassed to ask for help to carry a vacuum cleaner. I mumble some excuse about a cracked collarbone.

"It's cool," the assistant says. "I like to get out of here now and then." She picks up the phone on her desk and stabs a button.

"I'm carrying something out for a customer," she says, grabbing a pink ski jacket off the chair. This is followed by a curt "Yeah," then "No," another curt "No," and then a "Yeah."

Out in the parking lot, I point out the van. "I was at the dollar store first."

"No problem," she says, "January thaw, huh?"

"Yeah, no doubt." I try not to look at her. They're going to knock her glasses off her face, read her mind, and then wipe her memory.

I pull open the back door, and she gasps as Packard, Greg, and Rondo jump out, pull her and the vacuum in, and slam the door. I take my time walking around the van, sly eye on the storefront. Then I get in the driver's seat. Sophia's filing her nails in the passenger side, pretending I'm not there. Fine. I crawl over the hump into the back.

The shop girl glares at me from the swivel chair they have her on; Greg's got her on one side by the upper arm, not quite a squeeze—reading her, no doubt. Rondo's on her left, and Packard's on a crate in front of her and they're firing questions at her.

I pick her glasses off the floor and try them on. It's just like Marty said—all four of the highcaps have blurs over their heads, like heat off cement. The shop girl's still glaring at me.

"Concentrate," Packard says. "The Dorks."

"I don't know!"

Beside her, Greg nods, confirming that she told the truth.

"Who *does* know?" Packard asks.

She shakes her head. "Just let me go!"

"None of them know," Greg says. "They suspect the Dorks are using their glasses, but they don't know for sure. Her name's Janie."

Janie turns to glare at Greg now, clearly offended that he's reading her.

"Oh, that's interesting," Greg says, apparently reading her some more. "You can even tell a dead highcap with those glasses. The waves keep coming off a highcap's head hours after he dies."

"Where's your customer list?" Packard asks. "You must have a database of some sort."

Janie crosses her arms.

"Yuppers," Greg says, rubbing his buzz cut. "Flash drive," he continues. "Avery keeps it. Usually in his pocket."

Packard asks, "Who's Avery?"

"Owner," Rondo says. "I got the visual."

"Listen, Janie," Packard says. "The Dorks are likely using this product to identify and kill highcaps. How would Avery feel about that?"

Janie swallows and straightens up. "He'd say if they are, it's not the glasses' fault. The glasses don't kill."

"But what if the glasses are the only link? Would he be willing to turn over his list for an investigation?"

"Nope. Never."

I don't need to be a telepath to see that she's 100 percent confident of this.

Greg nods. "Avery's customers rely on him for secrecy. It's his brand promise. Avery doesn't break his brand promise."

"Fine," Packard says. "So we get the flash drive."

Janie snorts.

Greg holds up a hand to silence Packard. "Even if we get the flash drive, it won't help us." Greg's nodding. "Thing's fully encrypted. Not only that, but Avery has committed key portions to memory. So even if you broke the encryption, it wouldn't make sense without Avery's knowledge. He guards it with his life."

"That's his brand promise to customers, so fuck you," Janie says. "Avery doesn't break his brand promise of secrecy."

"True that." Rondo's nodding. "Strong on the brand promise, this guy."

"You can do anything you want to Avery, but you'll never get that customer list," Janie says defiantly.

Packard says, "Maybe we'll take off his glasses and read him."

Jamie smiles.

Greg squints. "Yow."

"What?" Packard asks.

"Avery doesn't need to wear the glasses," Greg says. "His contact lenses have the special glass. And the chip that distorts highcap signals is implanted in his body."

Packard looks stunned. "Surgically implanted?"

Rondo and Greg both nod.

Janie holds her hands over her ears. "Stop it!"

"Surgically implanted in his body?" Packard asks. "He'll always be immune to us?"

Greg widens his eyes at Packard. "Exactly. She thinks you'd have to kill him to get the chip out, but you can't read a dead man's mind. She's convinced he'll guard customer names and product formulas with his life."

"Goddamn," Rondo says. "That's some serious dedication."

Janie pulls her hands off her ears. "It's his promise. Our customers care about that shit."

"Because they're all paranoid," Sophia observes from the front.

"Where in his body is it implanted?" Packard asks.

"Nobody knows," Greg says.

"How the hell does your company operate?" Sophia asks. "What if you need to do something with billing or shipping?"

"Information on an as-needed basis, and deleted after use," Greg says.

"So I guess you're shit out of luck," Janie adds.

Sophia looks at her watch. "We're pushing it."

"Yeah," Packard says.

Janie looks alarmed. "What are you going to do?"

Packard asks, "Who does your shipping?"

Janie presses her lips together.

"They switch it up," Greg says. "Randomized. Fake account names."

"Hurry up. They're going to notice she's gone," Sophia says.

"They'll think she's smoking," Greg says.

"Fuck you!" Janie says. "I hope the Dorks kill you all."

Packard quizzes her about the back of the store, security. Whether outsiders ever come in. Plumbers, techs, delivery. All negative.

"Nurses for a health screening?" I try.

"No," Greg says. "Wait. State accountants. Auditors."

Janie's shaking her head, eyes closed, fighting the read now. I'm surprised she doesn't know how to skunk her thoughts with an earworm song. "They're being audited by the state. Sales tax problems. Auditors were there last week. But they're not coming back. Audit's done."

"We have to let her go back," Sophia says.

Janie casts a careful glance in Sophia's direction. Sophia's playing the good cop, paving the way for Janie to allow her creepy, memory-cleansing gaze.

"Where does Avery live?" Packard asks.

"Nobody knows," Janie says.

"Good God, can we release her already?" Sophia scrambles over the hump and shoulders past me, somewhat roughly, and helps Janie out of the swivel seat. It's weird to be wearing the glasses, and seeing the blurs over all their heads.

Packard opens the back door and she hops out, then helps Janie out. Sophia apologizes to Janie; they exchange a few words.

I'm the continuity, so I get out too, just in time to see Sophia lock onto poor Janie's memory. Janie returns her gaze. She seems to think Sophia's trying to communicate something, and then her face goes dull. Sophia's focus intensifies, brown eyes so dark they seem opaque. I used to think Sophia sucked the memory out of people, but Otto explained that she blurs it, like taking her finger and smudging it beyond recognition.

Greg leans out the back, reaches into Janie's ski jacket pocket, and pulls out a pack of cigarettes. Squatting in the back of the van, he lights up.

"What are you doing?"

He hands the lit cigarette to me. "When Sophia's done, put this in her hand and give her the glasses, like she dropped them. Get her attention off the van so Soph has time to sneak back in."

Packard glowers at me. "I hate those glasses."

"I bet you do," I say, eyeing the haze over his messy copper curls. I pull them off.

Sophia breaks eye contact and slinks back into the van as I stick the cigarette between Janie's first and second fingers. Then I hold the glasses out to her. "Hey! Don't lose these."

"Oh!" Somewhat unconsciously, Janie takes them and positions them on her face.

I quickly bang the door shut. "Thanks for carrying that out. I couldn't've done it myself."

"Sure." Janie gives her cigarette a questioning look, then she takes a drag. At that point, I know we're home free.

"Sorry to put you through all this, you know . . ."

"No problemo," Janie says.

"Well, have a nice day." I smile and walk to the front, get in the driver's seat, and watch her meander back in the direction of the store.

I wait until she's in, and then, with a shaking hand, I start the van, and drive off as normally as possible. The gang will stay in back and out of sight until we're clear. I wouldn't mind if they stayed out of sight the whole way home.

A couple blocks down, I pull off my wig and scratch my head all around. I remind myself why we're doing this. And that we took—what? Five minutes of her life? Is that really such a big deal?

And I'm thinking I should order some of those glasses.

Chapter
Nine

A NEW TEAM OF TAX AUDITORS will be reviewing the Paranoia Factory operations: Shelby and Simon and me. This is not completely surprising. We disillusionists are masters at infiltrating people's lives and workplaces. And then there's the fact that we're not highcaps.

I spend a boring yet exhausting few hours back at HQ waiting for everything to get arranged. Phone calls are made; emails are sent; pizza is ordered and eaten.

It turns out that the state subcontracts tax audits to private companies, and somebody knows somebody who has the power to fix a work order of some sort.

Eventually the story is hammered out: the team of state tax auditors that was sent last week screwed up. The three of us are the replacement auditors, charged with redoing the sloppy work of our predecessors.

In truth, we're going in there to *figure something out,* as Packard puts it. "Products were shipped; customers were billed. The information is there," he says. "And if nothing else, get that flash drive."

After dinner, Packard and I head to the office supply superstore where we're supposed to rendezvous with Shelby and Simon. Packard picks out a nerdy, wire-rimmed pair of reading glasses. "For Simon," he says.

"As if he'll wear those," I say.

Packard tosses them into the cart.

Simon's going because he's good with numbers. Shelby's going because she's an immigrant; apparently paranoid inventor-CEO Avery is more likely to trust outsiders— another tidbit Greg pulled from Janie's mind. And I'm already involved. Plus, I have bookkeeping experience from the dress shop.

The office store's nearly closed. I select a neon-yellow folder with a kitten on it and throw it into the basket.

"What's that for?"

"The papers from the real auditors."

"They all use leather-bound folders."

"I'm the deviant auditor. It'll add verisimilitude."

He thinks about this. "Okay. I like it. Now, let's see . . ." He pulls out the shopping list Sophia and Greg made. They visited one of the real auditors—yet another person who got the ol' *read 'n' revise*.

Packard tosses three *Accounting for Dummies* books into the cart. "What's wrong?"

"I hate when Sophia revises," I say. "Even a day. It seems worse than Ez invading our dreams."

"Wait a few nights and you might change your mind on that."

"How would you feel if Sophia did that to you? If she revised even an hour?"

"This is about catching killers."

"It doesn't bother you when she does it to innocent people? Takes their day or whatever?"

He pushes his hand into a bin of brass brads and pulls it up, letting them run through his fingers. "When you see people's motivations like I do, innocence isn't a word you use lightly. Or often."

"Okay, how about *relatively innocent*?"

"That's not my concern."

"Not your concern. That's admirable." I pick out a fancy pen.

"Yeah, well, the whole knight-in-shining-armor thing never worked so well for me."

Something stops me here—something sad beneath his flippant tone. "No?" I say, hoping for more.

He ignores me. I think about the dream, the sense that he needed to protect that place. "Tell me, Packard."

He turns to me. "About my knight-in-shining-armor days? My tireless work on behalf of the weak, the down-trodden, and the stupid?" This, like it's a joke.

"In the dream, you were concerned about protecting that place. The kids in that place."

"You're back to that?"

"What happened with you and Otto?"

He grabs the pen right out of my hand and puts it back. "Accountants use pencils."

"Why do they have pocket protectors, then?"

"For pencils." He consults the list. "We need brief-cases." He leads deeper into the store.

I catch up to him. "Tell me your and Otto's secret and I'll never mention how you deceived me ever again."

"Mention it all you want. I know what I did to you."

"Come on," I say.

"I can't tell you, even if I wanted to. Which I don't."

"You made a pact of secrecy?"

He stops and turns to me. "Yes, we made a pact. What-ever you think of me, I'm good for my word, and I take my pacts to the grave." He turns into the portfolios aisle.

"It's not telling if you dream the memory."

He continues down the aisle without answering.

"You and Otto and the castaway kids, that school like Peter Pan Island. The stairwell."

"Right," he says.

"What happened in there?"

"Boyhood adventures," he says casually.

"It was more than that. I was in your head."

He picks up a briefcase, pops the clasp, and opens it.

"How did those bodies get embedded in the wall? Were they highcap children you couldn't protect?"

He sighs theatrically. "And the tragedy haunts me still." He shuts the briefcase and puts it back.

"Ez asked me if you were ever in a war zone."

He pulls out another briefcase, as if I'm not even talking.

I say, "I know the memory of those corpses in the wall is real, but at the same time, it feels metaphorical, doesn't it? A secret that's buried. Bodies entombed. It's bad to keep secrets like that. It always feels better for secrets to come out. To just relax and remember them clearly, start to finish." I'm copying the way Ez used the power of suggestion, when she painted that picture of me giving her the descrambler bracelet.

He unsnaps the clasps.

"That one hand seemed bigger than a child's, though," I say. "Pushing out. The hand, the truth, all coming out."

"Like a zombie."

"You felt so wary, and all that dread. Alone in the school stairwell, with glass stuck in your foot. How did those bodies get in there? And what happened next? It would be such a great relief to relive it," I say. "Replay it start to finish, in a clear and open way."

He freezes, midinspection. I'm guessing he's finally realized what I'm doing—trying to charge up his stairwell secret.

"And then there was a crack in the wall, right where you didn't want one—"

"It won't work," he says casually. "I can't blame you, though." Gently, he places a briefcase into the cart between us. "You certainly can't afford to let your memory of us last summer run loose in a dream. You work so hard to hide it, even from yourself. The power of it."

He's doing it back to me, but I keep going; it's what Ez

would do. I say, "You lit your lighter and held it up to the crevice so you could see in. You didn't want to see, but you had to, and there were fingers showing, like a body was embedded in there."

He rests his fingers lightly upon the top of the shopping cart's metal caging. "I'm thinking about that afternoon you came to the empty restaurant, that day after the Alchemist. You were so alone." He pauses. I was. I'd never felt so alone. "Nobody saw it, but I did. I always see you. And you came in that door and came up to me and everything was new."

My blood races; he's two feet away, on the other side of a shopping cart, but I feel his presence, his heat, his maleness. It's like he charges the air around us.

"And I touched you." He runs a finger along his side of the cart. "Your skin was electric—I half thought there should be sparks." He lowers his voice. "I know you felt it. You looked so beautiful. And then you came closer."

He starts to roll the cart sideways. I clamp down hard on my side, stopping it, shocked that he'd talk so dirty in an office superstore. Then I realize that he hasn't said anything dirty at all.

He leans in and talks low. "Your skin was so warm, and you smelled like girl soap, and you were trembling. I could feel you tremble with my lips."

The trembling wasn't about fear; it was about the aliveness of being with him. And how the brush of his lips felt kinetic. I curl my fingers into the cool metal crisscross of the shopping cart. "I'm thinking about the stairwell."

"I'm not. I'm thinking about how you sighed this little sigh when you sank into the feeling of us together. We both sank into that feeling together—I'll never forget that. And then you pushed your hands under my shirt and slid them across my back, and your palms made that skin-on-skin sound."

I swallow. The lights are too bright.

"The slide of skin on skin. A kind of whisper." He rolls the cart aside now, and there's just blank space between us. We're too close. "The heat of your touch, the whisper of it. And I remember how it felt to hold you, and how holding you made my prison walls seem to vanish for once."

I take a half step back, unable to breathe, overwhelmed by this raw confession.

"There you are!" Shelby's voice cuts the energy between us.

She's a clashing heap of mittens, scarves, and a big floppy knit hat; Simon trails behind her in his shaggy coat. She steps right up to Packard and launches into complaints about us having to pose as auditors. "With our large target load, and now this? Is too much!" Her accent thickens with emotion as she recounts her oppressive duties as a disillusionist.

Packard wears his listening face, brows drawn slightly together, but he's not listening; he looks a bit dazed. Rosy cheeks. Simon gives me this look; he senses that they've interrupted something.

They did. Packard let me into his secret life for a moment. The secret life inside him.

I try to focus on Shelby's complaints. Packard's nodding, and then he lifts his gaze over her head, and our eyes meet, and this sensation plunges through me. He'd felt happy. Less confined—even in his prison! I'd never thought it meant all that much to him because, minutes later, he'd refused to apologize for making me his minion. But it did mean something to him.

But then, if he'd felt any kind of connection or warmth toward me, why would he refuse to apologize?

The answer hits me like a thump on the chest—he was simply trying to charge up the memory. *This was about Ez, not Packard and me!* I turn and storm off.

God, I am so gullible! I fired at him and he was simply

firing back, trying to charge up the memory. Exploiting my emotions—and doing a damn fine job of it. I round a corner and head for the copy area.

I stop in front of a shelf stacked with reams of paper in all different colors—pink, yellow, magenta, electric blue.

"Justine."

I turn and there's Shelby, pink lipstick vivid against her dark curls and crazy knits, expression in a question.

I say, "Why, after all this time, do I continue to be surprised that he'll do anything to get what he wants? Do I look gullible? Because apparently, I really am."

"You are *not*," she hisses as the store closing announcements come over the loudspeaker. I look away and she grabs my arm. She has a chipped front tooth that sometimes gives her a sexy, dangerous edge; other times it lends her vitriolic oomph. This is one of the vitriolic oomph moments. "Of all people, no. You are not."

"I am. I know what he is, and he can still dupe me. There is no limit to that guy." She fingers one of my coat buttons as I tell her what he said. "Like it meant something to him," I add. "It was a vulnerable time for me, that kiss. A raw time, you know? And he could sense that. So he gets hold of that one little genuine thread and works it, just to get his way. You know what it's like with me and Packard? It's like in the Peanuts cartoons where Lucy holds the football for Charlie Brown, and tells him to run up and kick it, and then at the last minute she pulls it away and he falls. And then she begs him to try again, she promises she won't fool him again, so he tries again, but she pulls it away and he falls again. He gets duped over and over, just like I fall for Packard's manipulations over and over. I won't let it happen again."

"Because you are afraid." She tilts her head, chipped-tooth smile. "You love your grudge against Packard too much. You are afraid to lose control, I think."

I give her an outraged expression, just a bit of a bully-ing edge. "No, it's because I don't like falling."

"Pfft."

"He just doesn't want us to dream his secrets tonight."

"What secrets?"

I haven't told her about the schoolhouse dream; it doesn't feel like mine to tell. "I'm not entirely sure," I say. "But I can't believe I fell for that talk when it was all smoke and mirrors. But I guess it's fitting. Packard as smoke and mirrors. He was a momentary diversion for me, on my way to Otto, who is my ultimate perfect mate."

"In other words, not real. Otto is fairy tale." Shelby smirks at her own cleverness.

"Helpful hint—most girlfriends pretend to like their friend's boyfriends, and act happy for them, or else they zip it."

"Such a friend is useless. You and Otto, you comfort each other. That is all."

"We fit."

"Your fears fit."

"I'm happy with him. Some people prefer that to grim-ness, believe it or not." A sterner store announcement sounds. "Come on," I say, leading toward the front. "You are going to meet your perfect mate someday and cringe when you think back on this whole conversation."

"Pfft," Shelby says.

We get into a checkout line behind Packard and Simon. I immediately engross myself in the magazine covers.

Shelby pulls three briefcases from Packard's cart: one black, one brown, one tan. "Boring," Shelby says. "All."

"This isn't a fashion show," Packard replies. "Pick one and scuff it up. Read those books, too—you need to know the terms. Tech services'll be couriering your lap-tops to you later, so don't go to bed until you can work the software." He lowers his voice. "Assume this guy has surveillance wherever he puts you. The screens'll be nonpeekable, but you need to act right."

"This'll be fun," Simon says.

"Have mine sent to Otto's," I say, flipping through *Midcity Business Journal*.

When we get up to the front, Packard chooses four chocolate nut clusters from the impulse item rack, one for each of us.

"Goody," Simon says.

Shelby unwraps hers and pops it into her mouth. "Thanks."

He holds mine out to me. It would be too weird not to take it, so I do. "Thanks." I put it in my pocket for later and I go back to my magazine. I like finding chocolates in my pockets when I least expect it.

Packard untwists the bright foil ends on his chocolate as the cashier rings us up. He extracts the dark Orb and smells it and I secretly watch him, wishing he wasn't such a manipulator.

He brings the chocolate to his mouth and bites. The planes of his cheeks move as he chews, jaw moving, teeth crushing. His Adam's apple shifts with his swallow. Eating seems so shockingly carnal and animalistic all of a sudden.

He takes another bite, and I watch, a hungry beggar outside a candy-store window.

Chapter
Ten

OTTO LIVES in a classic stone building nestled between an old-century hotel and a yesteryear department store that caters to Midcity dowagers who no longer care about money or hipness. I love just walking into his building—it's like a grand fortress full of heft and history.

It's not our night, but I want desperately to forget the stirred-up memory of that kiss with Packard. I need to get things back to how they're supposed to be: me with Otto.

Sammy the doorman tells me that Otto's home. Good. I walk through the marble atrium and head up in the paleo-space-age elevator. *Otto and I are together; get used to it*, I think, in silent response to Shelby's naysaying.

The doors slide open and I step into his foyer, surprised the lights are all off. "Hello?" I make my way around the tall table and head toward the fire glow, dancing on the hall wall. "Otto?" I pause at the threshold to the grand living room; firelight casts a pulsating glow over the ornate woodwork and furnishings. It's weird, because Otto would never leave a fire unattended.

A voice from the shadowy corner: "Justine." Only then do I make out his dark form, hunkered in the armchair by the velvet-curtained window.

"Hey." I move across the Oriental rug, pattern barely

visible in the licks of light, toward the chair in the corner, like a dark throne. I kneel before him. "Hey," I say again softly.

He closes his eyes and shakes his head minutely. That alone tells me all I need to know. The headaches. The pressure. It's bad tonight.

"I thought it was getting better," I say.

"It is," he whispers.

But not enough.

"The ones we've released so far, they've made a difference, haven't they?"

"Of course."

I straighten and kiss the top of his head, on his hat. "I wish I could take it away."

"My head?" he jokes wanly. "Please do."

"The pain."

"It's okay."

"Yeah, right."

He sits still as a mountain, half his face in darkness, the other half glowing pale in the flames.

I settle onto the chair arm and kiss the light half of his face, brushing his hair back from his jaw with one finger. I whisper, "Helmut and Simon are at the end of their targets. That's two less, maybe three—Vesuvius is finishing one. We're making progress. . . ." Only like forty more to go, I think.

A long silence leaves me feeling helpless, wishing so badly that I really could take away the pain and fear.

"I can feel them, sometimes," he says, fingers on his forehead, "trying to breach their prison walls. I can feel their will to break free of my force fields."

"It's okay. You're okay."

"I'm not. If they all surged to get out at the same time, the sheer pressure of it would explode the veins inside my skull. I'm sure of it."

"Otto, don't," I plead, imagining him holding his head in agony, bleeding out his ears, his eyes. "Don't even visualize that."

"What if somebody figures it out and unites them? An orchestrated surge would kill me."

"You have no proof of that except your imagination," I say, though it's not the wildest idea. Gently I rub his neck, but not too hard, ever since we read about the woman who got a vein star episode from her neck being pinched in a beauty salon hair-washing sink. "You're spiraling. You need to get control of your thoughts."

He says nothing.

I rub in circles. "How long have you sat here?"

"I don't know."

"An hour?"

"Maybe."

Two or three, then. Christ, if there was ever a perfect reminder of why we're crashing violent highcaps, it's this. Otto, destroying himself to keep them imprisoned. At the very least, the stress of maintaining those force fields with his mind is spiking his blood pressure, a factor that has been linked to vein star episodes. My heart beats in my throat; I pray he doesn't sense my unease.

"What's the nature of the pain?" I ask.

"Pressure," he says. "Sometimes hot pressure, and sometimes dull—a dull spike that protrudes from my midbrain area to behind my left eye. And there's a tingly numbness behind my right eye—"

He goes on in minute detail. We're both connoisseurs of the varieties of cranial pain, and I listen, horrified, until I come to my senses. "Enough. Stop it." I squeeze his shoulder. "Let me do something."

"What?"

I move around the back of him and touch his hat. He sucks in a breath.

"Will you let me?"

A pause. Then, "Okay," he whispers. "Okay."

I pull it all the way off and kiss the top of his warm, darkly luscious curls, which smell faintly of his rosemary-mint shampoo.

"What are you going to do?" he asks.

"I'm going to relax the area."

"How?"

"With my fingers. Lightly."

A silence.

"Really lightly," I add. He doesn't like people touching his head, but sometimes he'll make exceptions for me. Moving stealthily behind him, I rest my hands on his head and rub gently. "I got this from a healer." A half truth. Shelby and I got massages together the other day, and even the lightest touch felt oddly calming. It gave me the idea to do this on Otto. Relaxation is good for any condition.

"Be careful," he says.

"Of course."

With vein star syndrome, one of the veins in your head deteriorates in a way that causes it to bulge out in a star shape, hence the name, but it can shrink back to normalcy just as quickly. Because of this, you never really know if you have it. A normal scan might just mean you're between star flare-outs. Then, without warning, you could get a bulge so fierce that it leaks or bursts. A burst is typically fatal. A leak can be too, but sometimes leaks subside, or they can be repaired if you get yourself to an ER stat.

It's the ultimate ticking-time-bomb condition. And it can be hereditary.

My mom died of vein star syndrome, so I'm more likely to have it than most. Terror of vein stars used to rule my life; most days I felt sure I was one heartbeat away from a bleedout. Every head sensation sent me to the ER.

Then Packard taught me to zing out my fear, and my paranoia about vein stars stopped.

Too bad he didn't warn me that it would forever change my neural pathways.

There are times I wish I could go back to the old way—terrified but free. But being here with Otto makes me grateful I don't have to sink into that dark, hopeless hole again and again. Actually, the hole he's in seems deeper than usual.

Otto was abandoned as a child, so vein star could run in his family just as well as mine. What if he has the hereditary weakness, *and* he's stressing his craniovascular system by holding prisoners? We have to hurry up and release them, release the pressure.

I move my fingers over his thick, silky hair, and the curves of his skull beneath it.

"Soften your shoulders," I command.

He softens. Takes a deep breath. Good. That will tell his parasympathetic nervous system to ratchet down, which should help.

"You're okay," I say, warm into his hair. "You're okay."

But not really. I can't believe I ever zinged him, ever attacked him. Packard says I generate twice as much fear as any other human or highcap he's met. How in the world did Otto endure it? If I zinged him now, it would destroy him.

This thought wobbles me.

"You're okay," I repeat firmly.

He shakes his head.

"Yes," I say. "Let this work."

He puts his hands over mine and pulls me down to him and kisses my cheek.

I smile. "What are you doing?"

"Come here."

I climb onto the chair with him, half on his lap, and

give him his beret. He puts it back on and I snuggle into him, the way I love to do.

"This is what's working," he says. "This is what's helping."

"This?"

"Just this. When we touch."

I gaze into his brown eyes and sense the truth of it. I put my hands on his arms, push them up under his sleeves.

"I touch a lot of people during the course of my day, Justine, but when I touch you, it's different. When I touch you, I'm not alone."

"You're *not*," I whisper, with all the seriousness I have in me. "I'm right here." I hold his arms under his sleeves, thrilled and honored that I actually help him. He makes me feel safe and good, but I make him feel not alone. I lay my head on his chest, awash in his goodness.

We sit entwined as the fire roars. I could stay forever, I think, ensconced in his strong arms, safe in his fortress penthouse.

We need each other. We fit.

And sure, it's not all breathless, pulse-pounding excitement, but when you're a lifelong hypochondriac, breathless pulse-pounding excitement is something you don't mind leaving behind. It's this that I've always wanted. Just this.

He gets up once and brings back lemonades and teriyaki crackers. Another time he gets up to put more logs on, and then we squish back together.

"Maybe we can just stay like this for the rest of the week," I suggest.

He draws a finger down my cheek, my neck. It's a new touch. Slightly playful. "Stay how exactly?"

I give him a saucy look. "Like this."

His eyes gleam as he snakes his hands around me, one down into my jeans back pocket. He pulls me closer and kisses my neck, light little kisses that make a feathery sensation inside me. "How about like this?"

Softly, I say, "That would be good."

"Or this?" he says, finding my mouth.

I kiss him back, sliding deeper into him, and we move together in a deliciously heavy rhythm that rolls his erection against my thigh. I kiss him deep and dirty, sucking his tongue into my mouth.

"Mmm," I say as we shift and move against each other.

"Do you know what I'm thinking?"

"Not precisely."

He pushes his hands under my sweater, draws his fingers up my bare stomach. "You don't know what I'm thinking?" he asks.

I smile into our kiss.

"I suspect you do."

I grab his wrists, because the sensation is too much, and I gaze into his eyes. A question.

"I want you to stay tonight," he says.

"I'm here," I reply. And then, so that he understands it in the deep way that I meant it, I say, "I want that, too." It's sort of a weird exchange, but our meaning is contained in touch and tone now. He presses into me, sighs into our kiss, and we move against each other in a wavelike rhythm that builds, then swells and breaks, then builds again, all deep currents and power. He pulls away and pushes up my sweater and I help him, tearing my shirt and bra off in the same go.

When he pushes his whiskery face into my breasts, I tense a little for the excitement of it.

"You," he says, in a way that makes me feel slightly roguish, as I maul him through his clothes, trying to get the sudden, unbidden thought of Packard out of my mind. Quickly I start unbuttoning his shirt. I feel strange, like there's an unformed, unfinished, sad little emotion bottled up in me, and I need to fuck it away.

He rises and I slide back into the big chair. My heart pounds as he stands up to his full height and roughly pulls off the rest of his clothes. I try to focus back on him, on his body, taut as a tree trunk. He kneels down in front of the chair and slides his hands up my thigh. "What is it?" he says. "Where'd you go just now?"

I sit up, kiss his neck, and take his warm, smooth cock into my hand. "Here," I whisper. Then I lean sideways, over the chair arm, cock still in my hand, and fumble for my purse, pulling out a condom. Letting him go, I unwrap it while he nuzzles my neck and moves around on me everywhere but where I want him. Because I want him in me—badly. I finally pull out the condom and unroll it over him, leaving the little bit at the top like you're supposed to, and smoothing it down. I love touching him. I can't believe we're going to do this, after all these months of being apart, and the chaste dates. I say nothing, so as not to jinx it.

Otto looms above me, hand on each of the armrests. "Are you sure?"

"Of course," I say. "Are you?"

With the firelight behind him, his face is completely shadowed, but I don't need to see his expression, because he leans down to kiss me long and strong, his thick hair brushing my cheeks, making a kind of erotic cave for my face.

I lay back, head hitting the backrest; he stays with me, between me, kissing my neck, my ear, but not in me. My whole pelvis sings to attention as he presses a hand onto my belly, and lower, reaching his thumb onto my clit. We kiss like that, and I want to fuck his thumb and every other possible part of him. He draws nearer, presses me back.

"Oh, Justine," he says when I reach down to guide him into me. The slow, sure way he pushes into me feels like a kind of heaven. An all-encompassing, fully complete, and perfect heaven. I let out a whoosh.

He stills. "Too hard?"

"Too good." I touch his hips in the darkness, moving with him, gazing into the velvety blackness of his face. We move slowly together, luxuriating in each other's bodies. Eventually his breath becomes ragged. He props himself up over me and moves into me from a higher angle that's a whole new language of goodness. I moan, possibly loudly; it's like he's plunging into my very core. I rise; I want every part of him in me, and touching me. We luxuriate in each other until the fucking takes on its own rhythm.

"I need you," he says. "I need you."

"I need you, too," I whisper as he lowers onto me, pushing into me. Our movement catches fire.

"Oh, God, I need you." He spreads a hand over my shoulder, grips me there, and pushes faster, harder. I'm on the brink of coming—I feel it taking over, that glorious autopilot where sensation drives everything and it's too late to think. I still can't see his face, but I feel him, feel the state he's in: lost, senseless, transported like me.

"You're the only one who makes me feel better," he mumbles, panting, covering me with kisses. "The only one who stops the darkness."

I try to conceal my shock—try to keep moving and not appear to waken from the sexual dream, but I have. *The darkness?* What does that mean? Does he mean his fear of darkness? Is he talking about the stress of the prisoners, battering against his mind? Or something else? I think what Shelby said, about him seeming grimmer. If anybody knows grimness, it's her.

I kiss him, but really, it's killing me that he'd be suffering and alone in it. And what does he mean, *stop it*? Not light the darkness but stop it, as if it's a force.

"Oh, Otto," I breathe. He's lost in the fucking. I feel

sure he doesn't know what he just said, which is probably for the best. Though now I'm too worried and freaked out to enjoy myself. And I wanted our first time back together to be so perfect! I try to get back in the mood, but it's no good, so I make a decision. Clutch his hair.

"Oh-oh," I say, squeezing my pelvis violently around his cock. "Oh!" I do it again, and thank goodness he starts getting off, and doesn't know. He pushes deep, then jolts inside me, ecstatic, as I fake on. He comes exuberantly.

"Oh," I say, hating myself for what I just did. But he'll never know.

After, I scoot over to make room for him and he sinks in beside me.

"That was amazing," he says.

I touch his cheek. "It was." But all I can think about is what he said about me stopping the darkness. I alone help him. I marvel at that a little. I've always been so hopeless, barely even able to take care of myself, but now here's Otto, looking at me full of faith. He needs me, and hell if I'll let him down.

He pulls up the quilt and tucks us in together and we sit there naked and cozy.

After a long, lazy span of watching the logs burn and shift, he says, "I heard about what you did today."

My first feeling is guilt. "What did you hear?" God, why am I always so guilty around him?

"The lead. The glasses. Brilliant work. Absolutely brilliant."

"It was more blunder than brilliance."

"You followed your instincts, and you took the suspect to the place he needed to go."

"It was luck he revealed anything. Seriously, he revealed the secret of the glasses in spite of me."

"No, not in spite of you—*because* of you. Sometimes

the best interrogators let the wind take them. You went in there, and when you came out, you had the information."

I want to say, *I wasn't interrogating him,* but I know Otto meant it as praise. "I can't help but feel like I screwed him over," I confess.

"One of the many things I admire about you," he says, "is your empathy."

"Empathy for the guy I just screwed over? I doubt he'll be thanking me."

"Maybe not. But others will." His eyes shine. "Keep your attention on the big picture, Justine. Sometimes, extreme circumstances call us to do things we'd prefer not to have to do. But the Dorks are killing people. They're killing more often now."

"I know. We have to move fast."

"No, you have to move smart. Let it take as long as it takes. I read the report on the manufacturing operation you're infiltrating tomorrow. If you head in there with any sense of urgency, you'll spook them and squander the lead. Move in there and lie in wait. Let the opportunity or the moment come to you."

I nod grimly.

"Like a spider," he says. "Your job is *not* to create the moment. It's about having everything in place when the moment arrives, and being ready to strike."

"So I'm a spider?"

He laughs his rumbly, sexy vibrato and takes my hand, kissing my knuckles.

About an hour later, the doorman rings up that a package has arrived for me. The laptop. It's late, but I fire it up and spend the time it takes to get familiar with the software while Otto reads.

It's midnight by the time we're washing up for bed. Otto reminds me that Covian is going to be released from the hospital tomorrow. Covian's family had to go back to Oklahoma, so Otto's going to pick him up. Apparently Covian's healing beautifully, and driving the nurses crazy.

"Driving them crazy how?" I ask, trying to be mindful about not brushing my gums too hard. Eroded gums can lead to heart disease.

"With his mania to get up and out of there. He ruined several wound dressings trying to walk around. Thank God he's all right."

"It's not your fault he was shot," I say for the umpteenth time.

In bed, I prop my head up on my hand and trace the curve of his biceps as he stares at the polished bronze chandelier, which casts a warm glow all around us. This is the ultimate man's bedroom, I sometimes think. All the furnishings are as solid and darkly burnished as Otto is.

"I have something for you," he says mysteriously.

"What?" I'm thinking something dirty, but he grabs a book from his nightstand. "Bedtime story?"

"Of a sort." He shows it to me. *Autobiography of Benvenuto Cellini.* "Renaissance sculptor." Otto opens the book to a ribbon bookmark. "I think you'll find a particular passage in here every bit as interesting as I did."

I settle back to listen as he reads aloud. It seems the sculptor made enemies of the Pope and the Pope's son back in the mid-1500s. Then the Pope's son threw Benvenuto in jail.

I lay my head on Otto's shoulder and close my eyes, luxuriating in the warmth of his voice. He's like a warm, living mountain that resonates goodness. I also find it pleasantly coincidental that Otto, whom I see as a type of Renaissance man, would read to me from a book about a Renaissance man. Soon we get to this passage where Benvenuto is in his dungeon cell eating a meal. Suddenly, Benvenuto notices something sparkly in his food. He is alarmed; he assumes he has just ingested pounded diamonds.

I lift my head. "Oh my God!"

Otto reads on. Benvenuto has heard that diamond dust can kill a man. Otto pauses to tell me that, according to his online research, the tiny particles supposedly lodge in the intestines, creating tiny perforations that become increasingly inflamed, leading to horrible pain and infection. He returns to the text. Benvenuto is freaked; he's already eaten half the food.

I grab Otto's sleeve. "Where did you find out about this book?"

Mysterious smile. "Am I not a detective?" He reads on.

"Do you think we should be reading this before bed?"

"It ends well," he says.

"It better." I shift so his arms circle around me, and the book is in front of me. I read along with him and we excitedly discuss the details. Benvenuto tries to crush and grind a larger shard, and soon determines that he has consumed glass, not diamond dust. He thanks the Lord for the poverty of the Pope's underlings.

I sigh my relief. "What a story!"

Gently Otto closes the book. "I know," he says. "The Pope's son, killing with diamonds."

"What a horrible way to die."

"You can borrow it for Ez if you like," he says. "Seems right up her alley."

"It would be almost too much."

"Isn't that the point?"

"Right," I say, taking the book, running my finger over the cover. That would be the point.

Chapter
Eleven

I'VE GOT HIM in a bear hug at the top of the steps. He twists and struggles and I nearly lose my footing, then I jerk him backward and we fall together on the broken concrete—me on my ass, him on me, on my balls. Pain shoots through me, but I keep hold. He's already torn away a lot of the wall. More of the bodies show now. I can't let him back down there, but he's not so easy to keep hold of these days. He's nearly my size now.

Henji pulls up and off, but I grab his arm and jerk him down top of me. He fights me, all knees and elbows, hair in my face. We roll. Glass shards gouge my back. Blood in my mouth.

He tries to get away again and I grab his sleeve, but it rips. I heave up, swing an arm around the back of his neck, and wrap my legs around one of his legs, trying to keep him down with me, but he pushes up, hand on my throat, knee in my balls. Pain. I can't breathe. Coughing.

I feel fuzzy. The tiles on the ceiling look funny, the words go double. *Riverside Elem,* spelled out twice, diagonal, then floating back together again. He needs to be protected. I can't let him see in the wall.

"Who are they?" Henji yells, voice cracking. I keep hold of him. "Who are they?"

He thinks it's Goyces. He's right.

But he's not sure. Maybe it's not too late. The glass grinds deeper into my back as we wrestle. He finally gets the hard side of his forearm past my chin and smashes it down into my throat. Choking, I twist his finger until I feel a pop, and he cries out and heaves off. I grab his pants pocket, but he pulls away, ripping it, and clambers back down to the broken wall and starts pulling it away.

I jump up and try to stop him, but he's too strong, too crazed. The concrete parts like rubble when he digs in his hand. He gets hold of something and pulls it out. One of the bodies.

Shit!

He jerks it out of the wall, lets it collapse onto the stairs—a dirty body held together with clothes and something else, like dirty tissues and rags glued to its skull face. *Skin.* All stone-dusty from the wall.

"Who?"

"Leave it, Henji!"

"No!"

He's brushing pieces of rubble off the body. I grab his arm, but he flings out of my grip; he has more strength than ever.

He brushes dust from what's left of the Goyce's shirt— one of the bowling league shirts they always wear, the circle patch over the pocket that says the name in cursive. He's ripping the shirt. I try to stop him, but he's crazy now, ripping off the name patch. When he has it off, he comes at me, holding it. "Does that say *Goyce*? It does, doesn't it? It says *Goyce!*"

"No, Henji!"

He smashes the little patch against my cheek. "Say it!" He pushes me against the wall, pushing and smashing the patch into my cheek. Blood in my mouth. "One of the Goyces! I'm not dumb. It's from a Goyce!"

He's right. One of the Goyces from rabbit night. The first Goyces.

"It is, isn't it?"

Hands on my shoulders. Jerking.

"It was one of the Goyces from rabbit night." He jerks my shoulders and I shake him off.

"Hey!" I try to get away. A stronger jerk. "A Goyce from rabbit night!"

"Justine!"

I open my eyes. He's over me, looking at me wildly. "Henji?"

Otto's gaze darkens.

"I mean—" I'm disoriented. It's Otto. I'm in Otto's bed. I was dreaming.

"He told you?"

"What?"

"He told you!"

I look at him blankly.

"What were you just saying?"

"It was a dream."

Otto grabs my shoulders and pulls me up. "I heard you. You were dreaming about the Goyces."

I shake my head, trying to shake out the confusion.

"He told you. What did he tell you?"

"I don't—"

"I didn't hear wrong! Don't lie to me." He sounds a little out of breath, dark curls wild under his crooked beret. "You know about the Goyces."

"No, it was a dream." I draw back until my shoulder blades hit his paneled headboard.

"A *Goyce from rabbit night*. That's what you said. I heard you."

"Yes, but I don't *know* about them."

"What did he tell you?"

"Nothing," I say, heart racing.

"How could you possibly dream that dream?"

"I didn't. It's Packard's dream. I was dreaming *Packard*'s dream. Just these bodies and you guys called them Goyces."

He leans nearer to my face, as if proximity will make things clearer.

"Otto, it's Ez, the dream invader. She got us."

"Ez?" He stills. "Both of you?"

"She linked to us," I say, wishing very badly that I'd told him when I had the chance. "She conferenced us."

I watch the emotions flow across his face. "That was you . . . sharing Packard's dream?"

"Yes."

"You saw Goyces?"

"I saw a decomposed body, and you guys kept calling it a Goyce. Otto, what's a Goyce? What happened with you two?"

"So you don't know." His failure to hide his extreme relief says everything about the enormity of what I just dreamed. He switches on his bedside lamp.

"What the hell happened in that old school?" I ask.

He takes a deep breath and sits up. "Ez has you two conferenced?"

"Yes."

"How long? How deep? Can you feel her yet?"

"No, it's nothing, and she's nearly rolling. It's nothing."

He frowns. "She has you two and you didn't see fit to tell me? You call it nothing?"

"I didn't think . . . Oh, Otto. I'm so sorry."

"Why wouldn't you tell me? Did Packard threaten you?"

"No."

"Then why?"

I see all my rationalizations now for what they were—excuses not to tell. "I didn't want you to know. I wanted to solve it and have you never know."

There's a new tightness in his expression; even his eyes seem smaller. I reach up to right his crooked beret, but he pushes away my hand. Like he doesn't trust me to touch his head now.

A hoarse voice: "Why?"

Panic rises in my chest. *Here it is,* I think. I kept it from him when I shouldn't have, and now he's angry.

"Why?"

I go on incoherently about feeling guilty for causing it, and the Dorks, and the stress of the imprisoned highcaps, but I know that if I'm not honest now, he'll never trust me again, so I dig deeper. "Because the dream invader, you know, she plunges you back in old memories and scenarios. And because Packard and I were conferenced, I felt scared that my old memories of when we were close, when we were almost, you know . . ."

"Yes, I know," he says impatiently. "Together."

"I thought they'd be the ones Ez would grab and stir up and explore, and I would be reliving that whole time with Packard—with *him* following along in my mind. It felt so . . ." I pause. "Like cheating. That reality isn't my reality anymore. I didn't want to go back there with him riding along. I just wanted to unlink us before you ever had to feel upset about it. Because you have so much to deal with."

"To prevent me from being upset. To protect me from *you* reliving your past."

"I know it sounds so . . ." I can't find a damning enough word.

His eyes look cold, stony. "You felt it was best to keep me in the dark to protect me."

I have nothing to say. Of course he's right.

"What do I care that you have a past with Packard?" he demands. "What do I care of memories? I care what you do *now*. I care who you *are*."

I feel small and despicable under his anger. *Who I am* is not looking so good. "I'm sorry."

"One thing! One thing I asked of you!" His eyes are so cold, I can't see into him anymore. "What was the one thing I asked of you? The one thing?"

"Never keep you in the dark."

"That's right. Because managing me, and lying to *protect* me, is the best way to destroy me." He flips the quilt off himself and gets out of bed. "My not knowing suited you, and everything else be damned." He grabs his trousers. "Your only allegiance is to yourself. Just like Packard."

"What are you doing?"

"I don't know."

"Are you going somewhere?"

"Apparently so."

"Where?"

"Out."

"It's four in the morning."

"I'm aware of that."

"What about the Dorks?"

He shrugs on his long coat over his bare chest. "I will not be kept ignorant. I will not be managed."

"Otto, at least take one of your bodyguards."

"If I can't walk in my own city alone, then I really do have nothing." And with that he strides out of the room. Part of me wants to run after him, but it would be futile. I listen to his steps down the hall, then the soft thunk of the elevator doors.

I rest my hand on his side of the bed, move it under the sheet, searching out the last of his warmth. What have I done? Don't keep him in the dark—it was all he'd asked. A dangerous dream invader had Packard and me linked up; Otto deserved to know that. Even Packard warned me to tell him.

I go to the window and look down at the empty sidewalk, pale under the streetlights. A bus rolls by; from up here it looks like a fat, white rectangle. A dark figure emerges out onto the sidewalk and trudges northward, hunched against the bitter wind.

I think about calling one of the bodyguards to head out and follow Otto, but that would just be more managing him. He's right about so many things.

The dream seeps back down the sides of my consciousness. Packard, keeping Otto from some truth—*protecting him*—those were the words in the dream.

I press my nose to the cold window, feeling so ashamed. I pretended to myself that keeping the Ez problem from him was in his best interests, but it was all about what I wanted. He was right about that, too.

People love Otto because of the way he looks at you, the way he inspires you to rise beyond yourself. It's such a wonderful feeling. I didn't realize until tonight how awful it feels when you let him down, and that warm regard drains away.

He disappears around a corner.

He deserves so much better. I have to find a way to make this right.

Chapter
Twelve

At 6:30 A.M. Shelby, Simon, and I meet with Ken—the one highcap accountant anybody could locate—at a coffee shop by the river. The wind's not coming off the lake for once, and the river's sweetly putrid scent fills the air. The Midcity River never freezes.

Ken gives us a mind-numbing tutorial on tax audit terms and processes. Afterward, we ride in my car to the Paranoia Factory, and Simon takes the opportunity to fill me in on his Ez investigation, which has hit some *suspicious dead ends*, as he puts it. "Two of the people the cops originally interviewed are missing," he says. "Vanished into thin air. I also reinterviewed the suspect—"

"Ez?" I say. "You went and saw Ez?"

"Any investigator worth his salt would."

"That is *not* okay."

Shelby harrumphs in the passenger seat. "Reopening target cases. Down this road you will find ruin. Both of you," she says.

Simon smiles. "I thought you liked ruin."

"Ez could be guilty," I say. "It may be as simple as that."

"Then that's what I'll find out," Simon says.

Shelby opens the visor mirror and arranges her thick dark hair into a bun that sits high on her head, like a black pillbox hat. With her black suit and black cat's-eye glasses, she looks ultramodern and quite hot. I almost never see her wearing all one color. She glares at Simon in the rearview mirror. "You look like idiot with bow tie."

Silkily he says, "This is my accountant disguise." In addition to his bow tie, he's slicked back his hair, and he's wearing a pea-green sweater vest.

"Is not Halloween."

While Shelby's look is intense, Simon's is a little crazy. "What matters is how we act," I say. "We're not here to convince them we're auditors; we're here to put them on the defensive and get them focused on financials while we focus on customer data."

I merge onto the tangle, cranking my wheel to the right. Around and around we go.

"Simon is a talented bluffer," I add, "so if he puts his mind to it, I'm sure he could wear a panda suit and get results." This little speech is designed to ease my mind as much as Shelby's.

"Pfft. Panda suit," Shelby says.

Simon says, "It's true. I would find it motivating."

"Motivating." Shelby says. "Does not make it good idea."

Simon has an arcane theory on why she's wrong.

"Stop smiling with your idiotic face." Shelby bends dashboard Gumby over, clear in half.

"Oh, Shelby," I say as I wing the car off to the left. "Gumby does not like when you do that."

She snorts.

We're near the top now, where the sleepwalkers reportedly jumped from. Around and around we go. The city passes in a panoramic blur of gray lake, gray sky, and soot-blackened buildings.

The plan is to spend a week nosing through the company books, trying to find shipping and mailing lists; it's hard to believe that Avery's key-chain flash drive contains the only copy of all customer lists, and that it's so heavily encrypted. Simon wants to drug him, copy the flash drive, and *decode the hell out of it.* Packard called that a last resort. After all, Janie thought the information wasn't decryptable off the flash alone. What if she's right? Drugging Avery would blow our cover, and then where would we be?

I breathe easy once we're off the tangle, heading west, and I give them Otto's spider lecture. "We wait. We bide our time. And only strike when certain." I picture him alone out there, vulnerable to the Dorks. I've called him several times, but of course he hasn't answered. If the Dorks shot him, surely we would've heard. And it's after 9:30; he'd be at his office now.

Ten minutes later we arrive at the Midhaven strip mall. I drive around to the back and park by the dumpsters, as instructed. I straighten out dashboard Gumby, then I reach over Shelby's lap to grab my stun gun from the glove compartment.

"You have yours?" I ask her.

"Always." She pats her purse.

"Simon?"

"Naah."

I can't figure out if he's being sarcastic or what. "You need to take this seriously. We don't know how fanatical and dangerous these people are."

The Paranoia Factory offices are on the upper level. Simon rings the delivery bell. Then he looks at me and says, "What's up with the angry glum bit this morning?"

Shelby rests a reassuring hand on my arm. "It will go back to normal," she says.

"What will?" Simon asks.

"Girl stuff," Shelby answers.

Simon rolls his eyes and rings again. Before we got to the coffee shop, I told her about the Otto blowout. She was sympathetic—especially for a person who dislikes Otto and thinks everything is doomed anyway.

Mr. Avery Koznik himself opens the door; I recognize him from the photo we got. He's a big guy with a blocky head and shoulders, even a slight Neanderthal look, but his gray eyes shine with intelligence. That didn't come through in the photo.

Simon makes the introductions; we've agreed he can be the leader.

Avery gives each of us a steely glare as he shakes our hands. His short, choppy, nut-brown hair is very road warrior, likely cut by himself. He couldn't be more than thirty-five, though his short-sleeved shirt and slacks—and especially his big, black work boots—are things an old man might wear. It's like he's part nerd and part thug. I've never met a person like him. I almost don't know what he *is*.

We give him our business cards, which have our real first names and fake last names, attached to extensive false identities that are only subtly different from our real ones—a Packard trick. You always want to stay close to the truth. Avery probably already checked us out. He would've gotten an email and a phone call yesterday about the supposed screwup, with the names of the new team to expect.

"We're clean, that's my message to you," Avery says, dropping the business cards into his breast pocket. "If you find anything, it means that *you're* not." He leads us up a narrow staircase.

"You've got a lot of false fronts for a clean operation," Simon says.

"Secrecy is our brand," Avery hisses. "Our customers are people who value anonymity, live under the radar, and that's what they like to see in a vendor. Let me ask you, have the cops found anything illegal about our false fronts? No, but I'm sure they've tried. And you won't find anything, either."

"We'll let the numbers determine that," Simon says.

"The numbers didn't determine that I was out of line the first time, but I'm getting a second fleet of auditors, due to your people's screwup. I have half a mind that this is harassment, because I should never have been audited in the first place."

"You have accounting idiosyncrasies that raise a red flag," I say.

"I think I have products that raise a red flag."

Of course he's quite right. We head down a slim, low-ceilinged hall.

Simon says, "If your products raised a red flag, you'd be getting a visit from the Toy and Game Commission."

Avery stops and turns at the lone door at the end of the hall, eyes on Simon.

Simon eyes him right back.

My heart pounds. What the hell is Simon doing, antagonizing him like this?

After a spell, Avery says, "Interesting." Just that. Then he opens the door and ushers us into a barren room with an even lower ceiling than the hallway. A lonely coat-rack stands next to a metal folding chair, and a bare lightbulb dangles into the center of the space. The windows and walls are bare, save for three doors on the far side. The place would be the perfect setting for an avant-garde play about bleakness.

We hang our coats on the coatrack and Simon starts telling Avery what we need—a workspace and certain sorts of files. Avery listens without comment, then turns and heads, somewhat robotically, through the center door.

"What was up with that comment of his?" I ask Simon. " 'Interesting'?"

"A bit of a bluff, a bit of a challenge," Simon says, seeming unconcerned.

Avery trundles back in with a card table and two folding chairs. Apparently we'll be working in this room. As he sets the stuff up, I smile over at Shelby, but she's eyeing Avery rather intensely. Or maybe it's just that she looks so intense today.

"Thanks," I say as I take my chair.

Avery hmphs. He won't be helping us, but he won't hinder us, either; that's the feeling I get. Simon and I start plugging in our computers.

"Is nice, this place," Shelby says to Avery.

Avery straightens, regarding her with piercing eyes. "Where are you from?"

"Velozabad, western city in Volovia," she replies in her usual monotone as she sets her briefcase on the table.

He says, "My mom was from Speka."

She stills. "I know Speka, yes. Is north."

And then Avery says something in a language that sounds vaguely Russian to my ears. Shelby replies—in that same language, it seems.

"Please, slow down," Avery says to Shelby. "I barely speak it."

"Accent is good, I think."

Avery eyes Simon and me. "Just FYI, I was born here, so you can tell the state that they won't get an immigration charge to add to this harassment."

Simon gives him a smile and hands him a printout of files we need to rereview or review.

Avery examines it with a frown. "I don't see why we need to do this over, or why you'd need this other stuff."

"We have to be thorough," I say.

He eyes me with that formidable gray gaze. "Perchance to harass?"

I smile. "I assure you, we are not here to harass."

He stays staring, all mistrust and challenge. "It'll take me a while." Then he departs again, shutting the middle door behind him.

Simon and I reposition our tables and chairs—Rondo told us that after Avery set us up, we should move, just in case he's positioned us in front of cameras, though I can't imagine where they'd be. In the cracks in the white walls? Too tiny. But then again, this is a place that manufactures protection for the paranoid. I'm thankful our computer screens have special filters so you can only read them from straight on.

"Hmm," Shelby says, taking a seat.

"What was that all about?" I ask her.

"Nothing," she says. "Enchanted to meet you and so forth. Volovian dialect. I hoped never to speak it again."

We pretend to work, examining files. It's tense, being here, knowing we're probably being monitored. Whenever we find encrypted material surrounded by non-encrypted material we make copies of it for the people who actually know something back at HQ. Packard says the context can help our people crack the code, especially if we get the flash drive copied. Sometimes we bang on our calculators, and we keep the Internet radio on all our computers at the same time to foil any listening devices. Even so, we turn it up when we talk about anything sensitive, and we have code words. The flash drive, for instance, is *the final figure,* and customer names are *baseline data.*

Now and then, Simon knocks on Avery's door and asks for a few more files. Different people come in and out, but Avery's made it clear that we're to deal with him only.

"This guy is some piece of work," Simon whispers angrily.

I give him a shushing look and turn up my computer radio.

"He's a surgically implanted freak of paranoia."

"He is a formidable foe," I say. "Don't mess it up."

At noon we ask Avery for recommendations on neighborhood lunch places, the idea being to mix with Paranoia

Factory workers. Avery tells us about a hotdog and burger joint. He addresses Shelby in the Volovian dialect again, and the next thing I know, he's joining us for lunch.

Avery and Shelby walk several paces ahead of us on the sidewalk. It seems clear, even when they're speaking Volovian, that he's pressing her for information on her past. She tells him her story, in English, about how her parents were killed and she left and came to work at a hotel.

Simon and I hang back.

"I feel like you're being dangerously casual in there," I say quietly.

"I feel like you're being awfully white-knuckled."

"People are dying."

"Don't worry; we'll get the list. This asshole has no fucking clue what he's up against."

Something in Simon's tone makes me study his face. It's his poker face. He's up to something. "And?"

Simon slides me a sly gaze.

"Oh my God," I say. "You're working an angle."

"Well, Justine, it's good to see you don't have your head *completely* up your ass."

"What are you up to?"

"It's not actually formed. I'm working *out* an angle. Actually a couple angles. This thing's full of angles, you know."

"Our angle is to stop the killing."

"Our angle is to be free," he hisses pointedly. "Or have your highcap boyfriends fucked you too far into oblivion for you to remember that?"

"Fuck you, Simon." I look over at him and wait for him to look at me, so he can feel the heat of my glare. When he does I say it again. "Fuck you."

He smirks.

"We need to get free," I say, "but I'm thinking about other people, too. You should try it."

"Oh yeah? Okay. Let's think about Avery. Has it occurred to you that once we get the customer list, the man's life isn't worth shit?"

This stops me. "No," I say. "Nobody's going to kill Avery."

"So they'll allow him to keep making antihighcap glasses, and everyone lives happily ever after? Is that really what you think?"

"I'd think they'd reach some sort of agreement instead of killing him."

Simon kicks a stone; it bumps over the curb and lands in the gutter. No answer. Is he right? I get a new bad feeling to add to my double-wide cache of bad feelings.

Avery and Shelby stop in front of a dirty plate-glass window with a neon sign that reads LENNY'S. Avery's smiling for once; he seems proud of the little place. Who would kill him? Not Packard or Otto. And Sophia, Rondo, Greg, the others—none of them is going to move on their own. Simon just wants to stir up trouble—especially if that trouble is between me and Otto, or me and Packard. He has a problem with both of them. He has a problem with authority.

We enter the long, narrow space; fryer smells hang thick in the air, and grease glistens on the yellow tiles that line the walls. Three small tables to our left are occupied, but the counter to our right has a row of open stools. Avery directs us to specific seats, putting Simon on one end, then me, and then Shelby. He sits at the very end next to Shelby. Apparently she's the only one he wants to talk to.

We order from Lenny himself, who has a thick black beard stuffed in a hairnet. Avery recommends the hot dogs, and insists we each order a Fizzy Yellow, which turns out to be a locally produced citrus soda I've seen around, but never tried. After Lenny sets us up with the beverages, he wanders away to start things sizzling.

Avery takes the opportunity to taunt us on the futility of our mission.

"When you're in the business of helping people protect their privacy, and stand up to oppressive forces—natural or man-made—you learn pretty fast to stay on the up-and-up. You'll find that I didn't take half the deductions I could've. Not half."

He seems to be in quite the grand mood as he passes silverware rolls down the line—Shelby, me, and Simon on the far end. "You'll find out that the auditors who came before weren't incompetent as you imagine," he continues. "I'm just that careful and law-abiding."

Simon leans forward to address Avery across me. "I hope you are, my friend." His manner is jolly. Is this his accountant persona?

Avery leans forward and eyes Simon. "I am." Avery directs us to watch Lenny, who is slicing real potatoes into French fries and throwing them into the fryer. "None of the frozen crap," Avery says. Apparently the burgers and hot dogs here are genuine, too, whatever that means.

I'm wondering what Simon's angle is, and if I should get him thrown off the project. My allegiance is to catching the killers and making the streets safe. And making things right with Otto.

Lenny slides our baskets in front of us. Simon and I pass the ketchup back and forth, and are simultaneously horrified that Avery and Shelby both load their hot dogs with horseradish paste, and nothing else.

"Yuck," I say.

"Is good," Shelby says.

Simon grabs an abandoned newspaper while Avery asks Shelby more questions. I stiffen when they stray into the area of her career.

"With your background, Shelby," Avery says, "coming from a place where public institutions turned against

the people, I'm surprised you'd choose to be an enforcer
for this arm of the government."

If he only knew what she really did.

Shelby slides a glance to me. "I do because I have no
choice."

Avery looks over at us now. I eat more fries as Shelby
amends this with her usual spiel on how there is no
freedom, but only prisons of one kind or another, and
their walls merely change shape. This is a subject she
can go on about endlessly. *Good,* I think. That'll shut
Avery up.

"Does not matter in end," she continues. "Happiness.
Pfft. Is illusion."

"How can you say that?" Avery replies, shakes pills
out of a bottle—antacid, it appears—and downs them
with soda. "Of course it's true that we're doomed . . ."
He screws the cap back on, lowering his voice, speaking
furtively only to her.

I munch a fry. Then another. They're the best fries I've
ever tasted.

Shelby's body language and occasional pffts tell me
she's disagreeing hugely with him. Their voices grow
louder. "You operate under illusion that happiness is
possible."

He slaps the counter lightly. "Of course I accept it, of
course it is an illusion, but what do you do with that?"

More mumbling.

With a smile I flip the page of the newspaper. Nobody
wins this argument against Shelby. Her dismal world-
view is a cosmological phenomenon, like a black hole. If
you don't tune her out or change the subject, she will
pull you down. It's one of the things that makes her a
powerful and dangerous disillusionist.

Avery gives it his all. I hear him say things like, "One
dungeon or another, of course it is true . . . unhappiness,
no question."

It's amusing until I realize Shelby has been uncharacteristically silent. Nodding. Leaning away from me. Closer to him.

Avery gestures fast and furious. "Plummeting . . . destined for misery." It seems he has his own sound track. "I'm destined for misery." He growls a little louder now. "Fine, but I'll choose my own damn misery—I won't let a human, government entity, or highcap choose my misery and despair for me. Those who would have us . . ." More mumbling. ". . . crash them down in flames alongside us. . . ." Something something. ". . . pull them to the deepest pit of misery."

Shelby's leaned even closer to him. I munch my fries, barely tasting them. Simon shuffles his newspaper. He's wary, too.

Finally Shelby speaks. "A fascinating and stirring view, Mister Koznik."

Avery says, "Please, call me Avery."

"Fascinating, Avery. And stirring."

He pays similar compliments to her view. "*Your formulation,*" he calls it, "is not only fascinating and stirring, but utterly enchanting."

I stuff some fries into my mouth, catching Simon's eye.

"Houston," he mutters under his breath," we have a problem."

After lunch I fire up the accounting program on my computer and proceed to stare senselessly at a column of numbers. Just weeks ago I had everything almost perfectly managed and buttoned up. Now I have the frightening feeling that things are spinning out of control—the exact feeling I've spent my life trying to avoid. The highcaps are being hunted and killed. My relationship with Otto is imploding. The memories I've worked so hard to pack neatly away might start leaking from my brain—*while I sleep*—for Packard's and Ez's entertainment. Or worse, I'll visit Packard's and Otto's boyhood chamber of horrors once again.

And then there is Shelby, who seems dangerously fascinated with Avery. And Simon's up to something. I become aware of a tingling above my left ear. How long is it since I zinged? Is the stress of all this exerting inside-out pressure on the vascular network inside my skull?

I sit up and take a deep breath. Staring into my screen, I perform a positive visualization. We get the list and everything we need to decode the names, and help solve the case. The killers are brought to justice. I imagine the relief on Otto's face, eyes soft again. And the warmth and trust is back when he looks at me. Because we want the same things, and he believes in me, and he needs me.

And maybe I'll urge my fellow disillusionists to step up the pace—hell, I'd take five cases a day—ten, if possible, to get the highcap criminals turned and released once and for all, freeing Otto's craniovascular system from stress and impingement. He'll understand that he can count on me. He'll see that my not telling him about Ez was just a stupid mistake.

I make a change in one number and the numbers in another column all change.

The door opens and Avery stomps out. "Shelby, are those glasses prescription?"

"Magnifying." She adjusts them. "One point five."

He disappears, then comes back out with three boxes, setting one in front of each of us. "I want you guys to have these. On the house. Starter kits. Antiradiation insoles, antielectromag tabs, and antihighcap glasses."

"Well," Shelby says. "Thank you."

I open mine up from the end, pull out insoles, some shiny stickers, and the glasses, wrapped in plastic. "Wow, thanks." I hold up the insoles. "You put these in your shoes?" Obviously I don't want to pay special attention to the glasses, but I'm thrilled to own a pair.

Avery nods. "They minimize the effects of geopathic stress on the human nervous system."

Simon unwraps his glasses. "Are these 3-D?"

"Anti*highcap*," Avery says. "They protect against high-cap invasion of your privacy and person."

Simon smiles. "Highcaps, huh?" Like it's a big joke. Simon's good—I remind myself that it's important not to forget that.

"I don't care if you believe or not," Avery says non-chalantly. "My message to you is, they're out there. This is not a joke. They're reading your minds, they're tele-porting things out of your pockets, and your home, and committing all kinds of other crimes against you without your knowledge."

"Uh-huh," Simon says.

Shelby examines the glasses through the plastic. "Most citizens, I think they have two minds for highcaps. They half believe, I think."

Avery points at her. "Exactly. But that's changing. Al-low me." He unwraps them for her. "Most of them do it subtly, or just don't mess with you. They don't want you to know they exist. But then you've got mass murderers, like the Brick Slinger last summer—you know that was a telekinetic highcap, right? Don't answer. My message to you is, these would've saved lives. And there are your telepaths hanging out at the ATMs, the telekinetic pick-pockets. They say certain highcaps can erase memo-ries." He tilts his head at Shelby, angling the glasses toward her. "May I, Shelby?"

"Most certainly, Avery." She pulls off her cat's-eye glasses.

Avery freezes for a second, so openly dazzled with her beauty that I feel uncomfortable, like I'm witnessing some-thing private between them. I glance over at Simon, who widens his eyes while flaring his nostrils.

When I look back, Avery is gently settling the glasses

over Shelby's smiling face. He steps back. "They look—incredible."

The glasses are dark like Shelby's dark hair, and mannish in a way that heightens her femininity. And then she smiles, revealing that crazy chipped tooth of hers. The effect is alluringly feral. Avery swallows with seeming difficulty.

"If nothing else, you really ought to wear them when you're out in public," he says hoarsely. "Concerts, malls." He mentions the blurriness, except Avery calls it a *field distortion*. "Best of all, you'll be protected from their influence."

"The glasses protect you?" I ask. "Like a shield?"

"Oh, no. Shielding is so dense, so . . . yesterday. I know they're my own product, but I have to say, they're brilliant." He smiles. "These glasses run on the principle of *information*. See, the highcap power travels via waves—think of it as a kind of natural electromagnetic signal that's transmitted the way radio signals are. All information, when you get right down to it, is carried that way." He explains how the holographic chip in the glasses will protect you by setting up a counteractive signal that adds proprietary information to that highcap frequency, or wave, counteracting highcap power within your personal space. He talks excitedly, touching his forehead a lot, like his brain's on information overload. I'd think he was mad if the glasses didn't actually work.

He tells us that once a highcap is hooked into you, say invading your dreams, or prognosticating you, it's too late. "They have to pull out on their own. They've already set up the feed, if you know what I mean."

I do.

"Amazing," I say, wondering how he knows so much about the effects of these glasses—and how he tested them. Did he have highcap cooperation? Was it willing cooperation?

Simon's got his sticker open. It's black with a yellow skull. "This is very punk rock, Avery."

"It's a tab. Antielectromag tag. Similar principle." He explains how it adds harmonizing information. He turns to Shelby. "The insoles, now, those *are* gross shields, but you need that. You don't want to know what's down there."

Simon sticks his electromag tag in the middle of his case. "Got anything for extraterrestrials?"

Avery glowers. "When and if their existence comes to light, I will study them, and I will develop something." He tromps out of the room, closing his door firmly behind him.

Simon smiles.

Shelby narrows her eyes. "Do not disparage him. He gives these out of kindness."

"It *was* kind of him," I say, turning up the radio.

"Yeah, he's a fucking humanitarian," Simon says. "Him and the you-know-whos."

Shelby lowers her voice. "He did not make the glasses for killing; he made them for protection." With a huff, Shelby turns to her keyboard. This isn't the best scenario. She already distrusts Otto and his supposedly growing grimness, and dislikes his having us disillusionists and countless highcaps as a kind of secret police at his command. And now there's this attraction between her and Avery.

I lower my voice. "By taking the *baseline data,* we're helping him out of a dilemma," I say to her. "We're helping him keep his brand promise, *and* we're saving lives."

Shelby just stares at her screen.

I feel Simon's eyes on me, but I won't look at him.

"Right?" I say.

"Do not worry," she mutters in her usual monotone, "I am with program."

I finally meet Simon's gaze. We both heard the implied *for now* in that.

I take little breaks to call Otto now and then, but he doesn't answer, and I feel more despondent as the day wears on. It's so unlike him to ignore me. Is he okay? How deeply have I damaged things?

That evening after I drop Shelby and Simon off, I swing by the government building, hoping to catch Otto at work. Gone. But one of his commissioners suggests Otto could be working off-site today. Off-site?

I try his home, his favorite coffee shops, and a restaurant he works at sometimes. *Nada.* So I swallow my pride and leave a message for Sophia. She'll know where he is. But will she tell?

Chapter
Thirteen

"YOU'RE HERE!" Ez rises from her chair behind the coat check window. "Where have you been? I want you to look at my liver area." She eyes a couple leaning over the railing a few yards away. "Maybe when they're gone. If you stare at it long enough, it looks like it moves on its own—like it expands, and then it contracts by the tiniest degrees." She watches my eyes for reaction. I give her none. "And sometimes I can feel the sensation of it all the way up to my throat. Is that a bad sign?"

"Did the Klosamine come?"

"Yes. And I'm doubling it."

"Don't, that's too much. That can actually make the next generation of organisms immune."

She gasps, still awash in fear from the last time. *My* fear. It's a horrible and devastating power that I wield. I catch sight of the photo of Otto on the wall behind her, and feel bad all over again.

"What? Shit! Something else is wrong. You just thought of something bad, I saw it in your eyes!" She fixes me with her pixie gaze. "Come on, out with it!"

"I thought of something bad, but it's not connected to you."

She narrows her eyes. "Of course you'd say that."

"It's true."

"How do I know that?"

"You don't."

She screws up her lips and fixes me with a silly look. "Touché."

I snicker. "Look, stop focusing so intently on the feeling and it'll go away. Okay?" A woman in furs trundles up. "Okay? I'll be right back." I head down the staircase to the bar below.

Stop focusing on the feeling. That was helpful advice, and I'm not here to be helpful. What was I thinking? I should've acted secretly concerned. I have to stop this compassion thing.

I buy myself an ouzo. Up above on the catwalk corridor, the woman's handing over her coat. Even though Ez hasn't asked about the field descrambler, I have this crazy urge to give it to her.

I think about what Packard said—that she collages memories to create action. Maybe that's why she keeps trying to get me to discuss handing the thing over—so that there's a memory of a conversation to stir up. Could that be enough?

I smile as I sip my drink. She really is sparky, and fun to be around, which is pretty impressive considering she's been isolated in that booth for three years. It takes a certain amount of inner strength to handle something like that—and to handle the fear I've been filling her with. I don't need Packard's psycho-sight to get the sense that she doesn't add up as a sicko killer. I've dealt with plenty of lowlifes and depraved murderers at this point, and Ez doesn't have the same feeling in any way. Is this really a woman who turned people into murderous cannibals for the fun of it?

But an innocent woman wouldn't be invading our dreams and trying to control us, and certainly Otto wouldn't have sealed her up without proof. While we were screwing around at the Paranoia Factory, I read the *Midcity Eagle*'s online archive from the summer of the Krini Militia. It really was horrible how those people were eaten, and there was a great deal of evidence against Ez. She reportedly fled to Brazil. No doubt Sophia revised her friends and family to believe that, just as Packard's friends and family were revised to think they saw him die all those years ago.

I go back up the stairs. I think about what Otto said: *Extreme circumstances call us to do things we'd prefer not to have to do.* Until I'm presented with evidence of her innocence, I have to work on disillusioning her.

Up top I head down the balcony past a chatty little group toward her little window. Nobody's recognized her in there—not surprising, when you see the murky photos and police sketches of her. I suppose one day she woke up and found herself in there. What happens if she contacts her old friends, or tells the world who she is, and pleads her case from the coat check booth? Does she meet an even worse fate? Are there rules? Consequences? We disillusionists never get answers to these questions.

I set my drink on her ledge. "I brought you something," I say, low, so the couple gazing over the balcony rail won't hear.

"Is it what I most want in the whole wide world?" She raises her eyebrows. "You know how happy that would make me."

I do know. "Sorry," I say.

She frowns a pouty frown. "Well, can I just see it? What harm would it be for me to see?"

This suddenly makes a weird kind of sense. What harm would it be? I hold up my arm.

Her face lights up. "It's the bracelet? That's the descrambler?"

"Shhh," I say, feeling happy that she's happy.

"Let me try it on."

"No way." I lower my arm, letting my sleeve fall over it, shocked that I just showed her. What was I thinking?

"The bracelet all this time?"

"I won't give it to you, though. Ever." And I'll be zinging her with my other hand, too. Shit! Why did I show her? She can picture it now. Packard warned that she could gain limited influence during the day. "I have this for you instead." I pull out Otto's copy of *Benvenuto Cellini*.

"Another book?"

"I knew you were interested in the ingesting of diamonds—"

She goes a little pale. "No. I really wasn't."

"You have to hear this. It's a fascinating anecdote."

"No." She puts her fingers to her lips.

"You'll love it, Ez." I launch into reading the passage about Benvenuto in the dungeon. She resists, but she's simply no match for me. I'll get her in the mood, I'll zing her, then I'll go. Soon I reach the passage where he's sure he's eaten the diamonds, convinced he'll die a grueling death, and Ez and I discuss this thing I learned on the Internet today: that tiny shards of pounded diamonds get these barbed fishhook-like edges that can sink into the intestine walls over months—one person suggested it would be like a stinging jellyfish living inside you. Ez looks like she's going to fall over. I don't blame her. The idea of it terrified even me, and I never had perforated organ fears.

I sense that her attention is turning inward. I should take her pulse right now and zing her.

"You wouldn't be able to even do an operation on that sort of thing," she says vacantly.

"Not unless they figure out how to transplant intestines."

"Or maybe they could bypass it. Maybe do a modified gastric bypass down to the distal end?"

I bite my lip. This is not my area of expertise.

"What is this, book club?"

Ez blinks, as though she's coming out of a trance. "Simon!"

I spin around.

Simon grins. "Hello Ezmerelda. Nurse Justine." He's still in his work outfit, but he's added his big ratty coat and the antihighcap glasses, and his black hair, once slicked back, is now disheveled sideways, seeming to defy physics, for a look that's insane, and bit menacing.

"Well?" Ez says. "What happens? Justine?"

"What?" I say.

"Does he survive?"

"Oh. Cellini realizes it's glass," I say. "Which is digestible."

She gapes at me, eyes so wide in her small, fine face that she looks downright doll-like.

"Glass is digestible?" Simon says. He comes up right next to me, so we're both at her window. "Are you guys discussing a book? Is that what you're doing?"

I show him the cover. "Do you know it?" I ask.

"No."

I give him a hard look. "Well, then . . ."

Simon ignores my hint and smiles at Ez. Shit.

There's a door to the side of the coat carousel. Nobody would've passed through it for years, but Simon could; he was given a descrambler for the Belmont Butcher, who has a high-security setup just like Ez. And now he's wearing antihighcap glasses. He wouldn't be wearing them if he wasn't planning on touching her.

"We're having a private conversation about it," I say.

"But not *overly* private," Ez says.

He's clearly not leaving, so I take the opportunity to inform him how swallowing diamond powder is like having a stinging jellyfish living inside you for months. I go on to talk about the crazy strong squeezing muscles of the intestines. Simon wears an amused smirk, as if it's all just a lark. He's messing everything up—a hypochondria attack requires a serious attitude.

I look at the place on my wrist where my watch would be if I wore one. "Sort of getting late," I say.

Simon gazes at me, all innocence. "You have to go? Too bad." He pulls a deck of cards from his pocket.

She smiles. "Rematch?"

I raise my eyebrows at Simon. *Rematch?* I push away from the window. So much for interviewing the suspect. He's been socializing with her.

"Oh, duh, your coat. Sorry, Justine." Ez retrieves my coat from the carousel.

I could still take her pulse and zing her, but thanks to Simon, her mind's not in the right place, and I don't see myself getting her back on track. I'm a little bit relieved, but at the same time, disappointed, because I won't get to feel that wonderful peace. I try not to think about that too much. I throw a couple bucks into the tip jar.

"Nice to see you again, Nurse Jones," Simon says.

As I pull on my coat, I stare levelly at Simon. "If you don't mind, since you missed your follow-up visit to the clinic, I'd like a word with you. A bit of a heads-up on your condition."

"I hardly think a broken arm is a condition." He lifts an arm. "It's healed up fabulously."

I bore into his eyes. "I really don't want to tell you the results of the test in front of Ez."

His smile is a challenging one. But just then, a large group, maybe a dozen, trundles in the door. We step back as the first approaches Ez's window. "I'll walk you to your car, Nurse Jones."

We get out of there. The sky is starry, and the street-lights illuminate tiny crystalline snowflakes riding the chill breeze. "What is this?" I demand, heading toward where I parked. "You're playing *cards* with her? This is beyond investigation. You're just after her."

"I can't make a friend?"

"Not this one." I turn a corner. The sidewalks are unusually empty, considering it's only a bit after seven o'clock. The Dorks.

"Loosen up," Simon says. "Why not go do somebody else and crash Ez later on? Give me more time with the investigation."

"Are you even investigating? Because this is important to me."

"Of course I am, but in the meantime, we've been having some fun, me and Ez. She's been in there for three years. How about you let her have some fun with me while she's still badass?"

"I can't. Unless she's innocent, and I'm not seeing proof that she is."

He snorts angrily.

"Sorry, Simon. I can't."

"I can't," he mimics. "Don't you ever hate yourself?"

I stop, spin around. His eyes gleam behind the anti-highcap glasses. "Here's the situation. Ez has her dream invader hooks into Packard and me. Know what I'm saying? She's got us conferenced. So she's fast-tracked."

Simon cranes his neck up, incredulous. "What?"

"I messed up, okay? I let her touch me while Packard tried to pull me away, and she got us both. Our sleeping minds are totally conferenced right now. Don't tell anybody."

Simon laughs. "You're conferenced together? You and Packard and Ez?"

"And she's already been screwing around in our sleeping minds."

Simon flicks his bangs out of his eyes with a jerk of his head. "Start sharpening the ol' chompers yet?"

"That's not even funny." I continue walking.

"It wasn't a joke. Has she been trying to work you in any way that would seem like she wants you to eat people? Does she talk about meat when you see her? Steak tartare?"

"Don't."

"I'm not trying to be funny. If she has a cannibal mania, or whatever kind of sickness makes a person do that, she'd be working you in that direction. Has she?"

"She's been making suggestions."

"About?"

"She wants us to hand over our descramblers."

"See? She goes right to getting free."

"Maybe it's step one. With your two days of investigation or whatever it is you've been doing, have you come to any different conclusions than Otto, the high-cap master detective? No."

"Yeah, I have."

"Only in your own mind. If you'd found something you would've told me by now." Everything is so complicated suddenly—too complicated. "Think about it, Simon. Ez has taken the power to command us as sleepwalking zombies. We have to crash her and make her break the link. It's a matter of survival." I say it as much for myself as for him.

"Even if she's innocent?"

"How long am I supposed to wait for you to find evidence of that?"

"I think she's innocent."

"If she's innocent, then why is she messing with our dreams? Why is she deepening her hold on us?"

"She wants to get out."

"Easy to say when you're not the one who'll be dining on guts if you're wrong."

"I'm going back up there."

"What? To ruin all my work?"

"Nobody's ruining your work."

"You already ruined my work. I didn't get to zing her because you interrupted."

"You still could've zinged her." He gives me a quizzical look. "What's wrong?"

"You took her mind out of it." I shrug. "She's rolling anyway. She's not even all the way sane now."

"She's sane enough for me," he says as we reach my car.

"To fuck?"

"That's right."

I give him my most damning gaze. "You would take advantage of her partial sanity and her loneliness like that?"

"What about my partial sanity? And my loneliness?"

"You are sick. And you're not going in there." I grab his wrists. They're bare. "Where's your descrambler?"

"You won't find it."

"You're not going in there."

"Or what? Otto will seal me up? Oops, he can't. Because I'm wearing these glasses now. These fucking things are the best thing since sliced bread. Otto can't touch me and Ez can't compromise me, either." With a smirk he leans on the passenger door of my Jetta, pretends to arrange his hair in the side mirror. "Until I want her to. I understand there are certain benefits to it."

"Packard can still cut you off and let you turn into a Jarvis."

"All the more reason to spend my last days having fun."

"I'm sure he'd manage to send some thugs over to beat you up in the meantime."

"Packard's sworn off that shit."

I narrow my eyes. Why does everybody assume Packard's out of the crime business?

"Anyway, I'll take my chances," he adds.

This, of course, is pure Simon. Always taking chances. Always on the losing end. Which is why I've slipped out my stun gun.

He realizes it seconds before I show it. He smiles, thinking about how to get to his, no doubt.

I say, "Don't move. Just tell me where you have the descrambler."

"I've taken precautions," he says.

"You never take precautions." We both know how this will end, but we have to go through it. "One. Two." He lunges. I press the button.

"Uh!" He crumples. I grab a handful of ratty coat, trying to break his fall, but his chin still hits the side mirror on the way to the ground.

"Shit!" I whisper. "Sorry." Quickly I straighten him so he somewhat looks like he's sitting and leaning against the closed door, though his head is lolled to the side, and his butt has sunk awkwardly between the tire and the curb. His descrambler turns out to be in his coat pocket— a chunky silver chain bracelet just like mine. He's starting to rouse. Quickly I pull off his glasses, too, unlock my car, stuff them both under the backseat, then lock it back up.

Heels click up the walk.

I crouch next to him and brush the black hair from his face, heart racing. "Hey, buddy."

A voice behind me: "Everything okay? Do you need an ambulance?"

I look up at a tall woman in a long purple coat. "He's a fainter and a bit of a drunk, but it's okay. I'm a nurse."

"Fuck you," Simon mumbles. "She's not a nurse. She never will be a nurse."

I smile up at her. "Back to his old ornery self."

"She's an agony nurse," Simon says.

"Thanks," I say to her.

The woman laughs nervously and clicks away, slightly faster than the clicks of her coming.

"Where're my glasses?"

"I'm sorry, but your glasses have been detained. I won't be a sleepwalker under Ez's control. I have more than enough problems without that."

"Fuck it. I'll go in without them." I watch him come a little bit more to his senses. He jerks his hand to his pocket and realizes the descrambler's gone.

I back away. I'll stun him again if I have to.

His expression darkens. "I'll get another pair. And I'll get another descrambler."

"Not tonight you won't," I say.

He stands uncertainly, one hand on the hood of the car. "Just like Packard. You're just out for yourself."

"Look who's talking," I say. "Don't you dare reverse my work with Ez."

"Good little Justine always wanted to be a nurse," he says in a mocking voice. "Now she's an *eeevil* nurse. Now she's an agony nurse. Attacking her victims."

I feel a little ill. "We're helping people."

"You're contorting so wildly to pretend you're on the *good* side, you're like a fucking sideshow act. Reality check, sister. We're the bad guys. We work for a power-hungry megalomaniac. Otto's a megalo*maniac*."

I smile hotly. "A megalomaniac would've killed people like Ez by now instead of going through what he's going through."

"People like Ez? You mean people who've been imprisoned indefinitely without trial? Who look very very innocent? To both of us?"

I'm taken aback by his seriousness. It's new. He turns and storms back toward the club.

I shove the stun gun back into my bag, get into my car, and sit, feeling like hell. What if she is innocent? I reposition dashboard Gumby, making his little green arms go over his face. His happy hopeful face just seems fake. "What am I going to do?" I ask him.

I've never needed to see Otto so badly. He's the person who makes it all make sense, my anchor when I'm adrift in doubt. He wouldn't have sealed her in there if she was innocent. I click on my phone, and my heart skips a beat when I see that there's a text from him.

I turn on the engine and the heat and settle in to read it.

at mayoral conference, recharging and revitalizing. need solitude w all that has happened. will talk when I return.

I read it again and again. *w all that has happened,* he wrote. Meaning all that's happened with us? Or is he talking about the Dorks? Why a text and not a voice mail? That can't be a positive sign. I write back: *Otto, I am so sorry. I miss you. Can we talk? When will you return? xxoo*

As soon as I hit send I think of different, better things to write, but it's too late. And it would be too flaky to send another message now. I feel panicky, like things are growing distant: the sun, the moon, my dreams.

Have other people heard from him? I call Jimmy, his chauffeur. He's in Atlanta; Otto's given him a vacation. He knows nothing.

I'll call the people at Otto's office tomorrow, but they'll probably only give me the information they provide the public. To them, I'm a consultant Otto uses now and then. This is one of the things I hate about being in a secret relationship with him. I try Sophia. Still voice mail. Did she go with him?

I call Covian. Voice mail. I leave a message for him to call me; he probably has his phone off. But surely Covian saw Otto this morning. Otto was determined to bring him home from the hospital and see him properly settled in.

Just for the heck of it, I swing by his place—a little Monopoly-type house in the Irish quarter just south of the tangle. I get out of my car and walk up to the door. All the shades are drawn, lights off. Covian's probably sleeping. But maybe he isn't. And he saw Otto more recently than I did. Maybe Otto said something. Maybe Covian could give me a read on his state of mind. I raise my hand to ring, then pause.

How thoughtless can I be? Only a desperate girl makes wounded guys get out of bed to answer questions about her relationship. I lower my hand. Covian will return my voice mail.

Back in the car, I read Otto's message again, searching for further meaning. Another thing a desperate girl does. *Need solitude.* Is he deciding whether to keep me? Of course he is. I attacked him once before, and he let that go because I was trying to save people's lives. Or so I thought.

He has such a noble nature, holds himself to such high standards—my deception could be more than he can tolerate.

Packard's at my place when I get there, stretched long across my couch like a lazy pasha, owning it as only he can. It's deeply irritating—not the least because he looks so magnificently male.

"You can't break in here like this," I say wearily as I set my keys in the dish by the door. "You're not welcome." I only half mean it. I look back to find him eyeing me with a serious glint. "What?"

"I spoke with Otto."

My stomach flips. "When?"

"This morning."

"What did he say?"

"That you dreamed about the Goyces." Tenderly he asks, "How are you doing?"

My vision steams, blurs; I blink back the tears, praying he doesn't notice. I haven't cried all day, and he has to ask how I'm doing. I cross my arms. "Fine."

"Oh." He stands and comes to me, enfolds me, crossed arms and all. "Oh," he says simply. It feels good. Like home.

I pull away. "He hates me."

"No," he says.

"Even *you* told me to tell him. But did I?"

"You did your best."

"No, I didn't." I sniff and wipe my nose. "Don't act like you're not a little happy."

"Happy? To see you sad?" He rests his hands on my shoulders. "Don't be dumb. I hate seeing you sad."

And of course I know that, and because I know that, the hot tears start drooling down my cheeks.

"Stop, Justine. Come on." He shakes me loosely. "Come on." It's supposed to be funny, the way he's shaking me. It is a little. "Come on now." As soon as he gets a smile out of me, he goes serious, eyeing me with grim fire. "People will always disappoint Otto. Nobody can live up to his expectations, because he sees in black-and-white, when things are really very gray."

"I should've told him."

"You were doing the best you could."

"Was I?"

He lets me go and shoves his hands into his jeans pockets. "You always do."

I close that line of talk with a taut wave. "He didn't say anything else?"

"Not much. He was on his way to pick up Covian."

"Did he say why he changed his mind about the conference?"

Packard looks confused. "The conference?"

"That mayoral conference? He's in DC. He went to DC."

"Otto went to that conference in the middle of the Dorks problem? And this Ez situation?"

"He wanted solitude. I got this text—"

"Otto sent a *text message*?"

"Obviously he doesn't want to talk to me."

Packard stares over my shoulder, seems to study my

St. George and the dragon tapestry, a cool old thing I bought with my disillusionist money last fall. I wait, noticing faint lines across Packard's forehead.

"What?" I ask.

Packard snaps out of it with a quick shrug. "He should've stayed, that's all. Look, we need to discuss that dream. You dreamed about a Goyce. I need specifics."

"Bodies entombed in the walls. You two fighting."

He fingers a button on his shirt, rolling his thumb around and around. "Come on. I need to know what you understood of it. Please." The way he says it— *please*—reveals a level of desperation that surprises me.

"Fine. It started out with you and Otto—or you and Henji, both as kids, in a fight at the top of those stairs. I got that it was Riverside Elementary. Riverside Elem—"

"Elem," he whispers. "The rest of the tiles fell off."

"And Henji was getting at the bodies. Kind of pawing through the wall, as if the wall disintegrated under his touch. I didn't know he could do that."

"It's a part of his power that he rarely uses."

"He yanks out one of the corpses and he rips the little name patch off the shirt pocket and he's saying, *It's a Goyce!*" I'm thinking about that patch. I'm trying to picture it. There's something off about it, but it's like, well, trying to remember a dream.

Packard's words pull me back. "You said it was a Goyce from rabbit night."

"Only because that's what Henji called it. It's not like the dream had a monologue of what rabbit night is."

"Say more. I know you can."

I sink into the chair and close my eyes. I'll give him this. "I understand that a Goyce is a dead body. The guy's name in life, or the name on a patch on a shirt. In the dream, you knew more bodies were there, and maybe he was putting it together." I study my hands, trying to reach back further. I come to it again; there's something about the name on the patch, like a snag in the smooth flow of my recollection.

"And?"

I look up. "I felt you again. What it was to be you. Bewildered, young. The panic as Otto began to figure it out, and you wanted to stop him and you couldn't. God, the way you felt—so vulnerable. And the dread, like this horrible thing was being uncovered. Your need to protect him."

He flushes and looks away. What in the world happened back there?

I don't press him on it. "It's horribly invasive, Packard, what Ez does. And I won't say anything to anybody, okay?"

"I know." There's this long pause where we sit there, silent companions, knowing each other's minds. It's nice. "Thank you," he says.

I stand. "Are you hungry?"

He looks surprised at the question.

I happen to know he's always hungry. And I want him to stay awhile. "Come on. I made some lasagna the other day." I head to the kitchen and he follows. "And if you're nice, I'll serve it on kebab skewers."

He clutches his heart. "No!"

I pull out the pan and heat it up in the microwave. "I can't believe I'm feeding you when you snuck in like you did."

"I'll stop," he says.

"You'd better."

He works on setting two places at the coffee table. I'm not set up to have guests, but he makes it nice—it's all those years trapped in a restaurant. And somehow, as we're sitting across from each other, balancing our plates on our knees, it's more than nice. It's perfect.

I tell him about the Shelby-Avery connection, and we marvel about it, but agree she can be trusted no matter what. And we talk about Ez some more. I assure him that whatever Ez stirs up is safe with me.

"I think she'll go on to different subjects now," he says mysteriously.

"Okay. But I should tell you, Simon thinks she's innocent."

Packard squints. "Simon needs to back off."

"Unlikely. Let's just say he'd like to fully insert himself into her case. And he had a descrambler." I load one last succulent bite onto my fork.

Packard lets out a hiss. "Right. For the Belmont Butcher."

"I took it away. Hopefully he can concentrate on somebody low security for a while. Simon thinks if she was really running cannibal sleepwalkers, she'd be pushing us in that direction more. Wouldn't you agree, if that's her big thing? She's focused on the descrambler, but not on cannibalism at all. Do you think that's suspicious?"

"You're still on that?" He puts down his empty plate and wipes his hands. "She's increasing her access to our memories. She's controlling our dreams, and soon she'll control our actions at night. We'll be her puppets. Disillusioning her is the only sure way to make her let us go.

"It's in her nature to keep the link. We will be at her *mercy*." He gives me a hard look. "Do you want to be even less free?"

This is a rhetorical question I don't bother answering.

He says, "Sometimes you have to be a bad person to save yourself, and it takes a little chunk out of your soul, but you do it anyway."

He's talking from personal experience. He's talking about what he did to me. I know this with uncanny confidence. "There has to be another way," I say.

"There isn't. Choose. Do you want your freedom or your morals?"

"Goddammit." I stand and go to the window; the

snow is falling heavily now, thick flakes swirling in the streetlight beams. "I don't want to give up more freedom," I whisper. If I say it louder than a whisper, I might cry. I close my eyes, hoping he didn't hear it in my voice. Everything is so complicated. Choices and dos and don'ts swirl as madly in my head as the snow outside my window. "I don't want to, but . . ."

"But?" I hear him moving behind me, the rustle of fabric like he's putting on his jacket, denim on the outside, and a white woolly lining. The sound of snaps. "Okay." More snaps. "Fine, then," he says. "Get zinging. You have until Monday—four days from now—or I'll cut you off."

"What?" I spin around. "You wouldn't!"

He tilts his head, eyes flat. "I appreciate dinner, but it doesn't change anything."

I stare, incredulous, as he pulls on his black knit hat and leather gloves. "We have to unlink her from us. And we have to disillusion all the people on the list of violent highcaps. That is our task. That is what we will do."

"So I finish with her or I'm a Jarvis?"

He twists his scarf around his neck. "That's about it. If she's not rolling and ready to hand over to Vesuvius on Monday, you're out."

"You won't!" It's like he's changed into a different person.

"I'll do anything to be free and stay free. Anything. You'd do well to remember that." He crosses the room and leaves, shutting the door quietly behind him.

He wouldn't.

But actually, he's always chosen his freedom over everything and everyone. I stare at the door, rigid with resentment. He's just made my decision for me. Because I'm his minion. I no longer rule my life.

After all these months, it's still as outrageous and stunning as when I first discovered it. I think about what

Shelby always says: *There is no such thing as freedom, Justine. Only prison walls that forever change shape.* Her way of making me feel better. Not exactly effective.

I move to the window just in time to see him emerge from the lobby below, walking proud. He heads up the sidewalk, gets into his old Dodge, and slams the door. The sound penetrates through my closed window and into my chest.

I wait for the roar of the engine, the white puffs out the tailpipe. Nothing. A minute. Another.

In spite of my anger, I don't like that he's just sitting there. Doesn't he realize he's exposing himself to the Dorks? Their eyeglasses can pick up the highcap blur through a car window, and he knows it! He needs to get indoors, behind a wall.

I look around for the bodyguards, but all I see is the swirling snow. And then this weird little question emerges out of the night sky of my mind: was that threat Packard's way of freeing me?

I adjust my posture, as if to get used to this new thought. The threat did free me from having to make the hard choice. Was that why he did it?

After a tense ten minutes, he starts up the car and zooms off.

Chapter Fourteen

SUMMER. MONGOLIAN DELITES. I kiss Packard, and something shifts in me, relaxes in me. A warm glow flows through my heart—relief, heat. I smooth my palms over his muscular back, enjoying the warmth of his skin, smiling into his yummy lips. I want to kiss him and taste him everywhere, and I'll never get enough of him, because he makes me feel alive.

I eat him up a little bit, pull him into me. He groans, and his passion turns me on like crazy. Breath harder and faster now, my shoulder blades thunk against the wall. I love his happiness—I can feel it as strongly as my own, and I let him overwhelm me with hard kisses that glow inside me. Warm lips on my neck, my ear. He whispers my name. I grab his hair, pull him to me. God, I love him. I want to spread out under him and wrap around him at the same time. He presses into me, and we move together and it's heaven, consuming each other. I just want to roll with him and be happy and free with him. Everything is right when we're free to love each other.

Packard.

I roll over, thrumming with happiness, wanting to stay in that fragile, bright love, wanting the spell to last. I slide my hand over the cool, smooth pillow, and I realize I'm not at the restaurant; I'm in my bedroom.

I sit up.

Love? Packard? No! Happiness, okay. Intense happiness. Aliveness. A kind of freedom. But *love*?

Is this Ez, messing with my memory? Can she do that? I try to think what Packard said.

Shit! Was Packard inside my mind that whole time? Did he experience that dream memory from my point of view? Feel what I felt?

Of course he did. I felt his fear and guilt in the school stairwell plain as day. I rub my temples. Was it even real? Did I believe I loved him then?

I stare out my bedroom window at bare, cold tree branches. I'd brought myself to forgive him during that kiss. Maybe I felt fleeting love, and maybe Ez found it and blew it up big. She didn't bother dredging up what happened after the kiss, of course. Where he refused to apologize for making me his minion. If there was any seedling of love there, he killed it with that.

Fine. Let him make it into whatever he wants, and let him go ahead and brandish it at me and try to manipulate me with it. I'll tell him that's what he killed. *Anything you felt in the dream is just a memory of what you killed!* I'll say.

Still, the idea of facing him mortifies me.

Five-thirty in the morning. There will be no more sleeping now.

I go back over the dream, which was like a memory, but more. It felt like being there. And made me totally horny.

One wool sock lies on the floor next to my nightstand. I grab it and tiptoe around the cold floor looking for a match, body still humming with crazy craving for Packard and an intense desire to help Ez. I feel this outpouring of affection for Ez and I just want to be free to help her.

I freeze, clutching the wool sock. Help Ez? *What the hell?*

Coffee. I stumble to the dark kitchen and start up my coffeemaker; then I go find the other warm sock and my jeans and a Midcity Warhawks jersey and put it all on, as though being fully clothed will buy me distance from the dream. And then I get a very bad feeling. I race to my dresser and scatter through scarves and jewelry on top of it and, with a great sigh of relief, I find my descrambler bracelet where I left it.

Later, at my kitchen table, I click through my messages. Nothing from Otto. Nothing, nothing, nothing, I ignore a voice mail from Shelby and reread Otto's old text message.

at mayoral conference, recharging and revitalizing. need solitude w all that has happened. will talk when I return.

I find myself smiling at his use of the word revitalizing. *Recharging and revitalizing.* It's a unique Otto usage—I don't think it's quite right, but it makes me like it all the more. This is what's real now: me and Otto.

Packard seemed surprised that Otto had gone to the mayoral conference. It's true that Otto isn't a conference type, and he hadn't seen the sense of going to it earlier, but I can understand him going now. He probably has new bodyguards and drivers to get used to, and there's the cranial stress of the prisoners, the emotional stress of the Dorks, and of course, the blow of my keeping him in the dark. Who could blame him for wanting to recharge and revitalize?

Knowing Otto, he'll duck most of the events and stay in his hotel room. Thanks to this force-field power, he can reinforce any room to achieve the kind of silence you can usually get only on a mountaintop. He can sit in silence like that for hours, and then he emerges full of energy. *The cone of silence,* I once jokingly called it, like in *Get Smart.* He'd enjoyed me likening it to that.

I read his text over again. Just recharging and revitalizing, and then he'll be back. And I'm a resourceful person; I'll find a way to make things right. I will not fail him again.

I click to Shelby's message, and I'm annoyed to learn she won't be riding with Simon and me. She's going to take the bus into work. Great. The commute had been a convenient meeting time for us—and today, of course, I could really use a buffer, considering how badly Simon and I left things. Stun-gunning and taking his stuff and all that.

I pull up in front of his place at eight sharp. It's an ugly 1970s fake Colonial apartment complex just west of Mongolian Delites—not the best area. At all. Simon saunters out in another ridiculous accountant outfit. This one involves a bow tie and argyle vest, and he totes a bright yellow-and-green lunch cooler along with his briefcase.

He flops into the passenger seat, slamming the door. "Got another one." He flips a chunk of black hair out of his eyes and looks straight ahead.

I pull away from the curb. "Another what?"

"Highcap."

"Killed?"

He nods. He still won't look at me. "Where's Shelby?"

"Took the bus. How's Ez?" I ask him.

"Good," he says.

After an uncomfortable silence, I say, "Put your seat belt on."

Instead of putting it on, Simon turns to me. "We need to move. We're drugging him today."

"No," I say. "Drugging him is our last resort. We agreed."

"We're not getting anywhere."

"We've been there one day," I say.

"Don't need to taste much to know it's cottage cheese." He sits back, and his hair falls over his eyes.

"We're not drugging him today. If it doesn't work, we're screwed."

"What if it *does* work? And we get the flash drive copied and all our answers sooner?"

"What if we get the flash drive copied and it's unusable, but in the meantime, he freaks out and destroys all the records and warns his customers?"

Simon sighs. "Little Miss Fear-'n'-stuff."

"It's called being *prudent*." I look over. "Really, Simon, like you're so concerned over highcap deaths. Do you *want* Avery to freak out? Is that your angle?"

"If I wanted him to freak out, he'd be freaking out."

I look over at him. "Put on your goddamn seat belt."

He clomps his feet up on the dash in defiance of my order. "I have other things to do besides sit in that office. Like investigate the truth about Ez, not that you care. Did you know I've now identified *four* interviewees from Ez's case who have missing persons' reports out on them? I have a pal in the cop shop who ran it. The former interviewees went missing at different times. *Four* people. You know what the odds of that are? Very slim. And what connects them? They all had knowledge of Ez's case. They were all people who could corroborate her story or not. At the time of the investigation, they said she was making up the relationship with that Stuart Dailey guy. But you know, time has a funny way of eroding people's will to keep up a lie. I think Mr. Stuart Dailey knows that."

I feel cold.

"Would you like to hear my theory?"

"Are you going to put your seat belt on?"

"No." Simon adjusts his bow tie. "I think ol' Stuart's back in the cannibal business, but he's smarter than ever.

He's not leaving gored corpses around for the authorities to find. As for victims, why not go for the very people who could put him away for the crime three years ago? Bet he'd send a few cannibals to eat Ez if he knew she was still around. And think about it—if the authorities believed him when he said he didn't know her, they wouldn't have deemed it necessary to send Sophia to revise his memory to make him think he saw her off to Brazil or whatever they did with her other friends. Though, even if he did find out where she is, it's not like his people could touch her. Anyway, I bet this time around he's not even having his sleepwalkers file their teeth. You know, human teeth are perfectly fine flesh-ripping tools without being filed. He's working totally under the radar."

I watch the road bleakly.

"The whole thing practically screams she didn't do it."

"I think your cock screams she didn't do it," I say.

"I need time," he says.

"It's too late. She's deepening her hold on us, and meanwhile, Packard's announced that he's going to cut me off if I don't get zinging her and have her rolling in the next four days. For good."

Simon looks over at me. "He said that?"

"Yes."

"Well, how about if you tell him to fuck off?"

"Like you have?" I ask.

"He won't let you turn into a Jarvis."

"The man who has always chosen his freedom over other people? Over potential bloodbaths in the streets? Won't let me turn into a Jarvis if I told him to fuck off? Really?"

Simon fingers the crease on his brown wool trousers. We've both heard Packard say it dozens of times—that he'd do anything to be free. *Anything.* Deep down, I don't believe it, but I've called it wrong about Packard so many times. I hit the tangle. "I have an idea," Simon says. "Zing Avery."

I almost hit a guard rail. "What?"

"Tell Packard to fuck off, and zing Avery."

I give him a dirty look and almost miss my exit. "Right. The disillusionist version of Russian roulette. Why don't *you* zing him?"

"Seriously, I think you could zing him safely," Simon says. "I think he'd be compatible. Look how he washes his hands all the time, and did you see him taking antacids and shit at lunch? He's obviously a hypochondriac."

"I'm not zinging somebody Packard hasn't cleared. I may as well pour liquid drain cleaner in my ear."

"Look, remember how Packard used to say we're compatible with maybe one out of seven random people? I think you have a *six*-out-of-seven chance of zinging Avery without blowback. And that would help us with this case. He'd be a little destabilized."

"And only a one-in-seven chance of my turning into a Jarvis."

"Come on, I'll zing Avery, and *then* you zing him. It'll be a rush."

I look over at him. He's jonesing to gamble, looking to take crazy risks. "How long since you've zinged?"

He ignores the question. "I'm tired of Packard telling me who to zing. I'm thinking of jumping ship. Maybe I'll start today. Zinging Avery will be my first step to free-agenthood."

"You can't."

"You don't even like me. What do you care if I fry my brain?"

"There's a big difference between not liking a person and wishing vegetablehood on them."

"You'll wipe the drool off me, won't you, Nurse Jones?"

"Stop it." Simon's making me nervous.

"Nobody hates being Packard's minion as much as you do," he says. "Nobody wants to be free as bad as you. I know you think disillusioning people is messed up."

I'm silent.

"Well, guess what? It's within our power to walk away from it, declare our freedom right now. We could be free right *now*, just by telling Packard we're done. This is the end of zinging people at his command."

"Even if we both successfully zinged Avery, which I will *not* do, we'd be free of Packard for what? Three weeks, tops? And then we crawl back, begging him to show us somebody safe to zing?"

"No. We'd keep going. Whenever the dark emotions build too high, we'd decide on our own goddamn people to zing. We'd say *Fuck you* to Packard until we fried."

"So we'd zing random innocent people? How is that supposed to appeal to me?"

"Oh, come on. One zing doesn't disillusion. They'd recover."

I pull into the little spot next to the dumpster, shut off the car, and get out. I want to be my own person more than he imagines. I hit the buzzer. "Is this all about getting me to stop zinging Ez?"

"Don't you care that's she's innocent?" Simon asks. There's an angry edge to his voice, and something else there. Desperation?

We're buzzed in. We go up and find Shelby alone at the table, working away at her computer.

"Morning, Shelby," I say as I start plugging in. I say it in a sort of pointed way.

"Good morning, Justine," she replies nonchalantly.

Simon spreads out his paper files.

"How was the bus?" I ask.

"Good."

I'm not understanding the bus bit. Did she want to speak with Avery one on one? I give her a look of humorous intensity, a look that digs. She straightens, lips pursed, like she's offended by my silent query.

"Early bird gets the worm," she says finally.

I plunk down my coffee mug. "What's the worm symbolize?" I ask.

Simon snickers. "Do I get a guess?"

"Is symbol for goal," Shelby says. "For baseline data."

"Yeah?" I raise my eyebrows.

Shelby purses her lips again and starts typing.

I let my suspicious gaze linger on her head.

Simon says, "I'd settle for the rest of the shipping figures. Doesn't seem to me that we got them all yesterday." We've always felt this is our most profitable area of investigation.

"I'll ask him," I say, eyeing Shelby. "He's in there, I assume?"

"I believe so," she says, not looking up.

"Yeah." I go over and knock. Avery opens up right away. He's in a blue turtleneck sweater, which softens the nerd side of his nerd-thug equation. Actually, it softens the thug side, too. In short, he looks more normal, though there's still the matter of his piercing gray gaze, and his home-style haircut.

"I thought they were in the packet," he says when I ask about the shipping figures we want.

"Those are way too generalized. We need to match the order to the deposit to the shipping order. It can't just be, *Here's some orders, and then they were shipped."*

"It's not *that* generalized."

"It's as if you dropped your tracking number the second you went to shipping. Honestly, we just need to track it through."

He glowers. "Let me see about it."

The rest of the morning is taken up by our pretend work. At around noon, Avery comes out of his office

with his coat. "Falafel day at Lenny's, people. Your best
lunch bet around here."

Lunch with us again?

"Wow," I say. "Thanks."

"I don't want you getting all light-headed from hunger
and fail to recognize our total compliance with the di-
rectives of our oppressors."

"Well, with an invitation like that . . ." I snap my
computer shut.

Lenny's is about as busy as it was yesterday. We take
the same seats we had before in the same order, too:
Simon, me, Shelby, then Avery. Avery suggests two
falafel sandwiches each, and then he and Shelby strike
up a conversation, part Volovian, part doom and darkness.

Simon reads the paper and I watch Lenny cook. If
things were different, Avery would make a really fantas-
tic disillusionist. We don't have a paranoia guy. Helmut
usually covers paranoia, though obviously I handle it
when a target is predisposed to health paranoia.

I grab part of Simon's newspaper. As usual, the Dork
killing made front-page news. The blue clothes specula-
tion is still going. I think about Otto, and how it both-
ered him not to be able to level with the cops about the
true connections between the Dork murders.

There's a sidebar that goes to the main story that pro-
files the woman killed by the Dorks the day before yesterday. The photo shows her with her nine-year-old
daughter. The two of them lived behind her tailor shop.
Her husband was killed and the shop burned during the
worst of the crime wave, and she'd finally finished repairs
this past year. A tailor. I wonder what kind of highcap
she was.

And I'm wondering what kind of person Avery is, too.
Janie at the vacuum cleaner store said even if he knew

for sure the Dorks were using his product, he'd never give up the names. What is his rationale on that?

Shelby looks over. "Oh, poor little girl." She pulls the paper toward her.

"An orphan now," I say. "Goddamn Dorks."

Shelby and Simon fall silent, expressions carefully neutral, but I have no doubt they're shocked at my jumping on the subject.

Avery shakes his head darkly. "Some people," he says. "Just disturbing."

"Is despicable, yes," Shelby says softly.

"In what world is this ever okay?" I say.

"No world," Avery says. "At the same time, it's a symptom of a larger sickness."

"And that makes it right?"

I feel Simon stiffen next to me. In excitement or dread, I don't know. Probably both.

"No, it doesn't make it right," Avery replies with pointed intensity. "I merely made an observation. Sneezing is a symptom of allergies. It's not right or wrong. It's a symptom."

"Sneezing doesn't have a mind," I say.

Avery fixes me with steely gray eyes. "Everything is a system—that's my message to you. Everything is a system. Doesn't matter if it has a mind."

"If sneezing had a mind," Simon says, "I might like to date it."

Avery unfolds his napkin and leans forward to address Simon. "If sneezing had a mind, I think me and sneezing would find a great deal of common ground."

Shelby smiles. "A taste for drama. You both have very much of that, I think."

Avery slides off his seat, grabs two white squeeze bottles from an empty table behind us, and plunks them down on the counter. "Garlic sesame butter. You put it on the falafels. It's delicious."

"Thanks." I turn the page of my newspaper. *System*, huh.

Lenny delivers our pita baskets: half moons of pocket bread stuffed with tomatoes, cucumbers, some other veggies, plus crispy brown falafel balls.

The rest of lunch is uneventful and we go back to the office.

At midafternoon, an older woman bursts in the door bearing paper plates of cake. She introduces herself as Linda from the assembly and shipping area, and sets one in front of each of us, along with plastic forks and colorful napkins, just as Avery comes out his office door. I thank her, wondering if he'll be mad.

"Cake," he observes. It's the kind where layers of yellow cake alternate with white frosting.

Linda turns to us. "Grumpy Pants hates cake."

"Mostly on a conceptual level," Avery explains.

Linda touches his arm. "Conrad's tenth. It would mean the world to him if you'd—"

"You think I'd forget? I have something. Don't tell him."

She tweaks his cheek and leaves.

Shelby and Simon dig in. I toy with mine; I'm not a big cake fan, but it was nice for her to bring it. *I should bring something to Ez*, I think. *I want to bring something to Ez.*

"Of course I have something for him," Avery mutters as soon as Linda's footsteps have faded. "That man has given a decade of his best hours to the mindless drudgery of packing my products. Of course I have something."

I stare at my cake. We'd noticed that he pays his people pretty well; we'd assumed it was in exchange for secrecy, not a sense of debt.

Avery continues, "The mindless drudgery of a manufacturing machine I myself created. I find it distressing just to look at that goddamn cake."

Shelby smiles up at him. "The man would be no happier with a million dollars and endless freedom. Cake marks another year in journey that would be the same outcome. Ends the same."

"Right, it ends the same," Avery says. "So why settle along the way? If it all ends the same?"

"Actually," I say, licking frosting off my finger. "It doesn't end the same. You could either get the agony of an awful disease or the shock of sudden death. There's a big difference."

"Mine will be sudden no matter what," Simon says. "I'll make it so."

"Me, too," Avery says. "Sudden and violent. It's the only way."

"You guys say that now," I say. "The bewilderment and panic as the body shuts down? All systems going slowly offline until your consciousness itself is just a thing? You'd hasten that? No way."

"Maybe I find a way to beat the odds," Simon says. "There's always a chance."

"Of cheating death?" I say.

"Or of it being different somehow," Simon says. "There's always a way out of anything."

"Good luck. Your body is destroying itself right now. It's probably using the cake as a fuel to destroy itself right now, but you won't know until it's too late."

"Is always too late," Shelby says. "Cheat death and you only change decoration in your dungeon."

Simon reaches into his green lunch cooler and pulls out a sixer of Fizzy Yellow, the soda we all had at Lenny's yesterday. "Thanks for getting me addicted to this stuff, Avery."

I take the one he hands to me, thinking it might be a good time to change the subject; this discussion is revealing a bit too much of our group's weirdness.

Avery addresses Shelby. "You're thinking of decorating the dungeon, and I'm thinking about desecrating it."

Shelby smiles. "Is still dungeon."

"Guys?" Simon opens a Fizzy Yellow for Shelby and she mumbles her thanks. He opens another and passes it to Avery, who takes it and turns back to Shelby. "Yes, it's still a dungeon, but at that point, it's my goddamn dungeon."

"Dungeon nevertheless. Desecration is merely a form of decoration."

Avery laughs, beaming at Shelby. "You guys are nothing like the last government auditors, that's for sure."

I'm staring at the bottle in Avery's hand. *Shit.*

Avery catches me staring. "What is it?"

"You look good in that sweater," I say. This flusters him. Which is what I wanted.

Shelby gives me a quizzical look; I can see the second she realizes what I've realized—knockout drugs in the soda. Like the pro she is, she betrays nothing. She simply picks up a folder and hands it to him. "We completed December."

Avery looks at the folder. "Thanks."

Then Shelby turns away from him and begins to type. Avery heads into his office.

I turn on the music, glowering at Simon.

He widens his clear blue eyes. "It's almost the third day."

I say, "It was going to be a joint decision."

"*Was,*" Simon says.

"You had no right," I hiss.

"We could have that thing today," Simon says. "Think about it."

"You should not have." Shelby shuffles some papers.

I whisper, "You are so off this project."

"You know he's giving us cleansed data," Simon whispers back. "There is no other way."

I huff out an angry breath.

"Oh! I gave him wrong folder." Shelby pops up, walks across the space, and knocks on Avery's door, then she simply pulls it open and walks in.

Simon's mouth falls open. "She wouldn't."

The sound of breaking glass comes from Avery's office, followed by Shelby's plaintive apologies, then Avery's mumbled assurances. Scrambling.

"That didn't just happen," Simon says.

"Oh boy," I say.

Eventually Shelby comes out. She maintains that it was an accident—she'd handed him the folders and hadn't seen the soda bottle. We spend another tense hour pretending to work. Avery doesn't get knocked out, of course. He'd only drunk a sip. We cut out at around 3 p.m.

"Are you on his side or what?" Simon demands as soon as we're out by the dumpster. "Do you think you didn't just single-handedly ruin our plan and raise his suspicions?"

"No," she says.

"Quiet." I unlock the car. Simon slides into the back, and Shelby goes around front.

"I was trying to further the investigation," he says once we're on the road. "You were trying to fuck it up, Shel."

"*You* were fucking it up," she says.

I say, "Both of you were out of line."

Simon says, "I didn't realize you were the boss."

"I didn't realize you two were so willing to compromise our only chance to save people's lives."

"Nobody is compromising," Shelby says.

Simon leans up between us. "Do you think he doesn't suspect anything? He saw Justine look at the bottle, and then you go in and knock it over? You think he's not having it tested right now?"

"Shelby's not an idiot." I turn to her. "You gave him the wrong folder at the outset?"

"Yes."

I nod, impressed with her quick thinking. We ride in tense silence until Simon's. He gets out and slams the door.

I turn to Shelby. "What's going on?"

"I could not let it be."

"Do I need to know something?"

"Not officially," she says.

"Unofficially?"

"I do not know."

"Are you with us on this?"

A pause. Then, "Yes."

I pull out and make a U-turn, heading toward her place, not entirely thrilled with that hesitation. "There's no time to find another way to catch the Dorks."

"I am aware. I do not want more people killed."

"I like him. I do," I say.

Her pretty lips tighten in a secret smile. "He is good man."

"What if we, you know, *fired* you? Just got you out of it? Let Simon and me do the dirty work. Let us be the ones."

"It would be complicity all the same. To not warn him."

"You can't keep preventing us like this. I mean, Simon shouldn't have done what he did. But going forward."

"Do not worry," she says sullenly.

"You're with us." More a question than a statement. "You're with us on this."

Her pointed look is a loud Yes.

I smile wistfully. "You remind him of his mother."

Tiny Shelby smile. "I am sure I do not."

We drive in silence. She's in a good mood, for her. She hasn't even bent Gumby. When we're almost at her place, she turns to me. "I am so sorry, I have not asked. Have you heard from . . ." She stops short, like she doesn't want to say his name. Like it would hurt me too much.

I shake my head. "It's bad. This feels so severe. He doesn't even want to speak with me!"

"You do not know."

"It's not too late for you, Shelby. Let us kick you off the case. I just don't know how this can work. How can you be on both sides?"

She traces a shape on the passenger window. "That is my question to myself, yes."

I choose my words carefully as we near her ramshackle apartment building. "Will you tell me if anything changes?"

She sits there, pondering the glove compartment.

"If you're not with us anymore?"

"If I am not with you, yes, I will tell you." She gets out, not looking back.

I swing by the government offices and head up to the mayoral floor, hoping to get information. I find Sophia in Otto's office suite, sitting behind her desk in the front room. Her red hair is in a chic, almost sculptural blowback style, and her green suit has a slight shimmer. I'm relieved to see she didn't accompany Otto to Washington, D.C.

She raises one unnaturally perfect brow. "What do *you* want?"

I bite my lip. What I want is something more than text messages, but I can't say that. Nothing would give her more glee than to know Otto's angry at me.

I say, "Can you tell me the name of the hotel Otto's

staying at? I didn't get to ask him, and I need to send some stuff."

This is quite true; I want to have orders of egg foo yong and egg rolls delivered to his room from an area restaurant. He often forgets to eat when he's revitalizing.

She makes very little effort to conceal her smile. "You don't know where he's staying?"

"Would I be asking you?"

She smiles. "I'm sorry, I'm not sure if I can give out that information."

"What are you talking about? Of course you can."

She stares at me and I look away. She laughs. "Oh, Justine, if I wanted to snatch your memory, I'd snatch it. As for Otto, he is a man of his word. He says what he means, and when he *doesn't* say something, it means he didn't intend to say it. He must not want you to know."

"Of course he wants me to know."

"That doesn't appear to be the case." She sits tall, polite professional smile, polite professional words. "Can you think of any reason he wouldn't want you to know where he is?"

I wait, wondering how much she knows.

She says, "Because that does seem to be his communication, doesn't it?"

"Quit screwing around."

"I can send over these urgent items myself if you like. And I'll let him know you have been inquiring about his whereabouts when I speak to him next."

"When will that be?" I ask, hating to crawl to Sophia like this. "When did you speak to him last?"

"I'm sorry, but I cannot reveal my communications with the mayor."

I do a mean little sniff-laugh, like she's pathetic, and all this is maddeningly inconvenient, nothing more. "So you're *not* going to tell me."

"I'm busy," she says into her computer screen. "Why don't you run along and pour your wretchedness into one of your victims?" She looks up. "I believe this interview is over."

My steps sound crisp down the marble hallway. I punch the elevator button. Of course she'll tell Otto I was trying to find his hotel. Like a stalker. Otto's too much of a gentleman to tell her what happened, but she'll smell blood all the same.

Chapter
Fifteen

I'M NOT IN THE IDEAL STATE of mind for visiting Ez, but it's not like I can take the night off, being that I only have until Monday to get her rolling. As I touch the descrambler bracelet, I imagine, as I have so many times lately, unclasping it from my wrist and handing it over to her, and the joy on her face.

Just to be safe, I take it off and fasten it around my ankle; as long as it's on your person, it works. It's only a matter of time until Simon gets his hands on one. It's probably only a matter of time until he tells Ez what we are. If he hasn't already.

Ez looks relieved to see me, so Simon hasn't told yet. Good. Ez is freaking about nanocites and obsessed with a zone of aliveness under her right rib. We discuss that, and she asks to see the descrambler bracelet again. I tell her I can't show it, and ask her about the Cellini book, which she has of course read. My fear is still in her; there's this uncanny way that I can sense it running through her veins like poison.

At one point she fixes me with her burning gaze and asks the strangest question: does Packard pull lots of night shifts at the hospital? She seems almost angry about it. Why? Does she think he was up all night?

Was he?

I run my finger around the edge of the ledge. Packard

told me it wouldn't work for us to sleep in shifts. *The dream link is extratemporal,* he'd said. *It doesn't matter when we sleep, only that we sleep.*

I inform her that I don't know his schedule.

Did he stop sleeping? No, with all that's going on, that would be madness. Though he'll do anything to stay free.

"Let's get a pulse," I say. She gives me her hand.

As I build up to my zing, I start feeling more disgusted with myself. I tell myself I just have to do it. I have no choice now. I press my thumb to her vein and watch the clock.

Packard sometimes asks me when I can ever forgive him. That's not something I'm ready to do. But ironically, it's the times I feel most trapped that I come closest to forgiving him. He was a prisoner just like me. He wanted freedom, just as I do.

I'm stoking, readying to zing her, pretending to find the vein, when I look into Ez's eyes. They're full of worry, and trust.

"What is it, Justine?" she asks.

And then it hits me: Ez is a prisoner, too. I'm a prisoner hurting another prisoner. She never had a trial and she's maybe innocent, and she trusts me and I'm secretly attacking her. I feel queasy. Again I tell myself I don't have a choice, but I'm tired of that.

I do have a choice.

I drop her hand, stare at her dumbly. "I have to go."

"What? Don't leave!" she says. "You're not done taking my pulse."

"I can't." I turn and walk—it's all I can do not to run for the exit sign.

"Come back!" she calls.

I push out the door into the night. The fear I stoked up boils uncomfortably at the surface of my energy dimension. It'll settle some if I give it time. Outside, I brace my hands against the cold brick wall, pulse pounding in my ears. I do have a choice, and my choice is to stop being a minion of Packard.

People have been telling me I am like Packard. I am—I'll do anything to be free.

Including risking becoming a Jarvis.

Everything feels so still—my heart, the stars, the icy air. Even the snow has stopped. I pull my hands from the rough wall.

I'm done. I'm making my own decisions from now on.

It's so crazy, yet so simple. *Packard doesn't get to boss me anymore.* Maybe I'll zing Ez again if I decide she's actually guilty, but it will be my choice.

And if I refuse, I have a little under a month until I turn into a Jarvis. Or I turn into a sleepwalking cannibal first. Or both.

"Fuck it," I say aloud, and I stroll down the sidewalk. I'm free. My own person. Nobody can make me do anything I don't believe in anymore. I smile. Laugh. It feels incredible.

And terrifying. The decision I've made is serious and dangerous, and completely the right thing. I don't know whether Packard gave me that ultimatum as a way of helping me or controlling me, but it doesn't matter. I'm ultimatum-free now.

My first act as a fully free person is to head over to Lenny's and order three orders of French fries. Lenny is still there. He sinks them into the fryer and we have a jokey little exchange about whether I'll be able to eat them all. Yeah, I'll eat them all.

I read Dear Aggie while I wait, and when the fries come, I drown them in ketchup and cover the ketchup with salt. They're just a little bit crispy. Delicious.

As soon as Lenny gets busy with another customer, I call Simon. "So guess what I did tonight," I say, unable to keep the smile off my face.

"What?"

"Declared my independence." I lower my voice. "I'm so done with being a minion."

"What? Just like that?"

"I'm a woman of action, my friend."

He whistles out a breath.

I pop a fry into my mouth.

"Are you going to zing random people or what?"

"I don't know. I haven't thought it through."

"You're just stopping?"

"I'll make my own choices from now on."

"But listen, you're not just going to . . ." He doesn't finish. He's thinking Jarvis, and so am I.

"Let the chips fall where they may."

"That's my line," Simon says.

"I know." It's all a bit dizzying, like I'm way up high on a tightrope. Will I be laughing as the weeks go on? Defiantly, I stuff another fry into my mouth, determined to enjoy this moment. The fry is delicious. The decision was right.

There's a long silence. "Maybe we'll figure something out," he says. "Kick around some ideas. I figured out spelunking. Packard figured out how to get free of Mongolian Delites. If we come up with something, then I'll jump ship."

Simon's not craving risk. He must have just zinged.

"I don't mind the odds," he explains, "but there's no upside to quitting this instant. I'm with you in spirit, and we'll see about the rest. And, oh, man, Packard's going to freak. If we figure something out and disillusionists start quitting, you know Otto'll stick him back in the restaurant."

"I don't want that," I whisper.

"And what about Otto and his imploding head?"

"I know, I know. I don't want Packard sealed back up, and I don't want Otto's condition to worsen, and I don't want to be a sleepwalker for Ez. There are a million reasons on every side of this thing. But Simon, in my heart, I had to stop. I mean, what about me needing to be free to follow my conscience?" I eat a double fry.

"You don't have to worry about Ez. She's harmless."

"I feel like you're right, but I need you to prove it," I say.

"I'm almost there. And just think—Packard's out of your life. You never have to see him ever again."

I feel hollow as the truth of this hits me. "Well, I'm definitely going to tell him I quit. I've been looking forward to it," I inform Simon. I haven't actually thought beyond telling him, and his reaction. Is telling him I quit the same as saying good-bye? The fry tastes like sawdust in my mouth.

"Justine, do something for me."

"What?"

"Wait to tell Packard. He might throw Vesuvius on Ez. Just give me a few more days."

"Fine."

We get off the phone and I finish my fries and read more Dear Aggie. Relationship problems. Those were the days.

After bidding Lenny good night, I make my way back to my car, feeling like a giant blob, thanks to all that grease. But a free blob. I sit for a long time in the driver's seat, not starting up. I'm tired, and I crave sleep, but I'm wary of it, because sleep makes me vulnerable to Ez's control. She wants that descrambler. What if I bring it to her, and she breaks out and starts running cannibals again? It's not like it's one hundred percent impossible that Simon's wrong.

Of course she'd gain control of me before Packard. As a highcap, Packard's mentally stronger, even in sleep. Tipping my head back, I close my eyes, wondering if I should go to an all-night movie or something. Just sitting with my eyes closed feels good, and I start to doze off with the pleasant sensation that I'm porous, like gossamer, as though it would be nothing for air or light or Ez's thoughts to flow clear through me. I wake up with a start.

Am I in danger of sleepwalking at her command as soon as tonight? Or am I just obsessing about it?

I decide to take precautions. I run a few errands, and an hour later I'm parking in the weedy parking lot on the side of Shelby's building.

I get out to the roar and exhaust fumes of the tangle; its overlapping masses of highway curlicues rise out of a sea of rubble and garbage on gargantuan concrete legs. Beneath is the dark, wild terrain of tanglelands—a dank, extensive network of highway underbellies and concrete caverns where dangerous people and dead bodies are said to dwell. As a rich disillusionist, she could live anywhere. It makes me love her that she chooses the building nearest the tangle.

She's going to fight me on my decision to quit, but I'm ready.

As usual, the door to the building is propped open. I head in and run up the scuffed staircase and knock. No answer. I'd thought she was going to be home tonight; she seemed rather intense about it, that she was doing nothing tonight. She stressed it. *Nothing.*

Another knock. No answer. When I call her, I hear the ring inside, which alarms me, but then she flings open the door, looking flustered. "Justine!"

"Were you asleep or something?" I ask.

"Sort of."

I breeze in past her. "You shouldn't nap this close to bedtime." I look around and fix on a heating pipe that goes from her floor to her ceiling. "Mmmm." I test it for stability. "This should hold." I pull my handcuffs out of my bag and turn to her.

She widens her eyes.

I smile. "That's right, Ez has deepened her hold, and this is what things have come to. I'm like fifty percent sure I'm going to be a sleepwalking zombie tonight unless you lock me up. And no way am I going to Packard on this." My gaze slides over her cluttered apartment—pillows, soda bottles, chunky black work boots. It'll be nice to spend some girl time with her. "I'm thinking you can slide your pullout over here, and maybe if I had one hand cuffed to the pole. It's gonna suck, but . . ."

She's looking at me strangely.

"I have this weird feeling sometimes that I want to help Ez. Nothing conscious, but deep down, almost preverbal, and I no longer trust myself in sleep. Are you hungry? Maybe we can order a pizza." I flop down on her couch. Pizza, wine, and then I'll tell her my decision. "Christ, I was just in my car almost dozing off, and I could almost feel her."

She lowers her voice. "She has deepened her hold?"

"I don't know if she's deepened it or if I just feel supervulnerable in general, like how things are with Otto. I might be obsessing. I know that's possible, being that this is sort of a brain thing. And what if her invasion activity exerts some sort of pull on the vascular structure of my brain? Like a kind of tidal pull? Shit, I wasn't thinking about that . . ." For the first time since I've arrived, I actually focus on her. "Is this okay? Is something wrong?"

"You cannot sleep over."

"What?"

She shrugs suddenly, seeming resigned to something. "You cannot."

"Why?" I look at her coffee table. Two bottles of soda. Chunky black work boots on the floor underneath. *Chunky black work boots.* My jaw drops. I scan the room. "Where is he?"

She blinks prettily at me. Then, "Fire escape."

I look at the window. Closed. He can't hear us, at least. "This is so out of bounds. Oh my God." I don't know whether to laugh or scold. In my frazzled state, it would probably be a little bit of both. I take a deep breath. "What are you doing?"

"Getting rid of you so that he can come back in."

"You know what I mean."

"I am not hurting our Dorks investigation."

"Jesus!"

"I am not hurting it. I give you my word."

"I can't believe you have him here."

"I kissed him."

I bite back my smile. I know this is not jubilation time. She sees it anyway and says, "I will kiss him again when you leave."

"Oh my God."

She narrows her eyes. "I know. I do not know what is into me."

"How about you getting the customer list? Any chance of that getting into you?"

"No, I could not."

"Why? If he falls asleep? It would be nothing to pull that little flash drive off his key chain and copy it. Little eensy beensy flash."

"No, I could not."

"He'd never know."

"I am not the kind to—" Abruptly she stops; then, "I would *not*." As if that's all she'd meant.

"You're not the kind to fuck a target to complete a mission? Like your friend Justine did? You're not the kind to lie to a man you've come to trust and adore? Or manage and manipulate him? Make him sorry he ever knew you?" *Like I did with Otto.*

She looks at the fire escape.

"I don't want you to, Shelby."

"You don't?"

"No. You know what? If it doesn't feel right to you, then you can't do it. Screw it all."

She puts her hand over my forehead as if to check my temperature.

"Stop it," I laugh. "We'll get the stuff without you. Just don't hurt us tonight."

"I will not hurt you. I will not hurt investigation, Justine. But what about . . ." She motions at my handcuffs.

"Okay, here's what I'll do. I'm going to go home and handcuff myself to my bed, and I'm going to throw the key across the room. Okay?"

"Oh, Justine, this seems quite dangerous."

"No, it can work, but you have to come over at six-thirty to unlock me. Can you do that?"

"Of course."

"Or, if I call in the middle of the night, like there's a fire or I have to pee, you'll come over and release me?"

"No, this is quite dangerous."

"It's fine. Six-thirty, got it? Unless I call."

She purses her lips.

"But if I call you, like, in my sleep, you'll know, right?" I say. "You have to make sure I'm fully awake before releasing me."

She nods. "I understand."

"Consider me gotten rid of."

Chapter
Sixteen

I WALK INTO Mongolian Delites so confused, so lost, and he's there. He looks at me with that softness in his eyes, and he sighs. I can feel the sigh inside me.

I go to him.

He takes my hand and pulls me into his arms with this steady force that's intensely satisfying, and we kiss—hard and long. I melt into him, lost and found all at the same time. A warm glow flows through me—relief, heat. I want to kiss him and taste him everywhere.

Don't be mad. Just for a little while, just for this moment, Packard pleads, pulling me closer. *I'm going to make things work out,* he whispers.

Warm lips on my neck, my ear. He whispers my name. I grab his hair, pull him to me.

Frenzied breaths, harder now, shoulder blades thunk against the wall. I love him and I love his happiness—I feel it as strong as I feel my own heartbeat, and I let his happiness overwhelm me, along with his kisses. I push my hands in under his clothes. I have to find his skin, his warmth, touch him everywhere. He's pulling off my shirt, kissing my little bra strap bulge, an area of fatness I hate, but he kisses it and loves it. He loves me. I want to be with him, but I'm so far away from him—I can't get to him. I pull and pull, but I can't get free.

Crash. Glass shattering. My arm is trapped—it hurts. Something's got my arm!

I jerk awake, heart racing, screaming pain shooting through my wrist. Cuffed to the bed. A yell from the street. Was there a car crash down there?

The red numbers on my clock say 4:07 a.m.

I lay back, ragged and bone-weary, feeling like my mind has been trashed, emotions flung from drawers. It was just a dream memory, I tell myself. Ez pulling out bits and pieces of my life. I take a deep breath, shoving everything back. It's winter, and I'm here in my apartment, cuffed to my bed frame.

I sit up, shoulder burning. I contort far enough over to flip on my light, and grab my book about a Victorian lady sleuth. Just as I'm getting into it, I hear the *bleep bleep bleep* of a siren on quiet mode. Red flashes illuminate the trees outside my window. Something's happening.

I pull as far forward as I can, but I can't see down to the street. Is it the police? Could there be a fire? I wait, listening. If there was a fire, somebody would've put on the alarm. I don't hear doors slamming, either. An accident out there, I decide. That would make sense, given the crashing sound.

I'm too apprehensive to fall back asleep, but sounds and sirens outside don't constitute enough danger to wake Shelby up and make her drive over and release me.

Sitting up, I settle my book into my lap and position my hand so that the bracelet part of the handcuff puts the least pressure on my wrist, which is rubbed pink in places. I read, trying not to think about Packard being privy to all my feelings during that whole episode last summer. Especially after the way he exploited my feelings in the office store. I'm also trying not to think of the vascular implications of Ez mucking around in my head, and I'm definitely trying to not focus on the tingles on the upper left side of my skull. If Otto were here, he would have calming things to say about the tingles, and the sirens, too. I miss him.

At 6:28, my front door lock clicks and creaks, and Shelby sweeps into my bedroom with a cup of coffee and a sheaf of papers, which she slaps onto the bed. "The list—three hundred twenty-two pairs sold."

"What?"

"Is shipping list for glasses. All customer names. All addresses."

I just stare at it.

"And coffee," she adds. "Now where is key? To release you?"

"Avery's customer list?"

"Yes." She looks around. "Where is key?"

I point to the corner where I threw it, a glinting jewel by the baseboards. She grabs it and comes over. The springs squeak as she sits.

"Oh, Justine!" she says when she sees my wrist. "Did you try to escape? Has her hold deepened?"

"I don't think so," I say, overcome with such sadness for my friend. She won't even meet my eyes as she fits the key into the cuff. She doesn't want to talk about how she got the list. Obviously she screwed him over somehow. She must feel like a monster.

She gets my hand free and I touch it gingerly, tears clouding my vision. I barely know what I'm crying about. Shelby ruining things with Avery? Me? Ez's plight? Packard?

"Drink." She hands me the coffee. I drink.

"I'm so sorry," I whisper. No way will I say something like, *You shouldn't have done that.* Saying something like that would just discount her sacrifice.

She peers at me strangely. "Sorry for what? What is wrong? Does it hurt?"

"I'm sorry you had to do . . . whatever you did."

"Yes." She bites her lip. "Perhaps I should not have unlocked you. Until I told you."

"Told me what?"

"For one, we do not have to go to office today," she says.

"Excuse me?"

She rises from the bed and goes to my dresser, pulling up a pink scarf. "He knows we are not auditors."

"Avery? He knows?"

"Yes." She winds the scarf around her neck. "He knows because I told him."

I sit up. "You *told* him?"

"Do not worry. I did not tell him about Otto and so forth. But he knows our mission concerning the Dorks, and he printed list of his free will."

"Just like that? What about his brand promise?"

"He made exception to catch killers." She adjusts the scarf. "We had several philosophical discussions before I determined he would be with me on this matter. And he is grateful to Packard also for saving my life."

I stand. "You told him about the *disillusionists*?"

"Yes. Avery does not approve, Justine. However, he makes this exception."

"I don't get it. Does he know what we're doing? Like with Otto's prisoners?"

"No, nothing of that. I told him only what is my story. And about our work to catch Dorks. I knew he would be with us. I knew his mind."

"You knew his heart."

"Pfft. Heart is a pump."

I smile. "I'm sure he agrees." I look at the sheaf of papers, recalling suddenly what Simon said. "Oh no."

"What?"

I tell her about Simon's speculations: that Avery's as

good as dead once we have his list of people who bought the glasses. That highcaps can't allow the glasses to be made ever again.

Her expression changes from alarm to disdain. "No." She shakes her head. "No, that was only if we took list, stole list. Avery acts as friend now. He *provided* list."

"Simon is no fool."

She waves this off. "Who would kill Avery if he acts as friend to highcaps? Also, only handful of highcaps would know."

I regard her incredulously. Is Shelby thinking the best of human nature? "Those glasses are dangerous to highcaps," I remind her.

"Is too late, genie of glasses is out of bottle. Avery is ally to highcaps. You will tell them?"

"Yeah, but you should warn Avery to be extra careful."

Shelby smiles. Positively glows. "Justine, Avery's whole life is for fighting and protection against things. Everything. He has several protective devices upon his person at all times."

I suggest Shelby drop off the list at Packard's herself. "You're the one who got it," I say.

She shakes her head. Avery's waiting in the car; they're heading out for pecan pancakes.

"Go," I say. "I'll run the list over."

After she's gone, I call Simon and tell him we're not going in.

Chapter
Seventeen

AN HOUR LATER I'm all coffeed up and cozy in a woolly red turtleneck, jeans, suede lace-up boots, and my black coat and hat. I head down the stairs with Avery's customer list locked securely in my accountant's briefcase.

Out front I'm surprised to see that the building next door is festooned with crime tape, and the second-story window boarded up—the window just kitty-corner from the entrance to Mr. K.'s jewelry shop. Another robbery. Clearly this was the source of the crash that woke me up last night.

I'll find out what happened from Mr. K. when his shop opens. Mr. K. learns about everything that goes on in the neighborhood just from standing in his doorway. He and I frequently bond over our disapproval of cheap new high-rises going up nearby, and the idiotic timing of the stoplight at our intersection. Yesterday I told him how eating diamonds can kill a person. He didn't believe me, but I suspect it's because he's in the diamond business. We had this whole jokey exchange where I told him he's going to have to put "do not take internally" tags on his necklaces.

I find myself wishing Mr. K.'s was open now. Anything to put off this meeting with Packard. I haven't seen him since I started dreaming of the kiss. Even though the memory is nothing but a hollow husk of the past, I still feel overexposed. Will he be amused at my feelings, and how easy it was to charge up the memory? Will he pity me for my gullibility? The incredible ease with which he can manipulate me? Will he be quiet and cool, full of knowing glances? Or will he work it and rehash it, thinking I'll fall into his arms?

Let him think what he wants. I'll deliver the list and leave. I wish I could tell Packard I quit, but I'll keep my word to Simon and wait.

When the time comes, however, I'll relish telling him about my self-declared freedom. Possibly more than the actual freedom.

Packard lives at the top of a warehouse building north of the river. His is the brightest, airiest living space you could ever imagine—a fishbowl, really, with more windows than walls, more skylight than ceiling, and more porch footage than interior footage. It's the home of a man who can't bear to be closed in again.

Francis opens the door.

"Francis!" I say. "You're out of the hospital." I barely stop myself from hugging him. Francis is antihug.

"Sprung me yesterday, little missy." Francis has Coke-bottle glasses and the thickest neck I've ever seen. I follow him inside, steeling myself for Packard's attitude.

Francis stops in the kitchen and grabs a water, asks me if I want something. I shake my head. Even the décor in Packard's place is light and bright, the polar opposite of the dark, heavy, gaudy Mongolian Delites décor. Packard hated the way the restaurant looked inside, but he could never alter it. Once Otto's force fields are in place, you can't change the look of a space in any real way. It just reverts.

We continue into the sunny dining room area, and

there's Packard, sitting with Carter amid jungle plants, the two of them bent over a laptop.

"Guys," Francis says.

Packard looks up. "Justine," he says, with weary indifference. "Everything okay?"

"Sure. Yeah," I reply. *Where's the attitude? The knowingness?* He seems . . . oddly passive. I don't understand. Was the whole thing just beneath his notice?

Packard tilts his head. "Don't you have to be at the office?"

"That's what I'm here about." I put my briefcase on the table and take off my coat. "I need a word."

Packard asks Francis and Carter to give us a minute. He motions lazily at the chair across from him and leans back, rubbing his eyes, like he's so bored and weary. *That's* how he feels about it? Bored and weary?

"Something's wrong," he says.

I settle into the chair, feeling foolish in ten different ways. "No."

"But not the dreams, right? They've been okay . . ."

"Okay?"

"Yeah. How are you finding them?" he asks. "What do you make of, say, last night's? What's your opinion?"

I finger the lock on the briefcase. "Of the dream?" Packard's asking *my opinion?*

"Yes, the dream." His green eyes are strangely bright and bleary.

"You want my opinion?"

A momentary hesitation, which he covers with an imperious tone: "I wouldn't have asked if I didn't want to know."

The imperious tone. He's bluffing. "Oh my God," I say. "You weren't there."

"That's silly."

"You haven't slept."

He waves this off. "Justine, Justine."

"Look at you! You weren't even there. You haven't slept for two nights, have you?"

Packard straightens up. "You honestly think I'd go without sleep at a time like this?"

"Yeah. Don't try to deny it. You haven't been sleeping—believe me, if you'd been there—" I stop here. Too late.

Sly smile. "What in the world have I been missing, Justine?"

I feel this rush of energy, and oddly, relief. The colors of the world go back to their normal saturation. "You haven't slept for like forty-eight hours."

"Actually . . ." He closes his eyes. "I think it would come to more than that, but I don't want to calculate it unless I have to."

"You can't not sleep. You can't do that. Packard . . ." He looks so weary! I want to go rub his shoulders, bolster him. Slap him.

"It's just for a few more days."

"People go crazy when they don't sleep."

"Not permanently."

"I don't like this. People die from no sleep. They *die*."

"Shh." He raises a finger to his lips, eyes on mine. "I'm fine."

"They die!"

"Justine, the human body can go eleven days without sleep, and I'm a highcap. High capacity. I can go even longer."

"This is dangerous. Oh my God—this is about the secret."

"You haven't gotten urges to get up and go to her yet, have you?"

"Don't change the subject. This is about the secret." He doesn't want me in that dream in a very bad way.

He draws his brows together. "You'd tell me if you

were getting urges, right? We can think about setting you up in a cell at HQ if you feel the urge to get to her, to sleepwalk—"

"I'm fine."

He regards me suspiciously. Even in his sleep-deprived state, he knows when I'm not telling all.

I pull the papers out of my case and slam them down.

"What's this?"

"The names and addresses of everyone who ordered antihighcap glasses," I say.

"The customer list?"

"Yes."

Slowly he lays his hand upon it, like he needs to confirm that it's real.

I smile.

"How'd you get it?"

"Shelby got it. Or really, Avery."

He pulls it toward him. It's a ten-page table: names, addresses, and dates.

"Avery's a good guy," I say. "He's an ally."

Packard riffles through the pages as though he's looking for something. "He just handed this over?" he whispers, stopping at a page in the middle.

"Avery agrees that the Dorks need to be stopped. Shelby determined that it was safe to level with him in a limited way, and she was right."

"Well, isn't that a hell of a thing." He pages through slowly now, from the beginning. Even his movements are more tentative than usual.

"Oh, Packard. You need to sleep."

"I'm fine." He asks me a lot of questions about Shelby's getting it and Avery's disposition.

"Everybody involved here needs to know that Avery's helping," I say. "He's not a threat. He's acted in friendship toward the highcaps, and we don't want him in any trouble."

"Agreed. This was generous of him. We have to thank him." He looks up. "Let him know how grateful we are." He snaps into action in the next moments, calling Francis and Carter back, instructing them to round up teams. He asks me to stick around and help.

"Sure," I say, rocking back on my chair as he makes a few quick phone calls and starts somebody at HQ printing maps. You can't tell anymore that he's sleep deprived. How long can he pull this off?

Once everybody's running back and forth at their tasks, he sits down across from me and curls his hands around a newly refilled coffee mug, the calm eye in the center of a storm he created. I stare at his knuckley hands, thinking about the dream. How he felt. And then he says something strange: "Just hold on for a little while longer, Justine. I'll get you out of this."

"What?"

He shakes his head. "Nothing. We'll get out of this Dorks mess. Okay?"

"That's not what you meant." What did he mean? Was that the lack of sleep talking?

He gives me a stern gaze. "What's up on the Ez front?"

"Things are evolving."

I half expect him to latch on to this, but instead he guzzles some coffee.

"Packard, look at you. It's bad when a person doesn't sleep."

"Sometimes it's good," he says. "Sometimes it gives you time to think." He bends a paper clip into a new shape; he seems to be aiming for a circle. There's something different about him.

"What's going on?" I ask.

He shakes his head, like his thoughts are far too immense to articulate. "If anything makes me crazy, it'll be too much coffee. I had this idea yesterday that people were following me. I got these glimpses . . . slightly surreal." He works the paper clip.

"I'm sure it's nothing." *Except Helmut's bodyguards.*

"Other than that, I feel fine."

"Have you heard from Otto?" I ask.

"No. Have you?"

"No. Aside from the text."

"Mmm." He sets the squarish circle on the table. Then Carter's back—he's made his calls, plus copies of the list. By the end of the hour, the list has been split into five geographical zones, which are assigned to five investigative teams—one highcap and one human each. Apparently handpicked humans with burglary and con-artist backgrounds have been standing by, waiting for this moment. The idea is to run down the names of everybody who ordered the glasses. They're looking for the Dorks first and foremost, but they're also replacing the glasses with fake pairs. Carter shows me one of the fakes. It's pretty convincing. He tells me they had a thousand made.

I'm to stay behind on the computer, researching the customer names to see if I can find photos, jobs, daily patterns, anything helpful to the pairs in the field.

People start moving out. Helmut's waiting for Packard. During a quick moment alone, I tell Helmut that Packard mentioned the strange sense of somebody following him. Meaning Helmut needs to tell Parsons that his bodyguard teams need to be stealthier.

Packard comes back with a can of Fresca for me and sets it on a coaster next to the computer. "Do I need to block WebMD.com?"

I smile. "Get out of here."

Most of the addresses turn out to be local—not a big surprise. I start Googling the customers. It feels good to perform a crime-fighting task that's not bizarre. People are in and out of Packard's place, and I strain for any news of Otto; I also keep my phone next to me every minute, wishing he'd call. I just want to hear his voice. I've left only one message today; I'm trying to restrain myself.

By bedtime, Packard's teams have replaced a good quarter of the antihighcap glasses with the fakes, and run down almost half the names, but there are no viable Dork candidates.

That night I handcuff myself to the bedpost once again. I have more memory dreams of Packard, and that kiss in the entrance of Mongolian Delites, though I seem to keep getting woken up from them by my noisy neighborhood.

I also dream of my mom, sitting at her kitchen table with all her anti-vein-star medications that everybody laughed at her for—until she died of a vein star rupture. I dream of the month our family spent in the bunker during the rodent flu scare, too. My parents told our school we were in Guatemala. I'd sit down there doing crossword puzzles and reading Arthurian tales, fantasizing about being rescued from it all—whisked away into a grander, more upstanding life by a noble hero.

That morning, lying in bed, waiting for Shelby to come and unlock me, I realize one person I haven't dreamed of is Otto. But that only means I'm not trying to suppress my memories of him. It's after seven in the morning in DC; he's probably having coffee and scones. He loves scones. I close my eyes, remembering his voice, his laugh, his confidence.

And just like that, it hits me: it's over.

This is the realization that I have, lying there in the dark. You don't ignore a person for days on end if you still intend to be in a relationship with them.

I stare at my ceiling, throat thick with tears. I'd made all these excuses, all these complicated reasons for why he hasn't been calling, but the truth is that I've lost him.

I've lost Otto. What's more, my backup plan of what to do to not become a Jarvis hasn't materialized, and I'm less free than I've ever been—I'm literally chained up. And what if I got a vein star blowout while I'm chained up? It really feels like the dream increased the vascular pressure inside my cranium. It occurs to me that there's a new area of numbness, actually. *Stop it!* I tell myself. *Stop it!*

Avery and Shelby come by promptly at six-thirty to unlock me, but it doesn't improve my mood. Along with a nice tall coffee, they have printouts on payment methods for me to deliver to Packard. Avery thinks they could yield a clue.

"Can you guys bring this stuff to Packard? I'm rollerblading with Ally in an hour," I say. "And Packard is really grateful to you, Avery. He told me that, and I bet he'd love to thank you in person." And also, I'm too upset to see Packard. I'm too upset to do anything.

"Avery cannot be seen going to highcap den," Shelby says. "Perhaps we will mail it. Would you prefer that?"

Reluctantly, I take the papers. I sit there, listening to their boots clomping down the stairs, then the faint clap of the lobby door.

I call Ally to cancel, blaming my security job, as I so often do. I didn't feel like exercising anyhow; I'm seriously concerned about my head. That numbness hasn't gone away. I would normally take aspirin for my handcuff-related shoulder pain, but aspirin thins the blood, which can speed cranial bleedout.

I force myself to eat a couple bagels and finish the coffee Shelby brought. I throw on a gray V-neck sweater and black jeans with boots.

My limbs feel leaden as I tromp down the steps, as though the realization that Otto and I are actually over has added a physical heaviness to my being. He's gone. And it's my fault.

Stepping out onto the sidewalk, I'm surprised to see Mr. K. outside his shop so early on a Saturday morning.

He stubs out his cigarette, motioning to workmen inside. "Updating the security system." He's surprised I haven't heard about all the overnight break-ins on our block. He points out scraping marks on the lobby door to our building. "Tried to get in through that way, too. And did you hear about Feethum?" He points to the still-boarded-up second-story window. "The same group tried to get in there. Four drug addicts. Scott Feethum clocked 'em and chased 'em off with a hockey stick."

"Drug addicts?" I say.

"Feethum said they were perverts, but the cops told us it's a ring of drug addicts that fences electronics." Mr. K. shrugs. "Feethum thinks everyone's a pervert."

"Maybe they're drug-addicted, electronic-fencing perverts," I say.

Mr. K. twists his lips in a semismile. "They hit this building again last night, but somebody called it in. Sirens scared them off."

"Shit!" I say, wishing I could talk to Otto. He would have a handle on all this. Insight. Advice.

Mr. K. lights another cigarette. "Cops say they're pretty out of it. Sounds like they're about to make arrests. Still, I don't want to take chances." He motions at his shop. "The Dorks and now this." We watch a guy in coveralls crawl into the empty display window and wire one of the black velvet display necks. Mr. K. suggests I stop back later and get a look at his new system—more state-of-the-art than his last, which was the ultimate state-of-the-art. He's always showing me things about his security system, thinking I'll be impressed since I'm supposedly in the security business. I always act duly impressed, while explaining that I'm not really on the tech end.

"Be careful out there," he cautions as I leave.

An hour later, I'm standing in the hall outside Packard's

door, waiting for him to come open it, trying to think if he's missed three or four nights of sleep by now.

"Justine!" Packard seems baffled and pleased to see me, but he's alarmingly pale, except for the grayish bags under his eyes. Weariness usually makes people look older, but Packard looks younger, oddly. Sort of vulnerable.

He ushers me in and I give him the papers, explaining what they are.

He studies my face. "Are you all right?"

"I'm fine. You need to concentrate."

He examines the list, then he calls Carter and reads off a few names, makes another call. He reads off a few more names. I'm shocked when I put it together that they're starting to haul some of the customers down to HQ.

"Great," I say. "How many exactly are you hauling down?"

"As many as it takes. The Dorks are on these lists somewhere." He sinks wearily into an overstuffed chair and looks up at me still standing there. "Got a problem with it?"

"No," I say, sinking into his couch.

Packard leans forward. "Now I know something's wrong."

I don't know what to say. I only feel this ache.

"Justine."

I stare up at the ceiling, willing myself not to cry. "Otto's finished with me. It's over. I should've told him about Ez like you warned me. And I didn't. He won't even talk to me—he's that disgusted with me."

"Don't think that."

"You know it's true. He refuses to speak with me *whatsoever*. I think that shows a new level of disdain."

He waves this off. "There could be any number of reasons."

"Oh, please. The man I've always wanted has finally dumped me."

"Man you've always wanted," he scoffs.

"Yeah. The man I've always wanted."

"You don't really want him."

"That just shows that you don't understand me. And the bottom line is, you don't get to tell me who I want."

Packard gives me his weary, you-are-so-clueless look.

"I can't believe you." I stand. "Screw you. I am so sick of being defined and bossed by you. And for sure, you don't get to tell me who I want. In fact, you don't get to tell me anything—" I so want to tell him I've quit being his minion.

"I can tell you this," he says. "Otto may be the man the frightened little girl Justine fantasizes about, but he's definitely not the man the brave, smart, grown-up woman wants—or needs."

I widen my eyes, incensed. "News flash: both Justines want to be with Otto."

Packard smirks.

"You think that's amusing?"

He yawns, shaking his head. "Mostly misguided."

His casual treatment of my loss enrages me, and my words come out sharp and hard. "I am done being defined and bossed by you."

He goes still, sensing something new.

"I am done." I stop, way too close to telling him. I cross my arms. "Last summer, you told me I should've chosen you instead of Otto, but you were wrong. You've always been wrong about that. Even though Otto hates me now, I still know I made the right choice, and you know how I know? Because he always cared what I wanted, in a way that you never did. You've always steamrolled over all the things I desire. This conversation alone demonstrates it perfectly. I tell you I want Otto, and you tell me I don't. The first day I met you, I wanted to be a normal girl not freaking out about my health, and you implied that you'd give me that, but instead you made me a minion. Ever since I met you, it's always been about what you want. In fact, I think you have blind spots in your psycho vision where it's all about what you want, and not about what you see."

"Justine, if you can just wait—"

"Just wait? For you to care? For when our desires and dreams line up to be exactly alike? Here I am, telling you I'm sad for losing Otto because he's who I've always wanted, and you think it's funny, and that I'm just misguided?" I wring my hands, aware that I should be directing my anger at myself, but I can't stop. "And you go on about me, *the woman this, the little girl that*. You don't care even to *know* what I want. Why can't one dream of mine come true? One goddamn dream? Because, you know what? Otto makes me happy."

This hush comes over the room, and Packard regards me strangely, almost like there's something new about the way I look.

"He makes you happy?" Packard asks.

"Not that you care."

"He makes you *happy*?"

"*Made* me happy. As you know, that's over."

"I'm sure he wishes he could be with you," Packard says.

"Are you kidding?"

"If anything, you're too good for him."

I laugh—the bad kind of laugh that might as well be crying. "You know what he said just before he left? That I'm just like you."

He regards me dimly and doesn't say anything for a long time. Then, "You were happy with him?"

"Yeah," I say.

He keeps that gaze on me, like he's memorizing my face. "So it would make you happy to have him back?"

"Of course. Not that it can ever happen."

He grabs a bag of red licorice off the sideboard and

tears it open, pulls out a deep red strand from the heart of it, and holds it out for me. I shake my head. He bites off the end and then he says, "Then I'll help you."

"What?"

"I'll help you get him back. I'll help you get what you want for once, okay? I care what you want, Justine." He bites off more of the licorice and chews. I watch his cheeks, his throat. I'm unsure, suddenly, what the hell I want.

"Don't look at me like that," he says. "I've been doing a lot of thinking. Remember? All the not sleeping? Making new decisions?" His smile doesn't quite reach his tired eyes. "There are things I'm going to change, and clearly I need to put this item on the list. On the top." He raises a licorice strand. "Item number one: help you get Otto back."

"It's not funny," I say.

"Oh, I know it's not." He heaves himself up, carries his licorice bag across the room, and slides open the door to the porch, holding it for me. I go out and he follows. Together we lean over the cold metal railing, looking down over Midcity's north side, a landscape of leafless treetops, brown rooftops, and gray roads. There's still snow on the ground—dirty mostly, with patches of white. He takes a deep breath and exhales in a pale cloud that lives a second, then disappears. He needed fresh air; I'd forgotten about his exhaustion.

A crow flaps across the sky.

"You have to respect the crows," he observes.

"Why? They eat roadkill and garbage."

"And they don't pretend different, do they? They don't play the finches' game—the cuteness and singing and all that. They'll never be a state bird, you know? But to the crows, that would be degrading. It's about who they are."

"They eat *roadkill*," I say. "And honestly, I don't see how you can help me."

He pulls out another strand of licorice. "What's the reason people love Otto?"

"Reduced crime?"

Packard smirks, watching the crow light on a branch. The bump on the middle of his nose looks bigger when you see him in profile. "Wrong," he says.

"His style? His idealism?"

A weary wave. Keep going.

"That he challenges people?" I try. "Has faith in people?"

"Faith in people. There you are. Here's the thing you need to understand about Otto—he relies on the faith of others. He *needs* to see it in people's eyes. People talk about how he believes in them, and how that feels, but it's a two-way street, a kind of feedback loop. Otto's faith in a person builds that person's faith in Otto, and vice versa. It's all looped, and the loop can't be broken."

Of course he's read Otto; he's probably been reading him for years. I don't know why it should surprise me, or make me feel so uncomfortable. Intuitively, what he's saying feels absolutely right. Packard. So good at reading and playing people. Except for me, oddly. "Why are you telling me this?"

"You can get back into that loop, but you can't do it with words. You have to show it in a big dramatic way. He has to feel it. Keeping him in the dark the way you did destroyed that loop. You said, *I don't believe in you or trust you.*" He lowers his gaze. His lashes look redder than usual under the bright winter sky. He grips the rail, and I recall how much I used to love watching those hands—strong, sinewy, oddly expressive. I think of his hands in the dreams. Boy hands, but the same. He says, "I never thought I'd be giving you relationship advice for Otto."

"Is that what you're doing?"

"Yes," he says. "I'm telling you how to get him back. Not that you've lost him." He twists his hands on the rail. "As a man who hates to be managed, can you imagine how he'd hate to be held captive? Even if it was just to protect him? Can you imagine how he'd hate that?"

"Wait, somebody's holding him?"

"Imagine if one person cared enough to figure it out. Believed in him enough to know he wouldn't abandon the city in the time of the Dorks, if that person—"

"Packard, what are you telling me? He's being *held*?"

"Listen before I change my mind. If that person freed him . . ." He squints at me, as if the brightness hurts his eyes. "Do you really think he's at a mayoral conference? Do you honestly think he'd leave Midcity at a time like this? And not return your calls?"

"Where is he? You don't have him. You wouldn't—"

"—of course not. I don't know where he is." He pauses here. "But if I had to guess, I'd look at Covian."

"But Sophia's spoken with Otto on the phone. She knows where he's staying."

He smiles sleepily. "She told you that, did she?"

I think back. "Actually, no. She never said it. She just said she couldn't *release the information.*"

"Of course not. She's got no information to release. She got a text, just like you. She asked me the other day if *I'd* heard from him. Sophia's got nothing."

"Oh my God," I say.

"Otto's staffers, they think he's at the conference. But really, has it ever felt right to you? Otto leaving during the Dork crisis? And as much as he hated that you withheld the Ez story, he wouldn't simply avoid you. He may be unreasonable, but Otto finishes things," he says. "He's a finisher."

"Covian has him. Whoa."

Packard speaks through a yawn. "Covian's a fiercely protective personality. And let's be frank—Otto was endangering himself, walking around the way he was."

"Like you care," I say, nodding toward Diesel's bracelet.

He smiles wearily. "Right. How can I strangle my nemesis with my bare hands if he gets himself killed by the Dorks?"

"That's not funny."

"Justine, I didn't vow to strangle him. I vowed not to take the bracelet off until I strangled him," he says. "There's a difference. For now, this bracelet, it's . . ." He pauses here, running a finger under the links. "I've been thinking about it a lot lately. The bracelet reminds me of Diesel, first off, but it also keeps me vigilant about the gravity of my struggle with Otto. And reminds me that I have choices. The bracelet means something, but it means more on than off."

I search his face, surprised. Impressed.

Packard chuckles dismissively. Does he think he's revealed too much? "Covian. He was well enough to leave the hospital, yet he's not at home. Otto wouldn't have brought Covian to DC; he told me he'd decided to use only human bodyguards."

"He told me, too," I say.

"So if Covian's not in DC or at home, where is he? There's only one place the Covian *I know* would be, and that's right here, gunning for the Dorks. He'd be trying to get on one of my teams. I wouldn't allow it, considering his condition, so he'd insist on supporting us in a dozen other ways."

"He'd be sleeping and breathing this investigation."

"Damn right."

"When Otto left that morning, after our fight, there were no guards with him at all," I say.

Packard raises his brows. "Can't imagine Covian enjoyed seeing *that*. Covian's not an idiot, but he is single-minded about protecting Otto. If I had to guess, I'd say he's got Otto in his house. Interior room. We have no reason to believe the Dorks recognized Otto or are specifically after him, so it's reasonably safe. It's what I'd do if I was Covian."

"Wouldn't Otto just claw through the walls or knock the house down or something?"

"He'd need to be bound to something not structural."

"Jesus. And you didn't do anything?"

"Covian destroyed his career by taking him, so why not let him keep him? And Otto was taking chances."

"You walk around in the open," I say.

No answer.

"Why are you helping me?"

Packard bites off more licorice, staring at the sky. "Can't I try to respect what you want for once?"

My heart skips a beat. I watch him chew. I have nothing to say.

"Go be the one who helps Otto. It'll mean a lot to him. The idea of the Dorks out there, hunting us—it's the kind of thing that would disturb him deeply. The whole thing . . . it's . . ." He pauses here. "It would disturb him deeply, that's all. Covian won't like you coming in, but he'd never hurt you."

"If I wear the glasses I'll have the element of surprise."

"Christ, no! You can't surprise him. He might think you're the Dorks." He turns to me. "Whatever you do, don't go in there with the glasses and surprise him. Okay?"

"Okay."

"Think of something else. Checking on his recovery or something. Get him to let you in."

"Okay." I push off and we head in.

I grab my purse, stunned by this new attitude of his. It's so unlike him. "Thanks, Packard." I follow him to the door, unsure what to say beyond thanks, so I say it again. "Thank you."

We come to the door and he turns. "I *do* want you to

be happy. I've had a lot of time to think, Justine. To reflect. I've realized things . . ." He seems to be searching
for the right words. "Now that we're on this, there's
something I should've told you a long time ago, about
what I've been doing. This whole thing with Jarvis—"
He's watching my hands, and I realize I'm gripping and
twisting the purse straps. I feel so confused.

"It's okay, you want to get going," he says. "This can
wait till you get Otto."

I don't want to go. What has Packard been thinking?
What does he need to tell me? Why, really, has he given
me this advice, this gift that will help me get Otto back?
"Okay," I say.

Without warning, Packard reaches out—I think he's
going to touch my cheek, but he slides his hand around
the nape of my neck and pulls me to him, kissing me
warm and strong, lips soft, breath like coffee. The kiss
takes me by surprise. My whole body wants to follow
deeper into him, but he pulls away, and we're looking
into each other's eyes, and the moment stops. And everything seems to fall out beneath me.

"Good luck," he whispers.

"Packard—"

He opens the door. "It's okay."

I stare at the open door. It feels like a closed door. And
I leave.

Chapter
Eighteen

I SIT IN MY CAR across the street from Covian's house, which looks as it did the first time I stopped by. Dark. Shades drawn. Garage door shut.

I'm here for Otto, but I'm still thinking about kissing Packard. Is it as simple as he says? That he wants me to be happy? The kiss felt like a good-bye kiss, and I didn't want to leave. Even now, I want to go back, to see what he wanted to say. Maybe kiss him some more. Is it those damn dreams?

I roll down the window, suck in the cool air. Otto needs my help. This is what I'm doing now.

I get out with the bag of cookies I bought on the way and shut the door. Lunchtime on a Saturday. The neighborhood buzzes with the drone of a chainsaw a few houses down, probably cutting firewood; I'm glad for the haze of distraction the loud sound creates.

I head up Covian's poorly shoveled front walk, avoiding the spots of ice, and knock on the door. I'm following Packard's advice and not wearing antihighcap glasses, though I did borrow Shelby's stun gun, so that I have two, in case Covian makes me hand mine over. Second round of knocking. My pretext is that I'm on a mission to see Covian and make sure he's okay after not hearing from him. And bringing cookies.

No answer after three rounds of knocking. And the

door's locked. I make tracks around to the small back-yard. The hedge is almost as tall as I am, and a small concrete porch holds a grill and two lawn chairs, both covered with snow. I knock on the sliding door in back, then peek in the crack at the side of the curtain, but it's just vague furniture shapes in darkness. I inspect the rest of the windows, and then I go back to my car and rummage around in my trunk until I locate a five-pound barbell and a blanket. Now I'm really glad for the drone of the chainsaw.

Utilizing my best *Yeah-I-belong-here* stride I go around back once again. I stand at the back window feeling nervous and shaky, and then I realize this whole caper has distracted me from my worries about my head—except now that I thought about it, I'm worried again. Thoroughly disgusted with myself, I hold up the blanket and smash the back storm window with the barbell, clearing the glass all around the bottom. Then I fit my fingers under the main window, which is unlocked, and force it up. Why break both windows? I'm a conscientious intruder. I fold the blanket and drape it over the bottom sill—another thing I've seen in the movies—and climb in.

"Covian?" I call. "It's me, Justine." I shut the window behind me to keep out the cold, and wander around, checking the rooms. "Covian? Hello?"

No answer. I continue on, through the dark living room, down the dark halls. He'd never hurt me, but it's still weird and scary to creep around his house. Finally I come to the basement door, just off the kitchen. I can tell it's the basement door because it's partly open, and the light's on, so I can see the stairs leading down, and an old wooden railing.

"Hello?" My stomach flutters as I grip the cool knob. "Hello?"

A sound—an *"unh."* Was it human? The house settling? I wait, still as a statue, straining to hear more, but all I get is the distant whine of the chainsaw and the hum of Covian's refrigerator.

Did I really hear it? I bend my head nearer, pull my stun gun from my pocket, and creep down. "Covian? It's me, Justine."

I stop midway, astounded. The basement floor looks like it's been torn up and rebuilt as a kind of insane maze. Concrete slabs, like chest-high walls, start and stop in random places, and in the middle is some sort of metal contraption—on second glance I recognize that it's a home gym, tipped over on its side, draped with chains and ropes.

I suck in a breath. Nonstructural. For Otto?

"Hello?" I go all the way down and pick around, checking behind every little half wall. Nothing. I rub my arms, panic rising. "Hello?" Nothing. "Fuck."

"Unh."

I look in the direction of the sound. Nobody's there. "Hello?"

A faint voice: "In here!"

Covian. His voice seems like it's coming out of the wall itself—a boxy protrusion. I move closer. The boxy part is man-sized, and it's pockmarked, too, like somebody was shooting at it. I tap it with my stun gun. "Are you in there?"

"Look down."

A piece of beige cloth waves out a hole in the bottom.

"Oh my God. Covian? Are you okay? How'd you get in there?"

"You have a phone?" Voice weak.

"Yeah."

"Call Packard. The Dorks have Otto."

I clap a hand over my mouth. Everything seems unreal. I fumble to press the buttons on my phone.

"Need a team," Covian continues. "Ambulance. Tools. Have to break the wall."

"Shit."

"They won't kill him. Took him. Carried him. I could hear—" Scarily long pause. "I'm sorry."

Packard answers and I give him the info. "You stay with Covian," he says. "I need you to get him to tell you everything he observed, everything he heard."

"The Dorks have Otto!"

"We'll find them."

"I'm glad you're on it," I say.

I spend the next ten minutes lying on the cement floor, holding Covian's alarmingly cold hand through the opening in what seems to be a small, man-sized room Otto made around Covian. Through labored breaths, he tells me how he'd tied Otto to the home gym to prevent him from touching the walls or ceilings. Yesterday afternoon Covian had come down to turn on a football game for Otto when the Dorks burst down the stairs.

Yesterday afternoon. They've had Otto almost a day.

Covian continues: the Dorks wore hoodies and face paint; all he can give me is height, weight, and that two were males. One could've been female, he thought. Covian went after them and they shot him in the stomach; he staggered back to the wall. Otto was struggling with other Dorks and the entire home gym tipped over. As soon as Otto had contact with the floor, he interfaced with the structure and used his power to make the box around Covian. That's what saved Covian's life. They'd shot at the wall.

The rest was a jumble. Covian thinks they must've picked Otto up at some point, and he's pretty sure one of them is named Henji. And he remembers shoes. Vans sneakers.

"Wait, what do you mean one of them was named Henji?"

"Henji," Covian says breathily. "After Otto boxed me

in, one of the Dorks yells out *Henji!* Mad, it sounded like." He pauses. I can hear him shifting around in there.

"Hang on, Covian. They're on their way."

"And later, *Let's go, Henji.*"

"Anything else?"

Covian thinks the Dorks picked the locks, judging from their quiet entry. And that they could be taking Otto to the river, or a place with Riverside in the name. Something about riverside."

Riverside Elementary, I'm thinking. Henji is Otto's name from that era. Is there a connection between the Dorks and what happened back at that school?

Banging upstairs. The door. I press Covian to tell me exactly what he heard about Riverside.

Silence.

"Covian, stay with me. Are you listening?"

"Only the word. I couldn't hear. I'm sorry!"

"Okay. Anything else?"

"I don't think they'll kill him. Why would they take him?"

"Don't say anything about Henji or Riverside to anybody. *Nothing.* Okay?"

He agrees. I force him to give his word, even though I don't think he'll be conscious much longer. I have the sense that he remained conscious out of sheer force of will, hoping to pass along these details as a way to help Otto.

I run up to the crash of glass as a sledgehammer comes through the plate-glass front window. "Hold on!" I open the door.

Carter and Rondo come in.

"He's in the basement. Got to go," I say. Sirens in the distance. I run out to my car and zoom away.

By the time I get Packard on the phone again, he's at HQ.

"They know he's Henji," I tell him.

"What?"

I give him the story with the Riverside and Henji details front and center.

"No."

"This reaches back there, doesn't it?" I say. "Henji and Riverside. Covian thought maybe they were taking him to the river or Riverside."

"What did they say, precisely?"

"He got the word, not the sentence."

"Damn."

"This is a clue. Can you use it to find him?"

"There's no more Riverside school building, if that's what you're wondering."

"How about the site where it was?"

"Condos. Look, I ruled this whole Dorks-Goyce connection out," Packard says.

"So you thought there could be a Dorks-Goyce connection?"

"I ruled it out. There were no Goyces on the list, and no family names related to the Goyces. It would be impossible, anyway."

"So the Goyces are a family."

"If nothing else, we can start looking for alibis during that game Covian had Otto watching. That gives us a way to cull the list."

"There are hundreds on that list."

"Hold on." More talking in the background. A door slams. Then he's back. "If they didn't kill him right off, it means they won't."

"Maybe they want to torture him."

No response.

"Oh my God!"

Packard says, "We'll get him back. In the meantime, we have to hope he holds out and doesn't relax his force fields. We don't even know where he's keeping all his dangerous highcaps, and even if we did, we don't have the manpower to guard them."

"I didn't even think of that."

"Well, we're thinking about it here," Packard says.

"They'd go free all at once," I say. "Midcity will burn if they get out."

"They won't," Packard says.

"It goes back to that school," I say. "There's something in that dream, Packard. I keep having this nagging feeling, like there's something we're not seeing. And the fact that the Dorks called him Henji and mentioned Riverside—"

"No." He lowers his voice. "I have experienced that dream and those events every goddamn night for years. I can sketch and catalog every bit of rubble in that stairwell. There is nothing to be learned in that dream." He calls for another laptop to be brought in; he wants somebody picked up from a Franklin address; he wants a large coffee.

"Maybe there's something outside eyes could see."

"There isn't." His refusal feels irrational. A sleepy mind fighting to stay on top of the day. "There isn't," he says again. "I have to go."

He clicks off, but I stay, holding the phone to my ear, not quite ready to end the connection.

Chapter
Nineteen

I DON'T KNOW HOW I get through the day. Otto's out there, in terrible trouble. Every few hours I call HQ for updates. They never have anything, just vague hopes that the next lead will pan out, and then the next.

I'm starting to get that they're fishing. By the end of the day they've interrogated, revised, and released fifty people. Result: fifty people are walking around Midcity remembering their day wrong. And I think about Packard: tired, weary, doing his best to get Otto back. I think about what he said about the bracelet, and I want to ask him about it. I want to see him; the sense of unfinished business between us is overwhelming. Like a madwoman, I clean my apartment top to bottom, as if outward physical order will calm the chaos in my heart.

Just before I lock myself to the bed frame for the night, I remember the druggie-fencer-burglars, and I put my stun gun under my pillow, just in case the cops haven't made their arrests. I toss the key across the room.

Exhausted as I am, sleep won't come, so I pull out my mystery book. As I read, I begin to focus too much on possible telltale sensations in my head. This, at least, is one advantage to being handcuffed to the bed: I can't go to the computer and read about my symptoms and freak myself out even more. Plus, it's been months since I visited the vein star forums; I have no doubt somebody has posted scary new information. I remind myself I wasn't feeling any head weirdness when I was in that tense situation at Covian's, and that sort of stress would bring on a vein star episode if anything would. This self-talk must work, because I drift off.

The crash startles me awake so violently that I shoot up in the bed, wrenching my arm. Was that from inside my apartment? I'm afraid to move. It's 2:10 in the morning. Another nearby crash jolts me into action—clumsily I grab my phone and dial Shelby. More cracks—like the cracking of wood. Somebody's smashing through my front door.

Shelby answers and I frantically tell her somebody's trying to get in, and I'm trapped on my bed, and why the hell didn't I call 9-1-1?

"We are calling 9-1-1 and coming there." A click. More crashes. I hold the phone tight, wishing she was still on the other end.

Another crash, and another. I grab my stun gun. Then a different kind of crash and a bang. The front door, hitting the wall. They're in. I sit in full alert, eyes wide.

Sounds in the living room. Heavy, plodding footsteps—more than one set. I'm so exposed, so vulnerable! Quietly as I can, I yank at my cuffed hand, like magically I'll get free. Then I maneuver around, trying to swing over to hide under the bed. Impossible.

In my state of hyperawareness, I can remotely track every movement and action of the intruders through sounds. Clinks of metal is them going through my keys and change dish by the door. Lower-pitched clinking; they're in my junk drawer.

I consider hiding under the covers—surely they're just looking for things to steal and fence, and then they'll leave. And if they're so out of it, like the reports said, maybe they won't think twice about a lump in the bed. But I don't want to be unable to see them!

Plodding footsteps around the living room floor. Another set down the hall to the bathroom. The creak of the medicine cabinet. The sound of a glass bottle, shattering in the sink. My perfume. Chains clacking on glass. They're pawing around in my jewelry and hair stuff on the ledge by the sink.

More crashing and smashing. My heart slams in my chest. They're nearing.

Brain flash. I grab handfuls of laundry from my floor beside my bed and pile it up with some pillows next to me, then I yank my crocheted blanket out from under the comforter. You can see through it. I curl into a ball in the corner near my headboard next to the pillows and throw it over myself, praying I blend in with the laundry. *Please be really drugged up! Please!*

I sit really still, peering through the gaps in the blanket. Soon a light form plods in—a woman with blonde braids and a shapeless white gown. She bumps into my dresser, then, with mechanical movements, starts to shuffle through my jewelry and trinkets. *Take what you want,* I think. *Take it and go.*

A man lumbers in and joins her at my dresser. He's wearing a loose printed top and matching printed pants. Two more women crowd in after him. One of them pulls scarves out of my basket.

Suddenly the one with braids walks toward me. I curl my fingers around my stun gun, think about lunging, until I realize she's going for my bedside table, inches away from my head. I fight to stay still even though my every instinct screams to scramble away. *Thieves are just like bees,* I tell myself. *Leave them alone and they'll leave you alone.*

She pushes my book and my glass of water right off the side. Crash. Up close she looks like she's about forty, and she breathes loudly through her open mouth. She examines my locket necklace, tosses it aside, pulls open my vibrator drawer and rummages through, movements more zombie than druggie. And that steady, rhythmic breathing, almost like she's sleeping.

Sleeping.

A haze of terror spreads over me. Sleeping. *No!* There's no way Ez could've linked to anybody else—nobody on the planet can penetrate the force field Otto sealed her in—not without a descrambler.

Unless it's somebody else turning them into sleepwalkers. With a sick feeling I revisit Simon's theory about the boyfriend, Stuart Dailey, being the culprit all along.

She shuts the drawer. The man comes nearer, as if to help her search my bedside area. The printed outfit is Spider-Man pajamas. I focus on Spidey's black, webbed face, willing them not to see me.

As if she hears my thoughts, the woman with braids turns her head, looks at me with dull eyes. She rests a hand on my arm, squeezes, and moans. All of them turn to me.

Fuck!

She tugs at my blanket; I clutch it to myself with my free right hand, which also has the stun gun.

"Help!" I yell. "Help!"

The man starts pulling the blanket away from my feet and I kick him; they seem intent on getting the blanket off me. Morbidly I wonder if they see it as a kind of food wrapper, like foil around a burrito. The woman with braids pulls harder on the blanket, so I just let go of it and zap her with my stun gun. She collapses on me and I shove her off onto the floor by the side of my bed while kicking Spidey, who is making headway with my feet. He seems impervious to pain. One of the other women crawls over the far side of the bed, and suddenly my stun gun hand is caught in the blanket. I kick and squirm like crazy. Spidey presses all his weight onto my feet and the woman peels up my T-shirt and lunges, face-first, at my bare belly. I scream as I feel her warm tongue on my belly, and then the searing pain of teeth breaking my skin.

Suddenly the room is lit up red. Sirens. The three sleepwalkers jerk to attention—including the woman who bit me. Blood drools down her chin. As if on command, they head back toward my living room.

I gape in disbelief at my stomach; blood oozes from a spot just to the left of my belly button. I want to stick my finger in it and see how deep it is, but I'm afraid to. I roll my T-shirt so it doesn't get into the wound, and I just watch the blood, feeling sick, pulling mindlessly on my handcuffed hand.

They're coming back. I pull the blanket over me but they rush right by, carrying equipment—sledgehammer, blowtorch, welding mask. They're going for the window. Spidey smashes the pane, and the three of them lumber out to the fire escape.

Rustling next to me—the woman with braids is waking up! She rises and heads toward the fire escape.

Sounds in the living room.

"Hurry up—in here!" I scream. "Hurry!" What's taking them so long?

She's nearly out the window as my room fills with blinding light. Flashlight beams.

"Police! Stop!" A cop darts after her and hauls her back inside.

Somebody flicks on the bedroom light.

I point. "Three more are getting away!"

A pair of cops goes out the broken window.

"Are you hurt?" A woman officer comes to my side. It's obvious I am; the front of my belly is bloody. She looks at it with concern.

"She bit me," I say in a strangely calm tone.

"EMTs will be here any moment."

I feel nauseated.

She asks me if I have a key to the handcuffs, and I point out to the corner where it is. "Please," I say.

She retrieves it as other cops march the woman with the braids out. The woman still looks asleep. What does it take to wake these people?

A different officer, this one wearing latex gloves, presses gauze to my wound. "Ambulance on the way," he says.

The first officer, who now introduces herself as Dana, unlocks me. She wants to know who locked me up and why. She looks skeptical when I insist it was voluntary, to prevent sleepwalking. I give them the story of the attack, leaving out the stuff about Ez and Stuart and us disillusionists. No, I don't know them. They broke down my door and attacked me. The cops don't seem overly shocked at the biting. Or are they just trying to keep me calm?

My stomach feels weird and quivery; I can't stop thinking of the blood I'm losing, and the feel of that woman's tongue on my skin. And saliva carries pathogens. What diseases has that woman picked up from other victims? What has she transmitted to me?

I pretend to listen to Dana, who's giving me information on filing domestic abuse charges for some inexplicable reason that I don't care about. My stomach is bleeding through the gauze, making bright red splotches. Somebody else assures me an ambulance is coming.

More cops arrive, including a pair of detectives. The lead detective, a no-nonsense woman named Sara, has light brown skin and short, salt-and-pepper hair. She wants me to repeat my story and I comply. Even through the haze of my medical trauma, I find myself thinking things like I'm glad I sleep in a T-shirt and sweats, and not something sexy or raggedy. And I have this sudden empathy for people who end up on the TV show *Cops*.

"She bit at you with her teeth?" Detective Sara asks. "You're sure about that?"

"Pretty hard to mistake," I say, staring at her tiny little dolphin earrings.

Sara exchanges glances with a pink-faced, sixty-something bald man whom she introduces as her partner, Al. Sara says, "We'd like to keep that detail out of the media for now."

It takes awhile for this to register. "Oh my God. That's what happened to my neighbor, isn't it? Scott Feethum. That's why he thought they were perverts!"

If Sara and Al are impressed by my deduction, they don't show it, and they won't confirm or deny it. They do imply that the blowtorch and sledgehammer are new developments.

"I can't believe you would make the neighborhood think it's harmless druggie burglars when people are actually in danger," I say.

Detective Al asks me again, more sternly this time, to keep the cannibal detail to myself.

I snort, wondering if they've made the connection to the cannibal cases three years ago, and how many of them understand that it was a dream invader running this show, or if they all still think it's Satanists gone wild.

"Any idea where they went off to?" Al asks. When I prove to be no help on that count, he tells me what a bad idea it is to have cuffed myself to the bed. While he recites a list of bad things that could've happened—things that even my habitually paranoid mind would've never thought of—a pair of EMTs pushes through the small knot of people to look at my stomach. One of them, a blond man my age with tiny glasses, pulls up the gauze and washes the wound with a stinging solution and some sort of wipe while I monitor his face for signs of shock and pity.

"Did it go through?" I finally ask.

"Through?" he asks.

"To my intestines?"

"No, this is pretty superficial," he says. "And organs like intestines tend to move around, like marbles inside a water balloon."

"Oh," I say.

He nods. "If this had been a dog bite, you'd need quite a few more stitches."

"I need stitches?"

"We'll let a doctor decide that. You were lucky." He sticks a butterfly bandage onto my belly, and more gauze on top.

"Because a dog's mouth is bigger?" I ask. "That's why it would be worse?"

"And a dog's teeth are sharper," he says, "made for ripping and tearing. Human teeth tend to hydroplane." All this talk is calming me down, even as we move onto the topic of saliva-borne bacteria. He's not nearly as concerned as I am, though another EMT brings up the remote chance of rabies. I'm just starting to freak out about that when Simon swings in.

"Justine!"

I jump out of bed, which kills my stomach. "Thank God!" I say.

He hugs me, shaggy coat and all. I'm feeling shaky all of a sudden. "She bit my stomach!" I give him the cop version of what happened; he can put together the rest.

"It's okay," he says, clutching me to him. "You're safe." He wants to see, and I pull the bandage partway off. The EMT informs him that while it's superficial, they're recommending transport.

The detectives are back with more questions. Did any of the people look familiar? What did they seem to be after? As I tell them the sleepwalkers were focused on my drawers and dresser a horrible thought occurs to me.

I go over and open the little box where I kept my descrambler. Gone. I look at Simon, who goes rigid.

"Something wrong?" Sara asks. "You guys notice something?"

"It's impossible to tell," I say. "They messed everything up."

"Do you have that bracelet of mine you took?" Simon asks hoarsely.

"That's still in my car. Under the passenger seat," I say. "Here." I toss him the keys and he takes off.

"What's going on?" Sara asks.

"He's worried about his valuable bracelet," I say.

Sara and Al are suspicious. They think something's up, and there are more questions, some repeats, and then I catch sight of Shelby and Avery coming up the hall. A uniformed officer won't let them through, because my bedroom is a crime scene.

I go to join them in the living room.

Shelby wraps an arm around my shoulder, and I tell her what happened. Avery stands next to her, monitoring the cops with his intense gray eyes, running his hand through his nut-brown hair.

"They took my descrambler," I whisper to Shelby.

"I know. We saw Simon going out. He thinks they wish to kill Ez. Under command of Stuart. We must go."

"I'm coming, too." I tell Sara that we're heading out for a bite. She and Al are suspicious, and they don't want me to leave, but they can't make me stay. I take their business cards, promising I'll come down to the station and make a statement later. I grab a sweater and jeans from my laundry basket and quickly change in the bathroom.

In a harrowing display of multitasking, Shelby explains the Ez situation to Avery while driving at crazy speeds to the Sapphire Sunset, which unfortunately involves taking the tangle. She leaves the Otto aspect out of it.

I watch out the window; the lights of the city stream

by as her car careens around one turnpike after another. I think about Ez, alone in that booth. Sleepwalkers trying to get in.

"Highcaps victimizing highcaps," Avery says. "I don't know what to think about that."

"Sometimes we don't know what to think about it either," I say. "But this one's obviously innocent. And those sleepwalkers are going to . . ." I tighten my grip on the door handle. "How did they know I had a descrambler?"

"Perhaps Simon's questioning of old witnesses led Stu to you," Shelby says as she barrels down a ramp. "Perhaps they spied on Ez and saw you breach the field."

"There are always people lurking around that booth," I say. "It would've been easy to eavesdrop. Could Stu have people watching her?"

"Man who commands sleepwalking cannibals can make people do many things, I think," Shelby says.

The street in front of the Sapphire Sunset is brightly lit and quiet. The building itself looks quiet, too. Even sleepy.

Shelby pulls up behind Simon's black beater and we hop out. There's still dirty snow around the sides of the building, and Avery spots the footprints.

We follow him around and down the steep, dark, slippery side of the building. You can see the lake beyond the rooftops, moonlight in the waves. My stomach wound feels wet, but at least I'm not freaking about my head.

Around in back we find a small window—the men's bathroom?—that's been thoroughly mauled. The bars are bent willy-nilly, likely through a combination of the blowtorch and the sledgehammer, and the glass is gone, aside from bloody shards around the edge.

"These nuts don't fool around," Avery says, knocking the last of the glass away with a piece of cardboard. He goes first, stepping up on an orange milk crate Shelby found.

"Once you're in, you want to go out to the bar area and turn right," I tell him as he scrambles in. "Take the stairs up to the kind of balcony catwalk thing!" I whisper loudly.

"We're right behind," Shelby says as he disappears.

I help Shelby through. "I like that he didn't tell us to stay here and wait," I tell her as I hoist myself over the ledge. It hurts when I use my stomach muscles. Did she bite a muscle? Should I have gone to the ER?

"Avery does not believe in infantilizing women," Shelby informs me.

Thumps overhead. We rush out the bathroom into the dim piano bar, rounding tables and chairs to get to the stairs. A thud, and a woman's moan. I take the stairs two at a time.

Up top outside the coat check booth, Avery's trying to shake off the two sleepwalking women, whose faces are attached to each of his arms; it's like they're human barnacles, clinging, biting. I rush over and grab the one woman's long brown hair and pull, which takes her mouth off Avery at least. Shelby jabs the other with the stun gun and she collapses, then Avery and I hold the other woman still while Shelby zaps her. The one who bit me.

Crashes from inside the coat check booth. I peer in to see Simon and the man in Spidey pajamas, both bloody, swinging at each other as they stagger through piles of coats and smashed furnishings. The sleepwalking man's eyes look dead, and his movements are clumsy, but he's an effective fighter all the same. I remember how impervious to pain he seemed when I kicked his face back in my bedroom.

Ez huddles in a corner, hugging her legs. Is she hurt?

Avery slams into the coat check room door with his right shoulder. "Is there a key?"

"Stop, you won't get in," I say. Blood on his left arm. Bitten.

"We have to try!" He bangs on.

"Stop!" Shelby grabs his shirt. "Is fielded," she says. "Force field! Human flesh cannot pass through."

"We need a descrambler." I spy one on the floor inside the room and I slap the window. "Ez!" I call. "Ez! Can you hear me?"

She looks catatonic. The men fight on, just feet from her.

"There are two descramblers in there," I say. Avery and Shelby peer in—I point out one descrambler near the door, the other under an overturned lamp. Spidey plows Simon into a wall, like a quarterback smashing up against a dummy.

I pound on the window. "Ez! We need your help. We need you to help us help Simon."

She holds her stomach, rocking.

Simon and Spidey careen to the floor, knocking over a bookcase. Spidey is on top of Simon, punching him. Simon fumbles around with his hand, grabs an iron, and smashes it, point first, against the man's ear. It stops him long enough for Simon to drive it into the man's eye, and still the sleeping man won't stop fighting. Spidey grabs the iron and they fight over the iron now. Blood is everywhere, but most of all on the man in Spidey pajamas.

"There has to be another way," Avery says. "It's a damn coat check booth. How do the coats get in?"

"There—" I point to the carousel. "And this gully for money. But no human flesh can pass." The iron flies into a paneled wall. The man tries for a head butt; Simon slips the worst of it. "And because of the angle of the gully, we can't fire our stun guns. There's no straight shot."

"Okay, okay." Avery whips off his belt and kneels on the floor, seeming to disassemble it and reassemble it. Feverishly he builds a contraption that involves a lever, a spring, a rubber stopper, and a bendy tube. His belt is some kind of James Bond weapon.

More crashes from inside.

Shelby screams. The man's punching Simon, who looks awfully floppy. Ez stands and starts punching Spidey's back.

Meanwhile, Avery's added another section of tube to his thing. He stands and slides it under the little semicirclular holes in the window, along the gully.

"What is it?" I ask.

"Corner-shooting tranquilizer dart gun." He aims. "Damn."

Ez is in the way.

I feel something brush my legs just as Shelby screams.

"What?" Avery says, still aiming.

"We got it!" I haul the woman off Shelby's leg. Shelby stuns her and she goes down. Shelby stares vacantly at her torn pants. A woman bit her. I know how she feels. I grab her stun gun and shock the other, just for prevention.

"You okay?"

"Yes," Shelby says morosely.

A low moan from inside the coat check booth.

"Direct hit," Avery says. I pop up and peer into the window. The man in pajamas lies on the floor. Simon grabs the descramblers, puts one in Ez's hand, opens the door, and pulls her out of there.

Ez looks dazed. I wonder how much of it is her injury—she's holding something bloody to her side—and how much is being out of that tiny room for the first time in years. She takes a deep breath and looks all around, then her legs give out. Simon catches her, but he's not much better off.

The three of us help them to the floor—Simon leaning against the wall, Ez laid out prone. She's got a bar towel. She's been stanching her wounds with it.

"Justine, you're a nurse," she whispers. "Help me."

I'm about to tell her I'm not, but I don't want her to be even more upset, so I say, "Let's take a look." I peek under her towel. It's so bloody, it's hard to see. Do we need an ambulance?

"Did he get my intestines?" she asks.

Simon takes her hand as I examine the area.

She groans. The blood isn't gushing as bad as I worried it might be. Even the worst of the three gashes doesn't appear to go deep. It's long, though, like the man tore a swath of flesh. "Looks like Simon stopped him before he could really dig in," I say. "None of these wounds look deep. Still, we'll get you to the hospital." I nestle the towel back. I've never wished so badly that I was a real nurse, and that I could truly help her. "Luckily, human mouths aren't as good at biting as a dog's."

"You can't let them go," she says. "They won't stop eating people."

Simon strokes her hair from her forehead. "We won't let them go," he says.

Behind us, Shelby and Avery drag the unconscious women into the coat check booth—no easy feat with just two descramblers. From their discussion, it sounds like a math story problem—it takes two people to carry a person into a force-field prison, and a body has to be touching a descrambler to get through, and there are two to bring in, et cetera.

"Hurry up," I say over my shoulder. We may not need an ambulance, but Ez and Simon both need attention—Simon possibly more than Ez. His face is grotesquely red and puffy, and blood from his mouth covers his chin and much of his neck.

"I couldn't believe they finally got in," Ez says.

Simon squeezes Ez's hand. "What do you mean, finally?"

"They've come by a couple times this week. Late, around closing," she says.

I'm shocked. "Like this? Sleepwalking?"

Simon hisses out a breath.

"Yeah," she says. "I could tell they were . . . like that. The one good thing about being in there. See, Stu—my old boyfriend. Long story. He's—"

"We know about Stu and you," Simon says. "God, did I lead them to you?"

Ez gives him a hazy look. "You knew?"

"Yeah," Simon says. "We're disillusionists."

"Dis—what?" She closes her eyes. "You're sure he didn't puncture one of my organs? Because I feel weird."

"You need to get checked out," I say. "But the good thing is that organs move around inside. Like marbles inside a water balloon."

"Marbles inside a water balloon." Ez says. "You always know how to explain things, Justine. You're a good nurse."

"I'm not really a nurse." I pull off my coat and place it over her. "I'm sorry—I wasn't honest with you. I'm not a nurse, and I don't really think you have parasites, either."

Her eyes fly open. "What?"

"I'm sorry," I say. "I only pretended to be a nurse."

"So I don't have parasites?"

"Unlikely," I say. "I was messing with your head."

"She didn't want to," Simon says. "We get sent around to mess with people, but it's over, because you didn't do anything wrong. You're innocent. You shouldn't be penned up. I won't let you get put back in there."

Ez stares into Simon's eyes. "You were sent to mess with my head?"

"He wasn't," I say. "I was. He was trying to help you."

She looks so small suddenly. "I thought you were my friend. All bullshit, huh?"

"No—Ez—"

"At least I don't have to go in your stupid dreams anymore. You and that guy."

I touch her arm. "Wait! Did you unlink yet?"

"No."

"Don't do it yet," I say.

Simon squints. "What the hell?"

"I need to revisit his dream. The one in that creepy stairwell again. Can you help me? I need to see that dream."

"I can't stir it up if the man won't sleep," Ez says.

I look at Avery's contraption, sitting on the floor. "What if the man was tranquilized?"

"Forget it," Ez says. "I hate being in him."

"Please, one more time," I say. "Tonight. Or, I guess it's almost morning. Just, in the next couple hours. I have no right to ask, I know—"

Ez moves and winces. "Yeah, you don't have a right."

Simon watches me, a question in his puffy, beat-up face.

"There's a clue to a kidnapping in that dream," I say. "Maybe. It's a hunch."

Shelby and Avery shut the door on the sleepwalkers. Ez consents to keep the link and try to pull up the stairwell incident if Packard falls asleep again.

It's decided that Shelby and Avery will take Ez and Simon to Midcity General, and they're to stay together until Stu is located. Shelby's going to tip off the cops on Stuart—with fervent instructions to wear gloves. Ez tells where to find a photo of Stu online to help the cops.

Before they're gone, I ask Avery for one of the tranquilizer darts out of his dart gun. "You can take the whole gun," he says.

"I just want the knockout stuff out of one of the darts," I say.

He gives me one—it's the tiniest dart I've ever seen, with a tiny pin nose. He shows me where to crack it open to get the liquid out. Packard has to sleep for Ez to get access to the dream. I'll have to sleep again, too. Can I?

It's nearly five in the morning. I swing by an early opening coffee shop for two nice tall piping hot decafs. I put cream in one, and the contents of the tranquilizer in the other. One cow brown, one knockout black.

Chapter
Twenty

PACKARD COMES TO THE DOOR looking mussed and soft, as though the lack of sleep has robbed him of his hard edges. He's surprised I've turned up at this early hour. "Justine."

Suddenly all I want to do is push my face into his chest, to have him hold me, to cry, *I was trapped! They tried to eat me!*

Instead I say, "I brought coffee," I give him his cup, hoping he doesn't notice how shaky my hand is. My legs feel like rubber.

Packard shuts the door and turns to me with a baffled expression. "You okay?" I bite back the need to tell him how it felt to be in that bed, attacked. How frightened I was. I'll upset and agitate him, and that's the opposite of what I'm here to do.

"Okay enough." I walk in past him, willing myself to snap out of it. This is about people's lives, Otto's life. He's out there somewhere, vulnerable and in danger, probably in pain. The way to find him is through that dream.

Packard follows me into the living room. I turn and soak in his piney smell, the fiery look of his eyelashes, the sound of his voice, and most of all, the way he looks at me. Sees me. I've never felt it from anybody else, and I don't know what it is.

He pulls the lid off his cup. "You sure?"

"Yes," I whisper, unmoored.

"We'll find him," Packard says. "We'll find him and we'll put this all right."

Otto. I settle onto the big comfy couch, asking about the investigation.

He stays standing, full of brief assurances on leads. I get the feeling it's not what he wants to talk about. He's got one hand shoved deep in his jeans pocket, clinking coins; it occurs to me that he's busying his hands to keep himself awake.

"I'm glad you're here," he says suddenly. "There's something you need to know, and it can't wait any longer."

"Yeah, I need to know what happened at that old school," I say. "And the Goyces."

"There's nothing there to help us."

"I think there is."

"And I think you have a vibrant imagination."

"Fine." I cross my legs.

He squints. "Just like that? Subject dropped?" He takes a sip.

I say, "Maybe I'll come back around to it."

"I won't," he says.

I smile at him, trying to decide if this is day five or six of no sleep. He regards me with a lightly suspicious air and gestures at the couch. "Sorry, but I shouldn't sit on anything soft."

"Oh, come on. I'm here." I feel horrible for what I'm doing, but the key to the Dorks is in the dream—I've never been so sure of an intuition in my life. Packard can't see the dream; he's too upset during it.

"I can't," he says, eyeing the spot next to me. He's trying to keep up his resolve, but he wants to sit. The lack of sleep has made him pliable. "I can't."

"I could kick you in the face every five minutes."

He laughs softly. "An offer like that . . ." He trails off. "Oh, maybe I can sit for a little while. But I should get to HQ." He settles on the couch, a chaste distance away, holding the tall paper coffee cup in both hands, elbows resting on his knees. He stares down into it.

"They've had him for over forty-eight hours," I say. "Shouldn't we have heard something from them?"

"They won't kill him." He takes a breath, like he's steeling himself. For what?

"There are some things worse."

"He's stronger than you know," Packard says. "Those years he spent in those caves. He withstood a lot."

"He was in the caves voluntarily."

"Voluntary is a state of mind. Otto knows that." He keeps looking into his cup with a troubled expression. Does he suspect? It makes me nervous.

"What the hell do they want?" I ask.

Packard shakes his head.

"This investigation feels like it's devolved into a process of deduction."

Softly he says, "It has."

"What about Riverside?"

"I had them check the old site for the hell of it. All around the grounds of the condos there." He rotates his cup in his hand, then drinks deeply from it. I exhale silently. He pauses, then drinks again. Good. He'll be drifting off soon. Time to get his mind on the dream.

"Packard, I want to go through your recollection of the Goyces coming out of the wall—that whole scene. I'm telling you—"

He looks up with a haunted expression. "Trust me, there's nothing there for you. Nothing. And I need to tell you this thing about Jarvis."

"About *Jarvis*? What about Jarvis? He's not worse, is he?"

"No," Packard whispers.

Jarvis? Whatever he has to tell me about Jarvis, it's not easy.

"Packard, I know you feel guilty about what happened to Jarvis, but we have to focus on Riverside. That old spray-painted, crumbly stairwell. The bodies entombed in the wall."

He peers at the bookshelf across the room, head tilted, as though he's having trouble focusing. The knockout drops are taking effect. He gulps some more coffee. "I shouldn't be sitting on this soft thing."

"That's silly," I say.

"Why am I so sleepy?"

"Hmm, let me think," I say brightly. "Maybe because you haven't slept for days?"

"I can't let Ez get in." He closes his eyes, drawing his brows together, as though he's thinking very hard.

"She won't. You have done such an excellent job of it, Packard. You've kept our dreaming minds apart. I know you're doing it to keep your pact, but I do appreciate it."

Little indents on his cheeks. Pain dimples. He's trying hard to stay awake, to protect his secret, but he's losing his battle. Does he realize he's losing now? "It's been sort of gentlemanly of you, staying awake," I say.

"No," he says. "But it has been good. I've made a decision."

"That's wonderful," I whisper soothingly. "You look sleepy," I say. "Drink some more coffee."

He sighs, complies. "I never pretended to be good," he says. "Except that one time when I let you think I would cure you."

"It's okay."

"It's not." He rests his head on the back of the couch. "Should've told you. Minute he let me out of Delites, but I wanted to be free. I thought it would be over. Just get through and then tell you. But it never ends."

"Shhh," I say. A long silence. I scoot closer. "We have

to talk about Riverside and the Goyces. Remember when Henji discovered them in the wall? And he knew the truth?"

"Stop," he whispers, eyes closed. "Please stop, Justine."

"You have to think about it." I push a reddish curl off his clear, pale forehead and this seems to soothe him, so I stroke his forehead again. He's drifting off. Carefully, I extract his half-empty cup from his hands and set it on the coffee table. There's something so sweet about him dozing, as though all his pricklers are gone. I have this urge to trace my finger over the little jut of his cheek-bone, down to his lips. He stirs, trying to rouse himself, rubs his eyes, and mumbles, " 's I asleep?"

"Shh." I lay my hand on his shoulder. My touch seems to calm him; again he closes his eyes. He looks so alone, even in sleep—furrowed brow, jaw clenched. When I take my hand away, the lines in his face deepen, so I put it back. "Come here," I whisper, coaxing him sideways. He nestles his head onto my shoulder. I slide my arm around him.

"Justine?"

"I'm right here."

He nuzzles closer, so that he fits perfectly against my neck; it's heartbreaking and wonderful, all at the same time. I kiss the top of his head. He feels so good. Too good. I close my eyes and just feel him—the good feeling of being with him, side by side. I'm tired, too. And my stomach bite stings. It was scary to be so vulnerable. I hold on to him, like he might comfort me. This is totally out of line, but I don't care. I need this for a little while, even if it's pretend.

I touch his hair. He stirs, and I adjust us so he's totally comfortable, watching him fight sleep. I lay my cheek on his forehead. "You just wanted to be free," I say softly. I sit there, slightly stunned at myself, but the old anger is far away now. "All you ever wanted was to be free," I say.

He shifts.

"Shhh."

"—falling asleep."

"It's okay." I hold him tighter.

"No—" With a jolt of energy he pushes away from me. "Ez."

"It's okay. A little sleep won't hurt."

He's fighting to open his eyes, and he manages a slit. "She'll get in." He shakes his head, bewildered, but sleep is reclaiming him. I pull him back to me.

"Shhhhh," I say, smoothing his hair. I kiss the top of his head, keep my face pressed to his hair, breathing in his scent.

"You don't know," he mumbles. "Jarvis."

Where is this energy coming from? "I know you feel bad about Jarvis. It's okay."

"You don't know." Packard pulls away, shakes his head vigorously, like he's trying to shake off the sleep. "An actor. Have to tell you."

"Jarvis was an actor? Like, on the stage?"

He shakes his head in frustration. "Hired him. I hired him." He scrubs his face with his hands, trying to rouse himself. "To scare you. All of you. Help me keep control. Not brain-dead."

"Jarvis isn't brain-dead? Yes, he is."

"No. He's not. God, why'm I so sleepy?"

"Wait—what are you telling me?"

"Not . . ." He closes his eyes again.

This haze of shock settles over me. "Not brain-dead? Jarvis is an actor? You mean, Jarvis is acting like he's brain-dead but he really isn't?" I shake him. "What do you mean?"

"Right. Just acting. No such thing as blowback. You don't have to zing anymore. No more zinging. You can if you want, but . . ."

"*What?*"

"Jarvis is an actor. Never any danger."

"I don't have to ever zing again? Or I can zing *any-one*? Is that what you're telling me?"

He mumbles unintelligibly. I shake him. "Don't fall asleep, Packard! This is important!"

"Zing anyone. Or not at all. You were never minions. Never."

"All this time?" The enormity of all this takes awhile to sink in. "All this shit about us needing you? You having to clear our targets? Us in a symbiotic relationship? That was all made up?"

"Made up." He pulls up his head, eyes me through slits. "Zing anybody, or nobody at all. All people are compatible with you. All contain all emotions." His eyelids lower. "You don't belong to me, Justine," he whispers. "You never belonged to me."

I hold him upright, digging my fingers into his shoulders. "But remember last summer when I quit? And my hypochondria came back twice as bad?"

"Imagination." He just shakes his head. His eyes drift back shut.

"No, stay with me! It came back twice as bad, remember? And if I hadn't zinged again, I would've ended up brain-dead like Jarvis."

"Reverse placebo. Suggestible. You're all suggestible."

"No."

"Only your imagination." He mumbles some more. ". . . never any danger."

"So we were never your minions?" No answer. I raise my voice. "If we stop zinging do we revert to what we were?"

A mumbled yes.

"And Jarvis is a fucking actor?" I let him go and he flops sideways. I grab his collar and pull him back up to a sitting position, slap his cheek. "Wake up! We were free this whole goddamn time? I was never your minion?"

He's out.

Again I let him go, and again he flops sideways. "Fuck!" I stand in front of him. "All the people I zinged. All the people we disillusioned. Not being able to lead my own life. It was all a *ruse*? You have no power over us whatsoever?" The layers of outrageousness pile up on one another. "All this time? All this agony?"

He begins to snore softly.

"You act like you care about me, see how I'm struggling, and this whole time it's bullshit? Jesus!"

No reply.

I flop onto the small side couch, but I'm far too steamed to sleep. I call Shelby and get her voice mail, but this is too huge to tell on voice mail, so I just say I have unbelievable news. I sink into the cushion.

This is what he tried to tell me the other day. For a few days now.

"Damn right you should've told us a long time ago," I say. "Can I be any more of a fool?"

Snore.

I mutter some more about his outrageousness, arms crossed. It's not the ideal state to get to sleep in.

How could he?

I was starting to trust him again. I wanted to trust him. I curl up, feeling bereft, like nothing's real, like nothing matters.

It's stupid. I should be happy; I'm free, after all. Isn't that what I wanted? Except I don't feel free at all.

Chapter
Twenty-one

MOLD. PIGEON DUNG. Stale air. Blood in my mouth. Something gouging my back. The ceiling comes into focus: RIVERSIDE ELEM. I sit up just in time to see Henji jerking the body out of the wall. It collapses onto the stairs—a dirty old body with scraps of clothes stuck on his bones and gray tissue on his skull face.

I call to him: *Leave it, Henji!*

No! He's shaking it, brushing it. I stumble down. I grab his arm, but he flings out of my grip. He's such a strong kid. He'll be big when he grows up. Bigger than me.

He's ripping the shirt. Too late now. I grab his arm but he's crazy now. Suddenly he has the name patch. He's coming at me with it. *It says* Goyce, *doesn't it?* Goyce! *I know it says* Goyce *on this.*

No, Henji!

He smashes the little patch against my cheek. *Say it!*

No, Henji!

He pushes me against the wall, smashing the patch against my face with force that gouges my cheek against my teeth. Blood pools on my tongue.

I sit up with a jolt, sunlight streaming through the windows, a ring tone sounding somewhere in the next room.

The patch. It doesn't say *Goyce;* it says *Joyce!*

Packard sleeps peacefully on the couch on the other side of the coffee table, twisted a bit unnaturally. The phone stops.

It's such a simple clue. The boys dropped out of grade school. They could barely read, and certainly couldn't read cursive. They'd mistaken a cursive capital *J* for a *G* this whole time. Surely Packard can read cursive now, but once you accept something a certain way for years, you cease to see it. This is what irked me—they kept saying *Goyce* when my dreaming mind read the badge as *Joyce*. Unlike Packard and Otto, I completed the third grade.

Packard was investigating the list for a connection to the Goyce family. No wonder he didn't find anything. There probably isn't even a name like that. It seems crazy that it would come down to that.

I have the clue and I'm free. Everything's new.

I grab my phone to check the time. Ten in the morning. Shit. As I flip it closed, it occurs to me that the last name Joyce actually rings a bell. Where have I seen it? Did I come across the name in my research? Back when I was looking for details to give the teams in the field?

I scan the room for Packard's laptop. If I can get to my search history I can probably find where I saw the name. And find Otto.

I walk into the dining room. The table's bare. I head to Packard's bedroom, flick on the light, and pause. I've never been in here. It's simple, spare, and clean, with gleaming hardwood floors and white bedding, and a stack of books by the bedside table. Nice. But no computer. Kitchen next. His counter's strewn with coffee cups, candy wrappers, and sections of the *Midcity Eagle*. I shuffle them around. Nothing.

I check the foyer and his leather case on the table by the door. Keys, wallet, papers. Would he have left the laptop at HQ?

I grab my phone and call Francis. He's there, of course. I have him check Packard's desk for the laptop. "I'm looking at it," he says, "but no sign of Packard."

I grab my purse and jacket. "Sleeping."

"Really?" Francis says.

Considering the amount of tranquilizer he drank, he'll be out for hours, but I don't say that. I tell Francis I'm on my way over to check the laptop. I have a lead to the Dorks' location. "Get a few guys together; this is a concrete lead."

He grunts. It's hard to say how seriously he's taking me.

In the car on the way over, I try Shelby. I can't wait to tell her we're free. Voice mail. I deliberate, then hang up.

I try Simon and he actually answers. "Did it work?" he asks.

"Oh yeah," I say. "You can tell Ez she can unlink now. You two doing okay?"

They are. They were released hours ago, and now Ez wants to make a picnic on the lakeshore, even though it's in the twenties. They're about to leave, and yes, Simon is fully armed, just in case Stu or his people show up.

"Wait, there's something else," I say. "Something unbelievable." I smile. I can't help myself. "Something unfucking unbelievable."

"I'm listening."

"Jarvis," I say, "is a fucking actor."

"Mmm," Simon says. "He never told me that back when. Back when he could talk. So what?"

"No. He's an actor playing the part of Jarvis, the vegetable."

For once, Simon's speechless.

"That's right. There's nothing wrong with ol' Jarvis." Telling Simon is deliciously fun. "He's an actor, hired by one Sterling Packard, to play the poor brain-dead wayward disillusionist, the bogeyman cautionary tale for all of us."

"No," Simon says, all breathy shock.

"Yes." I turn onto the bridge over the sludgy Midcity River.

"No way."

"Packard confessed. Jarvis is an actor. That nurse of his is probably his wife or something."

Simon's laughing. "You are shitting me!"

I smile. "We're free. If we stop zinging, nothing happens. We just go back to the way we were."

"Fucked-up, but free—"

"That's right, baby!"

"Whoa." He laughs. "Whoa!"

"And if we zing a random person? No blowback. No danger. Because guess what? All human beings contain the full array of emotions. The man's an actor. Seems minionhood is just a state of mind." It's both preposterous and fascinating, and a bit of a cruel joke.

"Wait. Jarvis worked as a real disillusionist for a year."

"Did he?" I ask. "Or was it an act?"

"Fuck. You know what this means, don't you?" Simon says.

"It means we're free," I say. "We don't have to zing anymore."

"Spoken like somebody who's never read a comic book. Hello, we're not just free, we have powers!"

I pull into the HQ parking lot. "Powers?"

"*Powers*. I can walk out onto the street and turn anybody I touch into a reckless person, at least for a few hours. Crap, Justine, you have an even better power. You can go around instilling fear."

"Health fear."

"No, think about it. When we zing, it's the raw emotion. We chat people up, direct them, but the zing itself is the feeling. And you have goddamn fear. You can walk the streets striking fear into people's hearts."

"Wow." Leave it to Simon to see that angle.

"There's gotta be something cool I can do with the power to make people reckless. I suppose it would have its applications in poker games. I could ruin political careers."

I smile. He's like a kid at Christmas. "We're free, Simon."

"Yeah, baby!"

I pull the phone away from my ear as he hoots, thinking about how many hours we spent complaining and scheming, looking for a way out, looking for leverage to use against Packard, anything to wrest back control. And now we have it. Just like that. I want to feel like he does. "I have to go," I say.

"Hey, next time you see Packard, tell him thanks for the superpowers," he says.

Once again I picture Packard, out on the couch.

"We're free," Simon says. I can hear the smile in his voice. "We're our own people."

"Damn right," I say, with an enthusiasm I don't feel.

Chapter
Twenty-two

I sit down at Packard's HQ desk and boot up the laptop. It takes me about half an hour of searching to find it.

"Harrington," I say aloud, even though I'm the only one in the little office at that point. Harrington is a name on the customer list, and when you Google Harrington, you get lots of Joyce connections. I dig a bit deeper and see that Deena Harrington's maiden name is Deena Joyce, and there are tons of Joyce cousins. I follow a link to a Joyce family reunion, and from there, to a Joyce family tree, where I discover that Deena's husband, Dern Harrington, went missing twenty-two years ago in July—the summer the abandoned Riverside school mysteriously collapsed. Further poking reveals that her father, Marcus Joyce, and her two brothers, Carl and Conner Joyce, went missing that month, too, along with several others. The bodies in the wall. Packard probably Googled each name along with Goyce to find connections. One wrong letter.

A little more research gives me three addresses. Families with children reside at two of them; the third is a rental property.

I go and find Francis and Rondo in the hall. "It's the Harringtons. The Dorks are the Harringtons."

Francis gives me a hard look through his soda-bottle glasses. "And you know this how?"

Rondo turns to me; quickly I skunk my mind with the Wham! song. "A tip. I can't reveal my source, but I have an address. It's real."

Rondo crosses his arms. "We'll put it on the list for somebody to run down."

"No," I say. "This has to be taken seriously."

"Then why are you skunking me?" Rondo demands.

I turn to Francis. "What would you do if you were one hundred percent sure you had the name and address?"

"Does Packard know about this?"

"He's sleeping."

Francis studies my face. "How is it that he's sleeping? He didn't plan to sleep until that dream situation was cleared."

"No matter how strong a person's will, he can't stay awake indefinitely."

Francis says, "Packard can."

"He's been up for days! Don't discount me, Francis. What would you do if you were one hundred percent sure on an address for the Dorks right now? Even ninety percent?"

"See, that's the thing. No offense, but this bit with Packard . . . and you're under a certain amount of strain considering your relationship with the mayor. . . ."

"Like I'm the hysterical squeeze?"

Silence.

Part of me wants to tell him I pulled it from Packard's mind in a dream, but would that reveal too much of Packard and Otto's past? How much of it has Francis guessed? He didn't know Packard and Otto back then. Nobody alive did. Except maybe the Dorks.

"Look, the hysterical squeeze has the ultimate lead. The hysterical squeeze is going to go over there herself if you don't want to help."

He's shaking his head.

"You have nothing. I have a lead. Humor me."

After a little more argument he relents. "What kind of place is it?" he asks. "You get a satellite view?"

I drop my car at my place.

An hour later I'm sitting in the old white van with Francis, Rondo, and two of Rondo's security firm employees—hulking ex-mercenaries in matching knit black caps. One wears a shark's tooth necklace around his ropy neck; it's so tight, it seems like it might burst off at any second; the other has a long braid.

We're parked across the street, a few doors down from the Harrington rental property—a blue rambler with no apparent exterior surveillance. Or at least, that's what Rondo has concluded after creeping around the neighborhood in his cable guy outfit. This lack of surveillance suggests that the house isn't the Dorks', but much to everybody's annoyance, Francis says we'll watch it for a while. We don't need that long. At 12:15 p.m. a man wearing antihighcap glasses emerges from the house. "Holy shit," Rondo says.

The man gets into the car and drives off.

"Were those black striped Vans he had on?" Francis asks. "Anybody see?"

Nobody is sure, but they could be the sneakers Covian saw one of the Dorks wearing. Magazines are put aside and the binoculars come out. Suddenly it could be something.

"Lunch run," Francis says. "See if he comes back."

Sure enough, the man returns twenty minutes later with a tray of three coffees, two large bags from Burger Qwik, and several newspapers clutched under his arm. And the shoes are black striped Vans, the same color and brand Covian saw.

"Three coffees, three Dorks. Thanks." Rondo turns to Francis. "How's that shoulder feeling?"

"Angry," Francis says, loading up a gun.

"Maybe one of the coffees is for Otto," I say. "Maybe there's only two guys and Otto."

Francis looks at me sadly, and then he tries to hide it by wiping his mouth. The mercenaries are doing gun-loading and belt-clicking things.

"Are you sure we shouldn't have the cops or more guys or something?"

"Don't you worry, buttercup," Francis says. "Anything more is extra time and a herd of elephants. We're going to get these sons of bitches now while they're eating. Eating cuts their awareness."

"You'll be careful though, right? I mean, if there's a danger and they freak on Otto . . ."

"Just you wait," Francis assures me. "We're going to freak on *them,* and we're going to pull Sanchez out of there." He wants to hit fast at every entrance while they're gathered around the food.

The mercenary with the shark's tooth necklace points out that the new moon was last night. "The closer to the new moon the better to start any military action," he explains to me, though he doesn't seem to have the buy-in that Francis did on the food thing.

As the girl, I'm to wait outside in the van and honk once if anybody else arrives. Or more, slide down in the seat, *then* honk. And on the off chance the Dorks run out, I'm to write down license plate and car details.

"The Dorks are going down," Francis says.

They have lots of guns of different sizes as well as a small battering ram that looks like a metal log with handles. Rondo and Francis will take the front, and the two mercenaries will go in back through the porch door. The mercenaries leave first, loping down the sidewalk; they'll come in from the other side of the block.

Rondo and Francis steal across the street, as much as two guys with a battering ram can steal, and creep across the lawn to the door. I roll down my window and sink in my seat. It's like watching a cop show except I'm scared out of my mind. *Be careful,* I whisper over and over, feeling like my entire body is suspended in air.

The whistle goes up—the mercenaries' signal—and then the high-pitched crash of breaking glass. Right after, Rondo and Francis bash in the door with a bang and then disappear, leaving the battering ram in the doorway.

I wait, straining to make out anything inside the dark rectangular hole where the door was. There's a pale area to the side that might be stairs or a table.

Please let him be all right, I whisper, clenching and unclenching the strap of my bag. I wait. A minute. Two minutes. Cars go by now and again, but nobody comes out of the blue house, and the ram just sits there in the open door. A jogger comes up the street, but he doesn't seem to take note that it's like twenty degrees and the neighbor's door is wide open.

I wait. The second hand on the dashboard clock clicks around.

What does it mean? We should've had a signal.

Movement at the door. A person? The ram disappears inside the house and the door shuts.

I stiffen. Who was it? One of our guys? A Dork? I would've thought one of our guys would've waved or given the thumbs-up.

I slide lower in my seat. A neighbor two doors down gets into his car and drives away. An empty school bus rumbles past. The Harrington home stays quiet. How could we not have developed a backup plan or at least a signal? And they turned off their cell phones before they went in.

I wait. Four minutes go by. Six. I consider calling the cops, but they never wanted the cops involved. I try Carter to get his advice on it. Voice mail. I try Packard. Voice mail. I dial Simon and he answers.

He's on the beach with Ez; at least something's right.

I tell him what's happening. He is very strong on my not calling the cops. He thinks I should creep as close to the house as possible and get a better sense of the situation. It's only dangerous if they catch me, after all. Simon'll call the cops if he doesn't hear from me in twenty minutes.

It sounds like a good plan to me. I look around for a weapon to bring. Nothing. My stun gun will have to do. I climb out of the van, shut the door softly, and start off around the block; I'll come at the house from the back like the mercenaries did.

I feel like a criminal, especially when I get to the other side of the block and have to traipse through a person's yard and up along their hedge. I hide behind a tree at the corner of four yards. The Harrington yard has no trees, though you can see tree stumps where they recently had them. Most of the snow has melted.

Still no sound or light from the house. The back glass sliding door is broken—it looks like the Kool-Aid Pitcher guy burst through it. If I got nearer, I'd be able to hear what's going on. I take a deep breath, put my head down, and dash up along the hedge and creep along the side of the house, stopping just shy of the bashed-in door. No sounds at all. It's weird.

I listen, watching the gray sky, gripping my stun gun tightly. Just quiet. What does it mean? Is everybody in the basement? Slowly I slide my head toward the opening. I feel the heat of the home on my cheek. And then the end of a gun barrel on my forehead. A hand grabs my hair, pulling me into the room. A sting on my arm where glass from the door frame scrapes. Somebody takes my stun gun, my phone.

Otto's voice: "No!"

My eyes adjust to the dimness and I spot him tied to an elevated chair. "Otto!" One side of Otto's face is covered in blood, his shirt is ripped nearly off him, and his cap is gone. The hair on the side of his head looks clumped, like his head's been bleeding. But he's alive. Relief and alarm rage through me. "Otto!"

It turns out to be a woman who pulled me in. She lets go of my hair, but she keeps her gun on me. "Where'd you come from?" She's maybe forty years old, all muscle-bound, wearing antihighcap glasses, of course. *Deena Harrington.* "You hear me?"

"I was out there. Waiting."

Otto casts an angry glance across the room; I follow it and see Francis, Rondo and the mercenary with the braid, all laying prone on the floor, faces down, hands knit behind their heads. Two Dorks, also wearing the glasses, stand over them holding guns.

"She was supposed to wait," Francis says.

Did the mercenary with the shark's tooth necklace escape? My spirits lift. Surely he'll know what to do, who to call. Then I spy him sprawled next to the wall, near the front door. He's bloody, and his neck looks severely wounded. "We need to call an ambulance!" I say. "He needs medical attention!"

"Not anymore," Deena says, practically squeezing my arm off.

"Oh my God," I say. "Oh my God!"

She gives me a jerk. "Cry and we'll kill you next. Heads up, T!" She throws my phone to one of the Dorks guarding our guys. "See who she called." Clearly Deena's the leader.

T is a short guy with a red nose and eyes that droop at the sides, antihighcap glasses riding down low on his nose. He checks my phone.

I turn back to Otto. "You okay?"

He just shakes his head. Does he mean, *No, I'm not okay?* Or, *Don't talk?*

"Two disconnects, and a connect to a Simon five minutes ago." T looks up. "Simon."

Otto's expression darkens. Simon's not the team player you want in a pinch.

Deena yanks my arm. "What do you have arranged with this Simon?"

"Nothing!" The strangest thought occurs to me here: I could zing her. I'm touching her, after all. But I can't bring myself to. For so long, I believed zinging random people would fry my brain. You don't just turn that off.

"Don't fuck around," Rondo says from the floor. "Call Simon and tell him we have things under control."

"Okay . . ." I can't tell if Rondo means it. I'm wondering if I should pretend to call it off, but really not call it off.

"No pretending," Rondo snaps.

Does he not want the cops there? Does he want the Dorks to *think* he doesn't want the cops?

"Just call it off, plain and simple," Rondo says angrily.

"Stop reading her mind." Deena thrusts a pair of antihighcap glasses at me. "On! Now!"

I put them on and Deena shoves me at T. "Call Simon. On speaker. Tell him things are under control and you'll call back later with details."

T redials Simon, puts it on speaker, and hands the phone to me, gripping my arm way too hard.

We wait. Deena frowns at us all from her post next to Otto, bound and bloody in his chair. T stands ready to take the phone back from me. The other Dork, a lanky fellow in a hoodie and antihighcap glasses, aims his gun at the three guys prone on the floor.

Ring.

I exchange glances with Francis, who nods, best he can with his face on the floor. The lanky Dork kicks his shoulder.

Ring.

I could zing this one, this T who's holding me now. I start stoking my fear. It still feels like Russian roulette, but Packard wouldn't have said it was safe if it wasn't. He was sleepy, not crazy.

Ring.

But is fear the right emotion for this situation? Isn't there some saying that you don't want a jumpy kidnapper? But I won't give him jumpy; I'll give him terror.

I'm stoking more than I ever have in my life—I feel it roiling up in me, cold-hot. I suck in a ragged breath as I move on, in my mind, to my hospital equipment triggers. It's so much fear.

Simon answers. "Justine?"

I swallow. "Well, it's a good thing we don't need the cops after all," I say as I start using my focus to rip the hole in T's energy dimension. "Were you making a sandwich or what?"

"You're cool there?"

"Yeah, we're cool." I'm feeling shaky. It's such a risk.

"What happened? Did you find Sanchez?"

I say a little prayer and let the fear rush into T. "Nah, it was a false lead. They busted in on a regular family, who is now pissed about their bashed-in door." I feel it whoosh out—hot jagged energy—so much fear! Every muscle in me tenses for the mind-crushing blowback. When I've given him half of the fear I've got, I let our connection close.

The blowback doesn't come.

"Too bad," Simon says.

"Yeah." *The blowback never came.* "You kids have fun."

"Later," Simon says, clicking off.

T pulls the phone away and clicks off, staring at it, eyes looking glazed behind the antihighcap glasses. "That wasn't right. That was a code." He crowds his pale face into mine. "Was that a code? The sandwich?"

"The sandwich?" I give him my alarmed-nurse trying-not-to-look-alarmed face.

"Jesus Christ!" T screams.

"Get a grip, T!" Deena says. "There was no code there."

"Yes, there was." He tightens his grip on me, positively vibrating with fear. My fear. *The blowback never came. I can zing anybody anytime. Or nobody.*

"Look at me," Deena commands. When T looks at her, she bores into his eyes. "There was no code. I heard it same as you."

But then T looks back at me; now that my fear is inside him, we're connected. I give him a new look, another one I use to freak my targets out. He lets my arm go and backs away. "It was a code."

The lanky Dork grabs my arm, gun still on the three guys. "T! The guy bought it."

Deena glowers at T, who's wild-eyed, like a cornered animal. The lanky guy and Deena exchange glances. They don't get why he's melting down.

Meanwhile I've ripped the energy hole between me and the lanky Dork, and I let go of everything else I have in me—the highest-octane fear on the planet. I know when it hits deep because he clenches my arm twice as hard. I'll have bruises tomorrow. It's okay, I think, as total peace and calm rain through me. Glory hour.

I turn to him. "Nobody's coming. Everything's cool." My unreassuring reassuring voice. There really is no end to my screwed-up specialties. "Nobody's going to be shooting poison into the windows or dropping on the roof from black helicopters."

He stiffens with a jolt that seems to reverberate through his bones.

T says, "What if there was something she was supposed to say on the phone that she didn't?"

"Pull your shit together, T!" Deena barks. "The woman lurched in here like a drunken bear. Carrying a stun gun! She's not part of the plan." She tips her head at me. "What's your name, honey?"

I give her a frown I don't feel. "Justine."

"Justine, here's what's going to happen." A calming voice—for the benefit of her underlings, I'm thinking. "Mayor Sanchez is going to gather all the highcaps in a stadium for a big announcement. All we want is for the highcap people to come forward and be known. A public announcement—that they exist, and here is their social contract with us."

"Gathered for a slaughter," Otto says.

"No, just an announcement. Does that sound unreasonable to you, Justine?"

"It will never happen," Otto says.

Audible breathing beside me. Lanky's respiration has sped up. He's also swallowing a lot.

Deena says, "We'd like it to be Mayor Otto Sanchez who gathers the highcaps and makes the announcement, but we don't need it to be. For every hour he procrastinates putting the event into motion, one of you will die." She eyes me. "Ending with you. Or maybe starting with you. It'll be a spur-of-the-moment decision."

"Let her go," Otto says. "She's no threat. She's not even a highcap."

"So we're moving ahead with the event?" she asks.

"It will never happen," Otto says.

She stalks over and grabs my hair. Yanks.

Horror in Otto's eyes.

"I'm fine," I say to Otto. "There's no problem here."

"What does that mean?" T demands. "No problem? She knows something. It's that call! They're coming!"

"Fuck!" The lanky one says. "We're fucked!"

"Shut up!" Deena pushes me to the floor. "On your belly. Fingers knit."

I comply, stretching out and knitting my fingers behind my head, facedown into the carpet, which smells like citrus chemicals. My stomach wound from the cannibal's stings—did it just open? Then Deena smashes her boot onto my knuckles, and that hurts, too. This would all concern me a whole lot more if I wasn't glorying.

"I want to check the perimeter, just in case," T says. "This isn't right."

"It's not," the lanky one agrees.

"Get a grip!" Deena pushes her boot harder onto my knuckles. "You're not going out to check anything."

The lanky one works his mouth. He's tasting my fear, buzzing with its vibration, its pitch. I used to avoid knowing my fear so intimately, but Packard got me to turn toward it and understand it.

"This is wrong." The lanky one backs toward the front door, nearly stumbling over the ram. "I say we kill and run."

"The fuck we do." Deena levels her gun at him. "Not one more step."

He freezes, eyes wide.

"Stop it, you two!" T plunges his hands into his hair, even his gun hand. "They're coming. We're running out of time!"

"He's right." The lanky one turns to look at the door. "Fuck! We're fucked! Why did we listen to you?"

"Away from there!" Deena yells, shoelace tickling my hand. I loop my finger into it. "One more step and I'll shoot you."

"Fuck you." The lanky one raises his gun at her, backing away. "I'm outta here."

"Stand down," Deena growls.

"Fuck!" says T. "Fuck!"

"Stand down!" Deena shouts.

"You said we could leave at any time," T says.

"Not now, you can't!"

"I can't do this!" The lanky one bolts for the door.

Gunfire. I curl my finger tightly around the lace. I hear a thud, which I assume is the lanky Dork. T yells. More shots. I stay down, eyes shut, trying to pull into an

imaginary little turtle shell as the fighting rages above
and on top of me. A shout. Deena's boot jerks; I hold the
lace tight. She stumbles. "Goddammit!" She shoves her
boot heel into my jaw. My cheek burns and the inside of
my mouth fills with blood, but I don't let go of her bootlace.

More shots, and Deena falls heavily onto my back,
knocking the breath out of me. A sharp pain in my chest.
Was I shot? I gasp for air. I can't feel my finger. I let go
of her bootlace. Hands around my neck. I cough and
tear at her fingers.

There's another shot and another. I feel Deena jolt,
then go still. Heavy. I lie frozen underneath. A sensation
of warmth on my back, like warm liquid, spreading over
me. It feels kind of good, until I realize it's either blood
or piss. I'm too freaked to move.

"Justine?" Francis's voice. The weight lifts off me. I
try not to think that it's her body.

I close my eyes, trying to collect myself. A hand on my
shoulder. "Justine," Otto whispers.

"Uh," I say.

"Oh, God, thank God," Otto says.

"I think I was shot."

"Where?" Francis kneels down beside Otto.

"The chest," I say weakly.

Francis says, "You weren't shot."

"Oh." I turn enough to look up at him, and then Otto.
"Am I covered with—"

"Stay still," Otto whispers. "Urine is actually very ster-
ile and germ-free."

"Uh!" I sit up only to see Deena, lying there dead, eyes
open. "Oh, God." I turn away, covering my mouth. The
other Dorks are dead, too. And the mercenary with the
shark's tooth necklace.

Otto rests a hand on my shoulder. "You're okay. You're
safe."

When I look at him, it seems like all the warmth is gone out of his eyes. "Have they been . . . Are you okay?"

"I will be," he says darkly.

I nod. The mercenary with the braid is on the phone. Francis eyes Otto. "You know we can't keep you out of it, buddy." They invent a story about the Dorks luring us here and we all memorize it.

"What on earth possessed you to bring Justine?" Otto says to Francis.

"She figured it out," Rondo says. "We were humoring her. We didn't think—"

"I knew it," I say.

"You're lucky we brought live ammo," Rondo says.

I spy a sweatshirt hanging over a chair. I get up and Otto helps. "I have to . . ." I point.

Otto understands. "Go. Hurry." Sirens in the distance.

In the bathroom I try to keep my mind empty of thought as I peel off my blood-and-urine-soaked shirt and drop it on the floor. I eye the shower, then force myself to put on the sweatshirt. My jeans are sodden, too, I realize with horror. But the pain in my chest has lessened.

I stumble back out to the main room. Otto extends an arm and I go to him, somewhat automatically. It feels good to be snug at his side.

"Are you sure you're okay?"

"I sustained quite an impact when they took me." He lowers his voice. "Several. At times I was convinced I had a vein star pin leak behind my eye, though it would've manifested by now . . ." He trails off. Clearly he's been thinking about this extensively. "I *am* feeling faint."

"You've been held captive for days. Have you eaten?"

"Barely."

It's here I notice that the blood on his neck is actually a wound. "Shit! Is that a big gash?"

"Yeah, but it stopped bleeding," he says, quite casually. "And I think my arm is broken. I can't move it."

"Otto!"

"It's okay," he says. "I'm safe. I just need my cap."

"We have to find it," I say.

He turns to me. "How did you know?"

"The dream," I say. "The Goyce dream." I explain about my gut feeling, and drugging Packard, and the cursive.

Otto holds me more tightly with his good arm. "When that cretin pulled you in the door . . ." He looks around. "I still don't know how this deteriorated so dramatically. The way the Dorks spooked."

I concentrate on straightening the sweatshirt, which bears the name of a hotel in Florida. When I look up, he's regarding me strangely. I touch the sticky side of his face. "If only you could look in a mirror. You are so bloody." I give him a sly smile. "The cameras will love it."

"You figured it out," he says, gazing into my eyes. "You knew."

Time was, Otto looking at me like that would have thrilled me.

The sound of sirens closing in spurs him into action. Using only his right arm—his left arm hangs immobile—he rips the antihighcap glasses off each of the Dorks and throws them onto the floor, then he grabs two pairs off the counter and tosses them down. Then he gestures at me.

At first I don't know what he means, but then I realize.

"Oh, sure." I take my glasses off and toss them onto the floor with the others, and Otto stomps them all with his boot, smashes them to smithereens, then kicks the pieces around to blend with the general mess of the house. "Never again," he says with a ferocity that surprises me. "Never again."

Chapter
Twenty-three

THE GROUP OF US spend a whirlwind afternoon in the hospital, getting X-rayed, poked, and palpated by doctors, and questioned by cops. Francis reinjured his bullet wound and has to go in for surgery. Otto gets a cast. A doctor examines my cannibal bite, and after that, a volunteer lets me choose clothes from their free bin to replace my bloody, piss-smelling stuff. I select a long printed skirt, a hoodie sweater, and pair of blue Keds high-tops, but all I really want is a five-hour-long bath and my own things around me. And I want to talk to Shelby, but she still isn't answering. Probably with Avery. I've never seen two people take to each other like that.

Most of all, I want to be alone and think. I can't think surrounded by all these people. But I have to wait for Otto and Rondo; there are the reporters outside the hospital entrance, and we're going to make our escape from them together. Apparently, the national and tabloid press got hold of the mayoral hostage situation.

When the cast is on, Otto goes out and makes a statement to the reporters. They still don't leave, so Rondo helps Otto and me slip out the back.

Soon enough, we discover that there are reporters camped out in front of all three of our homes, and one following us. Rondo does some fancy driving and suddenly we're checking into the Royal Arms, a grand old five-star hotel on the lakefront. One room for Rondo, and one for Otto and me.

Otto and me. And suddenly we're heading up in the lavish elevator.

After all that time I spent feeling sad about having lost him, it feels strange to be with him.

As soon as we get into the room I wander to the window and look down. Cars stream back and forth; exhaust billows up. Across the street, the lakefront parklands stretch out as far as the eye can see—a trashy tundra of frozen dirt, leafless trees, and boarded-up concession stands. In the distance, you can just make out the line of giant boulders defining the shore like jagged teeth, and beyond, the endless black of the lake.

"Hungry?" Otto says.

I spin around. "Famished!"

Otto's on the bed, half propped up. His arm is casted almost to his shoulder, he's bruised everywhere, and the alarmingly deep gash in his neck is heavily bandaged—two more centimeters over and he would've bled to death, the doctors said. I have this thought that he's probably too injured and medicated to have sex, and then I feel guilty for being relieved about that.

We order half the room service menu, and then Otto calls Sophia. He wants her to sneak over with a beret as soon as she's finished with what's probably turning out to be the busiest day of her life as mayor's assistant and press secretary. I take a long-overdue shower while Otto makes some phone calls.

The food's being delivered when I come out in a fluffy hotel bathrobe. It's only dinnertime, but it seems like midnight.

I give the room service waiter a nice tip and pull the cart in next to the bed. One by one I lift the silver tops off the plates. Grilled fish sandwiches, fingerling potatoes, gnocchi, warm rosemary bread, a selection of fruits and cheeses, and numerous chocolates. There's also a Scotch on the rocks for Otto and a decanter of white wine for me.

"Yum," I say, unfolding a bed tray for Otto.

"You don't have to baby me," he says.

"You were tied to a chair for three days, and you have like nineteen injuries. You are going to lounge in bed while you eat. And I'm helping you."

He relents and I start fixing him a plate. They'd wanted to keep Otto overnight, but he'd promised to have a private nurse with him. Me.

Standing there next to his bed while we waited for his discharge papers, I'd reminded him that I'm nowhere near being a nurse and never will be—something he continues to refuse to accept. I also reminded him that the neck is superclose to the brain—it seems like an infection could travel there pretty fast. We debated this: Otto believes proximity doesn't have anything to do with it, and that an infection could travel anywhere fast. We both really wanted to ask the nurse, but they were already unhappy enough about his leaving.

I butter a piece of bread for him, eyeing the bandage. It was a big chance to take, leaving the hospital. I show him. "Enough?"

"You are so good to me," he says.

I set the buttered bread on his plate. "Maybe I just don't want crumbs in the sheets," I say, trying to keep things light.

He gets his serious look. "I missed you. The whole time they held me, I imagined something like this. A kind of daydream. Being away with you."

"Bet you didn't have broken bones and a neck gash in it," I joke.

"No," he says, clearly not feeling jokey.

I concentrate on loading up my own plate, remarking at stupid length on how perfectly browned the potatoes are. Then I prop up a pillow and settle in on my side, putting my concentration on my food.

I don't know why I'm so ill at ease, so disconnected from Otto. Worse, I keep wondering if Packard's woken up yet, and what he's doing, and how he feels, and I keep mulling over what he told me, the outrageousness of what he did.

I've decided I should definitely wait to tell Otto about us disillusionists being free agents. The kidnapping experience was hard on him; I can't say exactly how, just that he seems less than he was. Less warm, less lively, less Otto. The last thing he needs to know is that his prisoners—and therefore his mind—might be freed more slowly. Or not at all. Who knows what the other disillusionists will do? Who knows what I'll do?

I shake the question out of my head, telling myself I'll worry about it later. I've had two near-death experiences in the last forty-eight hours, and maybe three hours of sleep. I need to recuperate, too.

From the bed, the view out the window is this panorama of the starry sky, with a crescent moon. And I'm clean and warm, and the food is delicious. I shove another potato into my mouth and chew, staring at the moon. It looks fake, like something you'd see on a greeting card. I kind of hate it.

Otto talks about Deena's plan. He thinks she wanted to gather highcaps in one place and kill them en masse, with herself as a suicide bomber.

"I couldn't let that happen," he says simply, taking my hand.

"It won't," I say. "We're safe."

He doesn't answer this; he just gazes soulfully into my eyes. "Have I thanked you lately?"

I smile. "Yes. A lot."

Just as Packard predicted, the rescue restored things; it was the grand gesture of faith that proved my commitment to him once and for all. He trusts me again. We're together again. It's almost perfect. One tiny notch away from perfect.

That tiny notch means everything, though.

"I need to revitalize," he says, letting me go to sip his Scotch.

"You want to be alone? To make your perfect cone of silence?"

"I can make a perfect cone of silence with you," he says. "You're like the beating of my own heart."

I touch his arm, just above the cast, and smile. I should probably kiss him. Instead, I pull a green top off a strawberry and feed it to him. Our eyes meet. Does he sense that something's wrong?

I pull the top off another strawberry and feed it to myself.

It's not like I'm conflicted about Packard anymore. Clearly he'll never stop duping me. How can I be with a man I can't trust? I find myself wondering if he heard about the rescue.

Otto's voice snaps me out of my reverie. "My sweet?"

I meet his gaze, feeling like he's seeing through me. "Yes?"

"What thoughts?" he asks.

I grab another strawberry. "Just everything."

He watches me for a spell. Then, "A woman died practically on top of you."

"And cannibal sleepwalkers tried to eat me, too," I say, and suddenly I just laugh. I can't stop.

He stiffens. "What are you talking about?"

I pour another glass of wine. "It's fine, I'm okay. Everything's okay." I settle back in and tell him the story of how the cannibals attacked me. I show him my bite and explain how Simon went back to reinterview the witnesses and found so many of them missing. That we suspect that Stu created new cannibals to kill them. We figured Stuart learned about Simon's investigation and followed him straight to Ez, and likely overheard something about the descrambler, maybe planted a bug, something. "He sent sleepwalkers after the descrambler so they could get in there and kill Ez. It was him all along. Last I checked, Simon and her are at the beach. Though they're probably not now."

He gets very quiet. I'm guessing he feels guilty about imprisoning Ez.

I say, "In a way, it's lucky that you had her in such a high-security prison. It saved her in the end."

He turns to me. "You had no right to free her."

I sit up, not believing he could mean that. "What?"

"You shouldn't have freed her."

I look at him like he's crazy. "She was innocent. She was hurt. She'd been attacked."

"Justine." He wears a serious expression, inky brows drawn together. "You can't randomly decide that one of my prisoners is innocent and release her."

"It was hardly random."

"It wasn't your call to make."

I sit up, outraged. "We should've put her back in there?"

"Yes, and alerted the police to the sleepwalkers and let them handle it."

"She's *innocent*."

"It doesn't matter, Justine. It's not for the disillusionists to determine guilt or innocence. What happens if tomorrow Carter gets assigned to a high-security prisoner, receives a descrambler, and decides to use it to release him?"

"She could've died in there. Her old boyfriend was the psycho all along."

"You and your friends can't simply go around releasing my prisoners."

I stare at him. Maybe he's exhausted. Nobody's at their best when they're exhausted.

Softly he says, "The system of law and order is designed to protect everybody. One person can't decide to change the rules."

"She was innocent. How is the system more important than that?"

"Law and order is more important than the immediate happiness of one person."

"Is law and order more important than the life of one person?"

"Sometimes it is, Justine."

For a wild moment, I think I don't know him.

"She's innocent," I say. "Even Packard didn't think she looked like a mass murderer."

"Well, if Packard says it, then it must be so."

"He was being sincere."

Otto glowers at the window, jaw set hard.

"Why would he make it up?" I ask.

"Packard's reasons for doing things are clear only in hindsight. You of all people should understand that."

I don't answer. Nothing about Packard seems clear right now.

"How many times has he duped you, Justine?"

"Enough," I say.

He picks at the gnocchi. "Me, too."

I turn to him. "When did he dupe *you*?"

"You were there," Otto says. "The dreams."

"Riverside Elem? The Goyces?"

"You still don't know?"

"That he duped you?"

He regards me carefully. "Maybe it's time you knew. It would put a few things into perspective."

"You don't have to. I know you have a solemn pact."

"No, it's time you understood how dangerous and foolish it is to believe Packard," he says. "It's time you knew that Sterling Packard duped me into massacring an entire extended family. Deena's."

I search his face for a sign that he's joking, exaggerating. Something. "No," I whisper.

"You saw the bodies," he says. "I did that. Twelve of them—all Deena's people. I killed them."

"Otto . . ."

"I didn't know, of course. But I killed them all the same, leaving her a widow. And leaving Tim and Brucey fatherless."

"Those were the other two Dorks?"

"You really haven't put it together? The school, what happened?"

Dimly, I shake my head.

"They were after us. The Goyces. Joyces, I know, but I'll always think of them as Goyces." He heaves out a deep breath, then winces. His ribs. "Until the Goyces started coming around, life at that old abandoned school, it was good. Just us highcap kids. No adults. We thought of Packard as the adult, though he was just a kid, too. But he'd been living out in the wild for longer than anybody—practically his whole life, so that made him an adult to us. Out in the wild leading a tribe of children. It had been going for years when my foster siblings and I got there. I'd run away with three foster brothers and a foster sister. We were eight, nine, ten years old, and we'd come from a terrible home—one of the few that would take in suspected highcaps, though there was never any admitting that we existed." Otto swirls the ice in his Scotch. Is he breaking the pact? It bothers me that he might be breaking the pact.

He continues. "One of the kids at my foster home was this sweet, lovely, very powerful telepath, Fawna. The couple running the home would keep her in a cage, and beat her bloody if any of us boys used our powers or left. Ingenious really, because we all had a protective instinct where Fawna was concerned, and it made us keep each other in line, and turn on each other for the smallest infraction. They had all kinds of booby traps in place for that cage, too. But one day we figured it out. We took her and escaped to seek out Packard and the school. We'd heard the rumors."

He's telling me the story. Should I stop him? Packard stayed up for nearly a week to protect this pact.

"It was magical, really. Urban ruins overgrown by forest at the edge of downtown. The river. The bridges. Packard took us in—he was maybe eleven at the time we arrived."

"Why was he outside so much longer than everyone else?"

"His dad was a thumper." Otto studies my face. "You didn't know that? His dad beat him?"

I shake my head, dazed at these revelations.

"Most parents of highcaps will get there eventually, but he started out with bad folks. We think he was outside before he hit six years old."

"A six-year-old?" With a surge of pity I imagine a little redheaded boy, scared and alone.

"Story is he took up with a bunch of river rat bums who got him stealing for them. Running cons. You can imagine how successful a six-year-old of Packard's intelligence would be at that. As he tells it, he was more or less supporting the bums. But the yoke of that chafed and eventually he left them, found the abandoned school, and set up there with telekinetic twins—One and Two, we called them. They'd never say their names aloud, these twins—they were that terrified that the big ear in the sky might hear and send them back to wherever they came from. By the time my foster siblings and I arrived, dozens of highcap kids were at the schoolhouse. Some of the kids would steal, some would scrounge, or guard, some kept us clean and dressed right so we wouldn't attract attention out in public. We even jigged electricity off the grid, thanks to one of the telepaths befriending linemen down on the bridge, asking questions and picking the answers out of their brains."

"Wow," I say.

"Peter Pan Island. In some ways, at least. My job was to make force fields to keep out the bums and party teens. We had a hidden entrance at the top of the enclosed stairwell—a little hole covered by trash. The scramble hole, we called it. You could barely see it."

I nod, thinking back to the dream.

"Bums and teens could get into the stairwell, but they'd try the chained doors, which were held fast by my force field, and they wouldn't see the scramble hole, which was the only thing not fielded." He nibbles at the edge of a chocolate. "The school still had books in the closets. The most popular were the travel books, with pictures of things like the pyramids and Stonehenge. We were all fascinated with Stonehenge. That's where I got the name Henji. Short for Stonehenge. Packard thought of it."

"Because you have power over buildings."

"The school was a good place for a while, though it wasn't perfect. Kids would fight. And there was this dream invader named Manly who would poach our stuff. That's how it started, I suppose. I had this box of treasures—the usual kid stuff: mouse skull, coins, a ribbon award. Manly got in there and took the coins. One day soon after, I was manipulating the wall—the whole school was built out of cement blocks roughly the size of shoeboxes. I was fooling around in the corner, playing with my force field powers, loosening the concrete, pushing my finger in and out, and I got this notion that I could suck the box into it."

I get a bad feeling here, thinking about the bodies in the wall. "So, you just knew you could do that?"

"It was a cross between a sense and an urge. So I set the box against the blocks and touched the wall and in it went. And then I loosened the concrete with my fingers and pulled the box out. Then I did it all over again. After that, I started hiding keepsakes and money for the other boys, in whatever parts of the wall they chose." He gazes out the window. The moon's moved on. "One summer—there were maybe three dozen highcap kids at the school by then—this telekinetic named Frank disappeared. We knew he hadn't left of his own volition; he wasn't a kid to do that. We'd thought the bums had gotten him, but Packard went to see them and looked all over and . . . nothing. A few days later another kid disappeared, and the next week another."

"God."

"We were all so frightened, Justine. Packard started us going out in pairs, but then another was gone." His eyes look pained. From the story or his neck, it's hard to tell. "Then one night, Fawna and Manly were coming in from something and they were just about to enter the stairwell when Fawna heard unfamiliar thoughts. She was so powerful for her age. Such an amazing little girl." He runs his finger through the condensation of his lowball glass, making a clear diagonal line. "They hid in the bushes outside the stairwell door and waited and listened. Fawna got a great deal of intelligence on the men. They would hide inside the stairwell and get kids coming and going. We'd let down our guards in that stairwell. Enclosed, but not protected. Fawna got that the men would come out after their night of bowling—they had a family league. They'd have a few beers and come out hunting us highcap kids. Worst of all, she learned that there was a bounty of $500 on highcap children, and these guys planned to eventually take us all. She managed to warn us inside there, kept kids from coming in or out, and the guys left. She and Manly got a good look at them, and the matching league shirts with the patches that said Goyce. Or so they thought."

"You must have been so scared."

"Terrified." He stares out the window. A bright star crosses the sky. A satellite. "There'd been rumors about some scientist doing vivisection experiments on highcap children. I felt sure that's where the kids were being taken. Some thought it was a government thing, or UFOs. Packard created new safety procedures, but the next week Fawna disappeared. We were all devastated. Fawna." He's silent for some time.

"I'm so sorry."

"It was the end of something, when she was taken. We were all a little bit in love with her. We didn't know what to do. We had telekinetics hurling things at them when they came next, but it seemed to just anger the Goyces. They'd sit out there in the stairwell in a line, sitting against the wall, smoking and drinking and talking, and we'd cower in the school. You can't imagine what it's like to be hunted like that," he says. "Vulnerable. Unseen by society. In some ways, this Dorks situation brought it all back. The powerlessness created by those infernal glasses. Those glasses . . ." He falls silent, picks a nut off a chocolate.

"Because they allowed you to be hunted again," I say.

"Soon after, Packard wanted to talk with me. Of course, Packard knew what I could do, sucking the boxes into the wall, and he asked me if I thought I could suck people into the wall."

My heart skips a beat. Packard.

"It had never occurred to me, but Packard wanted me to try to suck the Goyces into the wall the next time they came. He said it would be like putting them in jail. My main concern, I remember, was how they would piss." Otto plays with the terrycloth belt of his robe. "How would they piss if they were encased in stone? Naturally, Packard had an answer—they'd piss right into the wall. And he told me that once we had all of them in there, he would personally take them to a real jail for kidnapping." Grimly, he meets my gaze. "In hindsight, I wonder how I'd believed it, but we were used to Packard having the answers. Then came rabbit night. We called it that because there had been this influx of rabbits to our part of the river, so we ate a lot of rabbit, and that night everybody who hunted got several. A feast night, but after, we knew it would be a Goyce night. They were coming regularly on Tuesdays and Thursdays, and it was a Tuesday. Packard and I snuck down and hid in the scramble hole, and we waited, both so stuffed with rabbit we felt like we could barely fit in there.

"Soon enough, four Goyces came in and set up in a row along the wall, whispering and laughing. Packard nodded his head, and I pressed my hand to the wall and urged it to suck them inside. And it did. They sank into it, as if the wall was quicksand and gravity went sideways. I remember Packard's face—that look of concentration he gets."

I picture it precisely. That burning look. Otto may not have felt the enormity of what he was doing, but Packard would've.

"It was a shock to see them disappear. It felt wrong, even then. We sat there, God, it felt like forever. Then Packard climbed down into the stairwell, and he started talking, like the Goyces were alive in there. He told them how they shouldn't kidnap children, and he would take them to see that justice was done. Whenever I'd feel strange about sucking Goyces into the wall, I'd think about that speech. Of course Packard knew I needed that as a way to fool myself. That's the worst part of it. I knew it was wrong, Justine, but I colluded with him to manipulate myself. Do you understand what I'm saying?"

"Yes," I say.

"More Goyces came the next day to look for the others. We were on the lookout, and we went down there again, and as soon as they touched the wall, I sucked them in, but one Goyce was on the other side of the stairwell, and he'd seen it. I panicked. I felt like my head might explode. Packard put his arm around me and whispered to wait. He promised me the man would touch the wall, and the man did. And I sucked him in. It happened until they stopped coming. Twelve I put in there. Twelve men and boys, and the Goyces stopped coming. And one day Packard said he brought them to jail. I asked him how he got them out, and he said he pulled them out the other side. I never wanted to question that. I wanted to believe."

"You were only eleven."

"Don't make excuses. Eleven is old enough not to fall for that." Otto's eyes darken. "I wanted to believe him."

"You were alone. He was all you had."

Otto raises a hand to forestall further utterances on my part. "That winter, the entry started cracking. I think all those bodies in that small space affected the integrity of the wall, and then you had trees growing into it, ice freezing and melting. I could've reinforced it with my touch, but Packard had us using a different entry by then. *Switching it up,* he said, and we weren't supposed to go into the old entry ever again. Of course kids go everywhere, and one of the boys saw the hand and told everyone. Hearing it, something in me turned upside down. I threw up. Actually threw up, right when I heard. It connected with something deep in me, deep in that place where I knew what I'd done."

"Oh, Otto." I touch a dark curl, push it off his face. "You were just a boy," I whisper. "Scared. Doing the best you could."

He shakes his head, like that's no excuse.

"I can't even imagine—to learn something like that." I rest a hand on his arm.

"You can't imagine it. One minute you're a boy, and

the next you're a killer, and you have poison in your heart. And everything inside you is wrong. I stumbled down there, through the scramble hole. Packard followed me. He tried to keep me from looking, but he couldn't. I pulled every one of those corpses out. The shock, Justine." He takes a ragged breath. "We fought, and cracks began crawling along the walls, and the entire stairwell started crumbling. I know what the rumors are, but I never meant to destroy that school. But pulling those corpses out, it was as if my rage and horror radiated through the whole building. The kids got out, but it collapsed around us while we fought. Then it was gone and still we fought."

"God, Otto."

"He was our savior, really. Savior to all of us kids, but he made me a murderer. I wanted to kill him, and I almost did—we almost killed each other. Somehow I picked myself up and stumbled off and just kept going. I needed to disappear—not from them, but from myself. Have you had that? That sense that you want to crawl out of your own skin, just slither away, leave yourself standing?"

"I don't know—"

"If you don't know, then you haven't," he snaps.

There's this long silence.

"Did you ever find those missing kids? Fawna and the others?"

"No." Otto drains his Scotch. "You know the rest. I stowed away on the freighter. At first it was a geographical fix—try to shake the feeling by getting as far away as possible. But then I started wanting to make it up somehow. That's how I ended up in Vindahar, why I sought out Master Basenji, and he helped me hone my skills as a crime fighter. Packard stayed and became a crime boss." Otto turns to me. "I was just a boy, and think what he made me do!"

I feel suddenly so angry on Otto's behalf. "It's horrible!" I begin, but I stop short. Packard was just a boy after all, doing the best he could. He was trying to save his little tribe—and save Otto from the awful truth by taking it all on himself. That seems quite clear when I stop to think about it.

I realize, in a flash, that this is something Otto and I have in common—casting Packard as the bad guy. It's so much easier to make Packard the victimizer than to see him as the very real and complicated man he is.

He did lie to me—to all of us disillusionists—taking our freedom to buy his. But then again, he learned at a very young age that he couldn't trust anyone else. And he was likely damaged every bit as much as Otto by what he did in that ruined school. Maybe more.

Not that this all excuses him, but it changes something in how I view him, and I suddenly feel this overwhelming sense of unfinished business with him. I want to go and see him, have it out, ask him a million questions, tell him important things—what, I don't know. I just know I haven't been seeing who he is for a very long time.

"And then we made a pact," Otto says, startling me out of my reverie. "Lying there, after the fight, both so injured, it's what we agreed—to never speak of it. As though silence would make it go away. Then we threw the bodies in the river. Who knows how Deena pieced it together. And then she and her boys got those glasses."

"How did they find you?"

"Pure accident. They bribed a hospital official to get Covian's name and address. They thought he could identify them, and wanted to finish him off. They figured out who I was when they saw how I sealed Covian up. I don't know how—photos, rumors, other kids telling tales." Otto stares out the window. Two freighters move across the dark water, lit in red and white.

"You saved Covian's life."

"Covian," Otto says through a clenched jaw. The intensity I feel off him surprises me. It feels new. Exhaustion, I remind myself.

"Have you slept much?"

"Not much."

"Hey, the bandage. We were supposed to change it thirty minutes ago. What kind of nurse am I?"

"You're the best nurse in the world."

I put my hand on his stubbly cheek. Then I take away the trays and food and stick them outside the door and grab the stuff the hospital sent along with us.

I think about Otto as a little boy. Nobody to care for him, nobody to help him make sense of the world.

Carefully, I pull up the bandage. "You're okay now," I say. "I'll help you."

"How does it look?" he asks.

"The same. Maybe a little less red." After I clean the gash, I dab it with ointment, updating him on whatever light, fun things I can think of. I'm deeply horrified by the story, though. And I left Packard alone, drugged. He tried to save those boys. I think of the guilt I felt when I was inside his dream.

"It feels funny," Otto says.

"Of course it does. It's an open wound."

I put on a new bandage, keenly aware of Otto's gaze, deep brown eyes full of adoration and need. He wants me to look at him, to meet that gaze, but I don't want to, because I feel like it would be a lie. So I fuss with the bandage and then I get him to lie down all the way, and he's out almost immediately.

I text Sophia to tell her not to bring the hat until morning, then I pull my bathrobe snug and tight and curl up next to Otto and try to fall asleep, but I can't stop thinking about those children alone, and everything they went through. Packard having to make those decisions. The

weight he carried. Otto's own guilt. And what happened
to little Fawna, and the others who were taken?

In the morning, the sunrise wakes me. I look over at
Otto, sleeping peacefully, jaw finally relaxed, dark hair
burnished bright. Will he ever save and protect enough
people to make up for his guilt?

I tighten my bathrobe tie and pad across the room to
close the curtains. It's not even seven in the morning; he'll
need much more sleep than this. I sneak into the bathroom, more refreshed than I've felt in a long time. It's not
until after I wash up that I get it. Ez broke the link. I'm
my own dreamer again.

Quiet as a mouse, I put on my skirt and tennis shoes
outfit from the hospital and head down to the lavish
five-star lobby, where I'm served hot, delicious-smelling
coffee in a real china cup with a little red flower pattern
around its rim. I take a seat next to the grand fireplace
and sip, unable to stop thinking about Otto's story. All
those lives, all that hate. The horror of Otto learning
what he'd done. And Packard, bearing it alone.

Has he realized we're free of Ez yet? He'll be so relieved! I feel eager to go over and point it out to him, and
tell him firsthand what happened with the cannibals, and
the Dorks, and that I know now what happened back at
the school, and that I understand. Yes, there's still the
Jarvis thing. Why did he tell? I think about what Otto
said: *Packard's motivations are only clear in hindsight.* I
certainly can't imagine what possible advantage he got
from revealing his ruse.

I sip my coffee, wondering if I'm stupid to have this
little cockeyed speck of hope that he doesn't have a game
for once. I wander across the lobby window and look at
the cars and the street out front. The press is probably
still on the lookout for us, but they'll be more focused on
Otto than me.

Quickly, I scribble a '*back soon xoxo*' note, even though Otto hates those. I take the elevator back upstairs and slide the note under the door. Then I go down and buy a hat in the gift shop, sneak out alongside a group of tourists, and hop a bus north to Packard's.

As I ride, I fume at people who ask the driver stupid questions, get on without the correct change, or otherwise slow the bus down. At one point I get the idea that I could run there faster, and I actually consider it for a moment.

Chapter
Twenty-four

FINALLY THE BUS LETS ME OFF at the stop near Packard's. I round the corner and see Parsons, the head of the bodyguard team we hired, outside Packard's building. It's weird that he's still guarding Packard, now that the Dorks threat is defunct. When he sees me, he says something into his wrist.

I walk up. "Is Packard home?"

He gazes past me, all around the street. "You alone?"

"Yeah. Is he up there? I need to see him."

"I can't let you do that."

"What do you mean? Mr. Parsons, I'm Justine Jones. We met once, remember? I work with Helmut—"

"I know who you are," Parsons says.

"You need to let me see him," I say, just as Carter bursts out the door.

"Fuck that," Carter says.

I smile. "Carter!"

"You better not have brought him."

I stare, dumbfounded. "What?"

Carter's wound tight for action. He pulls a gun from his belt. "Otto. Otto's people."

"Carter!" I raise my hands. "What? I'm alone."

"You sure?"

"What are you doing?"

He kicks the door shut behind him. "What do you want?"

"To see Packard."

"Yeah. Fat chance." Carter jerks his head at Parsons, who wanders to a nearby car and leans in the window. Carter turns back to me. "Nice of you to leave him drugged for Otto like that."

"I didn't leave him drugged for anyone. I was trying to get at that dream. We were dream invaded."

"You couldn't have woken him up after? Given him a head start?"

"Carter, what's going on? Jarvis was an actor. We're not minions," I say. "Why are you being like this?"

"Because you have screwed him over for the last time. Because unlike you, I'm not about to forget that he saved my life. I would've been dead by now. You would've spent half your days in an ER waiting room. Do you care?"

"What are you talking about?"

He shoves the gun back in his belt. "I'm talking about the fact that he threw it all out the window for you. Because *you're* never happy. Because you care only about yourself. And how do you thank him? You drug him and leave him like an animal for Otto to come and get. Don't worry, I snapped him out of it. Like only a half hour ago. We're getting him out of here. He's not going back to the Mongolian Delites."

I squint at him, bewildered.

"Figure it out," Carter sneers.

I figure it out just as Carter says it. "The deal. If we aren't disillusioning criminals, Packard goes back inside. And now that we're free agents, you think we're going to keep crashing Otto's criminals? Packard scuttled the deal that keeps him free just to please you."

"He scuttled the deal . . ." I say.

"For you."

This haze comes over me, seems to envelop me. "He traded his freedom for mine. . . ."

"Well, hand the girl a stuffed monkey. She got it."

My eyes mist up. The little speck of hope expands like a flower inside me.

Carter says, "We're helping him clear out of here before Otto comes."

"Otto wouldn't put him back in."

"You got that right. Because Packard'll die before he goes back in there. And I'll fucking die making sure he doesn't."

"I have to see him." I fling open the door and go in.

"No!" Carter grabs my arm. I yank it away and start up the stairs. A man's coming down with a box and I duck under. Carter crashes into him. I race up the rest of the five flights. Packard's door is open and I burst in, with Carter behind me, rush through the foyer to the dining room, and freeze.

There are boxes everywhere. Packard stands in front of the table, hurriedly sorting papers and IDs into piles, not looking up. Seeing him, something uncoils in me. It's like I know him, recognize him. Like I've known him forever. "Packard," I say, going to him.

His angry gaze halts me cold. "This my official wake-up call?"

"No . . . No, I . . ." I feel confused, panicky. What have I done?

He waves Carter off. "It's fine." Carter stomps away, and Packard goes back to his sorting. "What?"

"You're leaving?" I ask.

"I'm not going back into the restaurant business." He stuffs a sheaf of papers into his briefcase. "Ideally, I would've gotten some head start here. It's a goddamn miracle I'm not sealed in there right now."

"I didn't think . . . I didn't think it through." I pause, hating myself. "Packard, I didn't tell him," I say. "He doesn't know yet."

He locks up the case. "How do you know Sophia hasn't heard, and that she's not telling him right now? Or any one of his people. Really, you are so clever at putting things together, and you didn't think this one thing through? I guess you have to care about a thing to think it through."

"Of course I care."

Packard continues packing. His hurt feels like a hot knife.

I see what he sees now: I left him like a sacrifice to Otto. He set me free and I left him vulnerable. My pulse pounds. Frantically I look around. "We can fix this—"

Packard gives me an incredulous glare. "Don't be naïve." He turns and runs a finger along the spines of the paperback books in his bookcase, extracts one, then another, starting a small stack on the table.

I move nearer, feeling panicky. "You traded your freedom for ours." *For mine.*

"It had to stop," he says casually.

"You sacrificed your *freedom*—"

"Only if he finds me. And he *won't*." He lifts a small carved wooden box from the bookshelf.

I feel sick.

He caresses the surface of the box, then sets it back in its place on the shelf. A man going on the run can only bring essential items. Packard's going on the run.

He's leaving.

"Packard," I whisper frantically.

"Stop it. It was overdue. My plan never went beyond using you all to get free of the restaurant. Then suddenly we had to keep doing it. It was getting old." He picks up the little box again, walks across the room, and nestles it into a suitcase full of clothes. "Disillu-

sioning people as a way of ameliorating Otto's ridiculous head condition—"

"What do you mean?"

He stands. "Otto's head condition." He practically
spits out the words. "There's nothing wrong with Otto's
head except that he's a hypochondriac. He can keep
those people behind their force fields just fine without a
problem. He doesn't need us to disillusion them. He
never did."

"What? But the cranial pressure, the headaches . . ."

"Please. It's imaginary. He needs a slap in the face, not
the service of disillusionists. He's a *hypochondriac,* Justine. You know how it works." He tosses a baseball cap
into the suitcase and walks off.

Stunned, I follow him into the bathroom.

He grabs an overnight bag from the closet, yanks open
a drawer, and throws in deodorant.

"It worked for me for a while. We just had to disillusion
the people on the list, which meant I had to keep the Jarvis
lie going. What's another despicable deed to me, right?
You know how it is—I'll do anything to stay free. To stay
living in Midcity. But you started to sense how wrong disillusionment was." He shuts a toothbrush into a plastic
tube. "You were never able to articulate it, but you felt
that it was wrong. For the record, I agree. It robs them."

"You felt that way the whole time?"

"Just lately." He twists a cap onto a tube of tooth-
paste. "Forcing people to turn robs them of the chance
to change and grow. Which is one of the few things that
set us apart from raccoons." He unzips an inner pocket,
puts in a razor. "Or to stay who they've become and suf-
fer." Helplessly I watch him pack. It's like an out-of-
body experience. "Basically, we've been robbing people
of an essential part of the human journey. I guess I
could've lived with it awhile longer," he continues, "but
I couldn't live with *you* living with it."

"Packard," I say.

"It was monstrous. I didn't see it before, but I do now. And you know what the worst thing is?" He stops, turns to me. "I did it to you."

Everything slows.

"I took your choices away. I took your life away. It was unforgivable, and I'm sorry as hell. I know it's too late, but I am sorry. I told myself that I was helping you, that it was for your own good, but it was never my right."

"You thought I'd be institutionalized. Or dead."

"Still wasn't my choice to make. To force you to be a minion?" He goes back to packing. "Forcing you to attack others . . . I should know better. I do know better."

Otto. He's talking about using Otto to destroy the Goyces. "You were just a child. You saved those children's lives," I say.

He spins to face me, bright with shock.

"He told me," I say. "Everything."

Packard blinks, seemingly unable to comprehend this. "Well," he says quietly, "now you know."

"You were a hero," I say.

He turns away with a derisive snort and folds a washcloth.

I feel sick. "Where are you going?"

"You know I can't tell you that."

Leaving forever. God, he can't—I can't—

He zips his little bag, and I feel the ground shift under me. He says, "If you want to do something for me, see if I can get enough head start. I won't ask you to lie, but—"

"Don't go," I say.

"I should stay? Fight? What's here for me now?"

"I don't want you to go."

He turns to meet my gaze. Maybe he see the tears starting. "Justine, you'll be fine." He touches my hair. "You'll be fine. You are the bravest, best person I've ever known. I *see* that. I've always seen it."

"I selfishly screwed things up for you."

"No. The opposite. You've given me so much," he says. "Things I thought I'd never have."

I turn my face to his hand, grab it, and squeeze it, like if I keep his hand, he can't leave.

He draws nearer, kisses the top of my head. I feel his warmth up and down me. "There was a time when all I could ever see was the way people were doomed to behave—their tendencies, their reactions to their own idiotic histories. Misery, delusions, compulsions, all of it. I would use that to control them. But you're not like that. The way you look at people, the questions that you ask—you make me remember that people can be more than all that. You make me remember that nothing's decided. Nothing's known. That is what you gave me."

Raw with feeling, I pull away, flattening his hand, warm between mine, and we look at each other—for how long, I don't know. His eyes still look bleary, and he needs a shave, but everything about him feels new. I have this crazy sense that I know everything about him, and nothing about him at all, and it's the most exciting thing in the world.

I think of Otto telling me the story of Riverside Elementary; of how I couldn't stop thinking about Packard after; of how I wanted to run out of that hotel room and just come here and tell him—tell him what?

The words come to me at last, flooding into me with certainty. *I love him.*

He draws a thumb across my cheek, stops on my lips, stops me from smiling. "I thought maybe if I waited . . ." He breaks off, eyes bleak, then smiles strangely. "Just give me my lead time, okay?"

I sniff. I laugh into his bleary eyes. "I can't."

He knits his brows.

I grab his thumb. "You can't get away from me."

He searches my face, cheeks ruddy. "What?"

"You can't get away from me, because I'm staying with you."

In the silence that follows, I touch his chest with my open palm. The air seems to thicken, pick up charge. "*You*. I won't let you go. I love you, Packard."

He pulses out a breath, gaze fixed so hard on me, the sensation is nearly physical. "What?" he says again.

I smile. He's an endless, dangerous person. *Because I love him.*

"Have I been crazy all this time?" I ask. "Because I think I have. Last night I felt so unhappy. All I could think of was you. All I can ever think about is you. Why am I always fighting it? Always fighting thinking about you, fighting this wonderful feeling about you. This aliveness. This love." I look into his eyes and smile like a madwoman. "I love you!" I can't stop saying it. "I love you. Love, love love."

"Jesus," he says, hands trembling along my waist. "Jesus!" And with a surge of feeling, he kisses me. "Jesus, Justine!" He kisses me all over—my lips, my face, my hair. He kisses me too fast to track—it's just this flurry of him. I laugh. I will never be safe—not ever again. Because I love him too much.

He pulls away breathless. Bewildered. Maybe he doesn't trust it.

"You," I say, putting everything into that little word, putting my palm to his. "*You.*" I rip a little hole between us, just to be more with him. No darkness flows through, but somehow, we're more together.

He grips my arms. I feel him so acutely now. "Justine," he says, and I know he sees me, and he knows me, and I'm home. He pulls me tight to him, and I wrap my

arms around him and squeeze. We're squeezing feeling
out of each other, and making the feeling as fast as we
squeeze it out. "You know I love you, too," he whispers.
"You know that, right? For so fucking long, Justine."

Hearing this, I feel like horses galloping in me. I realize that I did know—a secret, silent knowing that had
always been there, but to hear him say it is magical.

I'm aware of my own breath coming bigger, harder.
His heartbeat to my breast.

"It's decided, then," I say, smiling into his cheek, because it's a crazy thing to say, and because our embrace
is turning animal.

He grabs my hair, and he finds my lips and he kisses
me. I push him and he backs up, and we're against the
hall wall, lost in each other.

Lost.

Home.

I smash into him; I want to touch him everywhere, de-
vour him. His face is warm under my lips, hair soft against
my cheek. I pull him hard to me, fingers pressed into his
flesh.

I feel teeth on my earlobe. Butterflies in the pit of my
stomach. The stone of his erection between my thighs.

Vaguely I come to my senses. "We have to get you
away."

"Fuck it," he breathes, finding my lips. He pushes up
my skirt, and we maul each other. Nothing matters but
us. It's like another entity is controlling us. A tidal wave,
or a comet. Love.

"Come here." He picks me up, legs wrapped around
him and all, and carries me to the other end of the bathroom, where he sets me on smooth, cool marble. He has
my leg in his arm, he's nuzzling my neck, and I'm pulling
him hard to me, sucking his lip, his tongue.

I'm ready to come before he even thinks to grab a condom from a bathroom drawer. I push my hands over his

chest as he rolls it on, baffled and feverish, with the sense that we've left the whole world behind.

He hides his face as he penetrates me. He pushes into me and stays there, unmoving, and I grab his hair and pull him away to look at his eyes. They're shining with tears. I kiss the tears off his coppery lashes, his lids and coppery lashes.

And then he holds my face and we fuck in a wet, blind, mad way.

Chapter
Twenty-five

"SO WHERE ARE WE GOING?" I ask, buttoning his shirt. His eyes gleam. He looks wild. Alive. He looks the way I feel.

"What do you think about Mexico?"

I gaze into his gleaming eyes, wanting to kiss them. And his nose. And his lips and cheeks. "The beach, perhaps?"

He tilts his head. "What do you think?"

When he was trapped in Mongolian Delites, he dreamed of sun and the ocean. It's hard on highcaps to live outside of Midcity, but if Packard left, that's where he'd go. "I think it sounds perfect. If *you're* there."

He helps me down from the counter, kisses my forehead. "There's this old beach estate I'm in the process of buying. It belonged to a 1950s movie star—a central building and smaller estate homes. A place for any and all disillusionists to come and live. A few of them will join me later this month."

"And zing you when they want."

"Of course," he says.

Packard's the only one who can handle a zing. The only one whom it doesn't affect.

"Or we can all finally get psychological help or shock therapy or something."

"You might need psychological help after you see this place. It's pink stucco. And very wild."

I pick up his overnight bag and press it into his stomach. "I'm there."

He takes it, and we just stare at each other, and I know I'll never get enough of him.

I ask, "Will you be able to do it? Be cut off from Midcity?"

"I'll make it work." He touches my hair, then pulls away. "We have to go. I have to tie up some things. Hit the bank. We can't be stupid."

The boxes and books are gone from the dining room. Packard sticks the overnight bag in his suitcase and shuts it, then looks up.

"What?" I say.

He comes to me and kisses me. There aren't words.

A harrumph from the doorway. "Have you gone insane?"

Carter.

"She's going with me," Packard says, in a warning tone.

Carter very pointedly makes no reply. "Vesuvius found a trade for your car. Your new one's a red Chevy. He'll leave it at McGonah and Twenty-second within two hours. Keys on the front right tire if he's not there."

Packard turns to me. "Ready for a road trip?"

"In two hours?"

"Yeah, two hours," Carter snaps. "Or do you want to slow him down even more?"

"Stop it," Packard says. "Nobody's slowing anyone down."

"I'll be outside." Carter stomps off.

"That's so fast. I have to pack, and I can't not say goodbye to people. I don't want to slow you down, Packard, but are you sure it's so urgent?"

"It's urgent." He hoists his suitcase and takes a look around his place. A last look. "Come on."

I follow him down the stairs.

Everything seems like a dream. "Don't you think,

when Otto comes to understand that he doesn't need us to disillusion people, and that there's nothing wrong with his head, don't you think he'll release you from the bargain?"

"Absolutely not. It'll only inspire him to seal up more people, including me."

"But you were trying to help rescue him from the Dorks."

"Only to prevent his prisoners from running free—or being sealed up for eternity. He knows that."

"Come on, don't you think he'd be a little grateful—"

"No," he says.

I laugh. "Packard."

"It's not a joke." He turns to me at the bottom of the stairs. "I scuttled the deal. He'll be looking to put me back inside. Don't doubt me on this, Justine. I know him. I know people. You see the best in them. But I see how they really are."

We emerge into the bright winter day, the sky a brilliant blue. Carter's down the block, leaning against his car.

Packard tilts his face to the sun, eyes closed, cinnamon curls shining coppery. "I won't die in that restaurant," he says. "And there's no more reason for me to stay in Midcity. Especially now." He turns to me with a pleasant gaze, features soft. He looks more handsome, more kissable, lighter somehow. And then I get it. He's happy.

Carter comes and takes Packard's suitcase. Parsons will give me a ride to my place.

"Two hours," Packard says. "McGonah and Twenty-second."

"I'll be there."

Packard glances at the cars whizzing up and down the street. "Maybe we should stick together." He comes to me and winds his fingers around mine. "We'll get you everything you need."

I put my finger to his lips. "I'll be there. Let me pack up my life." And then I kiss him.

I have Parsons drop me off at the end of the block, just in case reporters are around, and I enter the building from the back. Up in my place, I scan through with a laserlike focus. Passport, laptop, my most favorite shoes, boots, clothes, books and jewelry. My Victorian lady sleuth mystery. I don't even bother to change out of my hospital handoffs.

Not fifteen minutes later, I'm driving over to Shelby's with two suitcases in the back of my Jetta. My car, my place—I'm leaving everything, and it feels exactly right.

"Good-bye, Gumby," I say, putting his arms upward. Happy Gumby.

I give her a call en route. Phone off. I try Avery and he answers on the first ring. "Yeah!" He sounds distraught, out of breath. Crashes and yelling in the background.

"Where are you?"

"Shelby?" he shouts over the din. "Is that you?"

"No, it's Justine. Do you know where Shelby is?"

"With a target. Iceboating." More crashes from his end. "Fuck! Justine, my factory! They're destroying my place!"

"Who?"

"The cops! They tossed us out, and they're smashing everything!"

"What? Since when? Who the hell ordered that?"

"How am I supposed to know?"

Avery's factory is only a few blocks away. I do a U-turn. "I'm coming to get you. We're going to talk to Otto."

"What if he ordered it?"

"He didn't," I say. He's sleeping, or at least he was an hour or two ago. Otto needs to understand that he's alive because of Avery.

And more than that, I need to tell Otto good-bye. I'll see Shelby and the other disillusionists later, but I won't see Otto—possibly ever again. He deserves a personal good-bye. I'll leave Packard out of it.

Grimly I think about Dad way out in the boonies. He deserves a good-bye, too, but there's definitely no time to drive out there. Then it occurs to me that Packard would gladly stop by on the way out. I know that suddenly. I know *him*.

A distraught Avery hops into my car, hair sticking up every which way, dirt and oil covering his clothes. Breathlessly he describes the destruction. That factory's his life.

"Otto will want to make this right," I say.

I slam into a parking space reserved for somebody named Kendall Cantrell just a half block down from the hotel entrance. Let them tow me. We hop out and rush through the noontime crowd. We're almost to the hotel entrance when I spy Otto walking out and heading in the opposite direction. He's in his disguise—no cap and dark sunglasses—and his gait is slow, hunched, cast arm tucked under his big overcoat. Should he be out of bed?

"Hey!" I don't say his name. I don't have to.

He turns. "Justine!" He strides toward us, looking surprised. "Where were you?"

I rub my arms; it's blustery here near the lakefront, with no buildings to block the wind. "I had some coffee in the lobby, went to see Packard, tried to find Shelby . . ."

He comes to me; I put up a hand as he comes in for a kiss. "Otto, you have to hear this. This is Avery, who owns the factory that makes the antihighcap glasses. It's because of him that you're free right now. Avery, tell Otto what's happening."

Otto isn't looking at Avery; he's looking at me. He knows something's wrong.

"Avery saved your life by helping us, and now his life is being destroyed," I say.

Finally, Otto addresses Avery. "I need to hear this," he says gravely, looking up the street, mumbling something about reporters. "Come." We cross the street at the light and head into the lakefront parklands. Smart. Nobody in their right mind would go strolling out there on a cold, windy day like today. It'll be obvious if anybody follows us now.

We walk along the paved path, heading toward the lake, as Avery tells the story. Otto asks Avery questions. Did the cops show a warrant? Are they searching for something? As Avery describes the violence, the destruction, Otto pulls off his sunglasses and puts them in his jacket pocket; he's looking at Avery, but he doesn't seem to be listening. He shouldn't be out of bed.

We pass Kotton Krazy, a little cotton-candy stand with a clown painted on the side. It's shuttered for the winter.

The wind blows stronger as we near the shore, and I pull my hoodie hood up and push my sleeves down over my hands, looking all around. "I don't see any reporters," I say.

"Good," Otto says.

We stop beside the jumbled rows of boulders, the size of monster truck tires. Otto places a foot on a boulder and glances at me, a question in his eyes. Beyond him, more boulders, and then the waves, whipping up into whitecaps. I pull the strings of my hoodie hood tight, wishing I'd grabbed a proper coat, but who needs a coat in Mexico?

Again I remind him that if it wasn't for the list Avery gave us, the Dorks would still have him.

"I'm grateful," Otto says, not even looking at Avery.

"And now he's in trouble because he helped us, Otto. He's a friend to the highcaps. Can't you call somebody? Call off the raid? The city needs to make this right." The wind blows clear through my skirt.

"Justine—" He turns to Avery. "I need a moment."

Avery shoves his hands into his pockets and walks over to a nearby picnic table.

Otto fixes me with a deep, tender gaze. "What's wrong?"

"Otto, Avery's factory—"

"No, us. What's going on? Last night I thought it was just the events, but then today . . ."

I shake my head. "Otto—"

He looks at me, eyes dark, hair whipping in the wind. I put a hand on his arm.

He shakes me off. "What's going on?"

"I can't be with you."

"What? Of course you can. We belong together."

I say, "I think we depend on each other for solace and we confuse that with affection."

"I never confuse it with affection," he says. "Neither do you. You fought to find me. You risked your life."

"And I'd do it again, but it's not love, and it can't be."

He dips his head, like he's not quite seeing me right, not quite hearing me right. "Is this because of what I told you? What I did to the Goyces?"

"It has nothing to do with that. It's just things I realized today. I realized I've been making my decisions out of fear. And . . ."

He stills, eyes glazed. "No—" He seems so far away, suddenly. Like a stranger. "It's Packard."

"I'm sorry."

"Packard did this."

"I did it," I say. "I realized it. I saw him . . . that's all."

"You're confused. You shouldn't make decisions after what you've been through."

"Otto, I'm clear for the first time."

Otto's eyes look distant, as though his thoughts are spinning far away. The wind whips his hair against the side of his face, his mouth, and he lets it. He's starting to make me feel nervous.

"I'm sorry," I say.

"You're telling me that you went to see him this morning, and all at once you realized . . ."

"Yes."

He casts a dour glance at Avery, who's huddled on the bench.

"I'm so sorry," I say.

He pulls out his phone, and I sneak a look at the clock tower. Forty minutes to get to the rendezvous spot.

"I need you out here," Otto says to whomever he's dialed. "Lakefront." He turns and waves at the street.

"What are you doing?"

"I'm handling this." He gestures Avery over. "Isn't that what you wanted?"

Did he have guys sitting in an unmarked car up on the road? Is he going to send them to investigate the destruction? "Otto, I want you to help Avery because it's the right thing to do. I'm not going to change my mind."

Avery comes up. Otto doesn't say anything, and there's this long, weird silence where Avery scuffs his foot against one of the boulders.

"I understand I owe you," Otto says to him.

Avery pushes his hands deeper into his pockets.

The tips of my ears are starting to freeze. Why are we standing out here? "We should go in soon," I say.

Otto casts a glance around. "Soon enough, my sweet." Slowly and casually, as if he's extracting a cigar, he slides a hand into his breast pocket, pulls out a gun, and points it at Avery.

"Otto!" I say, thinking he's playing some sort of joke.

Avery puts up his hands and steps backward, losing his footing in the boulder bed.

Pop! The sound sends a jolt through me. Avery falls into the rocks. Shot. In the chest. Then, *Pop!* His head jerks.

I gasp. Avery stills.

"Stop it!" I scream as Otto steps closer, casually shooting him two more times. *Pop. Pop.* A silencer.

Otto lowers the gun, eyes on Avery, sprawled in a crevice between two boulders.

And then there's just the wind.

"Oh my God!" I clamber over a boulder, near as I can get to Avery. Wave spray soaks his clothes. I grab his arm and his hair and pull, trying to get him unstuck from the crevice. I let go when I see that his face is half gone, all bones and brain. I clap my hands to my mouth. "Avery!"

I turn to gape at Otto, who stands stiff as a statue, eyes on the horizon. "What the fuck?" I search for Avery's hand, thinking to hold his hand, just in case there's life still in him. "Fuck!" I find it and grab on. Still warm, but his body is twisted all wrong. I don't know what to do. Did this just happen? I can't think what to do. I hold his hand.

A hand on my elbow. Otto. "Come out of there."

"Fuck off!" I yank out of his grip, but he grabs me again—hard—and hoists me off the boulders back to the dirt. I try to shake him off. "Get away!"

But he has his good arm clamped around me. It's like an iron vise around my chest, holding my back to him. I feel the hard outline of his cast on my shoulder blade.

"You killed him!" I claw at his forearm, kick his legs. "You fucking killed him!"

And then Sophia's in front of me. "Sophia!" I say. "He shot Avery!"

She smirks.

"It's not a joke. He shot him!"

She just gazes at me weirdly and says, "Maybe Avery shouldn't have had that antihighcap chip implanted in himself."

"What? He was a friend to highcaps."

She keeps gazing at me. Is there something wrong with my face?

Shit!

I clamp my eyes tight, trying to jerk out of Otto's grip. "Oh, no, you don't," she says. I feel her fingers on my eyebrows, my cheekbones, spreading the skin around my eyes to make my eyelids come open. I fight her with all the facial power I have, but she's digging into my eye sockets, forcing my lids open. I try to jerk my head around. "Get away from me, you freak!"

"Shh." Otto's chin comes down like a pike in the top of my head. "It'll be over soon."

"Fuck off! Fuck!" I squirm as Sophia comes closer, brown eyes and sharp womanly brows blotting out the lake and sky behind her.

"You can't do it!"

I can feel her breath on my lips. "I am doing it."

I jam my elbows back into Otto's chest—there's a broken rib there somewhere—fighting to get my eyes shut. Sophia's fingernails gouge the tender skin around my lids. Air on my eyeballs. I can't shut them!

"An hour?" she asks.

"Take the day," Otto says.

"An hour would probably do it."

"Take the day," Otto commands.

"No!" Frantically, I picture Packard, the way he looked when I told him I loved him. Our kiss. "I won't forget," I say.

Otto's voice sounds distant; something about my having coffee in the lobby. I start to feel fuzzy. I cling on to the vision of Packard. Fingers around mine. Happy for once. *I love you. I love you. You know that, right? For so fucking long, Justine.*

Sophia's giant face starts to blur.

Chapter
Twenty-six

THE 9-1-1 OPERATOR wants me to stay on the line, but I don't want to talk anymore. I hang up, hazy with shock. How could he? I climb over a boulder to get nearer to Avery's bloody, twisted body, clichés about dead people looking like broken dolls running through my mind. He does look like that, and I have this urge to right him. I pull on his arm, thinking to unwedge him, but he slips down farther, and I almost fall right into him.

What am I doing? I move back to the flat dirt and crouch, hugging my knees, tears cold in my eyes, or maybe that's the spray from the waves.

"It's okay," I whisper. But it's far from okay. I guess I'm saying it to his soul, like, *Things will be okay, don't be scared.* Not that I really believe it. I don't know anything. I don't trust anything.

For the millionth time, I picture him shooting Avery—the chest, the head. Twice more once he's in the rocks. I remember screaming, and then he turns to me. *You love to remind me that I'm a villain, but when I actually do something the least bit villainous, you act outraged.*

A giant wave sends spray up over the boulders onto Avery, a little onto me. His hair has a coating of ice. How long ago did I call 9-1-1? Why aren't they here?

Shelby.

With shaking hands I take my phone out of my purse,

hit her number, fingers clumsy as frozen steaks. Voice mail. I leave a message: "You have to get down to the lake-front. It's Avery . . . just hurry. The section of lakefront parklands across from the Royal Arms." I look around for a landmark. "Down from Kotton Krazy. You have to hurry. Wait—don't drive crazy, though. Don't hurry. Wait . . . shit. Just hurry up and get down here."

I hang up and dial Otto, squinting across the park-lands tundra at the upper windows of the Royal Arms. Are the lights on? Which room is ours? *God, please, let him be awake.*

My heart lifts when he answers.

"Otto, thank God. I'm across the street. Lakefront parklands. By the shore."

"What?"

"It's Avery, he's—can you just come out here?"

"What are you doing out in the parklands?"

"Otto—Packard shot Avery!"

"What? Packard? Avery?" Muffled movement. "Hold on, I'm heading out the door. Are you okay?"

"I am, but Avery's dead!"

"I'm coming," he says. Noise in the background. A slam. A ding. "Is Packard still there? Do you think you're in any kind of danger?"

"No, he ran off. Why would he shoot Avery? I don't understand—I just came out here and Avery was there and . . ." I stare at Avery's body.

"I'm on my way."

"The boulders past Kotton Krazy."

Sirens.

"Looks like someone called it in," he says.

I look up toward the road. "I did." Two police cars and an ambulance bump right over the sidewalk and head across the empty expanse toward me.

Frantically I wave. It's like they're coming in slow motion. Or maybe my mind is in slow motion.

I click off as two uniformed officers get out of the first car, and I point the phone toward Avery's body, twisted in the rocks.

He tried to help us. And Shelby loved him.

One of the officers asks me what happened. I don't know what's shock and what's temperature, but I'm totally numb as I retell the scene: Packard comes out of nowhere. He reaches into his jacket pocket, takes out a gun, and shoots Avery. The chest, the face. I feel sick as I think about Avery's intense eyes. His fear. Him and Shelby at the lunch counter.

More questions. What I was doing out here? Did the victim know the shooter?

I talk through my sniffles, eyes clotted with warm tears, as I recount every step of my morning—coffee in the hotel lobby. Afterward I'd wandered around the hotel, killing time, not wanting to wake Otto. Then I came out to get fresh air and ran into Avery. We'd taken a long walk. At one point, suddenly Packard came up behind us out of nowhere. Avery accused Packard of following him. Packard pulled out a gun—right out of his pocket!—and he shot him. The chest, the face. And then when Avery was lying there dead, Packard shot him twice more!

Even as I tell it, I can't believe it.

A burly officer wants me to describe the gun. An EMT tucks a blanket around my shoulders while I talk.

"Any idea why?" he asks.

Wiping my eyes, I shake my head. "Packard goes, 'This ends here.' And then he shoots Avery dead. And then he says to me, 'I hate those glasses.'" My vision starts to blur. Nothing's right.

The officer asks about the glasses. "Avery had a factory that made these glasses," I say. "Antihighcap glasses."

The burly officer says, "Hmm."

The officer taking notes looks up, seemingly bemused. More police cars roll up, and Otto gets out of one and lopes over, one sleeve flapping free, his broken arm a lump in his coat.

"Otto."

Suddenly he's by my side, a safe, warm presence. I've never been so happy to see him. He wraps his right arm around me. "Come here," he says, kissing the top of my head. His coat is warm and soft on my cheek, and I shut my eyes tightly. I just want to burrow into his warmth and safety as he solemnly greets various officers. He knows most of the force by name from when he was police chief. They speak in low tones. "Give me a second with her," I hear him say.

He kneels in front of me. "Look at me," he says. "You're okay?"

I gaze into his deep deep eyes. "I'm so cold."

He rubs my arm through the blanket. "Packard shot Avery? There's no question in your mind on that?"

"Two feet in front of me. He just shot him. I don't understand. Just because of the glasses?" I can feel a kind of hysteria creeping over me. "It doesn't make sense!"

He stands, clutches me to him again. "You don't have to make sense of it. You don't have to speculate on a motive. Just tell the officers what happened, all right? That's all you have to do."

I say, "Packard goes, 'You love to remind me that I'm a villain, but when I actually do something the least bit villainous, you act outraged.' Like it's all a joke. And then he fucking takes off."

"Goddamn him." Otto rubs my back. "God*damn* him."

"Should you be out of bed?"

"Don't worry about me, Justine."

Avery's sheet-covered body is on the shore now. Uniformed officers shine lights over the boulder wall. Searching for bullets? Clues?

The burly officer and his partner are back, slower with the questions. Like a machine, I answer. What I saw. What

Packard said. One, two, three, four shots. *When I actually do something the least bit villainous, you act outraged, Justine.* The whole world spinning out of whack.

Commotion up by the police line. A pink, red, and black blur.

Shelby.

Officers hold her off the shore. She's seen his black work boots poking out of the sheet. "Avery!"

"Let her through," Otto says.

Shelby rushes to Avery's side. I break away from Otto and go to her and touch her back. She wouldn't want more than that, but I need her to know that I'm there. That I'm always there.

"Let her ID him," Otto says.

An officer lifts the sheet from Avery's half-blown-off face, one intense gray eye still intact.

"No!" Shelby sinks to her knees, rests a glove on his chest, and just stays there, silent as a portrait, tears streaming down her cheeks. I sink down next to her.

"Who would do this?"

"Packard," I say.

"Packard?" she says. "You saw him do this?"

"I'm so sorry," I say.

Her gaze seems empty. "Packard."

"Yes." I tell her what happened.

"I will kill him," she whispers. "That is my message to you."

Chapter
Twenty-seven

CANDLELIGHT FLASHES in Otto's dark eyes as he reaches across the table, palm upturned. I lay my hand on his, and he closes his fingers around mine. His hand feels warm and good and safe.

We're at Ciappo's—a grand old classic Italian restaurant in the basement of an ancient brownstone; it's where we had our first dinner date last summer.

This is just what I needed. The past three days with Shelby have been a wrenching series of funeral activities and posthumous introductions to Avery's relatives and friends, many of whom had heard about her, which made things more painful. He'd told his family about her. He'd adored her.

Three days of long silent walks. Nights at her place, trying to make her eat and sleep. Trying not to look too hard at her new, darker brand of grimness.

These days have given me a new appreciation for Otto. He's been my rock, my ally. I squeeze his hand. "Thank you."

He smiles.

It took us some doing to get to our table, like an obstacle course of beaming, tuxedoed waiters and glamorous well-wishers. People have been stopping by all through our meal to express their admiration and gratitude. Kidnapped by the Dorks. Survived their grueling torture. Helped to subdue them. He's a hero all over again.

There's no longer any point to keeping our relationship a secret. That's impossible since the kidnapping and shooting, and anyway, the disillusionists are no more. Or at least, with Packard vanished and the deal off, none of the disillusionists are working to crash and turn Otto's highcap prisoners. We can't do it without each other. Or without Packard.

"You are such a good friend to her," he says.

"I wish I could do more. I wish I could've stopped him. How did I not see it coming? How could I have read things so wrong?"

"That's Packard's genius, Justine. It's not your fault."

"Again and again he fooled me. Even now—"

"Stop! Nobody can warp a person's understanding as Packard can. Packard could make people believe the world was flat if he wanted to." Otto squeezes my hand. "He's brilliant and deadly dangerous. I certainly wouldn't have let him out of Mongolian Delites if I'd known what he was still capable of. I would've put him somewhere deeper. Once I apprehend him, I *will* put him somewhere deeper."

I drink down the last of my wine. Everything's dark now. Otto. Shelby. Even her energy dimension has changed. Instead of the cool, smooth surface, she feels thick and grimy. I sometimes get the sensation of being slightly coated when I pull away, like her loathing of Packard seeps into my pores.

Of course, I have dark feelings of my own toward Packard, but I'm not planning on killing him like she is.

"She'll repair," Otto says, as though he's read my thoughts. "We all will."

"I feel almost guilty having a nice night."

"You can't be a strong friend to her if you don't take care of yourself."

The waiter comes with the dessert selection. We choose the truffle petites to share.

"An excellent choice," the waiter says, backing up two steps, and then spiriting off.

"A no-brainer," I mumble.

Otto raises an eyebrow. I smile.

"There it is," he says, meaning my smile.

"Stop."

"We'll all repair."

"You've been great," I say.

Otto's been laid up himself with his injuries from the kidnapping. I would've stayed with him, but he'd insisted I stay with Shelby. He put his car and chauffeur, Jimmy, at our disposal, he sent food, and of course, assigned bodyguards to both of us. He's constantly reminding me that Packard's out there somewhere, and we don't know what he'll do next.

The coffees come. Otto moves our waters aside, helps make a place for the cream.

It really is like my world has turned upside down. Life is unpredictable and frightening, just the way it used to be. They say you don't notice gradual improvement—the fading off of an annoying hum, the subsiding of an ache. Somehow, I hadn't noticed that I'd started trusting in life, trusting in myself.

And then the rug went out from under me. It wasn't the Dorks or the sleepwalking cannibals who did it. It was Packard shooting Avery.

Or who knows, maybe that was just the last straw. Now I just want to snuggle into Otto, stay warm with him, have him wrap his arms around me. Well, he only has the one arm to wrap around me at the moment, but that's enough. My noble, patient, strong Otto.

"It still seems like a dream," I say once the waiter's gone.

He tips a packet of sugar into his coffee. "It's jarring

when you realize you can never really know people," he says. "And how that makes this world a dangerous place."

I nod. But I'm safe with Otto. If you don't have safety, you have nothing. That's something both of us understand. Again I think of the shooting, and I get this stabbing pain behind my eyes. Sometimes I get that when I think about it too hard. "Stop." I put up a hand. "Stop. We can't talk about that."

"We'll talk about something else." He takes my fingers, kisses them. "How about that you look beautiful."

"That's all that matters," I joke.

He smiles, eyes swathed in warm crinkles. It's almost like his old smile. Maybe things will repair.

I take a deep breath. "Thank you for this," I say. "All of it." I splash in the tiniest bit of cream. Cow brown. Packard's phrase. I think of Packard too much now. It's just so outrageous. Like one plus one suddenly equals three. I put my hand to my head. I can't think about him. I smooth the skirt of my gown, pure black velvet except for ruby buttons where the straps meet the bodice. The gown was a gift from Otto—it arrived at my apartment via courier in a silver-wrapped box along with the dinner invitation for tonight. All just an hour after I'd called him to complain that Shelby had kicked me out, insisted on being alone.

Otto's wearing what is arguably the better outfit: coal-gray brocade vest under a black velvet jacket. He looks like a Renaissance king with his dark curls flowing down from his midnight-black velvet beret. It occurs to me that our outfits go together in a really cool way, and that comforts me. No, I tell myself—it's nearly perfect. We fit, Otto and me. We always have.

I pluck a cocoa truffle from its silver foil cup.

Otto holds up a hand. "Wait."

I pause, truffle midway to my mouth. "What?"

"Okay, eat that one."

I pop it into my mouth. "Yum."

He sips his coffee.

"What?"

"I have a surprise for you."

"Another?"

As he reaches into his breast pocket I freeze. I don't know why. He pulls out an envelope and slides it across the table.

"A letter?"

"Open and see," he says, selecting a nut truffle.

I pull it open and extract two pages.

"Read the white sheet first," he says.

I comply. "Dear Ms. Jones. We are pleased to inform you of your admittance to our nursing program, starting spring . . ." I look up. "Otto, what is this?"

"You got into nursing school."

I look at the insignia. Midcity U. "I didn't even apply!"

"I did. On your behalf."

"What? How?"

"I pulled a few strings. You'll have to do the work, of course. And pass a few tests." He taps the purple paper. I take a look. It's a certificate for one hundred hours of tutoring in anatomy and biology. With the mayoral seal on it.

"Otto! This is so thoughtful, but I can't attend nursing school. You know I can't."

"You can."

"Already I'm not going to be zinging targets anymore. I can't sit there studying diseases—it'll be like 24/7 symptom surfing. I'll be a basket case. You don't know how it was before."

"No, I don't." He takes the papers from me and puts them back into the envelope. "But I know you. And I know this is your dream. That's all I need to know."

I shake my head. "I can't handle it."

"I'll admit, I don't know how bad it was for you. I

wasn't there when it was bad, and I'm well aware that that madman wouldn't have tricked you into joining the disillusionists if you didn't have an unnaturally high level of fear—"

"Freakishly, unnaturally high. In the stratosphere. I'll be in a permanent state of terror."

"You handled it before."

"Barely."

"You handled it. And this time around there's one big difference."

Again, I have this flinch reflex as he reaches into his breast pocket. What is that? He pulls out a little velvet box. My heart pounds as he sets it on the table.

"You didn't have an ally before."

I stare at the little box, feeling so unsure.

"Go on," he says.

I've been so unsure of so much lately. I can't trust myself to think.

"Open it," he says.

I take a breath and lift the velvet cover. A ring. "Oh my God." A breathtakingly gorgeous ring, twisting bands of brilliant diamonds, like dancing stars in white gold, with a giant diamond in the middle that catches the light in millions of colors.

"You've never had me by your side before," he whispers. "Believing in you, loving you. You're always able to talk me down, expose the trickery of my mind. We'll do it for each other. I have to get used to holding those prisoners with my mind; you have to get used to going without zinging. We can do it together. We'll chase our dreams together. We can do anything together, Justine."

He rises from his seat and comes over to me, kneels beside me, hands on my thighs. "Marry me. Be the first lady of Midcity. Watch over the citizenry with me. Make a life with me."

A wash of confusion comes over me as he waits. I look

down at the ring. I feel the patrons of the restaurant watching us. Otto watching me.

I hesitate, not trusting myself.

Snap out of it! I tell myself. Am I crazy? He's who I always wanted. And it's when I think about being without him that it really becomes clear: I need him more than ever, and he needs me; we can navigate through each other's deepest fears and pull each other out. We can face the future together.

So I take a deep breath. And jump. "Yes," I say.

He stands and pulls me up, kisses me. People around us clap.

I laugh.

He says, "May I?"

I hold out my hand and he puts on the ring, best he can with one hand—I help him a little—and then he kisses each of my fingers.

"Yes," I whisper.

"Let's get out of here." He swings my velvet cape over my shoulders, then dons his own coat—a nearby waiter rushes up to help him while I grab the last truffle and pop it into my mouth. We stroll through the endless row of tables full of well-wishers and smiling citizens, and emerge into the cool night. You can see your breath.

He takes my hand and we climb the ancient steps up to the street and wander out to the sidewalk. A few parked cars, but no Jimmy with the limo.

I lean on a sign pole, looking at my ring. "It's beautiful, Otto," I say.

"You're beautiful," he replies, glancing up and down the street. "That's odd. Jimmy knew to wait."

The street is dark, aside from faint starlight. "Maybe he took it to get gas." I turn my hand this way and that, watching my ring glitter. This will be right.

"I had a man posted out here. And was that streetlight out before? Something's off."

He pulls out his phone and punches something into it with his thumb.

I'm looking up at the light. It's broken. "It's been shot out," I tell him.

He fumbles in his pocket.

A flash of silver behind him. Carter. I gasp as he puts a gun to Otto's head. "Up. Both of them."

"Carter!" I say. "What are you doing?"

Otto raises his good arm, and Carter pulls his coat half off to let him raise his arm that's in a cast.

"Carter!" I'm stunned. He's our anger guy, but this makes no sense. "Stop!"

Carter takes a gun from Otto's jacket, then one from Otto's boot.

A voice behind me. "Justine."

I spin around.

Packard strolls out of the shadowed alley at the side of the building, black coat flowing behind him.

"Packard!" Conflicting emotions spear through me, paralyzing me. My brain feels numb.

Like a dream, Packard comes to me, wraps his arms around me. "I've got you now." Warm breath on my cheek. "It's okay. Let's get out of here," he says.

I come to my senses and push him off. "Are you insane?"

"You were foolish to come out here," Otto says to him.

Carter mutters a threat.

Packard looks confused. "Justine. Come on, we have to go."

I back up toward Otto and Carter, pushing my hand to my temple, where the pain is.

"It's okay." He holds out his hand.

"*Okay?* You kill Avery, and you think I'm going somewhere with you?"

"I didn't kill Avery," Packard says. Sirens in the distance. "You know I'd never do that. You of all people."

"Me of all people? I saw you do it."

"No—what?" Then, slowly, "No." Pain in his pale green eyes.

"I saw you." It's only now I realize he's holding a gun. "Fuck! What are you going to do?"

"Justine, it's me. You know me! Think! It wasn't real. Why would I kill Avery? You've been revised."

"A revision," Otto says. "That's convenient."

I look back and forth between them, thinking back to the shooting. *You love to remind me that I'm a villain, but when I actually do something the least bit villainous, you act outraged.*

So real.

The pain stabs into my forehead. "How fucking gullible do you think I am?"

He levels his gun at Otto. "Tell her."

"Leave Otto alone," I beg Packard. "Don't."

"Tell her!"

Otto says, "I don't lie to Justine."

I place myself in front of Otto. "Don't you dare."

Packard goes white. "This is me, Justine."

Sirens from both directions. "Goddammit, Packard." Carter backs off Otto, keeping his gun trained on Otto's forehead. He grabs Packard's arm. "Let's get out of here."

Packard looks dazed. "You know me, Justine."

I flash on Avery, broken on the boulders. "Do you have any idea what you've done?"

Packard shakes Carter off. "I didn't do it!"

"My fiancée begs to differ," Otto says.

The far building flashes red.

"Come on," Carter hisses.

Packard blinks. "Fiancée?"

Our eyes lock. "That's right."

"It's me," he whispers, and for one searing moment, I don't know anything.

"Packard!" Carter. "You want him to put you inside again?"

Otto says, "Oh, I *will* put you inside."

Packard says, "Not if I blow all the walls down." He turns to me, and my stomach does a flip-flop. Something's wrong.

"God," I put my fingers to my forehead.

Packard looks bewildered. "Justine, what's wrong?"

"You're tormenting her, destroying her," Otto says. "You want to kill her, too?"

A screech of tires. "Fuck!" Carter grabs Otto's shoulder, holding on to him. What's he doing? "You're going down, Sanchez."

Packard turns and walks off, black coat flowing behind him, and then Carter rushes to Packard's side, walking backward, ready to shoot. "Not a move," Carter growls.

Together they head into the alley as engines roar and tires screech behind me. And then they're gone.

I turn just in time to watch Otto crash his fist into the window of the parked car.

"Oh my God! Otto!"

He pulls it out and looks at it. Cut up, bloody. And then he punches the other window, a throaty smash. "Damn him!"

I grab the back of his coat. "Otto!" But he keeps hitting the car, wild with anger.

Officers who've pulled up see this and they swarm around Otto. "Mayor Sanchez!"

They're trying to subdue him, which only makes him struggle.

"No, not me!" Otto's voice is angry, booming, and he pulls away from the officers. "Not me. Packard!" He tries to gesture in the direction of the alley, but they have his arm. "There! Packard! The fugitive! Go!"

A few officers lope in the direction he's indicated.

More officers gather around. It's not until they have him contained that I get it.

Carter zinged him. Anger. A diversion.

I go up to him, whisper in his ear, "This was a zing. Carter. Anger."

Otto gapes at me, understanding coming over his face. I see him struggle against the feelings. The strong emotions make you less crazy when you know they're not yours.

"You're okay," I whisper.

An older officer pushes through the uniforms. "Back off," he says. "The mayor's fine."

He is. He's straightened up, expressing shock at his behavior. Cumulative stress, appearance of Packard, threats to his fiancée, caught without a weapon. He charms them. He makes them laugh. Fights the anger.

I rub his back, looking toward the alley where Packard and Carter disappeared. The alley is empty now. Just flashes of red from the cop cars.

I turn back to Otto. "Let me see." I take his hand. His knuckles are bloody. I pull off my black silk scarf and wrap it around.

"I'm the luckiest man in the world," he whispers.

"No, I am," I say. "Luckiest woman."

Otto kisses my cheek.

So why don't I feel like the luckiest woman? Especially compared to poor Shelby. God, I have the freedom I so desperately longed for, I have a new career to build, and I'm going to marry the man of my dreams. It's a happily ever after if I've ever seen one.

I hold the scarf gently to his hand, and my ring sparkles brightly—a small, precious, fiery thing against the darkness. I don't know why it should make me feel so sad.